The Bismarck Folly
Part 1
Resurrection

The Minstrel boy to the war is gone,
In the ranks of death you'll find him;
His father's sword he has girded on,
And his wild harp slung behind him;
"Land of Song!" said the warrior bard,
"Though all the world betrays thee,
One sword, at least, thy rights shall guard,
One faithful harp shall praise thee!"

The Minstrel fell! But the foeman's chains
Could not bring his proud soul under;
The harp he loved ne'er spoke again,
For he tore its chords asunder;
And said "No chains shall sully thee,
Thou soul of love and bravery!
Thy songs were made for the pure and free
They shall never sound in slavery!"

Thomas Moore

Folly [noun]:
1. Lack of good sense; foolishness
2. A costly ornamental building with no practical purpose

Acknowledgements

My thanks to my wife Catherine, without whose encouragement this book would never have had the resurrection it needed. My gratitude to all those who withstood the barrage of questions necessary in the search for technical accuracy, all those years ago. There were many. In addition, and recently, I've mercilessly pestered both my youngest sons who are now at sea themselves as Officers in the Merchant Marine but who were not yet born when this story was *first* written.

Thanks to a more recent endless source of info for someone who has forgotten so much of how things were, the crew of the Navy-net, albeit unknowingly.

A further note. I hope for the early release of the six British ex-soldiers held unjustly in an Indian prison for doing their job. These men were some of the brave souls who risk their lives to guard merchant ships at sea. Being on anti-piracy patrols protecting merchant sailors from the scum who steal and murder for personal gain should not be a criminal offence.

Terminology and Acronyms

AWO: Advanced Warfare Officer, basically controls a ship's systems in battle.

Bandit: identified hostile aircraft.

Bikini Amber: heightened security state for terrorist alerts

BOST: Basic Operational Sea Training. First of a series of ship work-up courses.

Bogey: unidentified aircraft.

Bootneck/ Bootie: Royal Marines, navy slang

BMMP: Russian designed tracked armoured amphibious personnel carrier. UK equiv Warrior

BTR80: As above but wheeled

CMS: Combat Management System. Software for presenting data and taking automatic actions

Crab: Navy slang for RAF personnel, any kind

ECM: Electronic countermeasures. Jamming

ECCM: Electronic counter countermeasures. Anti-Jamming.

ESM: Electronic Support Measures, a passive means for the detection of enemy transmissions

FLASH: Highest priority signal, jumps the queue to the top every time.

ICABA: International Compressed Air Breathing Apparatus

Jungly helicopter: one which is painted olive green drab.

Jungly Pilot: RN pilot who has served with the Royal marines

Kreigsmarine. Lit: *war-navy* German navy of the Nazi era

LSM: Landing Ship Medium

LST: Landing Ship Tank

MEM: Marine Engineering Mechanic

MMSI: Maritime Mobile Service Identity. Series of nine digits which are sent in digital form over a radio channel in order to uniquely identify ship

MGCC: Main Gunnery Control Centre.

Muppet: Most Useless Person Pusser Ever Trained

PFDHEC: Pre-Fragmented Directional High Explosive Canister. A new shotgun like AA shell.

Pusser: 'The Royal Navy' as derived from Pursers issue. Or to be Pusser –strict adherence to rules

RIB: Rigid Inflatable Boat. Used by marines and boarding parties.

SAM: Surface to air Missile

SART: Search And Rescue Transponder

SIC: Subject Indicator Code. A formalised prefix on signals for routing/security purposes.

Sitrep: abbreviation, Situation Report

SSM: Surface to surface missile

WAFU: Wet and fuck-all use. Derogatory/familiar term for Fleet Air Arm ratings and officers.

Prologue. A Distant memory

Morning 27th May 1941. *Bismarck*, Eastern Atlantic

The ship shuddered and shook again, cups rattled and pencils fell to the deck. It was no small feat for over fifty thousand tons of Krupp steel to shake and rattle like this. The men sharing the compartment with him looked around at each other and up at the deckhead as dust and motes of paint rained down from conduits above. Max König had no idea whether they were outgoing shots or incoming shells. Probably incoming, he decided. Even as far down as deck five in the insulated after gunnery computer room they felt the shocks.

"Attention to duty." He said out loud, not in a 'shouty' voice but still one of authority, and the men returned to their work.

They were still receiving range finder information to process from the after director and it was important to crank out the bearings and elevation for the next salvos as fast as possible.

He knew that things were going badly because he had Mullenheim-Rechberg's word for it. When the voice came over the headset with the news that turrets Anton and Bruno were out of action along with the foretop control director, a chill ran down his spine.

The voice of the new First Gunnery Officer was grim but purposeful as he informed young Max that they would concentrate their remaining guns on the much older and hopefully more vulnerable British battleship *Rodney*. The secondary armament was to keep the destroyers at bay as they circled the crippled giant like a pack of wolves waiting for the moment to rush in and finish it.

Young Leutnant Max König knew that no one else in the gunnery computer room would be aware of the change in command structure, and wouldn't care less anyway were it not for the fact that with the change of gunnery officers came the loss of half their main armament!

Anyone with even minimal awareness could work out that they hadn't a chance this time. This was one of those *Titanic* moments where it becomes obvious to everyone in the know that they'd had it. An aberrant thought entered his head; the *Titanic* was about the same weight as us as well. He reflected that the torpedo that had jammed their rudder last night had, in a single fatal blow removed their ability to escape to Brest in France, and worse still, it had ensured that when they were caught, the

British gunnery officers would find a slow moving and easy target for their weapons. It had in fact been *Bismarck's* iceberg.

He returned his attention to the feeding of accurate fire control information to turrets Caesar and Dora. It was zero nine hundred hours and only twelve minutes had passed since the action had commenced and they'd lost half their main battery.

Just fifteen minutes later, Müllenheim-Rechberg informed him that his director had been destroyed too so Max passed a last message to turrets Caesar and Dora telling them to fire independently then sat back in his swivel chair and stared at the bulkhead in front of him. There was really nothing else he could do now except die.

The waiting was torture. An endless series of rumbles, thumps and shockwaves and flickering lights as their once magnificent ship was reduced to floating rubble. The engineers and designers who'd put *Bismarck* together had clearly been masters of their craft, it had been forty minutes or so since their last guns had been silenced and still she floated, Max noted.

For almost an hour König and his four men sat in a strange isolation listening to the 'crump' of impacts and feeling the shudders as the one sided battle raged above them. Communications were at best intermittent and often non-existent, the lights flickered occasionally adding to the mounting fear and sense of loneliness.

The telephones were down when the gunfire finally ceased, an event betrayed only by the lack of shuddering impacts. Unable to stand it any longer he sent his *Oberbootsmannmaat* or Petty Officer, to find out what was happening.

Erich Henzer had left the isolated compartment deep down in the ship and made his way for'ard. Staying on deck five was a good choice he discovered, no damage at all that he could see. When he judged he was beneath the bridge superstructure he started to climb. His plan was to find the first bridge officer he could, and report.

Henzer was a ten year veteran and despite the changes that had occurred since the Nazis had taken over in Germany he felt the Kreigsmarine had resisted much of it and so he still had confidence in the professionalism of the officers and senior non-coms, not like the strutting fools ashore.

The first living person he came across was on deck three, the armoured deck. He found a bleeding and clearly dying Petty Officer whom he vaguely recognised. There was smoke in the air but with no gunfire the ship was eerily quiet. He offered the man a smoke which was gratefully received and learned his action station had been the bridge.

"All gone." He whispered hoarsely. Henzer looked around the for'ard first aid post; stretchers, bandages blood stained and clean, clothing and three bodies all covered over. Chaos.

"What do you mean?" He asked.

"Bridge took a direct hit from a big one. All killed except me."

Henzer was getting spooked now despite his training.

"Where are the stretcher bearers and the doctor?"

The wounded man coughed gently and took another drag.

"Don't know. They started moving everyone up before the guns stopped. I am the last. Think they forgot me."

He coughed again and a gush of bright blood flooded the front of his already soaked chest bandages. A look of panic entered his eyes and he gripped Henzer's jacket with a quiet, pain filled intensity before he lay still. Henzer was horrified. He removed the man's claw-like grip on his jacket and closed his eyes.

Another deck up. Not just smoke but fires, unattended fires too, damage now obvious. Shit where was everyone? Up again. The main deck was just chaos, like a giant's junkyard with torn decking and twisted metal everywhere. He spotted a Leutnant with a bandage over one side of his face and eye, he was dragging a wounded man to a hatch which exited on to the upperdeck. Henzer quickly ran forward and took the legs to help lift him over the coaming. The Leutnant tiredly nodded his thanks and they sat the man upright propping him with a couple of lifejackets. The Leutnant's uniform was in tatters and he stood upright to stretch his back. Henzer took his chance, came to attention and barked out a report in his finest non-com voice.

The Leutnant's manner instantly changed.

"You have no time to spare Henzer, the order to scuttle is either about to be given or has been given. You must run as fast as you can back down to your dungeon and tell the others. Now man! Not a moment to waste!"

Henzer turned and ran. He tried to retrace his route but somehow he ended up on the familiar pathway he usually took from his messdeck. He dodged fires and falling debris, coughing his way through smoke filled passageways with a feeling of rising panic which he tried desperately to suppress.

Part of him, a large part he shamefully admitted, wanted him to give up and get back to the light above. However, the other part of him that made him a senior Petty Officer, would not allow such creeping cowardice. He pushed aside things which blocked his way, skirted fires roaring through open hatches and once had to double back and go around damage that blocked him totally. Breathless he arrived to give his news.

A rising bubble of fear began to fill Max as he and his men began to quickly make their way upwards. It was incredible that this ship of over two thousand men appeared empty and the feeling that they were the last ones below was steadily taking hold. More worrying was that they had no idea at what time the fuses had been fired on the scuttling charges, or if they had been fired yet!

The fear of being trapped in the hull of the ship as it sank swiftly to the bottom made his gorge rise but he controlled himself remembering that he was an officer, even if it was the most junior officer rank possible, and he should set an example.

He noted there was no apparent damage on decks four and five, the emergency lighting was constant and flicker free which was reassuring. They encountered no one as they moved rapidly upwards to deck three, the armoured deck.

The absence of even the sound of ventilation fans gave the ship a Marie Celeste like quality that had the young officer's imagination going overtime as he reached the nearest hatch leading up to deck three.

The first indicator of the danger they now faced was when Max signalled Petty Officer Eric Henzer forward and the young man knocked the hatch clips aside. When the spring loaded armoured hatch didn't budge Henzer repositioned himself with his feet on the ladder and pushed against the hatch cover with his back.

Letting out a high pitched yelp of pain, he quickly fell off the ladder and the hatch slammed shut but not before a jet of flame had charred the cotton shirt on Henzer's back in the half second he'd managed to lift the hatch a fraction.

Max and the others quickly stripped the smouldering remains from him and in the less than adequate light tried to assess the damage to Henzer's back.

"It is hot sir." Henzer reported sardonically before fainting briefly.

Max smiled at the man's courage and noted the blisters rising even as he looked down at the scorched back. Spotting a fire hose still curled on its reel a few yards away, Max ordered one of his men to see if there was still pressure on the system.

Seaman Renzel quickly reported that there was some pressure and dragged the hose from the reel and carefully opened the valve to gently let cold water flow over the burns. Henzer shuddered as the cold water took away the dreadful heat from his back.

Max soaked the remains of Henzer's shirt and draped it over the man's shoulders while ordering them to work their way further aft for the next upward hatch.

Five long minutes later they had tried a further three times to get on to deck three but each time they tried the heat was apparent and on one of them the roaring of the fires above sounded like a welding kit in use. Time was passing and König was starting to think that there really would be no way out and that they'd left it way too late to escape. How long did it take to scuttle a battleship anyway? Would they feel it when the charges went? He'd no idea.

Joseph Halke a young seaman spoke up.

"Sir, what about the communications tube between the computer room and the director station on the upper deck?"

Max thought a second. Damn but it might work he decided.

"Good idea Halke, I will buy you a bottle of finest schnapps when we get home!"

Halke beamed with pride and led the way back to the nearest access hatch. The narrow armoured shaft proved to be accessible and all of them began climbing up the seventy degree slope. Two minutes later the dread began to rise again when Halke reached the last access panel before the end of the tube but could not open the small exit hatch and had no room to manoeuvre. The best he could do was to rap on the metal lid with his wrist watch.

The claustrophobia, the heat and the lack of a decent airflow were pushing everyone to the edge of panic; Max began to silently plead for an end to the torment and didn't care what. Suddenly there was a scraping sound and the access hatch was opened up by someone. He was so relieved he nearly let go and slid back down the steep tube.

They found a place where the smoke from the fires wasn't so bad and then began to search for life jackets and a life raft. Henzer lay on his front with the cool air washing over his blistered back.

The man was in dreadful pain but there was no one to administer pain relief, just groups of men sheltering away from the fires raging around the upper works waiting for the moment they would have to enter the icy grey waters of the Atlantic.

Max König re-wrapped his diary in its oilskin cover and put it back in his jacket pocket. He'd always been a diarist and wrote in a basic code so that it wouldn't be obvious to anyone other than another mathematician aware of Fibonacci.

He looked out over the grey seas and took a deep breath of clean air but caught movement out of the corner of his eye. A heavy cruiser was moving parallel to *Bismarck,* at a range of just over half a mile his gunnery officer mind decided. He watched and then realised with horror that the periodic splashes were torpedoes being launched. He looked around quickly to check the same wasn't being repeated on the port side.

"Achtung! Everyone to the port side NOW!"

He grabbed Henzer's arms and Halke grabbed his legs and together they shuffled as fast as possible across the torn decks to the opposite side. A moment passed and then a series of thumps passed shockwaves through the deck under them and minutes later the ship begin to list.

Max was glad he'd had time to make a few last observations in his dairy because he didn't think he'd get much time now. He took charge of a party trying to launch a raft from the upper side of the ship and redirected them to the side which was sinking towards the water with increasing speed. As the water rose to meet the raft they clambered on and he ordered them to paddle like hell with anything they had. He turned and gave a last look at his home of the last six months as she slowly rolled over, hissing steam and defiance to the last.

A Recipe for Disaster

May 25th 1982 – Middle Bay, Falkland Islands

The crushing pressure was gone but the ringing persisted in his ears. He could feel. He knew that he was lying down and that there were no particular pain spots in his body. He breathed and immediately coughed. Smoke, bitter and acrid. He began to perceive noises around him other than the monotonous single tone.

Another thing he could feel, and alarmingly so, was that the deck he was lying on wasn't horizontal any more, it caught and pinched against his skin on the downward side of his cheek where gravity took his weight. He instinctively knew that that was bad news, very bad news in fact, but had yet to work out why.

He opened his eyes and panic shot through him like the touch of a live wire. He was blind! Seconds later the panic began to subside when he realised he could actually see. He could make out the yellowish glow of an emergency light through the thick smoke. Not good, the ship was on emergency power. A loud groan came from nearby and he coughed in response.

The deck lurched, trembled then jumped beneath him, more ear pressure, more deeply ominous rumbling. The tilt of the deck increased and suddenly he knew everything.

The war, the Falklands, the warning over the main broadcast, and lastly the bombs. A scream from nearby accompanied the sound of something heavy scraping across the deck. More coughing.

"Who's that?" Croaked a voice.

"Sub Lieutenant König" He coughed out.

The smoke was noticeably thickening and very much the biggest problem in their immediate future. Jonathan 'Jake' Henry König made his way over to the origin of the sound and discovered someone sitting on the deck tying a bandage around the lower part of his left leg.

An equipment locker was lying on its side next to him having sprung from the bulkhead when the bombs exploded.

More screaming, not far away but out of sight.

"Must get some ICABAs or this smoke'll kill us." He coughed out.

"Who are you and where's the nearest ICABA locker?"

"PO Herring Sir, this thing that fell on me will be the locker you're looking for Sir, I expect what we need will be on the deck just here somewhere." He coughed back.

Jake skirted around the wounded man coughing all the time, eyes streaming and stinging. He blinked rapidly to get a bit of clarity and spotted what he needed a few feet away. He quickly reached down and grabbed the straps of two of the breathing units and hauled one over to Herring.

He immediately turned on the air valve then set about getting the mask over his face, a memory of the grizzled Chief Stoker instructor at Dartmouth surfaced 'pull the straps but don't pull too hard or quick or you'll rip all that lovely hair out, if it ever grows back that is', so he pulled steadily on the straps and got his seal.

Blessed relief.

He quickly checked to see if Herring needed some help with his but needn't have worried, the PO was sucking in gulps of fresh air to clear his lungs of the poisonous fumes. Jake waited a few seconds but knew they needed to get to the upper deck, pronto if the increasing tilt under his feet was anything to go by.

Loud gasping screams from nearby.

"For fuck's sake help us somebody!" Croaked out a voice followed by a sob and a thudding sound on what must be the nearest hatch cover.

He helped Herring up and watched as he hobbled across and leant against the nearest bulkhead. Jake looked over to the hatch and even in this poor lighting he could see it was warped.

He shuddered to think of the pressures required to warp these natural strongpoints. Waste of time just trying to open it, he thought to himself as he searched the equipment on the deck. Then he found what he needed, a pair of crowbars.

He took his anti-flash gloves off to get a better grip and used the bar as a club to knock off the remaining hatch clips and then he inserted the curved end under the partially lifted rim.

He heaved. Nothing. He heaved again. Nothing. 'Shit,' he thought, this bloody thing is well and truly stuck. He gestured to Herring and shouted through the mask.

"Give us a hand will you Herring or we'll never get this bugger open."

Herring lurched away from the bulkhead and hopped across before bending down and picking up the other bar.

Together now they applied their weight to the bars under the rim of the warped hatch. It gave way after a third and final desperate try. Both men fell back as the hatch sprang open and clanged against the bulkhead.

More smoke billowed up from the compartment below. Jake could see very little but flames flickered here and there. He took a deep breath lifted his mask and shouted.

"Who's there?"

A cough and a groan from below and Jake knew he'd have to go down and help. The ship lurched again and another deep rumble reminded him that time was running out for them all.

Jake began to climb down and saw a torch jutting out from the bits and pieces that had fallen out of the locker. He reached over and grabbed it praying that it still worked; he flicked the switch and a strong beam lanced out.

He continued down the ladder shining the beam around. Visibility was crap because the light reflected back from the thicker eddies of smoke making it near impossible to see far. But it was a thousand times better than total darkness. Again he took a breath and lifted his mask to shout.

"Herring pass another ICABA set down will you or whoever's here will be dead before we can get them out, not sure how many there are."

A groan near his foot.

"Here Sir." Came from above, as Herring lowered an ICABA set by its straps. The flames were getting taller and spreading as ironically, the oxygen brought in by his entry, fed the fires.

Jake put the set on the deck and began to search for the source of the groan again. It was an overall clad young MEM cradling his right arm with his left. Jake needed no medical training to know the lad could not use it and began to wonder if he could lift him up the ladder without help. He got the set on the young man and again waited a few seconds to allow the fresh air to have its effect.

"Are you hurt anywhere else?" He said with a deep exhale before slamming his own mask back in place. A nod of the head then the lad took a deep breath himself and lifted the mask to speak.

"I think my right ankle is broken, I tried taking the weight but I can't." A quick breath from the mask. "Can you find Jonesy? He was over there a ways but I haven't heard him for a while."

Bloody hell, Jake was thinking, can it get any flaming worse? He quickly discovered it could as he stumbled over 'Jonesy'. Jake rapidly bent down and put his fingers at the side of Jonesy's throat. He felt around a little in case he was missing the right spot, but no, there was no pulse in Jonesy's neck. Then his own luck ran out.

There was an innocuous popping sound from behind the bulkhead in front, something whined by his ear at high speed then twin jets of flame sprang out in front just as he was standing up.

His arms caught the brunt and he fell back clouting his head against something in the darkness as he snatched them away from the flame.

The pain was indescribable, like sticking both your arms in a deep fat fryer up to your elbows he imagined. He screamed into the mask as quietly as he could, took several deep breaths and the picture steadied again. He moved quickly back to his first casualty. A deep breath.

"Right I'm going to lift you up as best I can but it's going to hurt like hell I think. We haven't much time, so 'sorry' in advance."

Another nod.

Jake reached down and placed the lad's good leg against his own boot and then reached for his casualty's good arm, prising it away from cradling the injured one.

A groan through gritted teeth was the response. Then he hauled the lad upright. Nearly dropping him as his own pain went off the scale.

"Feel free to help yourself with your good arm." He shouted through his mask.

After a struggle he got the lad within reach of Herring's hands above and then he was quickly hauled out with another loud groan as his damaged ankle bounced off the hatch coaming and his broken arm shared the weight of the pullup.

Jake quickly followed up the ladder and as an afterthought slammed the lid back as hard as he could and managed to get one clip on in a corner. He had no idea whether that would delay the fire at all but it was all he could do.

Now he had to get himself and his two wounded followers out onto the upper deck, which should be along here somewhere he decided.

The list was increasing alarmingly and as they at last made it to the upper deck discarding the heavy ICABA sets, it was nearing 30 degrees and rising as they watched.

They were on the damaged side aft of the bomb entry point he noted. He was looking around for life rafts as the water began lapping over the deck in front of him. The three of them hobbled and walked down into the water as it rose. Cold shock! Pain relief for his arms!

Jake quickly inflated the MEM's jacket and checked that Herring had his inflated before taking his own out of his waist pouch and sorting himself out.

They needed to get away from the side of the ship before it rolled on top of them and then out of the water pretty damned quick or they'd be dead from hypothermia a short time after. No pressure, he thought as he and Herring dragged the struggling MEM away with them.

He looked round in time to see a raft being paddled towards them with an officer in the bow. Then there was a huge sighing sound and he quickly looked back to see his home of just three weeks, turning fully turtle, her blue anti-fouling paint incongruous against the grey sky and sea.

Huge bubbles burst on the surface and bits of buoyant material popped up.

Then they were being hauled out of the water into the raft and he gave his first scream of many as his rescuers hauled on his burned arms.

"Ere grab his other arm Lofty before I lose my grip."

"Christ the poor bugger's burned all the way up, look at that will yer, 'is eights have melted onto 'im".

Jake leaned back against the side of the raft and felt the morphine Syrette taken from the chord around his neck and the sharp prick as it was stuck in his thigh.

He closed his eyes, blinking away the stinging salt. He hadn't liked the *Coventry* as much as the *Sheffield*, but losing them both without him so much as sticking two fingers up to the Argies was a bit much, he thought, as the morphine started to kick in.

He hadn't had a chance to get to know anyone on *Coventry* very well but it was a fantastic ship though, and he knew she had performed miracles to keep going and keep getting in the way of the Argy aircraft on their way to bomb the ships in San Carlos; but once too often, and by then her people were absolutely knackered.

She was the last Type 42 destroyer in the South Atlantic at this point, *Sheffield* gone and *Glasgow* damaged.

You could tell when the exhaustion started to take its toll, people took longer to do simple jobs and minds seemed perpetually fuzzy. Defence watches, four on and four off were a killer too, never enough sleep and not sustainable. However with the ship being the only '42' down there they were expected to be in three places at once.

He remembered his arrival and the interview with Captain Hart-Dyke. He hadn't known what to expect. He had been on the *Sheffield* when she was hit so they all wanted to know what had happened, he'd seen it in their eyes and heard it in the way they'd studiously avoided the subject at lunch in the wardroom before his captain's interview.

Captain Hart-Dyke was buoyant and charming, he explained his need for Jake since his last junior Warfare Officer was now on the hospital ship Uganda having his appendix taken out. Hart-Dyke went on to say that even when he was fit to come back to work, it wouldn't be allowed because of the rules governing the treatment of casualties under the red cross flag in time of war etcetera.

Jake hadn't minded because he was keen to do something other than just abandon a ship, which was all he'd achieved so far in this war. With deft and gentle probing Captain Hart-Dyke had managed to extract Jake's version of events without making it seem like prying.

Plainly he would need to know if there was anything he himself would have or could have done differently and if Jake's previous captain had somehow cocked up causing the loss of his ship.

Jake learned over the next two and a half weeks that *Coventry's* company thought the old man could walk on water and Jake came to think so too as the action unfolded throughout May and *Coventry* had done everything asked of her and much more.

Today had been dreadful though, they were supposed to be pulled back out of the line as the wheels were literally coming off both the equipment and the men, even the wardroom toaster had been robbed for something to fix the air search radar!

The skipper had had a tense conversation with the admiral when he got his orders to step into the Lion's den once more, rumour had it that he'd pleaded with Woodward to pull them out as they were just worn out, and that the admiral had promised just one more day.

Jake sat there in the raft having lost his ship again and really the cause was the same in both cases. Insufficient guns, no point defences which would have automatically destroyed the missile that hit *Sheffield* and which would have torn apart the pair of Skyhawks which bombed the *Coventry* just as easily.

A 'Dalek,' sailor-speak for a Vulcan phalanx point defence gun, on the *Ardent* and one on the *Antelope* too would have shredded the incoming jets, he mused in a poppy induced haze. Whichever way he looked at it, it was all about money and the admirals had bowed to the 'pencil necks' and taken second best rather than get fewer ships built.

He drifted off again as he waited for transfer to the hospital ship himself and vaguely wondered if the officer he'd replaced would think himself lucky to have his appendix flare up at just the right time. A last aberrant thought wandered in and out; bad enough losing one, bloody careless losing two ships.

Wednesday January 13th 2016

Georgetown, Grand Cayman

The old government house wasn't the ideal seat for the new administration, mused Andrew McTeal, Prime Minister of just sixty days.

The buildings were large, airy and set in the most delightful gardens imaginable, *but*. Always the *but*, frowning he swivelled the heavy leather upholstered chair away from his antique rosewood desk and towards the two inch thick Plexiglas windows that lined his study instead of the original French doors. The original architects hadn't given much thought to defensibility; he presumed they'd relied on the Pax Britannica back then.

He stood and wandered slowly towards the nearest window. Still deep in thought, his keen eyes swept the lush gardens and automatically noted the roving guards from the recently formed Ministerial Protection Police or MPP as they referred to themselves.

These men and women now kept him alive, albeit a virtual prisoner. They were a specialist unit trained in part by British SAS instructors for their close protection and counter terrorism work as well as Scotland Yard's anti-terrorist unit for the intelligence gathering and threat assessment.

They had all sadly been very busy recently, and he'd thanked the Lord for their skill and extravagant bravery on more than one occasion. He knew he mustn't let the 'fug' of depression take over and paralyse his mind.

He turned back to his desk with a last wayward thought about the MPP, the kind of protection you need when you have just snatched twenty seven billion US dollars from the funds of perhaps the most successful drug cartel currently operating in Colombia.

He lit a cigar and savoured the smoke, no going outside for a quick puff for him any more; these were really good a nice present from Raul on independence.

About seventeen billion had been electronically residing in some of Cayman's 600 offshore banks. The rest had been scattered in shell companies and corporation deposits around the US, Europe and the Far East, all traced though, from their Cayman origins.

How many times had he asked himself whether it had been worth it? How many times had he said 'no' in private and 'yes' in public? The cartel's revenge was still unfolding like a slow motion horror movie that he couldn't stop, switch off or better still, rewind.

McTeal was 52 years old and until two months ago had been the driving force behind the island's 'Independence from Britain' movement. Now he was Prime Minister and wishing he could wind the clock back to those relatively carefree and seemingly innocent days.

He had been, he only admitted to the mirror, totally unprepared for the realities of government. In fact he reflected that his own arrogance had persuaded him he was not only qualified but the best man for the job, such is the disease of the professional politician.

The joint approach from both the US and Great Britain when it came, shortly after, had been flattering he ruefully admitted, and the proposal appealed to his righteous self-importance and crusading attitude. The final nail had been the joint visit from Barrack Obama and David Cameron, the photo-op had been the cream on the cake for his self-importance.

Plainly they had read him like a book. It had all seemed so easy on paper, quite exciting really from the safety of this room as the experts had accessed the various banks and with a passcode and mouse click had electronically moved the money out of the reach of its owners, just like that. The experts had all been confident the money could be applied to ruining more trafficking rings. The experts weren't here now though.

Their initial reaction had been swift, barbaric and utterly ruthless. He stared at the framed picture of his family on the wall and looked down quickly to see the tremor in his hands.

He knew on a rational level that it was both fear and anger fuelling it and the one fed the other in a vicious cycle that left him no sleep at night and no peace in the day. Muttering to himself he buzzed the intercom and asked for more coffee.

McTeal was a handsome and impressive looking man, so they told him, his face was smooth and unmarked by childhood disease which was still common in the Caribbean. His skin though dark was not central African black and his eyes had a penetrating quality which had caused the most resolute witness to wilt under their gaze when he'd served at the Bar.

He stood a broad shouldered, slim waisted six feet two inches tall. He was a proud man, proud of his heritage and his personal achievements, proud of his island people and now fully aware that he'd likely die for them too.

The battles he'd fought at the Bar had never placed him in the frontline. It had been easy to wax lyrical about right and wrong, to wave an accusatory finger at the miscreant in the dock. Not anymore!

The world had turned and now he was in the front line experiencing the result of his own orders and actions. The battlefield was the whole planet, the enemy a guerrilla force who's prize was money not territory, who's fuel was heroin and crack cocaine. An insidious infection with almost unlimited finances, and whose mercy could be measured in Nano grams.

A young man entered the room quietly, quickly deposited the coffee on McTeal's desk and left. He'd be telling everyone about the boss's look of thunder when he got back to his desk in a minute.

McTeal checked his wristwatch by habit ignoring the three other clocks in the room, ten minutes before his next appointment. Too much time.

The drug barons had washed money through his islands for years, they all knew it. Everyone said it was impossible to stop it. Well what they'd meant really was that they were *sensibly* too scared to do anything about it.

He just wished he'd been too scared too. Sure the Caymans were not a good place to hide dirty money any more, well for now at least. But the cost to him had been appalling, his wife and two children slaughtered in the street.

They'd been dragged from the government sedan and after killing the driver, one had slit their throats and the other had filmed it. They then deliberately placed a gun at each other's head and pulled the trigger, but not before uploading a film of the murders onto YouTube. The cartels had endless supplies of men who would die for them if their families were given money to break out of the poverty trap that vast swathes of South America found itself in.

That had been the start of the most dreadful day of his life so far. Further cartel suicide murderers had killed his mother and father as they waited for the MPP to come and secure them.

While that was happening two ministerial colleagues, finance and security, were blown up by car bombs as they were driven to safety. The whole thing had been carefully planned to cause maximum terror and maximum damage –which it did.

While no one claimed responsibility it was plain where the orders had originated. The beatific Caymans indeed he laughed harshly, causing his secretary to peer fearfully around the door.

Worse still, this was just the start of the Columbian's pay-back, he knew that when they'd finished exacting revenge on everything around him, then they would come for him.

He lurched to his feet, overwhelmed by events he could no longer control. His eyes focussed. He was standing in front of the picture, he looked at his smiling wife, daughter and son.

"I can't give in." He whispered to them. "Or you will have died for absolutely nothing."

Saturday February 6th, 2016

Presidential Retreat, Haitian Island of Gonâve.

General Francois Lasseugue Farache, President of Haiti, sat quietly in his study. The only light in the room came from an antique oil lamp on the corner of his large ornate desk.

The gently undulating flame cast waves of soft light out to the farthest reaches of the room, revealing the richly ornate eighteenth century French style decor. There was only one other chair in the room and it sat empty in front of the President's desk.

He stared at it intently as if attempting to divine the next occupant's intentions. The positioning of the lamp was deliberate as was more or less everything the General did.

In its present position it cast a favourable light across his features making his skin appear paler than it was. The Haitian disease he decided; to try to appear black to the ordinary people and as pale as possible to the people that really mattered.

It wasn't a good idea to be too black or too white in this country. To his peers, the paleness of his skin denoted a considerable French heritage, a good thing if you wanted to get to the top with their support. To the general population his blackness was a sign of closeness to his slave heritage, essential if you were to last any time, since most of his soldiers were black too and they kept him in power.

He grunted to himself and sat back, the chair groaning in protest. He mentally acknowledged his ever increasing waistline but countered that admission with the knowledge that the chair had been picked for a much smaller occupant, one Jean Bertrand Aristide. And anyway, he further justified, Presidential duties inclined one toward larger meals and too little exercise. The thought of Aristide however, painted a smile onto his fleshy features for just a second.

The satisfaction he felt at having outmanoeuvred both Aristide, Boniface Alexandre and then Preval as well as the damned interfering Americans, was tempered with the knowledge that his position within the Junta, that now ruled Haiti, was not terribly firm.

Aristide had done most of the work himself, it had to be admitted, his excesses as the democratically elected President of Haiti had dwarfed even the myopic Clinton administrations' attempts to overlook them. The final straw for the Americans had been the beating up of two of their embassy staff at a demonstration in Port-Au-Prince, after Clinton had publicly warned Aristide that support would be withheld unless he changed his ways.

He'd been a major at the time, a dangerous rank really. A sort of in-between rank when it came to a coup d'état. The ensuing demonstration had provided Boniface's supporters the perfect opportunity to wreak havoc by severely beating the two lowly staffers and dumping them by the embassy gate.

Everyone knew how sensitive the Americans were about their embassies and so the 'Molotov' into the embassy compound on the same evening had finished Aristide in their eyes.

It had only required a little pot stirring in amongst the ordinary people, not too difficult when you had your men buying the rum, and the invoking of some totally erroneous memories of 'the good old days', and voila! Suddenly Aristide's grip on power was slipping. His end was sealed when he closed the House of Representatives claiming they were subversives, and then suspended the constitution.

Preval had been a bit harder to get rid of but nature had helped with the earthquake and then then storms. After that it had been plain sailing to mount a military coup and best of all, the Americans had stood by and watched, unwilling and unable to interfere to because of the widely reported events leading up to the coup.

The only fly in the ointment for the General was having to share power with his two principal allies in the coup, but that could all change tonight, he thought.

Pulling open the top right drawer of the desk he withdrew the nickel plated Walther PPK -he liked James Bond- and expertly checked the action and load before replacing it in the desk without closing the drawer. Hauling himself up out of the chair, he moved slowly across the polished wooden floor towards the closed, louvered French doors.

He stood listening as the sounds of the jungle nightlife competed with the slow measured tread of his own presidential guards as they patrolled the neatly raked gravel paths encircling the old plantation house. He checked his watch again and noted with annoyance that it was only three minutes since he'd last checked it. He understood his nervousness.

This meeting had been initiated by the 'absent party' and Farache liked to do the initiating himself usually. But the real reason for the nerves was simply that in a few moments, under an intense security screen, he would be meeting with the current head of a Medellin drug cartel. The blank cheque they offered would certainly be welcome, but what did they want in return?

Red Sea. König Marine survey vessel Kristina
[Midway between Jazirit Jabal Zuqar and Jazirat Al Hanish as Saghir]

"Captin!" On the bridge able seaman Arief Budiono shouted into his radio.

"What is it Arief? Is it important? You know I'm trying to get the kink in this tail sorted." He added with a touch of impatience. By 'the tail' he was referring to the seismic source array of multiple towed sensors and activators.

"There is a patrol boat Captin, heading directly towards us at high speed. Twenty degrees off the port bow *sah*."

"Shit, not again."

Captain Wilhelm Van Plasterk looked up and slightly off to his left. Dammit, he'd need to climb a little higher to see. He wiped his hands on his dirty dark red overalls, took his white hard hat off and wiped the sweat from his brow.

The big Dutchman marched up the afterdeck to the nearest ladder to the bridge. On his way he caught sight of Arief's patrol boat. He entered the air conditioned 'coolth' of the bridge and grabbed a pair of 'bins' from the rack and focussed quickly.

Problem was there'd been all sorts of shit happening around here recently, the Saudis bombing anything that moved or didn't, two different factions of nutjob Muslims having a go at the government or what passed for it, and each other.

None of them could agree whether it was night or fucking day. The last couple of days had seen visits from an Eritrean fast patrol boat, really fast that fucker thought Willy, forty something knots when he swept by with that 25mm auto-cannon pointing at us all the time -jeez that was scary.

He focussed the binoculars again and paused. No flag. Not yesterday's Eritrean, wrong ship, wrong shape, wrong direction of approach. This one was coming in fast too, these buggers don't care about fuel costs do they, bloody cowboys, he muttered under his breath.

Maybe they just forgot to raise the flag this morning? Something was nagging his memory, a memo, a message, something in the last week or so anyway, but he'd been so busy setting up the scanning and towed array he hadn't had time for all the paperwork on his overflowing desk.

He followed them in, only half a mile now. Figures standing on the foredeck. He focussed on them. No uniforms, just a dishdash and random robes, oh, and AKs all over. Something bad happening here, he felt a chill down his spine and thought of his wife and two daughters back in Holland.

"Arief run and tell everyone not to do anything to provoke them, ask the Chief to join me at the midships entry port. This is bad Arief, they aren't navy guys, I'm going to push the button."

Arief looked alarmed. As he should do, thought Willy as he made his way to the back of the bridge and along to his cabin.

There on the bulkhead by his bunk, with a plexi cover flip up cover was a black button. This was the activation unit for the SASS system. He lifted the cover and hesitated. If I'm wrong I'll get shit poured down my neck until I drown he thought.

Then he pushed it and reclosed the cover. One look at his desk and the pictures in the frame there and he headed down towards the midships boarding area.

The activated SASS beacon (Ship Automated Security System) should first send a satellite message to the country code programmed into it for this area, then dial the nearest Rescue Coordination Centre (RCC) and deliver a pre-coded message. In this case it would notify Jeddah, a useless five hundred plus clicks away.

As he climbed down the companionway and arrived at the starboard midships entry port Willy was thinking about their chances. The RCC at Jeddah would get the call, there was nowhere nearer that was set up as an RCC. They'd notify König Marine headquarters in Norwich England as a routine.

Willy thought through the next steps. Locally the RCC would check the location of the beacon originator and read up on the vessel sending it. Then they'd look at the map to see who should or could respond. They would see it was a toss-up between contacting Eritrean authorities or Yemeni. Being good Arabs they would contact Yemen. Willy mused; I wonder how good that relationship is at the moment?

Anyway if they got through to someone and if they had anything in the area they'd be here in about four hours maybe five by sea.

Chances of an airborne intervention were remote in his opinion, anything taking off in Yemen was going to be shot down including helicopters because no one knew who was flying the damned things and for whom; if of course there were any left now after the Saudi coalition had bombed the crap out of anything resembling a plane or helicopter when they intervened in 2015.

Even if they contacted Eritrea, it was still going to be a long wait.

So that was it then, no help no time soon and without a single weapon other than a galley knife, they could only hope for a low key takeover not a bloodbath.

The SASS system like many international ideas was great if you were in the North Sea or English Channel or maybe off Palm beach, he thought, but in the back end of the world utterly useless. He considered the English expression ... *'closing the gate after the horse has bolted'*. Very apt.

A Casus Belli?

23rd August 2016.
Breaking news. Rueters London

König Industries Marine released a statement which was issued at the company head Office, Norwich, England. This morning the CEO, Jonathan Henry König, confirmed that the MV Kristina had been taken by armed pirates whilst surveying the channel between Yemen and the Jazirat islands. Nothing is known as yet concerning the fate of the seventeen missing crewmen. Kristina is the seventh vessel to be taken in an eight week orgy of attacks in the area.

Related: European navies pull back from Gulf of Aden.
  George Moore May 2016
Related: Yemen patrol boats taken by AQAP militants Tariq. Malaqua Aug 2016

27th August 2016.
Breaking news. Reuters London

It has been confirmed this morning that YouTube images released last evening and reported on Al Jazeera, do in fact show the crucifixion of the Christian crew members of the missing König Industries survey ship MV Kristina. It is unknown at this time what has become of the twelve other mainly Indonesian Muslim, crewmen. The company has yet to issue a statement.

See HTTP://......Warning violent content and scenes of violence including murder.

Related: World piracy on the up again.
   Pjet Wolkrom May 2016

30th August 2016.
Breaking news. Reuters London.

The bodies of the twelve Indonesian crewmen missing from the König Industries survey ship Kristina have now been identified. They were deposited this morning outside the offices of a shipping agent known to be associated with König Industries Marine in the port city of Mocha, Yemen. A note pinned to one of the corpses claimed that the ship and its crew were working for the Great Satan and that Al-Qaida in the Arabian Peninsula

(AQAP) would continue to engage the enemies of the prophet wherever they found them. There was again no comment from König Industries head office.

Related: Tough talk but no action on Pirates Malacca straits. George Moore, May 2016

12th December 2016.
Breaking news. Rueters Amsterdam

A court in Amsterdam today awarded record damages to the widow of Captain Wilhelm Van Plasterk the murdered master of the MV Kristina, claiming in its judgement that the company had done little or nothing to protect its employees and had therefore failed in its duty of care. During the trial it became apparent that König Industries had made repeated requests to British and EU authorities for permission to carry limited arms on vessels operating in the Red sea and Indian Ocean. König Industries Marine will appeal the judgement.

Friday 12ᵗʰ May 2017

Outside European Court of Human Rights, Strasburg France

Ed Kirk, König Industries' Chief legal counsel held his mobile phone to one ear and shoved a finger in the other trying to shut out the background noise whilst he spoke to his client Jonathan 'Jake' Henry König.

"Well sorry about this Jake but you know my feelings." He pontificated. "I don't know what your reasoning was for having us take a softly, softly approach to this case but it sours my cream when I lose one that I'm pretty sure I could have won with just a little effort."

"Yes Ed I understand your point."

Ed could be a bit pompous sometimes Jake knew, but he was the bee's knees for corporate law and a good friend to boot. Jake parted the blinds in his Sofitel hotel room just about a mile down the road from where Ed was speaking and watched the lunch time crowds meandering along Rue Thomann.

"I'm sorry I've kept you in the dark over this but it isn't just about the killings on the *Kristina* or just winning a case Ed. It's an accumulation of incidents and factors that made me want to lose this one so it would provide a precedent and justification for later actions. Anyway, what's the English version of the judgement?"

"OK. Here it is." Ed removed the finger from his ear and moved away from the entrance to the weirdest court building he'd ever seen, trying to find a quieter area. He looked down at the summary page in his hands.

"They say that by failing to provide a policy with adequate contingency planning against assaults of a piratical nature, in that there were no measures advised and provided which would have allowed the crew the ability to repel a piratical attack on the vessel blah, blah, despite it sailing in waters where such attacks have recently occurred blah, blah, this is the cruncher Jake, they say König industries failed in their primary duty of care to the officers and men on this vessel in the persons of Captain Wilhelm Van Plasterk, deceased, and others named, and as such breached their Human Rights." He broke off to vent his spleen about the judges.

"What sticks in my craw Jake is that these 'holier than thou' backroom lawyers, few of whom incidentally have ever worked in a courtroom, would have been first to crucify you ...er, er sorry

Jake, poor choice of words, if you had toasted the guys that did this to Bill and the others."

He quickly did a mental review to check if anyone had been toasted just in case he'd screwed up again.

"Anyway they drivel on for about ninety pages. Now what this means of course is that they kick it back to the Dutch court who's verdict you'd appealed and then basically they will uphold their first verdict and award in favour of the plaintiff so the company will be down nearly £30 million for the various damages. I still don't understand why we only *played* at defending it and then appealed all the way up to the ECHR though?"

Jake drew a breath before answering; this was the key to the whole strategy.

"Suppose one of our ships was attacked again Ed, suppose we defended the ship with one of our security detachments. Suppose Ed, we deliberately sank the pirate vessel and killed its crew. Suppose it was written into company policy that no captain should readily surrender his/her vessel if attacked on the high seas and would be subject to internal disciplinary inquiries if they did. Do you think you'd be able to mount a reasonable defence of company policy after this judgement Ed?" The light bulb lit above Ed Kirk's head.

"Oh my. Damn right! Jonathan Henry you are a sly one. I knew you wouldn't mind the pay out to Billy's widow but I just couldn't see the wood for the trees. You going to arm our ships now?"

"Discretely, yes. I'm not out to prove a point, just to do what I think is the right thing, I'm going to put a full security detachment aboard any vessel known to be travelling through waters where there's even a vague possibility of attack. They'll have whatever is deemed necessary by Andy Evans in order to ensure they can fight off anything that might come at them, up to and including shoulder launched guided weapons and heavy machine guns if deemed a requirement. Meanwhile there's another project I want to brief you in on and this one will make your eyes pop Ed, a private Man O' War and not so discretely armed. So you finish off down there and meet me here, I'll wait in my suite for you."

"You're the boss."

Ed clicked his phone shut and went back into the two barrel-shaped buildings that made up the ECHR complex, weird or what? As he entered, his mind was already turning over the international agreements, the international maritime organisation documents and anything else he could dredge up that might have a bearing on arming civilian ships.

Jonathan agreed with every word the presiding judges had written about the lack of defensive measures, except that these same people would have objected shrilly had König Industries taken any precautions such as arming the vessels, which then injured the attacking pirates.

In fact they would have happily supported a prosecution, brought by the surviving pirates, against his company had they deployed any proper defensive measures such as 'things which can hurt people', was Ed Kirk's somewhat sarcastic elaboration. Jake did not consider stringing razor wire and rigging fire hoses anything approaching the defensive capability necessary to discourage the barbarous and inhumane activities that these so called pirates indulged in.

The European courts were brilliant at such judgements, they had you both ways and yet suggested no means by which his company could have complied without breaching a dozen other international conventions.

Well he didn't begrudge the money at all; it was the principal which was being tested here. He was glad the decision to move König Industries headquarters and as much as possible of their operation to Little Cayman had been taken. The facilities were almost ready now, and they'd be away from the ridiculous EU the fact that Britain had voted leave and was going through the tortuous process of disentanglement had not changed the decision, he'd still have people there but the legal headquarters would not be. He needed a chat with his good friend Andrew McTeal about which international agreements the newly independent Cayman republic signed up to. Being a lawyer Andrew hopefully wouldn't go 'flourish' mad and sign everything put in front of him.

Sunday 21st January 2018- Early

Geneva, Switzerland

Jake had to confess to a little nervousness. Nothing he'd done was wrong in his interpretation of things, or illegal as far as he knew, BUT it was going to be all about how other people construed what he was up to. That ultimately, would see the success or failure of this project.

If people misunderstood why he'd built this particular ship and if governments felt threatened by the change from national to private security in this arena, then it would be money down the drain.

Worst of all in his opinion, more merchant sailors would be placed at risk. Everything would go sour if he could not persuade these men that what he'd done, in fairness at great personal expense, was viable and even legal, but to him, most importantly, necessary. So it was all about presentation.

Meeting in Geneva today had been a great idea; he planned to introduce two of the key members of the project team to each other by personally giving a brief résumé of their achievements and fitness for their assigned tasks. They were both ex-navy men but not from the same navy, and they would become the foundation stones for the company of his new ship –if all went to plan.

He also intended to read a third résumé for a person who was absent from the meeting. Jake would explain that they'd meet up with the Chief Engineer who, having assisted with the construction, was now in the Crimea supervising the fitting out.

With him in Geneva was Reiner Krull, a six foot two inch, dark haired and slender south German whom he'd worked with in Plymouth whilst on the staff of Flag Officer Sea Training (FOST) for the RN.

Reiner's only visible concession to his forty nine years were the flecks of grey at the sides of his dark hair. When they'd met years before, Reiner had revealed his first encounter with FOST had been on the destroyer *Mölders* in the late 80's as a very junior officer. The memory of this still made him shudder, he'd told Jake whilst describing his first ever 'Thursday War'.

It was one of the features of the work-up period which had made FOST infamous and not just in European navies; the Americans had a healthy respect for it too. But since the purpose of those weeks of drills and exercises was to turn a green crew into a competent crew or a competent crew into an excellent crew it was right and proper that people respected it.

Reiner's second visit had been in 94' as a skipper himself, Kapitan-Leutnant of the fast attack boat *Tiger*. This time he'd been ready. He and his crew had scored high for more or less everything each and every time they were tested, even when the 'Fosties', the polite term for FOST staff, had thrown the odd spanner in the works. This throwing of a spanner in the works when everything seemed to be going well was how they'd earned their less than polite moniker of 'Green Slime'; this referred to their distinctive olive green foul weather gear.

His third visit in 97' as a Fregattenkapitän and Staff Officer German liaison, after FOST had moved to Plymouth. Jake who had been there a while already, met and immediately liked the new German officer. They had worked closely during that time and quickly became friends. Jake had seen Reiner work through tactical problems with a phenomenal speed and icy calm which had earned him the nickname 'Data' after the Star Trek android. His calm, efficiency and consummate logic meant he could easily dissect the arguments of ships officers who thought they'd handled the 'Thursday War' better than they actually had. Reiner was without doubt one of the finest naval warfare specialists that Jake had ever met and he'd met plenty. If all went according to plan Reiner would soon be Captain of König Marine's newest ship.

The other man present in Geneva was a seaman too, but his craft had been learned from the perspective of an ordinary sailor. Ken Herring or 'Kipper' to his friends, an ex-Warrant Officer had left the Royal Navy only seven years before having completed twenty five years' service man and boy. He and Jake had also met at FOST when Herring had been a Petty Officer and the meeting had been a navy classic.

Jake, by this time a Lieutenant Commander, had thought there was something familiar about the new *Fosty* who unusually wasn't a Chief or Warrant Officer. The nagging familiarity had continued until one day when they'd both been at HMS Raleigh waiting to fly out to a ship, part way through its first week of Basic Operational Sea Training (BOST), where things were pretty tense on board. Inevitably as they waited for the delayed aircraft, they had exchanged derogatory remarks about WAFUs of all ilk and Jake then finally steered the conversation to his hunch.

"Now don't take this the wrong way Herring, but I feel as if I know you from somewhere but I'm damned if I can think where."

This as both knew was a common feature of naval life where you met lots of people, stayed with them sometimes just for weeks and others for years, and then either never saw them again or met them and couldn't remember on which ship it had been. Herring smiled.

"I'll put you out of your misery Sir, you served with my dad on *Coventry*. In fact it was you who helped him escape after she was hit!"

"Well damn me, what a coincidence. We lost touch after the war you know, but I occasionally got an update on his progress from various places. How is the old bugger?"

As soon as Jake said it he regretted asking, it had been a long time and Herring senior would be heading for a state pension soon, no dammit, he'd be drawing it! If he were still alive that is.

Ken saw the quick hesitation and jumped in fast.

"He's fine Sir, he often talks about his time on *Coventry* and then the *SS Uganda* with you. Over a few tots he'll remember that day you saved him, you know how it is. It comes up each time the media idiots have these big anniversaries every ten or twenty years. They just dig up the old stuff and people like yourself and dad have to relive it with wall to wall TV and newspaper coverage each time the great day approaches."

Jake nodded in agreement.

"Bit of a stretch to say I saved him though, I just came round first, I'm sure he would have helped me out if it had been the other way round but I concur with what you said about the anniversaries, I try to avoid them if at all possible. But sometimes I get taken by surprise, then I end up reliving the only thing I'm famous for, Jonathan König, the guy who got sunk twice. Well anyway I'm pleased to hear he's still cooking with gas."

"Aye Sir, but he still hasn't forgotten you. I saw him last weekend and told him I was working for your guys and he asked to be remembered."

Jake recalled that Kipper Herring 'the younger' had got his promotion to Chief shortly after that conversation and he had been impressed afterwards with the way he had handled himself in some pretty awkward situations.

The last time he'd served with him had been in the late 90's when they'd both ended up in the Adriatic on another 42' and Herring had been a senior Chief trying desperately to cope with the demands that the reduced ship manning policy had made on him and his seamen.

With Jake as 'The Jimmy' and Herring as the 'Chief Buffer' they'd had the devil's own job to keep things together for that deployment, Jake's last as it happened.

They had formed a bond then, mutual dependency, mutual respect. Herring kept the lads on side and watched Jake's back and Jake tried to keep as much crap off their plate as possible and watched Herring's back. They'd stayed in touch after Jake had resigned, Christmas cards and the like, and he recalled being immensely pleased when Herring had made it to Warrant Officer.

When they arrived in Geneva, Jake had taken the pair of them to lunch at one of the finest restaurants to be had locally before telling them they were all off to the Crimea to visit the dockyard where their new ship was in its final stages of fitting out. Two pairs of raised eyebrows had greeted the location information and so Jake had amplified.

"Yes I suppose the location may at first seem a little odd but bear with me because it won't be the only 'oddity' you're going to encounter today. In fact you'll probably think it's the least of them by the time you return home." He paused and took a sip of wine.

"This is going to sound like a bit of a rant at certain points gentlemen but it is essential background if you are going to join with me and commit to this enterprise. You have to know how I'm thinking at this stage of the game."

He began his explanations.

"Over the years, I've cultivated a number of contacts in Russia. It was necessary to prevent a repetition of a rather embarrassing incident just after I took over the companies I inherited from my father. When Russia suddenly dumped thousands of tons of surplus aluminium on the world market just a week after I'd signed up for the next year's requirement, I faced a boardroom revolt which nearly lost me the Chair before I'd even got it warm." He shook his head.

"I won't elaborate on that fiasco, they were new to world markets and I was new to running companies. Anyway it was for that purpose but also for altruistic reasons too, since I bore them no ill will from all the time we'd been on opposing sides in the cold war. I was keen in my own little way that we would not be on opposite sides again. So I was pleased that Russia had started to turn the corner economically and, was no longer ideologically opposed to us."

Jake went on.

"Anyway, the shipyard where this vessel has been constructed is expert at the type of specialist alloy welding and fabrication of the materials used in its construction. They were after all, producing vessels for the former Soviet Navy made from similar stuff. Our missing Chief Engineer is actually one of the most experienced metal alloy fabricators anywhere on the planet and has been closely involved with design as well as construction. That was as soon as we learned exactly how capable he was; but I'll let him fill you in on the details later."

He paused for a moment to pick his next words carefully.

"Russia is sensibly no one's enemy by choice. To qualify that statement. I have to say the odd behaviour of the EU and the US back in 2014, and subsequently, has caused a rift which will take some healing if it ever does. Especially since Russia reasonably, in my mind, feels a little picked on. You didn't need to be a genius to see the reality of what went down in Ukraine, but the propaganda poured out by our Western media painted a totally different picture. In my position I need to keep abreast of things, spin-free information if you will. This has become increasingly hard to obtain through journalistic channels, it appears the age of the investigative journalist has mostly ended along with that of telling something resembling the truth."

He took another sip of wine before continuing.

"I am not a big fan of Mr Putin, but not because of Ukraine particularly, although I think he could have handled that better, it is because he plays 'switcheroo' with Medvedev for President and Prime Minister, which to my mind subverts the new democracy in Russia. However in fairness, he does have some rather unique problems and since I don't have to put up with an entrenched mafia and troublesome republics I'll decline to criticise too much."

He paused for emphasis.

"I see no logical reason for this continuing push in the West for another cold war, most especially since we are no longer in ideological opposite camps. The raft of sanctions that the US, EU and various countries have imposed over the years have made it difficult, but thankfully not impossible, to operate there. But we need not get into politics really, the area is safe and secure and the work quality has been outstanding. The local people have benefited hugely and we have built up a large measure of goodwill in the area and in certain ministries as well, since we pay in dollars and on time. I won't go into specifics at this point but certain pieces of equipment are of Russian origin anyway as you'll discover."

He paused looking them in the eye.

"So unless either of you has any deep and abiding conviction which will prevent you working in Russia or joining us, I suggest we get over to the airport as one of my company aircraft is refuelling as we speak."

Although it was no longer possible to fly scheduled to Sevastopol Jake's aircraft had a direct flight plan to Belbek, a Russian military field near Sevastopol so the twelve hundred or so miles only took a little over two and a half hours with no stops.

Sunday 21st January 2018 –Afternoon

Gulfstream G450 Enroute Sevastopol, Russian Crimea.

From Reiner Krull's perspective at the moment, things were a little out of kilter, so to speak. He sat in the luxurious leather seat of the Gulfstream G450 and stared out at the clouds passing below wondering what he'd got himself into.

That he trusted Jake wasn't in question, he just hoped that whatever was coming down the road wouldn't destroy their friendship if it all turned sour somehow. Their families had stayed close over the years since their FOST time and Jake had tried several times to get him to come and work for his shipping company after he'd inherited it on the death of his father. Reiner had always found a face saving excuse to say no, up until now.

He smiled as he recalled how Jake had sprung this ambush one weekend early last September as the families had got together for a BBQ at his house in Norfolk. He and Jake sat a little apart from the others and talked. He hadn't realised he was being interviewed almost until the end of the wide ranging discussions.

As usual they had righted all the world's wrongs over a beer or two and then covered recent events involving Jake's ship the *Kristina* before the conversation moved onto the world naval drawdown, except China and one or two other notables, and that was dissected.

Another focus of their discussions had been the reduction then removal of European states naval forces from the Gulf of Aden area, after the politicians had declared it safe, which clearly it wasn't. The ensuing predictable upsurge in piracy attacks on the now unprotected shipping in the Red Sea and out into the Indian Ocean was an obvious consequence.

This led neatly on to the topic of private security operating at sea from small security teams on ships and then on to Ghana's insistence on using private security for a piracy prevention mechanism in their waters.

Finally Jake worked the conversation around to his corporate security division and its possible growth to include the high seas, now that governments seemed to prefer to rely on others to do what they were duty bound to do i.e. protect and defend their sea lines of communications.

They had both been appalled at the arrest and imprisonment by the Indians, of six former British soldiers from another company which supplied security to protect ships transiting the danger areas. The Indians had behaved most bizarrely in this extraordinary case of a ship accidentally straying into territorial waters. The pair agreed that surely it wasn't in the Indian's interest to prevent such men working, and clearly the infringement of territorial waters had been unintentional. It seemed that the final convictions had rested on firearms licence technicalities of all things.

Jake and he had pulled that one apart as far as it was possible and concluded that there must be another factor somewhere, not made public, which would explain it. Clearly the person responsible for being in Indian territorial waters was ultimately the ship's master, but even moving down the chain of command it could only go as low as the Officer of the Deck. So plainly it was wrong to imprison the security staff who had no knowledge of where exactly they were.

Finally they talked through the possibility of the resurrection of the private warship as a going concern, as a 'gap-filler' where navies could no longer afford to tread. Really, Reiner decided ruefully, he should have realised that he was being interviewed a lot sooner, but the topics were of such interest he hadn't noticed how structured they were.

Sunday 21st January 2018 -Late

Sevastopol, Russian Crimea

On arrival at Belbek International Airport that evening, they'd been met by a company logoed utility vehicle. König Marine was stencilled on both sides in English and Cyrillic; it was the kind of vehicle with two rows of opposing seats in the back. The trio had thrown their overnight bags in the space at the rear and jumped in, Jake riding next to the driver.

When they got to the dockyard gates, a smartly dressed guard had stepped out of his hut and shone a torch at the vehicle. On recognising Jake he snapped to attention smiling broadly and saluting he pulled open the gates. Jake had waved from the front seat next to the driver who doubled as security and then added for the others.

"You know I can't get over being one of the good guys around here but I suspect it's something to do with the wages being generous and paid regularly in dollars." The driver smiled, nodding.

The others had smiled politely too but given that they were driving to see the object of so much private speculation, potentially the start of new careers, in a country neither had visited before and which was or had been recently a war zone, the smiles were a bit little 'copy and paste'.

Another five minutes of slow bumpy driving through a typically cluttered dockyard had brought them to their destination, a large newish hangar-like building only partially revealed by the occasional still working arc lights. A bitter wind blew off the sea bringing a stinging sleet with it.

Reiner and Ken stiffened when the driver got out and pulled a small pistol from inside his jacket, but Jake told them to relax. The guard had walked away from the vehicle towards the building talking into a radio as Jake explained.

"My Security Chief organised all this stuff, Andy Evans is his name; you'll meet him before too long. He insisted on personally recruiting the local security team for the whole project. Incidentally all these guys served in the Spetsnaz or in the case of the Team Leader, the FSB, and they all speak pretty decent English."

They learned that their current driver was part of a team of four who slept on the ship and kept it permanently covered. Security was taken seriously since the neighbours weren't good friends at the moment Jake commented, as the driver waved them in and opened a side door. Jake led on then, through a small reception area and past some empty offices of what used to be a covered frigate building complex.

Both Reiner and Ken knew that these types of place were ideal for all weather construction and safe from the prying eyes of anyone's satellites, so at least this part was familiar turf.

Finally Jake took them into the cavernous dock area where the echo caused by the slap of water on solid objects added another dimension to the pitch darkness. As they breathed in they got the standard dockyard mix, seashore, laced with oil, cut timber, paint and other unidentifiable but familiar odours.

They heard a loud click and then the sound of switches being thrown. Even in the sudden glare the shape of the vessel was unmistakeable. It takes a sailor's eye to find beauty in the hulking utilitarian form of a ship of war, but a beauty this was, by any measure. Reiner knew he would die with that image burned in to his retinas. The others were silent too and he recalled Jake standing off to one side grinning like a Cheshire cat at their surprise.

"Fuck a stoat." Was as much as Ken Herring could manage before lapsing into stunned silence.

As they walked around the end of the dock Reiner and Ken, still in a kind of trance, had just stared at the high, flared Atlantic style bows, Reiner noting the graceful line it bestowed on the vessel. He recalled looking along the length of the ship as they turned the corner and walked towards the gangway set halfway along its side. It was much larger than he expected.

Still, this was plainly not as large as the original and Reiner *had* thought 'warship' when Jake had gone through his recruiting phase so he wasn't surprised that it was a warship, just that it was **this** one. Reiner had automatically thought 'small' like a patrol boat of some kind, maybe like the *Tiger*, his first command, but this was in fact over a hundred metres long, as big as a modern frigate. He did a double-take at the oak leaf design on the ships' crest mounted high up on the bow and felt a twinge of apprehension. It had been many years since a ship had worn that coat of arms.

The guard on board was alert and had met them at the brow with pistol drawn until satisfied that all was as expected. Most of the interior fittings were still absent and the vessel had a sepulchral feel to it as their footsteps echoed through the hull on their way to Jake's cabin. Like the rest of the ship his cabin was sparsely furnished at the moment. He poured them glasses of his favourite Lagavulin whisky while they sat and swapped stories. It transpired that Reiner and Ken had met several times at FOST. The conversation was in danger of becoming a FOST reunion when the Chief Engineer joined them. Jake could see both Reiner and Ken had some serious questions but they could wait. He let Oleg introduce himself, the big Russian engineer's tale had been a lesson in the difference between East and West.

Oleg Ivanovich Scotnikov was an impressive man, almost the stereotype 'Russian' with his massive frame, steel grey crew cut hair and 'Stalino' moustache. The image was spoilt only by rimless 'Lennon' spectacles and an overt gruff kindliness that was entirely genuine. Reiner had taken to him immediately despite an adult life on opposing sides of the cold war. Scotnikov's story that night on the ship had brought home to the others how very fortunate they had been.

Oleg had been one of the last graduates of the old Soviet Frunze Academy which produced officers for the naval service. Even as Boris Yeltsin wandered around the Kremlin out of his head on cheap vodka, the wheels of the creaky replacement for the Soviet machine creaked around and spat him out a posting to Murmansk and the Headquarters of the Northern Fleet.

Having specialised in metal alloys and fabrication of the ultra-tough Titanium alloy used for the hulls of deep diving submarines, he'd been put to work as an engineer solving problems associated with the cracking of Titanium welds. As chaos reigned in Moscow the young Oleg applied his analytical mind to the task and had even worked briefly on the *Kursk* before tragedy struck her in 2000.

Inexplicably and devastatingly, Scotnikov been made redundant a year later. It was still his belief that it had to do with the unfortunate *Kursk* and anyone associated with it in any way, however the reason given was that he was really Ukrainian now and not Russian.

Returning home to the Crimea to discover that even as a highly qualified engineer, work was hard to come by and those who had been officers in the former Soviet military were often looked down on and discriminated against by the local Ukrainian elites as they went 'Western'.

At first the work in Crimea had been assessing the warships bequeathed them by the split up of the Soviet Union but after two years of that and other dead end jobs, Oleg had been made redundant again.

Since then his CV expanded to include labouring on building sites, repairing air conditioning units in the summer and motor cars whenever. No pension and no redundancy money from Russia or Ukraine, unlike Western navy men.

It had been a bitter blow, and with a wife and three children Oleg couldn't afford to be choosy about work despite having rising to the rank of Captain third class whilst serving in the navy.

Next of course in 2014, had been the return of Crimea to the Russian Federation but as that would take a day or so to explain he glossed over it.

Finally a stroke of luck came his way, the news that there were jobs to be had in one of the naval shipyards at Sevastopol filtered through and he dropped his spanner and walked straight there; jobs didn't go begging for long in the Crimea of today.

Only later had it come to light that he was not only well qualified but that one of his specialisations had been the fabrication of Titanium alloys for use in submarines. This fact tossed him high up the grade scales to senior engineer (local) without further ado, just on the recommendation of the König Marine senior engineer who recognised Scotnikov's unique qualification for the job at hand. That had been when Oleg started to meet Jonathan Henry König on a regular basis.

The König Marine British engineer had apparently been so impressed by Scotnikov's work and dedication that he'd recommended the big Russian be appointed Chief Engineer afloat, and that came with the rank of Lieutenant Commander and a big pay rise too.

Oleg sat quietly after his unusually lengthy speech, he was normally soft spoken and reserved but felt the others needed to know that whilst things hadn't been good for them always, he and others like him really had had the shitty end of the stick after peace was declared.

Kipper Herring broke the silence first.

"Well Oleg you thought you'd had it hard, I thought I was to be coxswain of a billionaire's posh yacht with semi naked girlies wandering around it, and look what I get, a flaming battleship!"

Laughter filled the night but then a serious mood settled over them.

"Let's take a walk gentlemen, there's plenty to see and you too will need to be familiar with every inch of her."

Up until that day Jake had deliberately kept everyone in the dark about aspects of his special ship, except of course the locals working on it. Not surprising really he thought to himself, they'd have thought me a basket case if I'd come right out with what I had planned.

As they wandered out on to the upperdeck and headed for the bows, all four men turned and looked back along the upperdeck, past the superimposed twin gun turrets towards the bridge area and signal decks above.

Then Jonathan Henry König, seemingly without effort, switched gears and became all business.

"I've got a bit of a speech now for you three gentlemen, during which I shall try to cover all of the questions that I'm sure you're dying to ask, by all means interrupt to clarify a point but please save incidental questions until I've finished. OK?" He looked around and collected the nods.

"Firstly, why build here in the Crimea? I mentioned the contacts I developed in the post-soviet Russia, well this one was well worth it. A note passed over my desk informing me that the *Alpha* class attack submarines were being decommissioned and sold for scrap, almost en-masse. Well you are also probably aware that they were constructed from Titanium alloys which made them ultra-expensive but also ultra-strong for deep diving. I was invited to tender for three of the hulls after they'd been checked for radioactivity."

He tapped his foot on the bare metal deck.

"At that time I had no idea what I wanted to do with the metal, but being in the shipping and shipbuilding business I reckoned I'd find a use eventually. If I were to try to buy the same weight of Titanium alloy today it would be ten times more expensive, so it was a good deal. When this project started to develop it became apparent that I had a use for some of the Titanium at last."

He paused and held his arms wide to encompass the ship around them.

"So this ship you're standing on is the only, sizeable, Titanium constructed surface vessel afloat at the moment, thereby making it the lightest and strongest hull anywhere."

Reiner's eyebrows rose at that point, a sure indication of surprise in a man who didn't give much away, thought Jake.

"The weight savings alone have been phenomenal, over thirty five percent total reduction of all up ship weight over steel construction, not to mention that Titanium is salt water corrosion immune too. Generations of sailors will spin in their graves, no more red lead paint and no more 'windy' hammers."

Kipper smiled at that.

"Now Reiner certainly has, and you Ken will possibly have guessed that this ship is indeed a smaller scale version of the German battleship *Bismarck* lost in action in 1941. I say 'version' because it isn't a replica, given that we aren't all one third sized crewmen."

He paused before plunging on.

"I'm sure one of your next questions would be why did I build a *Bismarck* replica? The answer for everyone else could simply be that I'm just an eccentric billionaire with nothing better to do with my money than indulge myself. That is true. I need not justify anything to anyone but you gentlemen at least deserve a fuller explanation of my motives.

There isn't really just one, but I'll try to explain some of the contributory factors. Firstly, I'm not actually a 'nutcase' as far as I'm aware. Some that I know may disagree but hey ho. There are some personal links to this vessel's namesake, for instance this."

At this point he'd pulled out of his jacket pocket a smallish plastic bag in which there appeared to be a somewhat tattered black note book and a folded sheet of paper.

"This gentlemen," he said taking the book from the bag, "is rather precious to me and my family; if you would please read a translation of the final pages Ken, Ivan, then I'll carry on."

Reiner read the original passage in the book and was deeply moved by it. He could without difficulty close his eyes and imagine the scene as the author had sat on the deck of the burning ship. He particularly noted the date. What Jake said next stunned him.

"That is the diary of Maximilian Johannes König, my Great Uncle Max, he was my grandfather's twin. He was one of only one hundred and fifteen survivors of the two thousand two hundred or so on the *Bismarck* during its last battle. Sadly he died of hypothermia on *HMS Dorsetshire*, the ship that rescued him." Jake stood up and took back the book with its translation and placed them in the bag.

"He was a sailor just like us. My grandfather told me he wasn't a Nazi and I believe him. Great Uncle Max, like many Germans, rather naively believed that the German people would come to their senses and get rid of Hitler and his thugs but, they all seriously underestimated the regime."

Jake could see Reiner nodding along with this.

"My grandfather and Max argued over this and when they parted for the last time, it was as my family left Germany in 1936 for Britain, all except Max who stayed behind hoping for change." Jake gave a reluctant smile and shrugged.

"They were on opposite sides in the war that followed. My grandfather was a respected marine engineer by then in ship construction and naturalised too; please note the last line where Max says 'you were right Kurt'. We think that is a reference to their disagreement."

"*Bismarck* wasn't a Nazi ship. A ship has no politics. Its owners were Nazis though but the design predates them. So you should know that I am not a Nazi and neither do I have any sympathies for their ideology. That hopefully, should dispel any doubts you might have on that particular score."

Reiner could understand that. He wasn't really political either, naval men seldom were. Politicians started and finished wars and like many western military people he was damned near apolitical.

Jake continued.

"But why *Bismarck*? Well it is such an awesome ship, truthfully isn't it? How anyone could look at her silhouette and not be impressed eludes me, but of course I'm a sailor top to toe."

He paused again.

"Between *Bismarck* and *Scharnhorst* I see two of the most aesthetically pleasing shapes that ever graced the seas, it was a real tug to decide which to build I can tell you. *Bismarck* though has been in my blood ever since I was a child and first read my Great Uncle's diary so in the end there was no contest."

He put the diary back in his pocket.

Reiner, like everyone else listened attentively to Jake's narrative unaware of this part of his friend's story and fascinated by the revelations as well as curious what was going to be next.

"But it wasn't for a long time after I bought the Titanium alloy that the idea of building this version of *Bismarck* popped into my head and hooked me. It sort of happened in a roundabout way as things often do."

"I had already been looking at the direction that privately security was going both ashore and afloat, indeed König Security Ltd is close to my heart and I am always interested in their ideas on how things are trending." He looked up at them.

"Some of our people are already training to serve at sea as security details on vessels navigating waters frequented by pirates, they will keep the ships safe, so the owners will get a significant reduction of their insurance premium as well as their cargo, ship and crew, home intact. Everyone's a winner except the entrepreneurs in small boats armed with AKs and the liberal progressives who want us to talk to them rather than shoot them."

They walked down the starboard side, past the bridge superstructure to just ahead of the seaplane catapult track.

"Anyway, consider why the ship is designed like this. With the exception of the Japanese, who for some reason seemed to favour a tall pagoda style superstructure, most everyone built them roughly this shape. This is the culmination of decades of development towards the pinnacle of efficiency for a naval artillery platform."

He lifted his hands and swept them in an arc encompassing the ship from bow to stern.

"Why reinvent the wheel? Really, why?"

He led them into the aft superstructure which on this version did not house the hanger but was instead offices and workshops.

"Why would we need a *Bismarck*? Consider this. Just from Britain's perspective, ninety five percent of our imports still come in by sea, therefore don't you find it odd that the UK government doesn't still have a sizeable navy to ensure the safety of its vital supplies, having twice before nearly starved to death when the supply ships were targeted? I do. I think it is a bizarre mismanagement of the worst kind."

He paused and led them back to the wardroom.

"They are happy to give away billions of taxpayers' money to other countries in so called *Foreign Aid* but not to fund their own police forces and their own armed forces." He sighed.

"It is also clear to me that since the ideology wars of the last century are over, the need for the four big black slugs to keep the peace, by which I mean the *Trident* submarines, has passed. Although it is also debatable as to whether they ever did. And yet that is what successive governments in Britain continue to commit to." He shook his head slowly.

"Sucking fifty billion or more from a shrinking defence budget for just four vessels which will deter nothing and no one, will never do the job for which they are designed and could not be employed in any other way, is the grossest dereliction of duty I can think of." He took a breath and carried on in a more reflective tone.

"I truly cannot think of a sensible or even plausible scenario where a UK Prime Minister would order a launch and I have tried, believe me. Consequently every other part of the UK armed forces and in particular the Navy is shrinking like an old party balloon." He paused to consider his next words.

"When otherwise intelligent people do something stupid, you know they are working to someone else's agenda. I leave you to work out who benefits most from perpetuating the submarine based nuclear deterrent, but it leaves me a commercial opportunity with this ship, and a residual duty to the sailors who risk their lives to keep us supplied."

"Hold on a sec boss, are you saying we don't need nuclear weapons?" Piped up Ken Herring.

"Not at all Kipper. What I am saying is that I cannot see the point of building more of the weapons we created to fight the last war, the ideology war. Oleg would probably be in a better position to advise us on how seriously the Soviet High Command rated the threat posed by Britain's independent deterrent and how much of a deterrent it was in fact. If you please Oleg."

Scotnikov who had no idea that Jake was going to spring that one on him, was understandably a little hesitant as he took a moment to collect his thoughts before replying.

"Gentlemen, please consider we were told that NATO were the aggressors, and maybe they were. Did you ever consider that? So we looked at things through a different prism as it were. Offensive and or defensive strategies of other nations were of course dissected and examined in great depth during my time at the academy."

He got nods all round for that statement.

"We considered the following." He ticked them off on his fingers.

"We had many thousand nuclear warheads and the Americans had many thousand nuclear warheads. The British Navy had one *Polaris* submarine at sea that could carry up to sixteen missiles, which we were told it never did. Would this one boat alter the outcome of a decision to prosecute a thermonuclear war after we had been attacked? The answer was resoundingly no. You see we were also told we would not be the first to use intercontinental nuclear weapons and therefore if used, it would be in retaliation."

He shrugged his big shoulders for emphasis.

"It was always considered that this one boat's purpose was to save American dollars and make Britain nuclear dependant on America." He sat back and folded his arms as if daring anyone to challenge his points.

Ken spoke up then.

"So you're saying you had a no first-strike rule too?"

Scotnikov turned to look directly at Ken Herring.

"Yes. The strategic weapons were always a separate thing since they were intercontinental and not tactical. You may know that the use of nuclear weapons on the battlefield was not ruled out for us and only thought of as another weapon in the arsenal.

Not the same concept as NATO eh, which had escalation as its route to nuclear?"

"Well I never knew that." Said Herring. "I'd always been under the impression that all your nukes were considered, what did you say 'another weapon in the arsenal'?"

Jake interrupted what was in danger of becoming a 'compare notes on the last forty years of the cold war' type conversation. This whilst fascinating, digressed even further from the point he wanted to make.

"OK Ken, thanks Oleg. That's pretty much what myself and many of my colleagues thought too when we chased these things around at staff college. Back in the cold war our contribution would have been just one last angry shot, since we would have all been supposedly nuked by then. As Ken pointed out the UK deterrent is not a first-strike weapon in any circumstance."

Jake brushed invisible fluff from his suit trousers.

"Today, despite what happened in the Crimea and Eastern Ukraine, Russia is no longer an ideological opponent, so there really isn't the least chance of there being a thermonuclear exchange, it's bad for business. Without ideology there aren't the same set of imperatives on either side. So perhaps you may think the Chinese would use them on us Kipper?" A nod for a reply was all he got.

"China may well be a threat but nuclear weapons possession is not the answer to that threat. They know we have a 'no first-strike' policy that really is set in stone so why would they be stupid enough to initiate a nuclear strike which to a large extent would simply nullify their overwhelming strength in equipment and numbers?"

He held his hands up for emphasis.

"It would be idiocy of the first water to play to an opponent's only strength and only a complete fool thinks the Chinese are stupid. They know that we wouldn't launch nukes even if they were marching in parade order along Plymouth Hoe! So if not Russia and not China, who then?"

As he had predicted Kipper was straight in.

"What about the rogue state scenario then boss? What if somewhere like Iran were to use them on us?"

"OK. Fair question Kipper so try this as an answer. Let's assume that a total nutter became boss over there, perhaps more so than the current incumbent, and then made nuclear weapons despite having signed 'N' treaties to say he won't."

He pointed to Kipper.

"Why would *WE* need an entire class of boats to deliver a response to any nuclear aggression of theirs? Knowing that their defences are less capable than either Russia or China we could simply use Tomahawk block IV or some other cruise missile with a nuclear tip, just how we armed them in the 80's. The newest ones though are stealthy, submarine torpedo tube fired, and have very, very low radar cross sections. This makes them nigh on impossible to detect with enough time to take them out, even with Iran's new S-300 missile system which Russia supplied."

Jake paused to let it sink in.

"No new technology per se and no new launch vehicle because various bits of what's left of the Royal Navy can fire them already, including our super sneaky submarines. They can also be air launched, or could be if we had anything left that could carry them now the Tornadoes are history. It would give us a precision capability rather than the 'sledge hammer to a nut' that a Trident D5, 6 or 7 is."

"But anyway, dial back a little. Let's for example's sake say that Iran was going to hit the UK. They'd probably decide to smuggle suitcase nukes into the country I think. They wouldn't need to bother with the diplomatic bag given how porous the UK borders are."

He shrugged as if to say everyone knew that.

"There isn't really another viable way to get at us is there? Leastways without their own nuclear tipped cruise or an intercontinental ballistic missile, neither of which they've got or are likely to get."

He let them weigh that up.

"Even if they got ICBMs, if they were mad enough to use them they wouldn't care that we had them too, because religious zealots aren't afraid of dying are they, so where's the deterrent? You are just left with revenge."

So imagine on day one they explode a suitcase bomb just outside parliament. Instant twenty five thousand year no-go area for a quarter mile around, beats Guy Fawkes all hands down. Let's assume they did not get the incumbent Prime Minister just so there's someone left to react. OK. So is he/she going to launch a Trident at someone immediately?"

Again the open arms asking for input but no one did.

"No, because she, I'll say she but it could be he, doesn't know where the nuclear material came from. So she calls the boffins at Aldermaston." He took another sip as he unfolded the plot.

"They take three days to examine the samples and sure enough they say we're pretty damn sure it came from Iran, so is she just going to launch now? No, because there is no immediate threat she'll have to go to parliament and then the UN Security Council for approval of her intent to act in retaliation, not self-defence. Also the Americans will want their say, because there isn't an on-going war. This is not swift stuff. Let's say that they get a UN Security Council resolution supporting a retaliatory strike, my personal belief is that they would not but hey ho let's just say they did. Is she going to launch now?"

Jake cupped a hand to his ear.

"Wait that's the telephone ringing, ah it is the Iranian president Madam Prime Minister, he says he must speak to you. He says that they have uncovered a plot to steal nuclear material and make bombs. Some misguided Iranian revolutionary guards it is believed, and they are busy pulling out finger nails to establish who, how much they got and where it is."

He could see them working through his arguments.

"Simultaneously an announcement of the same thing is going out on Al Jazeera, BBC and CNN. Is the PM going to launch now? No way. Will she be the PM who goes down in history as killing a million Iranians on 'just the likelihood' that their leadership is guilty?"

He paused before carrying on.

"Can you imagine it? A Trident D5 popping off above Tehran –if it got through. Perhaps the Russians have sold them the ABM variant of the S-300? So popping off a D5 when there is some uncertainty over who is actually guilty? Is she prepared to suffer eternal world condemnation? No they'd be back at the UN who would put the nuke option on hold, no doubt indefinitely. Can anyone see any flaws in that?"

Ruefully Reiner, Oleg and Kipper shook their heads and Jake continued remorselessly.

"If we are to deter religiously motivated terrorists, we should remember that they are not necessarily stupid. In our current scenario, even if the killers then detonated one device per day in five major cities across the UK, there's still no one to shoot at. It would be rated as non-state terrorism and the UN wouldn't sanction nuking anyone and we wouldn't do it without UN approval, ever, even though we'd been nuked."

He looked at each of them in turn.

"I just can't see us shooting despite us loftily saying we reserve the right to defend ourselves. You can't fight a stupid backward idea with nukes. So it isn't a deterrent really because the only kind of people who would attack using nukes now are religious zealots who all want to go meet Allah, or whatever name they call God, as soon as possible, so they don't care about deterrence, only nations do. The current set of nutters mould us like putty because they use our own liberal progressives against us like large bludgeons."

He held up a hand just in case someone wanted to chip in.

"BUT just in case there's a scenario out there where it could happen and in case someone fancies a shot, we should have the back pocket option through a nuclear cruise missile system."

He suddenly pointed to Reiner.

"Reiner did you as a German feel in danger of nuclear war every day throughout the cold war and after? Do you perhaps fear the threat of nuclear blackmail continuously? I ask you as someone from the only non-nuclear weapon armed power in the room."

Reiner shrugged.

"Although we have never had them, I can't say that we've missed them, and I wouldn't say that we live in daily fear of attack by them either." He looked around at them all.

"I'm not even sure what nuclear blackmail could be. How would it work? Say nice things about me or bang? Give me x, y, z or bang? I think the world is a different place and would not allow any country to do this. I'd say the same is the case for Spain, Italy, Denmark and Sweden, Brazil, or Vietnam or any of the hundred and sixty or so countries who do not possess them."

Jake continued.

"Thank you Reiner, fair points. Well none of us here could be considered pacifists I think. But if *we* can't come up with a viable scenario for using a nuke, what are the UK government thinking of by bankrupting the defence budget to have four submarines whose sole function is to fire lots of multi-nuclear tipped missiles? It would be a once and once only event, and with only a circular error probability of three to four hundred yards it is not exactly a precision weapon is it? Not much use for taking out a guilty party with a nuke I'd have thought. City buster yes, but I really can't see anyone sanctioning that, can you?"

He could see no argument from the others, so continued.

"Anyway, I think it is fair to say that the RN cannot police the seas as it once did with less than two dozen surface ships." He waved a hand dismissively. "Please don't get me started on about the two useless carriers we got fobbed off with and if the EU countries combined their fleets, as they have been trying to do for ages, harping on about 'ever closer union', even they would not be able to do so. The US Navy has also shrunk from a six hundred ship Navy to less than three hundred in just two decades and continues to shrink further. It too has policing issues and commitment clashes. Ditto the Russian fleet, which of course has shrunk the most but mainly because it was really only built up to challenge the others." He paused again.

"Of all the world's major powers, only China has significantly increased its navy since the end of the cold war, this too is really just to assert itself rather than through need. The problem is that the procurement, maintenance and retention of naval vessels is damned expensive with no discernible reward that Western politicians can point to when not at war. Endless patrolling using small multipurpose ships is expensive. Flag waving is passé nowadays. Jollies to foreign ports are too expensive without good reason. The world has turned gentlemen and international law isn't really global law." He saw a puzzled look on Ken's face.

"The United Nations Convention on the Law of the Sea Ken. Is it global? No. One of the non-signatories is the USA which resists, reasonably in my opinion, being bound by courts and institutions above the Supreme Court of the USA."

He looked around to see if anyone challenged his perception of the way things were but no one seemed inclined to disagree.

"So the pencil necks have their way and hack away at the military without considering that navies take time to assemble, you don't open a box and there's a new one; people take time to train, there's no instant sailor. Politicians forget this and all too many have never served anything except themselves."

He took in the nods of agreement.

"But there are a number of threats still out there which require, I believe, guns not long range missiles. I sincerely believe a vessel such as this and ones like her, perhaps less dramatically shaped though, when focussed on particular problems, could act as the stop gap between what is needed and what governments are prepared to pay for.

"We could ride shotgun for merchant ships in any area of the world where there is trouble. We can take contracts from shipping lines which feel threatened and need escorts and or security personnel. There are a number of opportunities for such a vessel and the European Courts have written our justification for us. Sadly it cost the lives of some good men to get that carte blanche. Hopefully we can prevent or at the very least reduce any further needless losses." He paused before adding his final bombshell. "This ship is armed gentlemen."

That drew a simple. "Shit." From Kipper followed by. "You mean this bloody tub is the real deal, guns an' all boss?"

Jake smiled at his surprise.

"Yes Kipper most of the guns are real. I don't want overload you with too much detail at the moment, but, those four twin turrets are AK130B1, one hundred and thirty millimetre dual purpose automatic guns, the secondaries are just eight of the twelve visible guns, the two midships mounts are dummy, but the others contain AK-176M1A seventy six millimetre, dual purpose automatic guns in twin turrets and finally, there are four thirty millimetre AK630M2B twin CIWS systems, the side by side variant, one for each quadrant."

There was a stunned silence as Reiner and Ken, looked around with a renewed interest, Scotnikov of course knew already.

"Now you can see why a good relationship with Russia helps when you want to use their top notch naval artillery. If ever used, I have promised an evaluation for them." He said with a smile.

"Each system required a turret re-design, obviously, and this slight change in design has produced the most powerful warship, gun armed, in the last fifty years." He said with a smile at the understatement.

"Arming it has also presented its own problems, not least, obtaining acceptance for the reappearance of the privately owned warship."

Reiner remembered having difficulties at this point. The idea of a private warship was *not* so alien to his orderly, organised mind after the preparatory discussions with Jake, but the extent of the weaponry was a big surprise, this was literally a pocket battleship! Reiner realised the hard bit for him was that warships usually served countries not individuals or companies; however he was of course aware of the 'Privateers charter' and its origins.

Jake continued and delivered a short résumé on privateering ending with a summary.

"So, currently non-naval vessels can be armed only if it is convenient to the major powers. I intend to change that equation Gentlemen. Of course at this time the UN sees itself as the world's moral compass and arbiter of all that is right and wrong, good and proper. It tries to dictate what can and cannot be done by nations, so that too is a factor. Effectively for us, for me, it is 'needs must' and we will be in the forefront of a shift back towards non-naval vessels being armed. I have two other projects which will result in armed non-naval vessels, but not necessarily of course as stunningly good looking as this one!"

He drew the meeting to a close with a change of tack.

"Consider this.   Instead of privateer or mercenary, think **Merchant Protector**."

Friday 30th March 2018

Hotel Manila, Manila Bay, Philippines

The wizened Chinese man looked out over Manila Bay from his private suite on the top floor of the old Manila Bay Hotel. He liked the hotel, old but dignified just as he saw himself. His business had gone smoothly this evening, the sweaty, greedy intermediary had oozed deference in such a cloying fashion that he had begun to feel nauseous. All done now though. He'd lit several joss sticks to clear the malodours.

In three days or so the MV *Pacific Olympian* would be close to the Malacca straits and preparing for transit and that was when his new and temporary business partners would take ownership. He had no idea how many the crew numbered or even who they were.

At a later date he would rue not knowing that Senator Paulus (Rep Illinois, influential and outspoken Chair of the Senate Armed Services Committee) had placed his nephew aboard that vessel, via a special request to the shipping line the young man had become a cadet for. The good Senator doted on the boy who by all accounts was a promising Cadet Deck Officer.

Xiao wasn't concerned with the crew or even the ship for that matter. What he was interested in were several securely sealed crates lying deep in number one hold, these contained green jade worked in the most fantastic sculptures and thousands of years old. They were the property of a certain peer of his in the less than visible world of Triad Shanghai, perhaps rival would be a better description?

By declining to make a choice of crew disposal when the ship was hijacked he had allowed the Indonesian pirates carte blanche, and their preferred internal security standpoint was that no witnesses meant no come back.

They were wrong on a number of counts.

Monday 2nd April 2018

100 miles East of the Singapore Straits, South China Sea.
17:21hrs local. MV Pacific Olympian

Young Colin Hayes, a nineteen year old first year Deck Officer Cadet, Pacific and Olympia Line, was excited. Ever since the Captain had called all the ship's officers and the Bosun to his cabin, before they entered the straits of Malacca, he'd been hyper. He had to squeeze in at the back to hear what the 'old man' had to say, as all the officers more senior to him, that is all of them, were in front of him.

The Bosun stood next to him, his dark face split by a toothless grin. Patricio was a small wiry Filipino man with no front teeth in his upper set. Truth be told, he had no reason to be there since he and the old man had worked it all out hours before.

Colin noted the Captain switch to his 'monotone' voice as he read from the 'Safe Passage' pamphlet for the Singapore and Malacca Straits, probably for the ten thousandth time. Colin wondered what all the fuss was about, a big well-lit and fast ship like this surely had no problems keeping the pirate scum at bay?

Then there was the emergency Ship Security Alert System (SSAS) and also they had radar scanning the waters, so really there was no threat but it was exciting to pretend. The Captain was at that point telling them all that the straits were maybe the busiest area of seawater in the world with over a third of the entire world's trading goods passing through each year.

Colin was trying to look cool and confident even though inside he was quite excited. He knew that the density of ships and cargo must be astonishing for it to be a third of all maritime trade. Gee a bridge watch here would be all binoculars and course alterations, he surmised, so they'd have to be real careful about avoiding collisions.

A buzzer interrupted the old man in full flow and he knew that the Second Officer up on the bridge at the moment was about to get a new asshole ripped for him.

"What is it dammit? I told you I was....oh, really? Uh huh, I'll come up, slow to five and aim to have them on the port side." He slammed the phone down still muttering.

"OK. We'll reconvene when this little drama is sorted, seems like there was a red flare fired by a vessel in apparent distress a couple of miles ahead. Ortez says they are down at the head and clearly well on the way to sinking, some sort of small fishing boat, looks like two or three on board."

"Bosun, take a couple of lads and young Cadet Hayes along with the Third, lower the tender and check out what's the problem. Be a pain in the ass if we have to pick 'em up and then drop 'em somewhere, but the rules of the sea etcetera, etcetera." He added, almost to himself.

Colin was doubly excited now, the tender was a RHIB, a rigid hulled inflatable boat or just RIB for short, so it was fast like a speed boat and you sat on a bench along the middle with a hard hat on and a life jacket. This was going to be cool like being in the Coastguard or the Navy.

The three visible 'fishermen' waved slowly at the approaching RIB and kept up a steady commentary for the ten heavily armed brothers lying in the hold below. One of the Filipino able seamen threw a line and one of the men caught it and pulled the RIB in close while miming 'brmm, brmm' with a shake of the head and mimicking the action of a pump.

The Third Officer assessed the situation and radioed back to the *Pacific Olympian* that he thought they could do with a pump out and maybe the Chief Engineer might see what could be done.

Captain Barnes inwardly fumed but the law of the sea was the law of the sea, and rightly so.

"OK Harris, lash on and drag them back here, we'll drift down slowly to speed things up." Harris acknowledged and the Bosun spouted some warp speed gibberish which the fishing boat crew appeared to understand and they lashed the two together for the hundred yard journey back to their own ship.

Nothing more was said until they arrived alongside the *Olympian* and tied on. The Chief Engineer was busy organising a portable pump to be winched out and onto the 30 foot boat's sloping deck before heading down with one of his grease monkeys to see if he could shake some life into the old clunker's engine.

At this point both the Third and Cadet Hayes had climbed back up and went to report to the Captain.

The old gnarled hands of the fisherman tapped lightly on the wooden bulkhead and the rest of the crew swiftly and silently rose up and began boarding the ship. One headed straight for the Captain's cabin where the SSAS beacon trigger was, and the others fanned out.

The Chief Engineer became aware of a problem when a sinewy arm appeared around his neck and an ultra-sharp gutting knife sliced across his throat. The Filipino crewman who'd been following the Chief's instructions looked around as he felt warm liquid splashing on his bare back. His look of horror was brief because the next stop for the knife was in his throat, his short gurgle went unheard against the background of ventilation blowers and other systems.

The first Captain Barnes knew that he'd been conned was when three men armed with machetes and hand guns pushed on to the bridge past the reporting Third Officer and Cadet.

He knew he had seconds to press the signal beacon button and ran to the rear of the bridge and down the short ladder towards his cabin. Risking a quick look behind him he threw himself into his cabin and slammed the door locking it. As he looked over to his bed he noticed a man standing in one corner. Then the gun fired.

Everyone on the bridge heard the gunfire and froze, except of course for the new owners of the ship who moved forward shouting and gesturing to everyone to head aft.

They were herded into the main dining room and put under guard while the rest of the ship was searched. After a few minutes when they'd combed it top to bottom and everyone was crowded into the dining room they were told to sit down and place their hands on heads. Everyone complied.

Meanwhile one of the original three fishermen went back to the little fishing boat and disappeared below. A loud whooshing sound preceded his rapid exit from below decks as the buoyancy aid deflated quickly. It had been the only thing keeping the little boat afloat since the hole in the hull was genuine. It had taken careful planning to get to this spot just at the right time.

The pirates had been following the *Pacific Olympian's* every move since it sailed out of Manila bay under the gaze of the old Chinese gentleman high up on the balcony by using pretty ordinary technology. AIS or Automated Identification System was rather like a civilian airplane's transponder unit, broadcasting its whereabouts to any station which could pick it up, the professional version allowed them to monitor ship movements worldwide, there was even a free but somewhat limited app you could download to your phone.

Merchant ships above 300 hundred tons gross and making international voyages have to have one fitted; perfect for pirates picking their targets without even having to go outside and look. Every course change, current speed and even nearby vessels, all provided to enable a perfect link up with the target. Easy really. Now they simply reprogrammed it to its new AIS identity with a 'hack' provided for the job, then when it uploaded its next broadcast, *Pacific Olympian* disappeared from the clutter of multiple ships and the new vessel emerged heading in the opposite direction giving out a false port of origin and destination.

Half an hour later the ship was underway north east into the South China Sea, it would be several days before the owners knew for sure something was amiss. Twilight hid the painters changing the funnel colour and logo, and the tent assemblers adding a new deck house and false derrick to match the silhouette of the ship which owned the stolen codes, a new port of registry on the stern and a name above it completed the make-over.

The real owner of that registry was in drydock in Shanghai having its bottom cleaned and propeller bearings sorted. The constantly monitored but extremely busy Singapore and Malacca straits had thousands of AIS returns and it would take days to sift through them to discover where *Pacific Olympian's* replacement had appeared.

For the remaining crew of the *Pacific Olympian* it was a tense time waiting to see what would happen next. They didn't have long to wait. As the sun set, one at a time they were ordered up onto the main deck beyond the sight and hearing of those still to come, a quick slash with a panga to an arm then a push overboard was the simple solution to the problem of the crew, except for Sheila Tong, a pretty Third Officer who was saved until last when she was gang raped before being thrown overboard, she didn't need the panga cut because she was already bleeding from her ordeal.

What they didn't know was that Sheila had been an Olympic hopeful as a youngster, long distance swimming was her forte, the water was warm, she'd kept in practice and the bleeding stopped quickly. More bad news for the pirates, was the burning anger which had boiled up as one after another of the 'filth' had abused her. This helped focus her mind on survival and revenge. As she went over the stern she saw the new port of registry and the newly painted name.

Young Colin Hayes and the rest of the murdered crew would have to wait some time for vengeance, but it would come. Sheila was fished out of the water as the finest catch ever for a little fishing boat out of Padang on the Raui Islands. The two man crew would have drinks bought them for months as they described the beauty that had appeared out of nowhere in the morning light like a '*djinn,* a spirit'.

The grief stricken uncle of Colin Hayes, Senator Paulus, would fly out to take personal charge of Sheila's repatriation to the states, her recovery, medical treatment including counselling, and her debrief, which included detailed descriptions of the leader of the attackers and several others, the new name of the ship and port of registry as well as approximate course and speed.

Senator Paulus, soon to be an acquaintance of one Jonathan Henry König, would know exactly who to ask for help in tracking down and dealing with the perpetrators.

Xiao Bong would discover too that he'd made a fatal error by acquiring something which was not his; he took two days to die when he was apprehended for a chat by the rival who'd lost something precious to him. It appeared that not all of his staff worked for him alone.

Friday April 20th 2018

Russian Crimea

The final descent into Belbek International, Sevastopol, was bumpy but as far as Reiner was concerned, couldn't be quick enough. He hated being away as the final touches were being made to the ship's fitting out but had been unable to avoid being dragged away to König Marine HQ at Norwich, England.

It was very different to the much bumpier landing in near blizzard conditions in January just gone. However this flight had been uneventful with plenty of time to reflect on the whirlwind of events of the last few months, all preparing for the big day tomorrow.

He had to be honest he'd been grateful for the offer from Jake when it came. Command of a new *Bismarck*, albeit privately owned, was going to be a monumental, and hopefully satisfying, challenge.

Being a First Officer on a Ro-Ro ferry wasn't a bad job as things went but it wasn't how he thought his career would pan out; besides how could it compare with this?

Reiner had got part the way up the promotion ladder in the German Navy. Then someone declared peace, the cold war was finished and governments the world over couldn't wait to swing the axe, Germany being no exception. After leaving though he'd quickly gained his civilian certificates and had had no problem getting sea going jobs since.

Tens of thousands of armed service jobs had gone across Europe within the first five years but the axe kept on swinging into the new century. Apparently there wasn't going to be any more warfare or any need for warships and armies in the brave new world, in spite of daily evidence to the contrary.

How long did the peace last Reiner reflected? For the West and NATO it went sour again less than six months later with the first Gulf War, then a year later in the Balkans with the break-up of Yugoslavia into its constituent parts.

That had been about the time Jake had resigned his commission he recalled. Fuming, so he told Reiner, he'd found himself on yet another Type 42 destroyer this time in the Adriatic, as First Lieutenant and with only two thirds of a normal ship's company to man it. This was all because some genius had decided that they didn't need so many men at sea, IF maintenance was done when the ship was back in the UK, which of course it wasn't!

That had been the very last straw for Jake, having the 'pencil necks' working out the manning levels on ships and rewarding MOD clerks if they saved money, which they did by not sending out the things that were needed, like food, spares and ammunition. The British MOD was really just trying to 'paper over' the lack of sailors to man the ships because they had made too many redundant, too quickly, Reiner decided. Later they sorted that problem, they'd just sold or mothballed the ships so it wasn't so embarrassing any more.

He considered the other side of the equation after the declaration of peace. For Russia of course it had lasted largely until the Chechen debacle starting in 1994 if he remembered correctly, and that hadn't been finally quenched until 2009.

Reiner had noted that the advent of Tony Blair as UK Prime Minister saw Britain get involved in anything military that it could or so it seemed, and usually at the behest of the Bush administration in the US, but occasionally without. With diminishing numbers of soldiers, sailors and airmen and a shrinking defence budget, the UK forces seem to have been propelled into any armed conflict that Blair could find, and usually with their hands tied behind their backs by ridiculous rules of engagement −as Jake had once explained.

The idea that warfare could be carefully controlled, graduated, and proportionate is plainly a politician's hedge, thought Reiner. Warfare as any serviceman could tell you, should only be a last resort but when used, should be overwhelming and *disproportionate*.

That was how to win, but winning didn't seem to be the aim of the politicians a lot of the time. It smacked very much of the Vietnam-Johnson-Nixon mentality, whereby if you bomb the enemy a few times in carefully selected areas then they'll come to the peace table and you'll get your way.

Then of course more recently, the shit hit the fan locally when the US and EU had fomented and funded the 2014 revolution in Ukraine and that had messed things up properly. No serious student of the military really thought that Russia had territorial ambitions in the Baltic states any more, or anywhere else for that matter, they were too busy trying to re-build a country ruined by seventy odd years of central government economics, and just trying to make a buck, and therein was the rub as far as the US was concerned he thought, rivals that wouldn't do as they were told.

From the side-lines it seemed like NATO were talking up the 'opposition bit' and rattling the begging bowl for more money citing the Russian bogeyman as the new reason. The media were on a roll, doing their usual scaremongering and using 'Cold War' as many times as possible in any given sentence. Reiner agreed with the aim of maintaining the NATO coffers but vilifying Russia in order to do it was beyond silly. Seriously, how did they think Russia would react?

The replacement of the democratically elected, albeit useless, president of Ukraine in Kiev with a US/EU approved one, had merely led to further polarisation in the country and the subsequent civil war which the West blamed on Russian re-kindled expansionism. Never mind that there were bilateral agreements *not* to recognise new regimes if they had replaced the old democratic one by revolution and not the ballot box, however that was apparently only for revolutions not organised by the US and EU.

The real irony for the western liberal progressives, had to be that they were supporting a regime which had a right wing nucleus full of anti-Semites and nutters who made Al Qaeda seem like 'softy wusses', as Kipper Herring remarked on reading about them. Still the levels of self-delusion these people could absorb without detonation was staggering.

Reiner had been brought up with the shame of what happened in between 1933 and 1945, after then of course half his country had been communist until 1990. There was a lot of baggage for your average 'thinking' German to carry around.

Dragging his mind back to the final crew list in front of him he was pleased at how well the recruitment had gone. Truth be told, there were many more applicants of appropriate qualification and suitability than they'd been able to select, he had been stunned to learn that nearly one thousand five hundred had applied for the forty seven positions.

With hindsight however, it was easy to predict the mass of applications given the rundown of navies in Europe and Russia, even America.

The next surprise had been when Jake had revealed where they'd all be based. He recalled the conversation back on the morning after they'd first boarded *Bismarck*.

'I have however had talks with, and obtained an agreement from, a recently independent Caribbean state. We will bear their flag as port of registry, and under special conditions, will wear their naval ensign.' Reiner had felt apprehensive for the first time then as he racked his memory for the name of a new Caribbean state. He did not actually feel like switching his allegiance to some tin-pot banana republic. Jake however hadn't let him have time to ponder the identity.

'Now I don't want you getting all 'twitchy' and paranoid about which Caribbean state, so I'll tell you now. The Cayman Islands. These were, until 2016 a British dependency. They have no standing military forces to speak of and no axe to grind with anyone in that region. Most importantly to us, their new Prime Minister is an old and dear friend of mine and my father's before me.'

It had been a relief to discover he had no objection to the Cayman Islands, and his wife had been really quite pleased. In addition they'd all be given dual citizenship which might be needed to resolve issues of a different kind at some point in the future.

Russian Crimea. Sevastopol Dockyard

The day had dawned clear, crisp and bright. Overnight rain had washed things clean again and the air smelled good as Reiner stepped out of the small door at the front of the huge frigate complex building which housed the *Bismarck*.

He was wearing just his blue denim work uniform at present as he did a final check-through of the complex procedure for getting the ship underway and out into the Black Sea.

With him was Ken Herring, similarly attired and carrying the ubiquitous 'Chief's clipboard' and pencil, as well as Simon McClelland, his First Lieutenant who carried a ship's tablet PC on which just about everything could be accessed on the *Bismarck,* including inventories and ship's diary. It was old versus new, pixels versus paper and graphite and the rivalry was keen.

Bets were accumulating over whose infallible system would fail first The ship's inveterate gambler George Bradley ran the tote and he had in the past, so 'Bullshit HQ1' reckoned, bet on who would hit the deck first, him or his mate when they got into a bar fight in Melbourne a few years before. George had then collected the winnings from his hospital bed.

All of them wanted the day to go smoothly and for the launch of the new ship to go off without a hitch let alone any scraped paintwork. Hence the repeated visits to checklists and visual checking.

Reiner was pleased to see that preparations for the ship's sailing were well under way outside the frigate shed. Bunting framed the front of the huge electric roller doors and hundreds of locals, workers and their relatives had turned out to see the new ship leave dock on its maiden voyage.

They were all settling themselves on two large multi-tiered seating platforms positioned on either side of the water that *Bismarck* would shortly pass through, if it all went according to plan. Already there was a party atmosphere even though the ship wasn't due to sail for another hour, and local food vendors had been allowed in to facilitate the celebratory aspects of the day.

The small dais from which the formal side of things would get under way was to the left of the big doors near the point where the three had exited the shed.

The PA system had already been checked several times but would be checked again noted Kipper on his clipboard while

Simon smiled and touched his tablet a couple of times and ordered one of the electro- technical team to re-check it in half an hour. Much to the amusement of Reiner, Kipper frowned and took out his radio quickly ordering the check verbally.

Satisfied that all was ready and the sea gates were open to let *Bismarck* out into Pivdenna Bay, the three returned inside to change into dress uniform which was deliberately similar to but not quite the same as that worn in the RN. Jake had discussed this with Ken, Simon and Reiner, they had agreed that a uniform was more than just the clothes you wore to work, and more so the dress uniform.

Taking a pride in your appearance and in your ship was necessary for 'unit cohesion' or in English, necessary in order to function as a team. A team you wanted to win and a team you would give your all to ensure that it did.

This did not happen automatically and could not be taken for granted even though everyone on board had served between eight and twenty eight years in various navies. Starting by making English the universal language 'on watch', English British that is, and not any of the other variants, all of the ship's company had to begin to pull together. As they settled in they now viewed this new career not only as an opportunity, but one which could ultimately lead to them going into action.

If they were to fulfil their primary role of protecting merchant ships in general, and not just their own vessel, then it could quite possibly, 'get noisy' at some point. If that happened you had to completely trust the man next to you or at the other end of the radio.

"Attention. Commodore in the mess." Came the slightly raised voice of Lieutenant Commander Simon McClelland as he got the nod from Kipper over by the aft door to the wardroom.

Jake stepped in wearing the dress uniform of a Commodore with the single thick band of gold on his cuff with silver thread at the edges. Instead of the full loop of gold that the RN had or the gold star of America, Russia and Germany, they'd opted for a gold circle like the inverse of the RN loop and roughly an inch across. No medals though. They had all agreed that their current set belonged to the past and therefore should not be worn with these uniforms. Only Jake and Reiner were in dress uniform as they would be on show, the rest were in standard sea going blue denim. He moved into the centre of the room where Granny Smith offered him a glass from a tray of champagne.

"Thank you Gentlemen." He said raising the glass, continuing the pretence of being invited into one of *his own* ships compartments.

"We won't do formality very often but it's nice every now and then to get out the best kit, if only to remind us that we are still in a disciplined service. Today is a special day for me, for the company and perhaps for the world at large."

"I don't want to overstate the case for needing us out there but if in its whole career, this ship prevents the loss of a single merchant sailor's life, then in my mind it will have been worth it."

"I know that if I had chosen a different nations vessel to be the design concept, maybe a US or British battleship, then this commissioning would probably *not* get the same attention it will, but I didn't and when word gets out people will be watching us, asking why this one particular design, not understanding and possibly sticking silly labels on us without knowing what they are talking about. That will be my burden not yours."

"In terms of equipment, protection and weaponry I doubt this vessel has an equal or ever will, given that it combines ultra-modern technology with older concepts of armour and mass gunfire, in a way that has never been done before from design to finished vessel. Think of this ship as a 'Merchant Protector'. That is our job. That is our purpose. Good luck Gentlemen."

He put his glass down.

"Right, that's my party piece done. Captain Krull please carry on as planned."

"Aye Sir". Reiner replied. "Gentlemen, dismissed to stations. Prepare the ship for sea."

"Aye Sir". They chorused in return.

*

Jake stood on the dais in the thin spring sunshine and fresh breeze as he delivered a speech about the guts and determination and the high quality hard work, that had gone into creating the vessel inside. He thanked them all and promised them more work in the future, though not necessarily like the vessel they had completed this time.

He announced that two further vessels would be designed and built at this very dockyard over the next three to four years, and that work on a vessel already designed would begin in two weeks' time. He stopped speaking as cheering started and carried on for some minutes. Then he introduced the lady at his side and stood back.

It was without doubt a poignant moment as Isabella Van Plasterk stepped up to speak in memory of her husband. She talked of his pride in the work he did in all the oceans around the world over the thirty years he'd been at sea.

"But I still see the same kind of evil which took my William; I see it all over the world, as greedy, evil and barbaric people kill and maim honest seafaring folk, apparently without any hesitation or thought of being held to account, and clearly with no fear of retribution."

She gathered herself pushing away images of her crucified husband that Al Jazeera had gleefully published and then syndicated to the rest of the world's press.

"I see myself as a gentle woman but even gentle women can be hard when they need be. So I wish this ship *Bismarck*, and its company safe voyaging, vigilance and good fortune. But if by chance one day they come across the evil creatures who deprived me of my husband, and my children of their loving father in that most barbaric way, then I hope they will act accordingly and demonstrate that when you sow evil, you reap in full." She stepped back and sat on the single chair.

The interpreter finished the translation and a cheer erupted both outside from the visitors and on board *Bismarck* as they heard the speech piped through all the compartments, not a few cuffing away a tear from the corner of their eyes.

Sailors are often quite sentimental creatures and the Senior Rates had named their bar 'The Willy Van P' in his honour and when the opportunity arose they would christen it with a suitable party.

Jake took the microphone again.

"People. When we leave I want you to enjoy this day and remember it. So without further ado I declare this ceremony over and I give you *Bismarck*."

Jake fairly flew off the rostrum as with a creaking and squealing the doors to the frigate shed began ponderously to part in the centre.

Mrs Van Plasterk was being escorted by his local agent so he legged it in through side door and in an undignified rush hurled himself up the sole remaining gangway which was promptly withdrawn and stowed.

Half a dozen seamen with a Petty Officer had mustered on the fo'c'sle in addition to the berthing parties. All lines were now cast off and as the doors finally creaked their last, Reiner up on the bridge took command.

"Helm, Steerpods from station keeping to very slow ahead if you please, steer for the gap."

He moved on to the starboard bridge wing put his cap on and stood at salute while the ship passed the cheering crowds.

Most of the assembled guests had not truly believed the stories that their loved ones had been telling them about the ship they were building over the preceding eighteen months and so the noise swelled as slowly the new *Bismarck* revealed its size and majesty as it emerged.

Cranes sounded their horns, ships nearby joined in and the crowds renewed their approbation in a spontaneous burst of cheering; the Russians built good looking ships too so they appreciated this one.

Nearby, the König Industries local Security Chief, was standing with the current local FSB chief. It was sensible to keep the new guy happy thought Yuri Predarovitch, you never know when you might need a favour and Pavel certainly still liked his vodka.

Pavel's report on the new vessel to his former bosses would probably wait until morning thought Yuri, noting how the vodka bottle next to Pavel seemed to empty without anyone touching it.

Bismarck slowly exited the dock and turned her bows towards the bay and the entrance to the Black Sea. Reiner moved back into the bridge and closed the door.

"Stand down ceremonial parties and secure for sea. Increase to seven knots now and then up to fifteen when you clear the bay if you please Mr McClelland."

Simon acknowledged and gave the necessary orders, he was Officer of the Watch for another hour then he could get some lunch. He moved over to the periscope-like roof mounted digital binoculars and had a good look all around before checking the radar repeater and ensuring both lookouts were alert.

Thursday April 26th 2018

Mediterranean Sea, 400km East of Malta, 500km North West of Benghazi. 18:30 local time

The Digital Selective Calling receiver (DSC) on the bridge of the 'Merchant Protector' *Bismarck*, gave a loud series of 'alert' pings. Lieutenant Julius Kopf the Officer of the Watch, who had been idly wandering around the bridge touching the various gizmos and gadgets that characterised the ultra-modern setup of the new ship, nearly wet himself thinking he'd set something off with his wandering fingers.

He was greatly relieved as soon as he realised what it was and walked over to the rear of the bridge to have a look at the DSC repeater screen.

At that point his complacency ended and with a muted 'Scheisse' he spoke into the mike by his lips.

"OPs." He said it clearly, still getting used to pronouncing his English carefully for the voice auto routing system. He waited less than a second before a voice came back.

"OPs aye."

"Bridge here. Are you getting the DSC alert?"

Which was a pointless question because the bridge just had a repeater from the OPs room.

"Yes I'm plotting the call now Sir. It was tagged as an all stations distress call, piracy code. Maritime Mobile Service Identity (MMSI) number is for *'Clovis Explorer'*, a Ro-Ro car carrier, South Korean; out of Gibraltar bound for Seoul. It should be on your plot now, we're listening on channel 16VHF sir. He says she's being fired upon by a small boat with a gun on it."

Kopf was just about to shut off and call the Captain when the alert ping started again and another message tripped across the screen. His first thought was 'it'll just be a repeat' but no, it was a new one. What the hell he thought?

"Bridge there's a new DSC alert. This is a distress call too, all stations, coded piracy. Err, the MMSI ID has it as the *Xin Ying Tan* a Chinese container ship out of Malta heading for Suez. No VHF on that one yet, plotting now sir."

Kopf looked at the bridge OPs repeater and saw the positions of the two vessels appear along with their Automatic Identification System (AIS) data which showed course and speed among other things.

Then *Bismarck's* position and finally all other vessels in the area squawking their AIS plots were added. A dozen other plots

74

appeared as the ops room added in relevant data. Both ships in distress were about thirty miles away, but which one should they respond to?

Before he could work out what course to order let alone call the Captain, the DSC alert pinged for a third then a fourth time. Kopf raised his eyes to heaven and sighed. Why my watch for fucks sake? He thought as he glanced around to see the helmsman and lookout both waiting for him to do something. Another ping from the repeater caused him to look at the plot again and now he could see a pattern emerging.

"OPs call the Captain now. I'll sound action stations and get us going in the right direction."

"Aye Sir, OPs to call the Captain."

Kopf hesitated a second or so then walked over to the covered buttons at the rear of the bridge, checked which to press and then pushed the Action Stations 'Surface Alarm', once, twice and a third time before using the Tannoy to confirm the order.

"Action Stations. Action stations surface action. Set state one condition X-Ray throughout the ship. This is not an exercise, I repeat, this is not an exercise." He briefly wondered if he should have gone the whole hog and set state one condition Zulu-Alpha and closed everything down, but for four Boghammers he really thought it would be a bit OTT.

Then he turned back to the helmsman.

"Full ahead, steer 260."

"Full ahead steer 260 Sir. Aye."

Kopf looked at the plot and noted the details of the three he hadn't checked. Number three was the Danish flagged *Maersk Mathilde* which was en route from Port Said to Antwerp, all details the same as before, OPs had heard a VHF call indicating another small boat attack. Four was *Xing Ning*, another Chinese container ship this one flagged for Hong Kong and headed to Felixstowe, VHF broadcast reported them under small arms attack too. The last made his blood run cold and dropped all the other pieces into place.

Number five, appearing almost at the centre of a circle drawn around the others, was a passenger ship. MS *Kristianstaadt* of the Skandacruise Line. She was big too, 88000 tons and carrying up to 1900 passengers and 900 crew. En route to Suez for an Indian Ocean cruise.

A noise behind him caused him to look up to see the Captain and Jake arriving on the bridge both wearing anti-flash gear.

Reiner climbed into his bridge chair and began swinging round the monitors to check what was going on, Jake stood off to one side and began using a viewer.

"Report Mr Kopf." Reiner said tapping away at his screens.

"Sir we have DSC distress calls from five vessels, four are cargo and one a large passenger liner. All give the code for piracy sir. We have managed to speak via VHF to two of the cargo ships and both report coming under attack from fast boats armed with a machine gun. It seems the hostiles are just shooting at them Sir, at present. The passenger ship though, included details suggesting she had been boarded by unknowns masquerading as migrants on a sinking vessel. I have ordered full ahead and a course change towards the passenger ship Sir; she's on a bearing of 260 degrees range nineteen miles."

Reiner looked up and nodded.

"Very good Mr Kopf, I have the con, you may take up your gunnery action station now."

"Aye, aye Sir." Said Kopf, and practically ran to the rear of the bridge and raced up the ladder up to the gunnery control room, which took up most of the space above the bridge and almost all the upper superstructure.

The whine of the *Bismarck's* two Saturn VMF gas turbines, each rated at 35,000HP, was clearly audible on the bridge now as they generated the electrical power needed to reach her top speed of thirty five knots, both guzzling quantities of diesel fuel per minute that would make even a hardened petrol head blush. The cruise diesel was in standby and the gas turbines, let loose, screamed their joy as the three and a half thousand ton warship fairly leapt through the calm seas and into the history books as the first commercially operated warship in over a century.

The two electric motors of the Finnish 'Steerprops' were mounted within the propulser units and truth be told they hadn't really had chance to do much testing or training yet on these azimuth props and on the superior manoeuvrability they gave the ship.

"Bridge OPs." Came a voice over the bridge speaker.

"This is the Captain, continue."

"Aye Sir. More information heading for the plot Sir and I have picked up two 'YouTube' videos believe it or not, which I'll send to your station sir. One from the *Xing Ning* and one from the *Kristianstaadt* itself. Isn't modern technology wonderful?"

"Thank you; see if you can raise the Captains of any of these ships, particularly *Kristianstaadt*, I'd like to talk with them before we engage. With the usual Mediterranean 'milky' glow-line on the horizon I expect we will need to get closer than ten miles to get a visual, how long OPs?"

"Twelve minutes at current speed Sir. Checking for comms now Sir."

Before he watched the video feed, Reiner issued instructions to the drone control. *Bismarck* was plainly too small to have full sized aircraft but technology had helped them again.

During the design phase a sub-project for the procurement of a recoverable seaborne drone had produced something which looked very like *Bismarck's* original Arado 196 seaplane but was smaller and unmanned. There were four aboard and each was capable of long endurance surveillance as well as carrying small air to surface precision weapons like the AT-9 'Spiral2' variant that Jake had ordered.

The small glass tube launchers of the missiles were discarded on release from the underside of the wing and the encrypted radio guided missiles could be operator controlled out to just over three miles from the drone itself. They used a variety of warheads like high explosive (HE) and Fragmentation (FRAG) but also included a third generation thermobaric or fuel air explosive (FAE) variant which gave lots of 'boom' for its size.

The Arado drones were launched from the midships catapult exactly as their full sized counterparts would have been on the first *Bismarck*.

"Drone control this is the Captain. Prepare two drones for launch, one with a recon and ESM pod and the other one FRAG and FAE. I want a full sea search first so climb quickly please. I also want ESM looking for any 'rackets' around those bearings," which is what they called bearing only emissions. "that might be these scum talking to each other. Next, prep the second pair both with frag."

"Aye Sir, launch Cyclops 1 with recon package, two with FAE and Frag, Cyclops three and four Frag. Drone control out."

Reiner spoke into his mike. "Guns." Then a click as the connection was made.

"Guns aye." Came Kopf's voice.

"I want Anton loaded with HE and Bruno with Flechette, Caesar and Dora to standby. Secondary guns to standby unloaded and the AK630's to standby loaded."

"Guns aye Sir. Anton Flechette and Bruno HE, AK630s to loaded standby.

Next Reiner switched back to OPs

"Are we in the Malta Rescue Coordination Centre (RCC) zone yet?"

"Aye Sir." Came the prompt response.

"Right, well get them on the Inmarsat and tell them we will be on scene for *Kristianstaadt* in less than fifteen minutes and will assess and report. We'll also provide a live video feed if they want. Make sure you give them our Caymans MMSI, it should tell them who we are and give them a clue as to how we can assist, oh and switch off our AIS. We don't want to give away where we are if the terrorists could be watching."

He had another thought.

"How long would it take them to get a patrol boat here if it was alongside at Malta now?"

"OPs, aye Sir, contact Malta RCC. Patrol boats Sir? Wait one. They have a top speed of 25 knots Sir, so it'd be easily over ten hours before they were on scene."

"OK. What about air assets then?"

"They have some ancient Allouette 3's Sir but they'd only have a couple of minutes on task before they had to turn back due to range limitations; they do have Beechcraft King Air 2000 but that's only able to drop life rafts. I suspect for terrorist operations they would need to call Italy to help them."

"How long before Italy could get something overhead then?"

"Coming from Sigonella, Sicily they could have an Atlantique maritime patrol aircraft on task in an hour I would guess. I'm not sure any air assets could do anything unless the Americans become involved, they have all sorts of stuff at Sigonella too."

"OK OPs. It's going to be over one way or another by the time any of them have anything on scene, unless there's a unit nearby already. Send them all our contact details and perhaps we'll get a call. One thing for certain, they should all have received each other's distress calls."

"Captain, Urwin has just watched the two clips. I'll hand over to him."

"Urwin Sir. The err, 'YouTube' just uploaded from the *Xing Ning* container ship shows a RIB of some kind and he's blatting away at them with some sort of big machine gun. Seems like one of the crew has balls the size of nine pound round shot Sir to hang over the side while he's doing that. The other one from the cruiser is only a few seconds long and we can see armed men boarding from one of the ship's tenders before the clip stops abruptly."

Reiner spun around in the chair to confer with Jake who, although not speaking was still a commanding presence on the bridge, clearly monitoring the situation as it developed.

"In my opinion four of them are likely just 'drive-by' shootings to draw attention from the main event which has to do with the cruise liner *Kristianstaadt,* but we'll get that confirmed in a minute or so I think."

Jake nodded his head.

"Concur. The hostiles have of course picked the point where they think their targets are the furthest away from any assistance. We plainly don't know what their intention with the cruise ship is, all we know is they have successfully boarded her. The clock is ticking on this one Reiner."

"OPs, Bridge. Sir we have the pictures from Cyclops 1, I'll highlight them on the repeater as I go through them. We have all five contacts on the plot now sir."

The pictures started appearing on screen.

"Four of them appear to be RIB types, with each having what looks like a jury rigged platform and a heavy machine gun mounted on it, possibly 12.7mm DShKs according to the security bods. The nearest hostile contact we have designated Sierra one and he attacked *Xing Ning,* at 035 degrees range 14 miles. The drone and radar has him moving away from them now and heading towards the cruise ship at 45 knots. This means he will pass less than eight miles to our starboard in the next couple of minutes Sir."

There was an audible indrawn breath before he moved on.

"Second contact, designated Sierra two is at 228 degrees south west of us, range 24 miles and is still circling the *Maersk Mathilde.* No contact from them since the DSC message several minutes ago Sir. We believe they were just broadcasting on channel 16 but it stopped abruptly, not surprising since they were saying that gunfire was impacting the bridge area."

"When Cyclops 2 is up send it that way first." Reiner instructed.

"Aye Sir. Sierra two first Sir with the armed Cyclops. Contact designated Sierra three is attacking the *Xin Ying Tan*, the one heading for Suez, he's bearing 157 at 19 miles Sir. Sorry, was attacking, now heading towards the cruise ship too. The Chinese are up on every channel that will listen, shouting for help and have fires in several places but not the cargo. He will now pass nine miles to our Port if he maintains current speed and heading. Contact designated Sierra four was attacking *Clovis Explorer*, bearing 335, range 27 miles is now trending this way in a wide curve rather than directly to the cruise liner."

"Wait one. I have the *Kristianstaadt* on sat-phone Sir, bringing you into the circuit."

"Kristianstaadt this is the Captain of the Merchant Protector *Bismarck* on your port bow range about sixteen miles, we will have a drone above you in seconds and be there ourselves within ten minutes. Who am I speaking to and what is your situation over."

Reiner listened as the tinny voice came over the bridge system. It sounded youngish and scared.

"Bismarck the Captain is down, I repeat down and gone. We have some security staff down too and I don't know about other crew. I am the First Officer, Jeff Bannister. The Staff Captain, second in command, is locked in the bridge with some others, I don't know where the Chief Officer is but I'm down aft."

He took an audible deep breath before continuing.

"There's about twenty of them, all Arab types wearing fatigues and those head scarf things. We thought they were refugees drowning. Their boat was sinking. We sent a tender to rescue them but they ambushed the crew and took it."

The words came out in a jumble of short staccato sentences telling a story of horror.

"It came back with our men held at gun point and they boarded shouting that Allah Akbar, or whatever it is they say. The Captain had gone down to see for himself and they just shot him straight away apparently, they didn't speak they just started shooting. They killed the Security Chief and two others too."

"Everyone else ran. I don't know what they are doing but they brought bags of stuff which may be explosives and groups of them have disappeared into the crew spaces and the passenger areas. They've started going through all the cabins now. I've heard them kicking doors in then demanding jewellery and money. They knew what they were doing Captain, some of them went straight down the M1, they killed an engineer en-route too and got his access card to the engine control room."

Reiner knew that this was no random attack. Anyone who was serious about attacking such a ship would have researched the best way to do it and clearly these bandits had.

They knew that there was a wide 'road' for want of a better word, nicknamed the M1 after the British motorway, which ran bow to stern below the passenger decks. This gave crew access to engineering spaces, the galley and storerooms amongst other things.

In all ships the engine room had total control of steering, engines propulsion, everything vital. When a ship left its berth the engine room handed control to the bridge -but could easily take it back with the push of a button.

"Now they've locked the bridge out of all steering and propulsion as well as closing down selected watertight doors. The rest of them are sweeping the ship and the crew has been ordered to muster in the main dining area aft which is deck three. All passengers have been ordered to their staterooms several have been beaten for not moving quick enough. There are armed men patrolling each deck I've been dodging in and out of cupboards trying to get an idea of what they are up to."

"OK. Have you been in touch with Malta Rescue Coordination Centre (RCC)?"

"Yes, we activated the SASS beacon straight away. They are sending a patrol boat but it is hours away and the Italians have a frigate and a maritime patrol plane on the way but again it will be hours, the RCC have been talking to us on the sat-phone too but as I say, any help is hours away."

"Roger that. You are aware of the other distress calls in the area aren't you? There have been at least five, repeat five attacks including yours. Some are on-going as we speak, all within a radius of 20 miles of you; we think it is coordinated and we think they'll head towards you as soon as they've finished messing with the others."

"Yes we are aware, we got the DSC calls from the others at almost the same time we were sending ours. We have no weapons not even a fucking taser."

His anger at being defenceless was boiling over, Reiner knew he would need to play this carefully to get good intel and cooperation.

"Our security is there to count people on and off and to stop passengers bringing booze on board. We aren't equipped to defend ourselves from a boat load of irate pensioners let alone armed nut-jobs that kill without even saying anything!" Bannister continued in a blurt of frustration.

His voice was getting a slight hysterical edge to it as the fear took hold and the horror of his situation unfolded.

"Listen Jeff. For a start we will make sure no others get to you. You're not on your own now. When we've got a decent idea of all the pieces of this puzzle, we will put together a plan to get you all out, or take them out, or both. OK? We have a full security team on board and these guys are experts. Ex SAS, Spetsnaz, Royal Marines, you name it; so all is not lost. So hang in there, I will contact you again soon. Stay out of sight and keep the phone handy."

"OK." Came the tinny reply, which sounded like it was in a cupboard.

I think I would be in a cupboard Reiner decided, no weapons, no defences, what a state to be in while wandering through a potentially dangerous area.

"Have the security team leader meet us in the OPs room Mr McClelland, your bridge."

"Aye sir." Replied Simon, who'd arrived unobtrusively and had stood to one side while the verbal exchange was going on.

Reiner and Jake headed down two decks to the OPs room to consider the next moves.

Down there already was Taff Elias the senior OPs watch keeper and his two sidekicks. They were checking nearby contacts and plotting the locations of the distressed vessels. The *Kristianstaadt* was right in the centre of a total of five near simultaneous attacks.

Clearly no coincidence this. Someone was pulling strings, that much was obvious thought Taff, but I bet they hadn't factored in a brand spanking new and fully armed *Bismarck* with a twenty man security detachment. You could see the other attacks were just chaff once you saw them all plotted, just meant to decoy or overwhelm responders was his guess.

The arrival of both Captain and owner was no surprise and he quickly turned on the large central holographic table which gave a 3D representation of the area around *Bismarck* showing all known traffic, air, surface and sub-surface, out to whatever the pre-selected range was.

Currently the setting was 50 miles which encompassed all of the designated targets and numerous merchant ships squawking their AIS identities. Immediately obvious was the position of the big cruise liner central to all the hostile contacts. Equally obvious was that she was the primary target. The question was what the bad guys were going to do with her once they had taken full control, which was inevitable.

As Jeff Bannister had said, these floating 'Gin Palaces' only had security procedures to stop passengers bringing cheap booze on board, and to ensure they didn't sail missing a few paying customers. Their main job was really just to verify that everyone who came on board where who they said they were, and that the crew members didn't have any business interests on the side like selling whole smoked salmon to a local hostelry. There wasn't even a Billy club or a taser to repel boarders let alone something that might actually deter or 'hurt them'.

This was obviously a well-planned ambush based on knowledge of the sea and maritime procedures and Taff wondered if his Captain and the ultimate boss Mr König, had the 'cahones' to take these bastards on, if they got a chance of course.

Reiner turned to Jake and formally asked for permission to engage if the opportunity arose. Jake nodded and turned to Taff.

"Make a note in the log please Mr Elias, I have given Captain Krull permission to execute company policy and engage those endangering civilian lives and illegally attacking merchant vessels on the high seas."

"Aye Sir, so noted."

The input from the Arados was seamlessly added to the hologram as it came in from the discrete directional transmitters on the small but immensely capable drones. They were designed by, and obtained directly from, a König Industries hi-tech division which produced them commercially for selected military and private security concerns.

Additional information could be called up or filtered out if the display got too, too busy. Things like the effective range of all surface, air and subsurface sensors as well as the weapons of course. This display went beyond the 2-D Star-Trek and into full 3-D. With the light cleverly controlled from the laser emitters, each surface contact was a NATO standard **V** with a stroke through the narrow end showing direction of travel and a clear colour to designate friendly, unknown or hostile. The Air contacts used a similar NATO set up but appeared to float above the sea. Again colour coded.

In translucent domed circles around *Bismarck,* her various weapon ranges were visible. For example, the furthest anti-air range of any weapon on Bismarck was displayed as a reddish translucent dome. A larger dome with a translucent brown tinge represented furthest any surface to surface weapon could achieve. The rings would expand or contract when weapons became available or were used. The drones had a cotton thin red line tying them to their controlling ship. The display also showed circles denoting the weapons mounted on them, and an operator could interrogate a circle for its weapon composition just by touching it.

At this moment two of the Sierras, were within the surface engagement dome, both flashing yellow meaning they were suspect or of unknown intent as yet. Reiner asked for radar back-track to be displayed as part of the process to ensure that he was engaging an enemy and not something like a speedboat bouncing along out of Malta. He also re-checked the current video feed, zooming in to show each with a crew of three and both with a large machine gun rigged in the bow. He now spoke into his mike and addressed the CMS directly designating them hostile and their chevrons instantly turned red.

The voice of the CMS unit asked for instructions for attacking these two now hostile contacts and Reiner spoke again delegating the task to Lt Kopf up in gunnery.

The weight of responsibility for the lives of perhaps two and a half thousand people pressed heavily on his shoulders now as he prepared to start an action which would have far reaching consequences, and not just for the ships involved locally. He studied the display for a moment more and then spoke into his mike.

"Drone control." A short pause and a click.

"This is the Captain. Prepare and launch drones three and four but stagger them by ten minutes. Cancel my previous and load with FAE and AS flechette if you please."

"Drone control Aye, launch Cyclops three and four with AS and FAE ten minute stagger."

Reiner looked up again and spoke in his mike.

"Guns." A short pause and click.

"Guns aye."

"Targets desig Sierra one and Sierra three are confirmed hostile. You are clear to engage with guns, Sierra one first."

"Guns Aye, engage Sierras one and three in order.

Reiner then said "Shipwide". Click.

"Do you hear there, this is the Captain. We are about to engage two hostile contacts. This is not an exercise, I repeat this is not an exercise. They have attacked merchant ships on their lawful occasions, they have therefore crossed the line. There is a situation developing on board a cruise ship nearby. Further sitrep to follow, meanwhile carry on and remember your training."

Lieutenant Julius Kopf had never fired a live round in his naval career. Correction, he'd never fired a live round at a target with a living enemy on board. He was surprised it bothered him briefly, but training takes over very quickly and before the aberrant thoughts had completely dimmed, his fingers were racing over the fire control panel.

He brought up a representation of the OPs room feed and checked the two designated targets. He then used a mouse to designate them with the Fire Control System (FCS).

He knew that the Saab Sea Giraffe, Agile Multi Band (AMB) system could do most of this stuff itself, and if required could be on fully automatic with regard to self-defence but he wanted the practice himself.

Both main radar antennae –unusual to have more than one– fed their information into the central CMS which analysed and categorised it before displaying the results. Information from all systems fed in seamlessly to give the most comprehensive picture.

He was, he admitted, a bit of a computer buff himself but even his grasp of CMS was tested by the algorithms working away in the background. It took time to be familiar and trusting of a system so he was doing things manually at the moment.

He could have switched his mike to CMS and given the orders verbally, but he'd do that only when he was fully confident with the manual methods. He spoke into the mike.

"Shipwide." A pause for the audible click.

"Do you hear there. This is Guns. Standby. Engaging. Out."

Turret Anton, the closest to the bow, smoothly and quickly trained to starboard, turret Bruno just behind and above did the same. Both pairs of guns began elevating then stopped.

They were now locked on their targets and the accelerometers deep in the keel at either end of the vessel fed in the information required to keep the muzzles pointing in the right direction at the correct elevation, so they appeared to move gently on their stabilised gimbals when in fact it was the ship moving. Like a predator sniffing the air they awaited the final commands.

Eight miles away a rigid inflatable boat or RIB, was skipping across the wave tops at 30 knots as it raced away from the ship it had mercilessly machine gunned.

The three young men on board were exhilarated, all had taken turns firing the big machine gun, it was a 'boys with their toys' thing. They heard nothing, they saw nothing and were utterly unaware of death rapidly approaching from over the horizon.

On the bridge there was a 'Ting, Ting' as the firing gong sounded. There followed a sharp 'crack' and the left barrel of Anton recoiled as the shell left the muzzle at one thousand nine hundred miles per hour on its fifteen second journey. Another sharp 'crack', the left barrel of Bruno recoiled too and spat its cargo at the distant dot on the milky horizon.

The smoke from both drifted rapidly away. The auto-loaders spat out the shell cases at the rear of the turret and loaded the next shells in each gun giving rise to an odd puff of grey smoke from the barrels.

The shell from Anton contained a new special round which could be used for anti-aircraft or anti-missile defence.

It had a laser proximity fuse designed to cause the shell to disintegrate at a set distance from its target but in this version the detonation blew through the front of the shell like a shotgun and sent its cargo of one centimetre cubes of tungsten flying forwards added to the momentum from the shell itself.

The result when the laser told it to detonate off the bow of the RIB, was quite spectacular and quite deadly

It had helped that the RIB wasn't manoeuvring at the time so for a single shot it was easy for such advanced gunnery systems to predict a future location.

The three men and the boat disappeared in a red mist and a cloud of shredded rubber. Within a fraction of a second the high explosive shell from turret Bruno hit the water where the RIB had been and exploded reducing whatever was left to even finer particulates as the remains of the 12.7mm machine gun began its five thousand metre drop into the Ionian abyssal plain.

Within a minute there was little left to show what had been there.

Lt Kopf sat back and stared at the live video feed from the drone. He zoomed in as far as he could but saw nothing remaining. He asked his number two for confirmation and having got it, he then designated Sierra three with the mouse.

The turrets quickly switched beam to train over the port side and the shoot sequence began again. The extra mile to target added nearly two seconds to the flight time of the shells but the result was the same.

Kopf was understandably pleased with the way the equipment had functioned, slick, seamless, accurate and a dozen other adjectives, but deadly above all.

In the space of a minute six young men had gone to discover whether Allah was waiting and whether he was pleased with them; and a certain raid commander was down a significant number of raiders without knowing why.

Julius knew that he'd been lucky and he could have expended much more ammunition if the terrorists had been manoeuvring, still he didn't think the boss would complain.

Back in the OPs room Reiner and Jake noted the track for Sierras one and three shiver for a second then disappear. They shifted their attention to the track and video feed for Sierras two and four and noted the position of Cyclops 2, the armed drone.

Reiner spoke into his mike again.

"Drone control." There was a click and an open channel.

"Drone control." Came back the voice of CPO Joachim Kempfe.

A big Dresdner, he was an electronics wiz who designed and programmed computer games as a side-line and who currently controlled their drone systems.

He sat with his partner in crime Petty Officer Luigi Abbate who cared for his four charges like they were his own children and maintained the catapult system too. Reiner gave him his instructions.

"Target Sierra two now and ensure they don't see you coming, no warnings please Chief."

"Target Sierra two, Aye Sir. Will be within engagement range in just over a minute Sir."

Joachim replied looking at the OPs screen repeater which showed his Cyclops 2 which Luigi called little 'Abriana', coming in at Sierra two from his south east, hopefully a direction they would not be looking in. The range circle surrounding the drone was a violet colour denoting an air-to-surface load. The plot ID also had a 'T' beneath indicating 'thermobaric' as the weapon type.

Joachim didn't think anyone would be looking up and if they did they'd be really lucky to see his charge flying now a mile high. A task made even more difficult with the thousand or so LED emitters on its underside which effectively made it disappear into the background.

'Clever stuff' had been Jake's comment when Joachim and Luigi had explained and demonstrated how an upward pointing luminosity detector told the LEDs on the underside how bright to shine down in order to be the same as looking at the background. With that and its whisper engine, which barely could be heard even on take-off, Joachim and Luigi were confident that the drone would remain undetected even crossing the peripheral vision of the boat's occupants.

The drone slid smoothly around until it was almost directly behind the RIB before Joachim spoke into his mike.

"Cyclops 2. Target Sierra two. One bird. Launch starb." Cyclops 2 received verbal its instructions and prepared the missile under the right wing for launch, then initiated the launch. The fibreglass canister fell away.

The recon drone picked up the flash of the rocket ignition of the AT-9 NATO code 'Spiral2' then lost it as the missile accelerated towards the boat with no tell-tale smoke trail.

At a pre-determined point the first charge broke open the container and sprayed a fine mist of fuel forwards and down, a fraction of a second later the leading missile component exploded and ignited the fuel.

Joachim watched the screen and saw the silent movie play out as the explosion flashed brightly for an instant. When it was done, the recon drone zoomed in the camera to check but there was nothing left of boat and men, nothing at all. He sat back in his chair and spoke quietly into his mike.

"OPs." He waited for the click then carried on.

"Drone control. Target destroyed one further package on board."

Taff Elias answered for OPs.

"Drone control Aye. Target destroyed one further package available. Standby for further instructions. OPs out."

He turned to Reiner.

"Do you want Cyclops 3 up Sir, she's FAE armed. Shall I ask if Cyclops 2 can get a solution on Sierra four before it gets too close to the *Kristianstaadt* say, no closer than ten miles boss?"

"Do it." Came Reiner's reply as he stared at the holo display now showing the other two Sierras as red chevrons since they were positively identified.

"Urwin get me that Chief Officer again please. I hope he's switched the ringer to vibrate, I'd hate for a cleaner's cupboard to suddenly start ringing like a phone box."

Geordie Urwin, Leading Seaman OPs and comms specialist started to make the connection.

"Aye sir, trying now."

The voice of Jeff Bannister on the *Kristianstaadt* came through the compartment speakers.

"Hello? What's happening *Bismarck*? I just heard a rumble in the distance, somewhere to my south west I think. It set some of these bastards scurrying about. I'm in an electrical inspection cupboard near midships on deck 3 and I can see a slice of what's happening occasionally."

"Good man." Answered Reiner with as much reassurance as he could convey.

"The noise was another boatload of your visitors disintegrating. We've taken care of three of them now, we may yet get the fourth before it gets to your ship, but it will depend on whether we deem it too close to you to destroy without alerting your visitors. We need to keep them guessing. What did they do when the boom sounded?"

"The one I think is in charge, started doing things with his phone. As far as I could see he dialled four numbers, listened but only spoke once. Then he started shouting at two of the others I could see. They ran to a pile of gear in long canvas bags, each pulled out a fat green tube, about a yard and a half I'd guess, with what looked like a gun trigger or something underneath and then went out on deck."

"OK. Good. Thanks for that Jeff. Now you stay safe......" He was interrupted by Bannister.

"Look I've just been talking to the Staff Captain on the bridge too. The raiders have been negotiating with him. They want ten million in gold lowered onto the ship's basketball court on deck ten, and they want all Muslim Brotherhood prisoners released from Egyptian jails. They've given us eight hours to comply or they will start killing hostages."

"OK, did the Staff Captain give you any orders?"

"Well he just said something didn't feel right about the demand or maybe the guy who made it. He couldn't put a finger on it. I'm a bit worried too, on my travels around the engine room spaces I came across some sort of explosive device stuck to the hull, and at that point it was about four yards below the waterline. It had a digital display that said 00.00 and a red light in one corner. Also, one of the grease monkeys told me he'd seen four or more of them too, he's hiding in various lockers and tool stowages. He also says they're all on the port side. The one I saw was as well. What do you make of that? Does that sound normal for this sort of thing?"

"That's brilliant intel Jeff, well done. Stay sharp and stay safe OK. Look we've got some of the finest security guys you could imagine and thanks to you we've got a clearer picture so I'll run it by them OK? Any news on the Malta patrol boat or the Italian frigate?"

"Err, they know about the demands now and they are going to stay over the horizon when they get here while they consult. Presume that means talking to politicians, which doesn't sound good to me. I don't think they're anywhere near yet anyway to be honest. They told us to ignore you, because you aren't official and you aren't authorised to take any action."

Reiner frowned. "OK so why are you talking to us then?"

"Well the Staff Captain wants to keep all his options open. Besides, as far as I can tell, you're the only ones who've done anything yet and the only ones likely to be in a position to do anything for quite a while."

"Right save your battery we'll get back in touch again soon. We will delay our approach a little while whilst we have a think about what you've said. Meanwhile, if the Staff Captain wants to talk to us, just tell him to call. Give him our sat number."

"I offered it to him. He doesn't want it. I think he's covering his back and he wants all communication with you to be deniable or something, if it all goes wrong. He's a bit of a pillock at times actually and way out of his depth with this, me too to be honest."

"Roger that Jeff. But I can see his point, we are the first of a new kind of 'Merchant Protector' ship so we have no track record or official status yet. However, this ship is crammed with gadgets that would put a smile on your face if you could see them, not only that but we are all ex-service and the commandos are all combat veterans. So don't worry, we've got your back, no one else is going to get near you and we'll talk to you before we do anything. *Bismarck* out."

Reiner turned to the others including the newly arrived Security Team Leader. These guys were part of König Industries regular security company and so did not carry ranks like *Bismarck's* crew. They were just hitching a ride to their final destination which was Little Cayman via Bermuda.

"Did you catch all that Arkady?"

"Yes Captin." Just like all the Hollywood depictions of a Russian speaking English, Reiner thought. Arkady Zotov must have been the one they had in mind. He smiled at the big man who looked like he needed extra pockets in his cammo gear, to put his muscles in.

"OK. So what is your assessment?"

"First the green tube. This conforms to the size of an Iranian Misagh 2, MANPADS or Man portable air defence system. We know that some have been captured by various factions and are in circulation but it could be another type of the same thing." Arkady placed a photo of the Misagh unit on Reiner's workstation.

"This means they are well prepared and our drone should stay at least 6.5 kilometres away, just over four miles, if there is a chance they can be seen. Next, the charges appear to be placed all along one side below waterline. This is a technique for quickly taking ships out. These vessels are very 'top heavy' I think you say. When blown it will cause a massive inrush of water along one side of vessel. Damage control will not be able to counter pump enough without sinking ship."

"Next the money in gold. Good idea, untraceable BUT they ask for too little in circumstance. Only ten million? They have nearly 2000 passengers to ransom. This gold would be only about 400 kilos I think. They also take passenger jewellery and money, but no need if they plan to die. Next they ask for prisoner release. They know Egyptians will not release prisoners, they know UK, US, Russia and many others will not talk to terrorists." The big Russian went on inexorably with his analysis.

"So this is impossible demand especially in short time. Also they have not done this a smart way if they want money and prisoners. They could have been on board and capture bridge easy if they wanted, I think. Then no alarm goes out *until* they want it to. They could have captured Captin and Security Chief and got into bridge, instead they kill them and make no attempt to get into bridge. No need."

"It is my belief Captin that they are playing for time until all is set and night has fallen, then they will leave the ship and blow it. I think this is to be a terrorist job like 9/11 and they want as many to die as possible; they want us to think they are playing our game and they seem to know the rules we play by and how to 'string us along', is correct?"

Reiner looked a little stunned by the clinical analysis, he glanced at Jake who also seemed to be mentally walking through the scenario that Arkady had just announced in his own inimitable style.

"Yes, string us along. How will they detonate Arkady?" Jake asked.

"Easy. They can use a timer, but there could be problems with that. But they will most probably use radio signal to detonate. It mostly depends if they want to join with the passengers saying hello to Allah, or maybe they want to get off and repeat the game again later. They may not be suicidal."

Reiner spoke into his mike. "Halshaw."

Then a click. The communications auto routing could target a headset wearer as well as a place.

"Captain here. Ian, I need you in OPs to talk about remote radio detonation signals and other stuff."

"Aye Sir on my way."

He picked another name. "Kempfe." Then the click of connection. It didn't need to make a sound but it was a help to know you were connected.

"Captain here. Joachim do we have an ECM pod for drones?"

"Yes Sir. We could load it on number four."

"Right, I need you to talk with Lt Halshaw about whether we could jam a signal and the distance over which we can be effective. Can you hand over to Luigi for a few minutes and get down to the OPs room ASAP."

"Listen up everyone." Reiner addressed all in the OPs room. "It is my belief that *Bismarck* can only remain a secret for a short while longer. I also concur with Arkady's assessment of intent. I expect they have men posted all around the upper decks now, some with surface to air missiles. Pretty soon their leader will work out that he has lost three units at least and he will conclude that someone is watching."

Reiner ran a hand through his bristle topped head, a sign he was stressed.

"I think if he is getting off he'll want to get on with his plan as soon as possible after dark which is?" He threw a look at Taff.

"19.45 our time Sir"

"OK. Thanks Taff. It's less than an hour and a quarter to sunset. In the ensuing alarm of the ship sinking and all efforts devoted to SAR, they could make their escape. I'd guess posing as a fishing boat or something with an AIS transponder on that allows them to blend into the background clutter. Perhaps their waterlogged sinking vessel is not as un-seaworthy, as they made out. Get Luigi to focus on the vessel they came from please Taff."

"Aye Sir."

"Anyway, that's what I'd do if I were them, they could be miles away before anyone gets around to looking at backtracks for the vessels in the area. The old Atlantiques would be looking for anything NOT squawking its position."

He paused a second then continued as if some tiny piece had just fallen into place.

"They might just leave a few passengers in the water to give people someone to rescue. Right, so I think our best bet is to leave Sierra four alone. Let him wonder what happened to the other three since one has arrived. Let them get on with setting the charges and let them think their deception has worked. Let them think frantic negotiations are going on to secure the release of the prisoners and get the gold to them." He glanced over to Jake and got a discrete nod of approval before continuing.

"My instinct tells me that when all is set, they'll transfer to the larger mother-boat to make their escape assuming I am correct and they are not going down with it. What we must do is prevent the detonation that we assume will follow as soon as they are at a safe distance, a hundred yards or so I expect."

Everyone was nodding away as Reiner precisely and concisely outlined their options.

"First thing to do is switch off all our upper deck lighting and secure any scuttles below decks to keep us totally dark. Then we need some options for taking out the trigger man. I expect it depends on what Ian and Joachim say about the electronic stuff as to whether we use ECM and shoot from the dark eastern side or whether we fry them with another thermobaric shot or two from a drone."

"Bridge." Reiner waited for the click.

"Captain here. Steer a course which keeps us out of their sight, at about ten miles again I suppose. We can come closer as the light fades and if we're in the darkest patch of sea. I suggest a figure of eight north and south but it's up to you Simon. Stand down from action stations for forty minutes, one in two to go and get something to eat and drink. I want everyone fed and watered and back at action stations in forty minutes. Clear?"

"Yes Sir. May I ask what's going on?"

"When you get Kopf back from his meal break to relieve you, pop into the OPs room and I'll bring you up to date, things are still not quite ready for the finale."

"Aye Sir. Bridge out."

"Right." Reiner spun his command chair around towards Ian Halshaw, Arkady Zotov and Joachim Kempfe. They were huddled over to one side of the OPs room having an animated tech-chat which involved much hand signalling and counting of fingers.

"I'll leave them to it eh Jake? I expect they'll come and talk English to us in a minute or so. What's your take on things?" Before Jake could answer Reiner spoke into his mike again.

"Galley." Click.

"Captain here. Can you bring some sandwiches and coffee to the OPs room please we aren't going to have time to come down?"

"Galley aye Sir." Said PO Steward 'Granny' Smith in his broad 'Brummy' accent. "On the way in a minute."

Jake waited until he had Reiner's attention again. He could see that the prospect of action had invigorated Reiner and his brain had shifted into that high gear which made most others look positively pedestrian when it came to thinking options through and making decisions.

"I'm with you so far in the summary of events as they've unfolded and are likely to unfold. I certainly hope to God we can pull this off Reiner, otherwise we may as well turn around and head back to Sevastopol and that breakers yard just beyond the frigate dock. Just a pity we haven't had time for any work up exercises."

It was clear to both that any error they made, any loss of life that could be pinned on their actions or even just laid speculatively at their feet, would be the death knell for the new *Bismarck* and the 'Merchant Protector' scheme. More importantly though if they got it wrong, then about the same number who had died on 9/11 would become victims again.

Once more, it was all because of some religious narcissists who could not tolerate competition for belief. Well they would be blamed but whether someone was hiding behind the religion for their own benefit didn't really matter, the result would be the same for the passengers and crew.

"What is it you English say? 'No pressure then?'"

"That's exactly it Reiner, no pressure old friend, and as usual the guys on the front line have to take the hand they are dealt and sort things out."

"OPs, drone control."

"Go ahead Luigi."

"Should be on screen now Captain. I zoomed in on the *mama* boat, recorded for a minute or so then pushed the frames through an image enhancer. This is what I got."

They all watched the film.

"Comments". Said Reiner. "Boss?"

Jake thought a second.

"Well it certainly looks seaworthy to me, it's riding high and is definitely a fishing boat, you can see the stern rig. They must have either pumped it out or had a water-filled blivet of some kind to make it look like it was sinking."

"I'm not sailor Sir but it looks OK to me." Was Arkady's input.

Reiner waited to see if anyone disagreed.

"So they've taken the time to empty the boat and bring it alongside. Right then, why keep it once they board the ship? Unless of course they plan to leave, well some of them at least. We have to go with Arkady's assessment I think; this is all a deception. Why would they bother negotiating for prisoners and money if they were on a suicide run? Just more deception. Provide hope. Politicians won't authorise a rescue if they think they can talk them out of it. Plus the bad guys cannot be aware that we are watching them and sharing all the live drone feeds with Malta RCC."

Another fifteen minutes crept by and then there was a call from First Officer Jeff Bannister.

"*Bismarck*, I've just had another wander around, carefully. They're all relaxed, they seem confident that everyone is under lock-down." The signal faded in and out briefly, and resumed with some static.

"All of the crew apart from the bridge staff, a certain grease monkey and myself, are sitting with their hands on their heads in

94

the atrium on deck three. Now I don't know if this is relevant but the ship's safe has been opened, the jewellery shops ransacked and anything they could get their sticky little mits on has been taken." He sucked in a deep breath and continued, the static briefly worsening as he moved his position.

"They've pulled their stinky little fishing boat alongside the port midships entryway and appear to be filling it with anything that isn't nailed down. Seems it wasn't in sinking condition after all. Now, I do speak a little Arabic but nothing near good enough to understand what is being said so I've asked the chap I found in engineering if he does and he reckons he's Lebanese, a Lebanese Christian in fact. So I've got him to go and secrete himself in the workshop behind the entryport on deck one where they've got their boat, in the hope he can pick something up. There's a service hatch there that he can sit behind to listen. I've given him one of the ships radios with the sound turned right down and tuned to an obscure frequency so he can tell me what's happening." He paused then as if unsure how to go on.

"Uh, have you any ideas how you're going to get us out of this then?"

Reiner answered.

"We're nearly there Jeff. But first we need a little code word to say you are not being coerced, I should have done this when you first made contact I'm sorry. Perhaps if you could call us *Tirpitz* instead of *Bismarck* if you get caught and they want you to pass on false information to us?"

"Err, yeah sure. *Tirpitz*, right. What's going to happen?"

"OK. First we are deliberately letting the last of the four machine gun boats get back to them. I know we said we would not let any more through but we have a reason. Anyway, we're nearly there with the plan, just a couple of things to finalise. We do think though that they intend to blow the bottom out of your vessel, all along one side to get it to capsize quickly. We also think they'll do that regardless of what the negotiations with the authorities come to. That will all happen when they leave your ship we think which we calculate will be as the sun sets or soon after. With me so far?"

"Shit yes! Yeah now I see it. Yeah, bastards want to kill us all not get a bloody ransom that's why all the ransacking!"

This last was said with panic near to surfacing. Poor devil, Reiner thought, skulking around on a bomb that was soon to go off was no one's idea of fun.

"Jeff look, we won't let them finish their little plan. We have our own, just waiting on a little tweak. You've been incredible so far, we are all deeply impressed with your bravery and tenacity. Just keep going for a little while longer and we'll get you out of there. *Bismarck* out."

Reiner closed his little speech in what he hoped was an encouraging tone and turned back to the room at large and for the ninety ninth time in the last ten minutes, or so it seemed, checked the clocks on the bulkhead in front of him.   They seemed to have stopped or were moving back slowly.

Granny Smith appeared carrying two big plates of sandwiches with everything from corned beef and pickle to smoked salmon and cream cheese. One of his helpers had two pots one with coffee the other with tea. They put everything on a table at the far end of the compartment.

"Grub's up gents." He announced gaily and departed with his helper.

Jake, Reiner, Taff and Geordie went over and helped themselves. I'm bloody famished thought Jake as he grabbed a corned beef sandwich and a cup of coffee. He realised then the hands should have had their evening meal an hour ago but they had held off when the current situation exploded right in front of them.

Then it was all business again as Ian and Joachim came over to lend their thoughts to the plan.   Between mouthfuls of sandwich Ian summed up their conclusions.

"We cannot say for certain that the ECM will jam the detonation signal used by the terrorists, although we're pretty sure it will, if the drone is close enough. We think that with night approaching the chances of seeing the matt finished drone with the smart illumination, will be very low order. And that if it gets within 500 yards vertical or horizontal, it will jam the signal. But we can't be sure. Also we can't be certain that if we used a thermobaric charge to obliterate the mother-boat that it wouldn't cause the trigger man to involuntarily push the button, if that is the kind of initiator they have."

"What else could they use." Chipped in the newly arrived Simon McClelland, as he grabbed a coffee and sandwich.

Ian Halshaw turned to face him.

"A timer possibly, but that means coordinating the setting so that you don't get blown up accidentally and if they want a simultaneous detonation, it's damned hard to achieve. They can't use a mobile phone either because we're hundreds of miles out to sea, a sat-phone is dodgy too because the signal may not reach all of the charges, or even any of them. Don't forget it would have to penetrate anything up to twelve steel decks and usually you want them out in the open for good reception. Notice how Bannister's fades in and out and he's on the decks above the waterline."

He paused to recall where he'd left off.

"However we do think that if missile detonation occurs without the trigger man having any warning, and as long as he isn't actually holding the detonator mechanism, that everything will be fried instantly so there would be no accidental explosion of the ship-borne charges. On that subject though, the drone missile launcher is a problem because there is a flash of bright light as the missile motor ignites."

"We think if the *Kristianstaadt* sent up a distress flare off to the south, it wouldn't alarm them particularly but the sound would draw all eyes that way and they'd focus on the pyrotechnics. If the AT-9 was then fired from the north at maximum range it is unlikely that anyone will see it or recognise it for what it was."

Reiner said nothing, just looked at his interlinked fingers for a second or two. Then he looked up, decision made.

"Thank you gentlemen that will be all." They left the OPs room looking less than happy that there was no easy solution for their Captain to use.

Reiner turned to Jake.

"This is what I propose Jake. We will combine our options. It will depend on clear coordinated timing. There is a danger that it will overcomplicate things but I think not." He stood up and began to pace.

"We should launch the ECM drone fairly soon so that Kempfe can get it into position on the dark side of the target, even directly above, since as night falls the lights from the ship itself will make it very difficult to see anything out at sea or high above. Next, we need to get Bannister to locate a distress flare and get him briefed to shoot it only when he's give the word and not a second before. Third, the drone with the hyperbaric warhead needs to be in position, I would say no more than two and a half miles west of the ship but slightly on the north side which will silhouette the target nicely for us anyway." Jake let the ideas percolate as Reiner wandered the OPs room.

"Lastly, *Bismarck* needs to be a precise calculated distance away I'm thinking two miles, given the velocity of the AK130 rounds but I'll check it. We have to be facing the *Kristianstaadt* directly but slightly to the north so any accidental overshoot doesn't hit the ship." Jake was fairly sure that the range check would be spot on if he knew Reiner at all.

"At the prescribed time the flare needs to go up." He stopped and turned towards Jake ticking the items off on his fingers one at a time.

"At plus one the ECM needs to start frying anything electrical in the boat. At plus two seconds, the drone will shoot, hopefully when all eyes are on the pretty firework. The AT-9 will take ten seconds to travel two point five miles. At plus eight *Bismarck* fires two flechette rounds. If we get it right, at plus twelve the flechettes will arrive along with the hyperbaric charge and will utterly destroy the boat and all in it without detonating the charges in the hull."

"After that *Bismarck* will close the ship rapidly and go alongside. Arkady and his boys will board and conduct a thorough search to eliminate any strays, and afterwards will make safe the charges. I am assuming the forensic people will want a sample to confirm origin."

"How does that sound Jake?" He waited for objections. There weren't any.

"OK. I'll get in touch with Mr Bannister and get him on board with the plan. Everything starts five seconds after the enemy fishing boat leaves the side of the cruiser, we dare not wait any longer than that for fear of them achieving a safe distance to detonate. Right now, I suppose, in the great tradition of all our services, we have to hurry up and wait."

About ten minutes later they had confirmation of the final murderous plan of the terrorists. Jeff Bannister rang to tell them that the boat Sierra four, had arrived alongside and that a heated discussion at high volume had taken place.

"My man says that they discussed the missing three boats and the head guy on the ship was quite 'nonch' about it but the senior guy in the boat wasn't happy. He was yabbering on about an imminent attack and saying that they should get off now if they have all the money and jewels, and just blow the damned thing up as soon as possible. He doesn't want to meet Allah yet and leaving now, gave them a good chance of escaping." Bannister again faded out then returned.

"Well apparently the head guy didn't like being told what to do and got real nasty with the other bloke and he must have pulled a pistol because the next thing he says is something like one more word and he's going to shoot the other bloke." He let out a big sigh.

"So it looks like you're right, the bastards are going to blow it whatever happens. What now?"

Reiner explained the plan, or as much as Bannister needed to know in order to get things going. He confirmed it was no problem to get hold of a flare too.

"So we'll call you when it is time to send the flare up and that will be very soon after the fishing boat leaves the side of your ship. You OK with all that Jeff?"

"Er, yeah I suppose so." Came Bannister's less than enthusiastic answer. "There's no other way is there?"

"Not that we can think of Jeff, the moment that fishing boat gets to a safe distance they'll punch the button and that will be it, nothing we'd be able to do apart from pick up a few who manage to get over the side."

"OK. How long do you think?"

Reiner took a deep breath.

"Ten minutes or so is our best guess Jeff. We have a drone up there with its camera slaved to that entryport. The moment that boat casts off we'll know it and that's when the clock starts ticking. So, you need to go immediately to get a flare, preferably a rocket parachute flare and then get up to one of the top decks and be ready for the call." Bannister agreed and went off to find a flare and link up with the grease monkey on deck ten forward.

Reiner stood up and announced that he was going to the bridge and would give the commands from there, Jake followed him up. They entered the bridge, which was now in red lighting to preserve night vision and picked up a pair of night vision binoculars leaving the periscope-like viewers to bridge staff and Simon as Officer of the Watch. They were now moving slowly towards the *Kristianstaadt* and Reiner asked for the range to target.

"Two point two miles, Sir." Was the instant response from Kopf up above in the gunnery station. He now had the feed from *Bismarck's* radar and the recon drone in the air just to the north of the stricken cruise ship. The accuracy of his ranging was in the three decimals range and he was confident that he'd get his shells on target as required. A bead of sweat was dashed away quickly so he didn't miss anything as he watched the fishing boat.

"As soon as we achieve two miles, go to station keeping with the Steerpods if you please."

Reiner observed carefully as another terrorist climbed aboard the fishing boat. That had been the fourth one going in that direction without anyone getting off. They're getting ready, he thought and moved over to the viewer which had a much greater magnification as well as image intensifying software, displacing Simon in the process.

He spoke into his mike. "Shipwide." Waited for the click and spoke.

"All hands, standby, standby."

Then closed the connection.

"Open the channel to Jeff Bannister and tell him to standby and keep it open!"

"Aye Sir." Responded Geordie Urwin, dialling the number.

Reiner focussed carefully now, he could see the shape of a figure standing just inside the fold out entryport, clever idea that entryport, he thought to himself. In the background he could hear his crew carrying out their orders as the distance clicked to two miles

"Station keeping." Ordered Simon McClelland."

"Aye Sir." Responded the helmsman and the Steerpods, using GPS linked to the engine controls, kept *Bismarck* exactly where she was.

"Pods set to station keeping." Reported Sid Buller on the wheel.

"Drone control." Said Reiner into the mike.

"Bridge here. Report."

"Both Cyclops in position and standing by Sir." Came the crisp reply of Chief Kempfe as he monitored the 'shooter' drone and made sure the jammer was ready to go on the other.

"Guns." Reiner whispered. Click.

"Bridge here. Report."

"Turrets Anton and Bruno loaded, trained and ready to fire Sir." Answered Kopf, with a slight note of excitement in his voice.

"Bannister standing by Sir." Reported Geordie.

Jake observed his friend as the final seconds ticked away. Such was his concentration he almost stopped breathing because he didn't want to make a noise and disturb the quiet whilst Reiner, apparently as cool as a cucumber, waited for the moment to order the strike.

*

Abu Mamluk took a last drag on his fortieth cigarette of the day and flicked it into the water at the side of the entryport. He checked his watch for the umpteenth time and reviewed the events of the day carefully to ensure he had missed nothing.

They had spent all morning and most of the afternoon steering the old fishing boat wide of any traffic at all, they didn't want to be seen by anyone before they chose to be seen. The four RIBs had been towed on a daisy chain behind them since it wouldn't be either practical or sensible to wear the crews out before they reached the target area and then they were released to carry out their own missions.

In the little wheelhouse the expensive satellite receiver stood out against the background of grime and clutter. It chirped and beeped happily as it maintained its internet connection and he could watch the approach of the target using the AIS system with an update every few minutes depending on which receiver stations were in range.

He had been only peripherally aware of this technology before but its existence was not a surprise, what was a surprise was that anyone, absolutely anyone, could track civilian ships and aircraft because each politely squawked its location to the world. He could understand governments and military units needing to know this information, he could understand shipping lines wanting it, but having it freely available? Perhaps they have no choice he mused, once out, there's no way to stop it being used by anyone is there? It was a recipe for disaster, as he was about to prove.

When the fishing boat had finally got into position the wait had not been long at all, thanks to the little box. They'd quickly pumped water into the rubber blivet in the hold so that the target ship would see just a waterlogged old boat full of desperate migrants apparently sinking.

He was counting on the gloom of the late afternoon and the fact that they would be on the darker side as the evening wore on. Clouds building up in the west would help shut the light down early too. They had a couple of boxes of red distress flares, the big parachute type, he hoped the cruise ship would not steam straight past, that would be embarrassing.

The man in Benghazi had said that there were foolish laws which prevented distress flares from being ignored on pain of prison and massive fines so he was confident that if they stopped right in its intended track, that the cruise ship would attempt a rescue.

A moment of fear had grasped what passed for his heart as the approaching monster appeared to ignore the flares and charged towards them. It was truly enormous. Perhaps it was still too light for them to see the flares? Perhaps they should have waited another half hour?

But then the giant cruise ship slowed perceptibly, the bow wave disappeared and she veered south. Brought up on traditional propulsion systems, none of the raiders had ever seen

Azipods in action before and could not have guessed the extra manoeuvrability and speed control they gave the massive cruise liner.

He had one more quick look around to make sure there were no clues for a powerful pair of binoculars to pick up on. He checked his watch again and looked at the AIS monitor for the last time. His little surprises should be starting their attacks any second now and he could see the four selected targets, all within thirty miles of this position.

The hidden Tuareg on the waterlogged and apparently distressed vessel, lay still and waited for their leader to give the order. They had discarded their traditional indigo robes and face veils so that they looked like the usual migrants, all except Abu Mamluk himself.

The man in Benghazi said that the ship would stop because they had to, because the Westerners believed that the filth that were crossing Libya on the old slave routes and buying passage on leaky dredgers and coasters and even hastily roped together oil drums, were refugees from war. He was right about one thing, the ship was stopping. They had no idea these people, no idea at all.

As he watched the cruise liner manoeuvre he reflected on how he had come to command this strike on this day. The discontent in Mali that had been spitting and fizzing for years, blew up properly in 2012 and full blown conflict had ensued. He and his followers, the number growing with his reputation, had a fine time initially, killing Malian soldiers and capturing many women and much booty.

Then the French came again and they were not so easy to discourage. Their Foreign Legion devils were every bit as tough as the ones who his father said came before, and better armed than ever. Many Tuareg had fallen.

He and his followers had quietly drifted away south east to Burkina Faso and had gone 'quiet', meaning they'd set up their tents and put away their guns -for now.

He had been a wanderer and slave trader like his father and his father before him, taking by force the dark coloured people from the south and bringing them north where the markets were.

The whites thought the trade had stopped in his father's time, but they knew nothing. He himself owned many slaves and had never ceased trading them.

But things had changed recently, instead of having to take slaves, they had started paying him and his brothers to move them north to the coast so they could travel to the lands across the sea where the white whores lived, money was easy to find and people paid you to do nothing. Fools all of them.

He didn't care what reason they came for, once these fools accepted and paid up they were introduced to reality, Tuareg style. Many never made it across the great wastes.

He had played this game for some time before the men of the Daesh came to spread their word which was simply 'obey us or die'. He'd seen others resist and be killed, so he carefully traded with them and swore allegiance so they did not kill him and his followers.

The new slave trade was organised by the IS gangs who had people everywhere down along the old slave coast and all the way to the east, selling the idea of moving to Europe, just pay and go, that easy.

He had decided to go along with things for now but when the time came they would just leave and fade into the deserts as usual. The land the whites called Libya was today not really a state, it had travelled back in time, it more closely resembled the tribal areas before westerners came and drew lines on maps.

The time had come. Today was his last deal with them. After this, he and his followers would disappear into the great deserts for a long time. Today they had become truly rich and if at the same time they helped Allah's cause, then so much the better.

Taking the ship, or what they needed of it had proved easier than expected. When the little boat had come away from the amazing hole that had opened in the ship's side he had watched from the small wheelhouse timing his move for when they were most distracted by manoeuvring close to his vessel. At which point he had calmly moved out from the wheelhouse bowed and then stepped on to the boat's deck through the opening half way along. The people who helped him on board wore smiles on their strange brown faces but not in their eyes.

He had simply walked forward to where the raised steering position was and put a pistol to the driver's gut. He told the frightened boat driver not to speak to the ship and to wait until his people had loaded all of their bags on board. Easy.

The radio squawked with increasingly strident voices from the ship demanding to know what was happening, why the crewman was not responding?

With the loading completed they moved the two hundred yards back to the side of the monster.

Waiting on the platform was the man in charge, an older man with many gold stripes on his shoulders. But it was the way he stood which told Abu that he was in charge. His cousin Abdhoul now came and pressed his pistol into the driver's gut and Abu moved to the midships boarding point when the boat nudged the fold out entryport.

With his weapon pressed into the back of a frightened Indonesian crewman he watched as the man tossed the line to a waiting seaman on the monster ship. Then Abu had calmly stepped aboard the *Kristianstaadt* as if he was the owner, which at that point he was in fact about to become. He walked towards the man wearing the white uniform and moved the weapon from behind his back. With studied calm he shot the Captain once in the forehead then once in the chest, before the surprised man fell Abu had turned and chosen his next target, the security chief wearing the Sherriff's badge on his chest. Abu shot him twice also.

The others ran away as fast as they could and Abu waved his men on and quickly began unloading the weapons and explosives. After that it was easy, he spoke to the bridge and got them to make the announcements to the crew and passengers. He'd been told but did not believe it, that these people were ordered not to resist what they called pirates. Laughable. So easy to get them to comply.

Right now he should be tumbling back into the sea with his bullet raked body leaking his life blood and his men dropping like flies as machine guns raked them. But they weren't. Foolish, gullible people.

So they took the ship and sowed the seeds of rescue, relief and an end to the nightmare by offering terms. They wouldn't be around long enough to accept even if the fools paid up.

The one thing that kept nagging at him was his inability to raise three of his four raiding boats on the sat phone. He knew his phone worked because he had used it to send the one word coded message to the man in Benghazi after he had taken the ship.

But three did not answer and then there was the boom in the distance from the south and west, was it thunder? There were certainly clouds building up so it may be. But the other boats were to call him after half an hour and only one had.

Then when the only boat he managed to talk to had come alongside the Libyan driver wanted to leave immediately. The coward was lucky he had not shot him on the spot.

Still, it was time to go now. He could not believe that the small amount of explosives his men had carried would be able to sink this monster, but he didn't care, the riches they had taken would mean they would never want for anything again.

Abu Mamluk stepped onto the fishing boat that had been moored to the side of the cruise ship and ordered it to move away a hundred yards or so.

As it chugged slowly away he readied the little box that the man in Benghazi had given him, he flicked the cover up and looked at the button. Then he heard a loud whoosh and a red flare burst high in the sky behind the ship, and then another.

It won't help, he sighed to himself, no one is going to rescue you people.

*

Unbelievable clarity even at this range and with poor illumination Reiner thought as he watched one of the terrorists flick his cigarette butt into the sea.

The terrorist then stepped on to the platform and looked around, apparently satisfied, he waved his arm and stepped on to the waiting fishing boat. This man was in full robes and clearly the boss. The lines were cast off and the boat began moving slowly away from the side of the liner.

Every single nerve in Reiner's entire body focussed on the fishing boat and the widening gap.

"Bannister, NOW!" Shouted Reiner.

A bright red flare blossomed above *Kristianstaadt*, followed quickly by another. Reiner looked at the man in robes who had his head tilted back clearly staring at the flare in the sky.

One.

"ECM NOW!"

Two.

"DRONE FIRE!"

Three, four, five, six, seven, Then.

"SHOOT!"

The percussive crack of two 130mm rounds sounded incredibly loud after the silence. Using flash-less powder meant all they saw was a bloom of smoke which quickly blew away.

Eight, nine, ten, eleven.

"Standby!"

Twelve.

Bright light, brighter than day blossomed next to the giant cruise ship, seconds later the thunderclap sound of exploding flechette rounds and igniting thermobaric warheads lashed *Bismarck*.

When the dancing purple dots allowed him to see again, Reiner scanned the area around the great ship and the vessel itself for any signs of listing, which, had the charges gone off, would probably be evident already. Of the fishing boat and those aboard there was no sign.

A whoop went up from the bridge crew which Reiner thought may yet be a little premature, but his eyesight was returning and still there was no evidence of listing. People started clapping and one of them was Jake König who came across and shook Reiner's hand.

"Bloody magnificent Reiner. Marvellous. Well done old friend."

Reiner's concession to overt emotion was to smile weakly.

"Helm, half ahead. Take us alongside the cruise liner, make sure you do a good job, we want an impressive mooring after the fireworks, not scraped paint."

"Aye Sir." Replied a slightly peeved Sid Buller on the helm. "Half ahead."

"Shipwide." Reiner spoke into the mike. Click.

"Security teams to the bow and stern. Berthing parties fore and aft, oh and well done everyone, it seems phase one was successful." He cut the mike as cheering erupted from various sections of the ship.

"Drone control." Nothing. He found it difficult to enunciate his English whilst wearing an inane grin and had to say it again.

"Drone control." Click.

"Recover the drones all bar the recon drone unless she needs to come down."

"Aye Sir." Said a happy, chuffed and relieved Joachim Kempfe.

"Mr Bannister are you still on the line?"

"Yes Captain. Wow! I nearly crapped myself when those bangs went off! Jees but thank you. That was something else, I mean really, we can never repay you for pulling our nuts out of the fire."

"Not a problem Jeff, but please remember, it would not have been possible without your coolness and bravery in such a desperate situation. You are to be highly commended and I'm sure your employers will reward you, as they should."

Replied Reiner in the understatement of the millennium.

"Now Mr Bannister, Jeff, our security teams will board first as there is still a slight chance that they have left men behind so I need you to speak to the Staff Captain and ask him to tell everyone to stay put whilst we comb the ship and check out the explosive situation. But if there are two or three deck officers or security officers and maybe an engineer or two who can act as guides it will greatly speed things.

He paused to let that sink in before continuing.

"Tell them that the security team will be fully armed and ready to neutralise any 'stay behind' terrorists. If we have even the slightest doubt then we will ask that everyone takes to the boats rather than risk losing anyone, sorry, I mean any more people. Oh and Jeff, tell him it should be OK to speak to me now."

Bannister's laughter had a slightly higher pitch than it would normally have but was heartfelt all the same.

"Will do Captain, I look forward to meeting you soon, out."

"OPs." He spoke quietly. Click.

"Geordie, inform Malta RCC that we have successfully destroyed the terrorists and their vessels without further crew casualties and no injuries to passengers. We are closing now and will commence a sweep of the vessel and assess whether we have the capability of making safe any explosives. As far as we can ascertain all the hijackers are dead."

"Aye Sir." Shot back Geordie's excited voice 'Eat shit and die motherfuckers' was his private thought and favourite quote from 'Full Metal Jacket' he couldn't wait to tell those assholes in RCC Malta that they could go back to watching vids now because the *Bismarck* had sorted their shit out. The patronising tone of earlier conversations, even when he'd just been passing them info, had really started to wind him up, this would be fun.

Reiner mentally ticked a box then moved on.

The *Bismarck* glided silently towards the loading platform and Jake wondered whether it was strong enough to moor their ship but Reiner ordered station keeping and light lines to secure them. With both ships able to maintain a geostationary position it should be possible.

As the ship entered the glare of the cruise liner's own lights, more high powered lamps were lit and *Bismarck* was bathed in bright light. From every veranda and balcony passengers began to cheer and shout loudly, waving madly to their rescuers even though they could not yet leave their cabins.

Jake turned to Reiner.

"Captain, you have an audience, why not step out on to the bridge wing and take a bow?"

Reiner looked uncomfortable but Jake was having none of it and pushed this reluctant hero to the port bridge door and out into the light.

He had never seen Reiner so uncomfortable, literally in the spotlight.

"Wave Reiner." Jake shouted above the noise of the passengers and the occasional big farting blare of the cruise liner's horn.

Minutes later, Reiner and Jake donned their uniform jackets and waited in line behind the security team.

As soon as the lines went over the security team positively bounded onto the platform. Reiner thought they were hoping there were still some terrorists on board, but he didn't think there'd be any since these guys appeared to have been motivated by money not religion, but you never knew.

Several of the ship's officers were waiting to act as guides and the detachment split into teams to search deck by deck.

Reiner and Jake stepped aboard and were met by the beaming smile of the Staff Captain who was a tall, balding moustachioed man probably in his early fifties by the look of him, thought Jake. Although broad shouldered and big boned he had gone to seed, a fact neatly disguised by the well-cut uniform. He stepped forward then hesitated, a little uncertain as to whom to approach.

Jake beat him to it and introduced Reiner as the Captain and himself simply as Jonathan König. Just then a tall gangly officer burst through the nearest stairwell door and walked quickly forward to meet them.

"Hi. Jeff Bannister." He looked at Reiner and Jake's sleeves and put his hand out to Reiner.

"You must be Captain Krull. Thank you again."

Reiner nodded and took over the introductions.

"This is Jonathan König, my employer, tactical advisor and the man responsible for putting us here at this time."

Jake shook hands with them both. The Staff Captain recovered his manners and ushered them forward.

"This way gentlemen, we'll go to my cabin." The security team member who was their escort spoke quietly into his boom mike.

"Tango Lima this is five. Mobile to Staff Captain's cabin with our Captain and bossman, over."

"Roger *fife*." Came Arkady's unmistakable murdered English. "Stay alert. Out."

As soon as they got into the Staff Captain's cabin the phone on his desk rang. Sorry gentlemen I must take this call. Head Office." This was followed by a shrug.

Jeff Bannister stepped in.

"Fancy a walk round the bridge Sirs?" This way, it's only just along here. He put a thumb up to the Staff Captain who nodded, and then escorted them on to the main bridge.

Both Jake and Reiner were shocked at the size of the liner's bridge.

"Good Lord, you could have a game of five a side on the port side and not disturb those on the starboard side!" Was Jake's comment.

Reiner was equally impressed and after shaking a few hands wandered around with Jeff as his guide.

A young female third officer approached Jake and coughed to attract his attention which was on some distant lights to the west.

"Sir, silly question, but are those real guns on your ship down there?"

Jake turned towards her and smiled. What a difference a pretty face makes on a bridge he thought better than the ugly mugs I have to put up with. He walked over to the port side and looked down at *Bismarck*, she was tiny compared to this hulking monster. A toy.

"Yes they are, almost all anyway." He replied.

"Wow." She said looking down. "I've never seen a ship like it before what kind is it?"

"You won't. I mean you won't see any like her nowadays, she's unique. She is my '*folly*'. I suppose it depends on your taste in nautical history but some seventy odd years ago a ship very similar to her but much bigger, sailed off to war. She was called *Bismarck* and yet would still have looked like a toy next to this ship!"

The girl looked puzzled.

"*Bismarck*. Yes I've heard of it.

"She's one of a kind this one, I had her built to protect merchant ships on the high seas so I guess you can call her 'Merchant Protector' class. This is her maiden voyage from her builders in Sevastopol."

"Thank heavens for that. If you'd had her built in Japan or Korea we'd have been stuffed."

"Thank you, young lady.

"The Staff Captain didn't tell us who was coming to the rescue, he didn't believe you'd succeed. I'm very pleased he was wrong."

At that moment the Staff Captain appeared at the bridge door and seeing them stepped in.

"My owners are of course grateful for your efforts and wish to meet with Commodore König at his convenience, in order to express their personal appreciation. Meanwhile your security people tell me that the ship does not appear to have any remaining terrorists on board –although to be fair it is so large it would take days to look through every compartment. They also tell me that the explosives are quite primitive and in the opinion of your security chief, will be easy to defuse and make safe."

He paused a second weighing his words.

"I have to consider both what is safest for the ship and what is practical, and above all the safety of the passengers. So clearly I would like the devices off my ship as quickly as is possible. Without them the threat to passengers and crew is minimal." He paused again searching for words which would not offend.

"I mean no disrespect but my company have asked me to ascertain whether your men have the required ability and qualifications to carry out this work Captain?" He addressed Reiner directly.

"You must understand my dilemma. It's a mammoth task to get all passengers and crew into the lifeboats and tenders and not without risk in itself. That would have to be a last resort and only in the event of immediate danger. Now that no one is around to trigger them, could we wait until we return to port or until the authorities send someone in order to have them defused?"

Reiner looked at Jake and gestured for him to answer.

"Captain…?" Began Jake.

"Alfonso. Alberto Alfonso, at your service."

"Alberto. Arkady Zotov was formerly a Major in the Russian Spetsnaz, he is an expert in all forms of commercial and improvised explosives; I have the utmost confidence in his abilities. His second in command is a former Royal Marine Captain and as I recall, also an explosive expert. They would have consulted before offering an opinion. Not only that but they are very practical people and not given to boasting. Plus you have to consider that having explosives in place with a detonator attached is in itself a very serious risk and given the primitive nature of the devices even more so. So on balance, I'd say we will all safer if you give the go ahead. It is of course your call. Meanwhile may I make a suggestion?"

"Certainly Commodore."

"I would suggest you sway out all of the boats, and launch anything that is recoverable. I would also respectfully suggest that you gather all passengers into the largest area you have. If you give the go ahead, while Arkady is defusing the explosives, I would be happy to go down and introduce Reiner and myself to your guests. As much as a gesture of confidence as any desire to meet them. How does that suit?"

"Eccellente Commodore that seems like sound advice. We will once more be in your hands please ask your team to proceed. I would say twenty minutes to gather everyone. Does that suit you?"

"I'm sure it will." Jake nodded to the security rating – Chandler wasn't it?

"Pass that on to your TL please Chandler."

A big smile.

"Roger that sir." Chandler stepped away and used his radio to brief Arkady, chuffed that the bossman knew his name.

Jake became aware that the young lady was still hovering and he turned back to her.

"I'm sorry I should have introduced myself. I'm Jonathan Henry König, and you are?"

She smiled broadly.

"Thank you Sir, I am Third Officer Isabella Roby and you know my dad!" She finished with a blurt.

Jake was stunned.

"Good lord you aren't John Roby's little girl are you? Heavens the last time I saw you, you were about this high." He held his hand at knee level. "I'm getting old. Is your dad ok?"

"Oh yes, once he recovered from the shock of his daughter going into the family business via the merchant navy. He's in Gib or will be soon I think, he's got the *Dorsetshire*, he retires next year; didn't get his flag but he doesn't seem that bothered."

"Good for him, he'd be bored witless pushing paper around a desk, I hope he's still there when I pass through, I'll make a point of going to see him. We served together on *Cornwall* and the *Cardiff* you know, he was a superb tactician as I recall.

"He said you were the best boss he had."

"That's very kind." He was a little nonplussed at the compliment and changed the subject.

"Well with your captain's permission Isabella, would you escort me to wherever the passengers will gather?"

Captain Alfonso nodded rapidly and smiled his permission whilst he set about organising ship's boats and passengers.

*

The cheers that swept the huge, two tiered main dining room as Reiner and Jake appeared, could be felt through the deck plates. They stood on the broad staircase which connected the two levels as Captain Alfonso had introduced them in a most flowery and complimentary manner. He explained that for their own safety they would stay here until the ship had been cleared of all trace of the terrorists.

"We are safe here." He pointed to the doors where König security guards faced outward watching access points carefully.

"It is down to the foresight of one man and the skills and daring of a second that we are here at this moment and not perhaps, on the bottom of the sea. It seems that intervention and rescue was immediately necessary because, it seems, they were planning to blow the ship up and us with her!"

He paused as an angry murmur swelled and shouts of shame were heard. Captain Alfonso waved his hands for quiet.

"Yes that's right. Now we were lucky, very lucky, that on its maiden voyage this brand new Merchant Protector vessel, which is alongside, just happened to be in the right place at the right time for us and the wrong time for the terrorists. I'd like now to introduce Captain Reiner Krull the officer in command and Commodore Jonathan Henry König, the far sighted owner."

He began clapping his hands and turned towards a smiling, savvy, Jake who waved to the audience, and a somewhat shy and reserved Reiner who came to stand beside him.

Jake made a brief speech in which he pointed out that Merchant Protectors were a coming thing and rightly so, but that they wouldn't all look like dressed up old battleships, which drew a laugh.

He looked up and nodded as one of the security men at the rear gave the thumbs up.

"My final present to you all is a ship cleared of explosives and terrorists and now I'd like to hand you back to Captain Alfonso."

Alfonso stepped back to centre stage and put on his solemn look.

"Some of you may know already but for the rest I have to tell you that Captain Jeffreys and Mohinda Kalkash, our Security Chief, were killed the moment the bandits gained entry. They both paid with their lives for obeying the law of the sea and coming to the rescue of what they thought were fellow 'mariners in distress'. So please join me in a minute's silence to their memory."

Everyone who could, stood up and bowed their heads. A pin dropping would have been audible, many realising now, how close they too had come to death.

*

Afterwards, Jake briefed Captain Alfonso, now officially in command of the vessel, that one of the explosive charges had been retained with its components separated in order that forensic analysis could be carried out, *Bismarck* would bypass Malta and hand it in to the police in Gibraltar in a day or so before carrying on with their own plans to cross the Atlantic and stopover in Bermuda. The rest of the explosives had gone down fifteen thousand feet to the Ionian abyssal plain where the terrorists had intended the ship to be. He confirmed there were no terrorist survivors but suggested all internal camera footage should be retained and handed to the authorities at your next port; there may be identity clues in there somewhere.

Alfonso agreed and walked them to the entry-port along with Isabella Roby who was going to have an interesting conversation with her dad as soon as she got some internet time.

The last of the security teams departed and Jake stepped aboard *Bismarck* once more, Reiner paused and saluted Captain Alfonso before being last aboard as was tradition.

Once more the ship's great horn blasted out into the night and newly freed passengers lined every rail cheering with camera flashes going off by the thousand, souvenir photos of this night would be spread around the globe by the following week as they all returned home.

Bismarck, now with running lights on, quickly faded into the distance heading west towards Gibraltar and almost blissfully unaware of the media storm they'd created.

"OPs." Click.

"Geordie, inform Malta RCC that we have successfully removed all explosive devices and disposed of all but one which we have retained for forensic analysis, and thank them for their help." The touch of sarcasm he felt was justified.

Geordie thought so too as he gleefully relayed the message.

18.30 Saturday April 28th 2018

RN Facility, Gibraltar. Type 23 Frigate HMS *Dorsetshire*.

"She's here Sir." The Officer of the Watch (OOW) reported to his Captain. "Just passing Little Bay now, ETA off the dockyard zone about ten minutes Sir."

"Righto I'm coming up. Wait five minutes then have the duty watch turn out on to the jetty with caps, along with yourself and the duty senior."

"Aye, aye Sir."

Captain John Roby RN was intensely curious by nature, he always fancied himself captaining the Beagle had he been born a hundred and fifty odd years ago, of course he'd not have had to cope with the problems that poor Captain Fitzroy had had with his mental health.

A tall man, he'd always had a stooped appearance throughout his adult life mostly due to the fact that the RN never built ships that were designed for six foot four inch naval officers, and if you didn't learn to stoop you were forever in the sickbay having your head stitched up.

He picked up his cap with the single line of golden oak leaves lining the peak and realised he wasn't at all bothered that there would never be a second row behind it.

His daughter had given him a sat-phone call on Thursday evening shortly after the news broke about the hijack of the *Kristianstaadt* and the deaths among the officers, which of course had nearly stopped his heart as it was trumpeted on the BBC world service news.

He was immensely proud of his daughter, she had chosen a life at sea but away from fighting ships, and whilst it had initially been a shock tinged with disappointment that she hadn't applied to the RN, the change that responsibility had wrought on her as she had first studied at Warsash Maritime Academy and then off to sea several times before finally qualifying, was reward in itself.

When she'd invited him down for her awards ceremony on qualification, she had insisted he attend in his dress uniform as she wanted to show him off to her classmates, a memory which still brought a smile to his face.

It was still there as he first stopped off at the bridge and borrowed a pair of binoculars, causing the leading weapons electrical rating who was up to his elbows in wires, to wonder what had pleased the old man. Then he made his way down to the midships gangway returning the salute of the Quartermaster as he stepped down on to the jetty.

He wanted to do this properly and he knew that *Bismarck's* crew would appreciate the gesture from an RN ship. He looked at the TV news crews and all the press being held back at the head of the jetty, he didn't give a buggery whether his bosses thought he should give this tribute, his daughter was safe and sound because of these men and this ship and he was damned if he wasn't going to give them the cheers they deserved.

He put the 'binos' to his eyes and looked to the south to see if he could make her out and yes there she was, past Rosia Bay and beginning to turn in towards the mole. Cameras flashed along the crowded end of the jetty and along the foreshore all the way to the point. *Bismarck* was making a rather dramatic entry with the setting sun behind her and he wondered if his old friend Jake König was milking this entrance, but he decided to be charitable and not cynical. They'd made good time to get here so it was unlikely Jake had been sat off the Trinity Lighthouse waiting for his moment.

Nearly here, he mentally noted as she turned their way on passing the outer mole, slowing perceptibly now and looking fantastic with the sun at her back and what a sight she was too.

John Roby smiled to himself as *Bismarck*, bristling with guns, manoeuvred herself the last hundred yards to be exactly opposite *Dorsetshire*. Flashy, very flashy Jake. The dockyard mooring party were waiting as *Bismarck's* Steerpods pushed her gently sideways, a most unnatural motion for a ship he decided. Clearly there was a small bow thruster as well, like parking a car nowadays he lamented.

It was time, the lines had been thrown and *Bismarck* nudged the jetty and settled, she appeared to be flying a Caymans Ensign so as far as he was concerned that made her legitimate. Since the Caymans were a former British dependency he decided it would be churlish not to give recognition for a successful cruise.

He nodded to the Officer of the Watch who then barked an order and a Tannoy announcement on *Dorsetshire* ordered all off duty hands to line the rails with their caps on and the duty watch came to attention on the jetty itself. There was a pause for a minute as the off watch sailors mustered and the *Bismarck* came to a halt.

The ship's company were chuffed to bits that *Bismarck* was berthing next to them, the cameras were flashing and many beers were likely to be forthcoming when they were swinging the lantern down the pub after they got home to Plymouth. Apart from which, these sailors wholly approved of *Bismarck's* method of dealing with pirates or terrorists or whatever they were.

A sharp command from the OOW followed.

"Salute."

Then Roby, the OOW and the Duty Senior Rating (DSR) all saluted. Next, the OOW ordered off caps and three cheers in the traditional fashion of the RN. The camera flash frequency intensified and he thought he'd probably be getting a quiet pithily worded note from some desk warrior in the admiralty which was the same as a good kicking by anyone else's lights. He wasn't bothered, he had a year to go and then he was going to be pensioned off.

The duty watch was dismissed and he took his cap off and stuck it under his arm so he didn't get saluted by everyone coming and going from his ship. He wandered along the jetty admiring *Bismarck's* clean lines and plentiful weaponry, and noting, the very modern additions of the radar arrays forward and aft. He was also impressed by the speed and efficiency of the berthing teams as they squared everything away, experienced men, well trained he decided.

It wasn't long before his shadow was joined by another and he turned to find Jake König standing next to him with a big grin on his face.

"Hello Jonno, good to see you again. How are you? Oh and thanks for that welcome, we all very much appreciated it. Seriously, I had no idea what to expect by way of reception committee, communications haven't been loquacious shall we say."

Roby laughed out loud and turned to pump Jake's hand.

"I can never thank you enough for saving the *Kristianstaadt* Jake, and of course my darling Isabella with her. Really. Such perfect timing is meant to be, it cannot be accidental surely?"

They fell into step and walked slowly along the jetty away from the flashbulbs, hands clasped behind their backs in the fashion of naval officers since time immemorial, and utterly oblivious to the press gathered at the shore end. Jake answered Roby's questions about the action and the decisions that Reiner and Jake had had to make to bring it all to a safe conclusion.

They were quite unaware of the police and customs visiting the ship and then the blue lights and sirens as the EOD crew arrived to take away the explosives they retained from the *Kristianstaadt* and all the digital photographs taken of each and every explosive charge in its location before removal.

"You need to play this one carefully Jake, the usual shit stirrers have been at it already. You know the sort of thing the 'Luvvy' press come out with. 'Was there another way?' or 'Brutal Mercenaries kill poor misunderstood terrorists, couldn't they have just talked to them?' etc. Then you have the 'red tops' with '*Bismarck* 5, terror boats nil' and 'DIY navy mallets bad guys'. All that kind of thing."

He breathed forcefully.

"Of course our heroic political masters sat back and sniffed the air to see which way the wind blew before dipping in with toned down comments about how fortunate it was that you were able to intercede, which was just as well for them because when the *Kristianstaadt* made an unscheduled stop in Limassol, passengers who were on there started giving interviews and were getting seriously peed off by the negative stuff from the 'Luvvies'."

He stopped and turned to face Jake.

"That First Officer was an absolute gem. He gave the clincher when he told them about how he'd had an Arabic speaker listening in on the terrorists and that they had no intention of negotiating, they just wanted to blow the ship up."

He sighed heavily.

"Things got a bit out of hand when one of the Aussie passengers who was being asked really loaded questions just stood up, walked over and popped him on the chin because, he said, it was upsetting his wife who was sat there clearly sobbing her heart out."

Jake just shook his head mentally thanking the unknown Aussie for doing what clearly needed doing. Roby continued.

"He then went on, shouting at them to get, quote, 'Their collective heads out of their arses and think about what *Bismarck* just prevented', topping it off with 'You'd have preferred it if they had killed us all wouldn't you? Make a better bloody story wouldn't it?" It was live TV so it all went out.

They resumed their measured pacing.

"There were plenty of others too which made good copy for the likes of the Mail, the Express and the Telegraph but you can guess what the Independent and the Guardian thought of it all, although they did manage to restrain themselves from calling you all neo-Nazis on a Nazi battleship much to my personal surprise."

He paused at the far end of the jetty looking out towards Algeciras.

"So the public on the whole support your action and the government started making nicer noises about it, but the metro elites think you're nasty people, pretty predictable really. No one has started yet with the embarrassing questions about the scarcity of nationally owned warships in the area but hopefully someone will soon."

"Thanks for that Jonno, I may see if I can prompt someone to ask that very same question sometime in the next few days in several different countries. Anyway, come on board and have a look, you know you're dying to."

"So transparent am I? Well I'm sure you have excellent coffee as well as more guns than you can shake a stick at; go on then."

They turned and strolled towards *Bismarck's* gangway causing the Quartermaster to have a mini fit as he frantically mustered a side party and piped aboard the two officers still engrossed in their discussions. Captain Roby stood on the brow and saluted the Caymans ensign at the stern as it hung limply in the evening air. It was only minutes to sunset when the ensigns on both ships would be ceremonially lowered.

Jake continued almost without pause as he made his way through the ship to his own cabin in the after superstructure.

"You know me Jonno, I don't look for fights and I certainly take no pleasure from killing, however I will not shirk my duty to other seafarers just to keep the 'Luvvies' happy. I suppose I should have guessed my detractors would have wanted us to parley with our hijackers but as I've said that was what the hijackers expected and wanted in order to have the time to blow up the ship and everyone on it, and make their escape, they were banking on it."

He recalled Roby was equally fond of peaty Isla malts so he passed Roby a crystal glass with a shot of his favourite Lagavulin whisky in it.

"So the 'Luvvies' would have had 3000 odd funerals to wring their hands at and to say it's all our own fault for upsetting people. It's bollocks Jonno, you and I both know it but these soft in the head wallys can't or won't see that there comes a time to say 'thus far and no further', and then stick by it."

"I'd expect nothing else from you Jake. I'm a little envious. You do have a freedom to deal with situations that all of us in the state navies envy and would love to have –again. And you have a bunch of your own lawyers on your side of the fence who will certainly watch your back and rein in any overt fallout, which of course never happens with us nowadays. If it had been a state owned warship instead of *Bismarck*, *Kristianstaadt* would have been blown up simply because they would have communicated with their government and the politicians would have mm'd and aah'd and dropped the ball –again."

He took a sip of his whiskey and nodded appreciatively.

"But I'm just warning you that there will be those who are desperate to hang you for this and will be watching to see if you trip up, and they don't all work for Allah."

They sat in the comfy Balmoral chairs that populated both wardroom and cabins and Jake used the voice activated comms to get Granny Smith to deliver a pot of fresh coffee.

"Very nice Jake." Nodded John Roby as he looked round, taking in the high tech LED screens which repeated the OPs room view of the world.

"But why guns not missiles? Not still on your Falkands hobby horse are you?" He clearly recalled a young Jake being told in no uncertain terms to shut up for expressing the view that misers in the procurement chain had deprived the Type 42's of that one weapon which would have made all the difference in both *Sheffield* and *Coventry*, a Vulcan Phalanx Gatling style close in weapon system would likely have preserved them. Of course in the aftermath they were retrofitted to all the other 42's.

Jake launched into his favourite soapbox subject with gusto.

"Come on Jonno, you know my views about how we were hammered in the Falklands for lack of guns. It is highly unlikely that any of the warships that were sunk would have been lost if each vessel had had just a single point defence mounting, and you know as well as I that the Type 42's were originally designed with one but the pencil neck purse-string pullers saved a few pounds by not allowing them. Four ships, nearly a hundred dead and the same number wounded for some spreadsheet warrior who's closest brush with danger was being goosed on the underground going home."

Roby could see he'd touched a still very raw nerve.

"You know the navy Jonno, they just go to extremes, from all gun to all missile when anyone with half a brain could see that that was stupid, the Type 22s didn't become good all-rounders until the batch threes which of course had '*gun*' point defences and a 4.5" '*gun*' at the front! We'd have been better off with the old Blake down there even though it had most of its AA guns swapped for the utterly useless Seacats."

Roby thought it time to change the tempo a little before Jake burst a blood vessel so he tapped the bulkhead next to his chair and got a solid sounding 'thunk' noise in return.

"How thick is the steel in these bulkheads Jake?"

Jake stopped in mid flow.

"Well it isn't steel Jonno, it's a Titanium alloy. All of the bridge and forward superstructure bulkheads, deckheads and decks are between four and six centimetres, all section bulkheads are three centimetres, all decks and the hull are four centimetres thick except over vital spaces where it goes up to eight. The main turrets have eight centimetre faces and tops with four at the sides and rear. In addition there's a Titanium Diboride composite sandwiched in the armour of many sections including turrets which actually cuts back on weight and increases resistance to penetration.

Jake sat back and smiled as the implications of what he'd just said visibly percolated through Roby's brain.

"Good lord she ought to capsize and sink with all that weight on top and what's the big idea with the armour? That went out of fashion several wars ago or was your design engineer on tonnage commission?"

"Thirty percent weight saving over steel Jonno and anyway, it's not a she, it's a 'he'. All German ships are male, unlike ours. It's hilarious listening to the conversations sometimes as the Brits invariably still call it she and the Germans and Russians call it a he!"

"Secondly, armour is coming back in vogue, the Arleigh Burke destroyers are all steel, no aluminium apart from the funnels, and have seventy tons of Kevlar armour around their vital areas; basically because it's about survivability and the innate vulnerability of vessels without any armour at all. You only have to look at the USS Stark and USS Cole incidents to see their logic."

He smiled cruelly before making his next remark.

"Have a good look at your ship tomorrow Jonno, it looks like someone has stretched grey clingfilm over a skeleton, the sides are so thin. I'm almost certain it wouldn't stop a round even from an SA-80 rifle."

Jake pressed his argument.

"It's all very well saying that defensive systems can cope with incoming stuff but we both know that a single hit from a modern anti-ship missile, especially if it was the big Russian or Chinese stuff, would sink or cripple *Dorsetshire*, however good your damage control teams are. Anyway, whilst ever they produce the majority of warships without armour, then they will build anti-ship missiles that won't defeat armour, which would be good news for us in the unlikely event that we had one hit us.

Our engineers have calculated that only the very largest ex-soviet missiles could possibly harm us and nothing in the NATO inventory. We might need a new paint job but nothing more and the composite prevents spalling."

Roby nodded.

"OK. I can see some of your arguments at least given that Gatling gun style point defences are the norm with missiles in a secondary role, but in offensive terms you're limited to a couple of dozen miles and I can reach out eighty or so with course correction built in."

"Perfectly true but that long reach will not help if your missiles don't hit or penetrate the enemy defences will it? Eight Harpoons Jonno, against modern anti-missile defences, jamming, decoying and point defences, you'd count yourself lucky to get a single hit and then only if you launched the lot at once to overwhelm the defences. One out of eight, so really *Dorsetshire* can only take on one over the horizon naval target with any hope of success, and how many incoming missiles can you shoot down with just thirty two Sea Ceptor missiles and no CIWS gun? Sixteen tops?"

He could see Roby was about to interject so he held up a hand to forestall it.

"Don't throw in the Merlin because I know the pusser hasn't decided whether to put the Marte missiles on them and even if it did they only have a fifteen and a half mile range which is inside the defensive missile range for most ships nowadays, making your EH101 vulnerable. Not just to missiles either, my 5.1" guns have new munitions which extend the range." He showed Roby a ship's datapad with the new munitions in schematic.

"We have one that is an extended range HE which uses a new propellant and gives another six miles on top of the standard rounds. Look the point is this; you can't decoy or spoof a shell."

He sighed and put his glass down.

"This ship is just about one of a kind Jonno, it's my flagship if you like, but even so I want it to be as tough as possible in case it ever has to fight. It could take on ships, aircraft or even land targets, the only gap is anti-submarine but all I can do for that is decoys and proximity alarms, however I can't see me fighting a submarine any time. There will be other Merchant Protectors soon but they will be more, conventional, shall we say."

Roby smiled.

"Good for you, now are you going to show me around this blasted folly of yours or what?"

The ship tour ended at the bow and they both turned back to look at the long sleek fo'c'sle and its two turrets with their twin guns.

"Damn but she's magnificent Jake, what is the barrel length for those monsters?" He pointed at the nearest twin 5.1" turret.

"In old money they're thirty feet long, new money nine point something metres."

At that point Jake's ear piece chimed and the QM spoke.

"Sir there's a runner from *Dorsetshire* with a message for Captain Roby, says its urgent Sir."

"Send him up to the bows QM."

Dorsetshire's communications rating walked swiftly forward and passed John Roby a message slip.

Roby nodded to the young lass and she turned away looking relieved. He tore open the message packet and then with a wry grin proceeded to read out the official communication from MOD(N) Commander in Chief Fleet, which basically said stay away from *Bismarck* and do not get photographed with her officers or the ship unless MOD(N) CinC Fleet says so.

"I told you Jake, we even have 'Luvvies' in the navy now. I hate the way they've brainwashed even the young officers coming out of Dartmouth. Gone are the traditions we learned and in their place is some bullshit PC charter to be nice to everyone always and they'll be nice to us. I'm glad I'm going actually, I really do feel somewhat 'dinosaurish' nowadays."

Roby screwed the flimsy up and was about to throw it overboard but then put it in his trouser pocket.

"I'm sure you must have had a fit too when that young marine officer allowed his team to be captured by the Iranians instead of calling their bluff and heading back to the ship they'd just searched and whistling up a Sea Skua armed Lynx to backchat them. It just makes them want to have another go because they think we're soft when it's our masters who are soft. Then there's teaching the pirates to treat hostages properly instead of us just running the buggers up a yardarm. Poor old Nelson will have attained supersonic rotational speed in his grave by now I expect."

Jake was next on the soapbox.

"The problem is that they can't see the way that it all plays to our enemies. They seem to have completely forgotten FDR's 'Speak softly but carry a big stick. I always interpret that to mean, try to avoid conflict if possible, ask them nicely to desist from doing bad things but if they don't accede, smack them hard until they do." He shook his head ruefully.

"We're being played like a Marlin on a long line. For years they've done nothing about immigrants, migrants, refugees illegal or otherwise -whatever they want to call them this week. There was more discussion at one point about what to call them than action to sort the problem. Refugees, genuine ones, arrive with everything they can carry including wifey and the kids but then they stop when they reach a safe country."

He paused to consider his next comments.

"Many of the ones coming across are just young males and they cross five countries to get to Germany or Britain. Refugees? Even families that do it are still not refugees despite one feeling for the little ones, not refugees by the standard definition anyway."

"So fine let's help. When the situation in their country of origin has stabilised they can go back surely? But no, once in the door they are here for good, which simply of course makes for more applicants with made up stories and the definitions of 'refugee' and adult become broader and broader as the 'luvvies' get in there. It is not sustainable and we'll all pay for their short sightedness in the not too distant future as they have no intention of integrating."

"My thoughts entirely," Roby threw in. "but I'd add a corollary, don't make stupid rules that you don't intend to enforce in the first place and don't allow law to be re-interpreted like all the human rights rubbish with the right to have a cat as family life. No, they have no right to go further or into Europe than Turkey. Anyway, I'd better get back now I've been 'warned' about the subversives on here." He added with a laugh.

"Yes, quite. I suppose I'd better organise some backstopping in the UK, EU and US at least. I can't imagine either the Russians or Chinese objecting to a boatload of terrorists getting vaporised. I'll organise a plane to fetch me and get together with the PR people and my lawyers. What a silly world it is at times."

"Too true. Look it was nice seeing you Jake and once again, a million thankyous for keeping my little girl safe."

They shook hands and parted as Roby was piped off the ship. On the jetty two hands were nonchalantly carrying the last of the crates of beer on to *Bismarck* observed by Kipper and a warrant officer from *Dorsetshire*, a crate from each junior rates mess and couple of bottles of 'Wood's 100' rum from the senior rates mess, another RN tradition working quietly in the background thought Kipper as he discretely observed, ready to intervene if there were 'issues'.

Jake headed straight for the communications suite in the OPs room and tasked a Gulfstream to be in Gibraltar as soon as possible. He went on to brief Reiner.

"So there it is, I have to whiz around now making sure the right things come out in the media and that not too many noses are put out of joint by our intervention. It beggars belief I know, but some of them out there would have preferred it if a) we'd never turned up when we did, or b) if we'd completely screwed it up and a lot of innocent people had died."

Reiner nodded sympathetically.

"So you'll re-join us in Bermuda then Jake, probably at the end of our work up?"

"That's about the size of it. I've got a plane on the way. I think it would be best if you just took the ship out and headed across to Bermuda at a steady rate. I've got that small converted mixed cargo ship 'Eliza' on its way to a mid-Atlantic rendezvous so you can both practice the replenishment at sea stuff. It's also got a tank of marine diesel to top you off and replenishment ammunition."

He turned back.

"I'm in half minds whether to transfer Arkady and his boys as well since Eliza is heading straight back to Little Cayman. What say you?"

"How about we keep a couple for advice and muscle when we're in Bermuda, you never know after recent events?" Added Reiner.

"OK. Keep four. Get Arkady to pick 'em and maybe Hugh Fraser to command. He's an ex Royal so he's probably better at the diplomatic shit than Arkady, oh and I think Andy Evans will join us there, he's been on a snoop."

"Fair enough Jake, we'll see you in a week then. I'll just request a mooring party from the harbourmaster and we'll be under way."

"Right you are and watch out for surprises Reiner. There's a good reason for the work up to finish in Bermuda."

Reiner walked away wearing a side to side frown instead of the usual single eyebrow, as he tried to divine what Jake's last words meant.

The sun had set some hours before and the press had got bored waiting for anyone from *Bismarck* to turn up at the end of the jetty so when she slipped at 22.00, they quickly headed off to the nearest bars to compose a by-line that they hoped would be syndicated, all speculative BS, so nothing new there then.

Bismarck slipped her lines quietly and without fanfare, moved away from the jetty and turned in her own length with the precision granted by the Steerpods, then headed out into the Atlantic for the first time.

Jake stared at her deep in thought until he could only make out the running lights. Then he turned and climbed into the chauffeur driven car for the short ride to the airport.

Thursday May 3rd 2018

Haiti, Presidential Palace Cabinet room, Port-Au-Prince

President Farache leaned back in his chair and let the warm glow of imminent personal victory suffuse him. He glanced down each side of the highly polished antique walnut table, taking in the gestures and body language of his ministers as they discussed his proposals. He was particularly searching for signs of hesitancy, he wouldn't see any open dissent of that he was fairly sure.

Nearly two and a half years of painstaking preparation had gone into this, he smugly reflected, vast numbers of man hours worked.

The Columbian's blank cheque had been as good as his word except it hadn't been a cheque or bankers draft; it had been cash in suitcases and holdalls, hundreds of millions of US dollars in a steady stream, he had no idea where Andino procured the cash and didn't care.

Thus he'd been able not only to build-up his armed forces substantially, but also to improve things for his people thus ensuring popular support. A spin-off from this had been the renewal of UN and US aid giving him even more cash to pour into the prostrate economy.

This had of course strengthened his presidency and made him a mover and shaker on the world stage. No one seemed to question the source of the newfound wealth or even how Haiti could have generated such sums, all in all things were going pretty well and that trend looked set to continue.

He turned his mind back to the meeting, his face betrayed none of his thoughts. General Gerard Guerrier had just finished his dissertation on the post invasion aspects of the military operation. Now was the time for the head nodding, these men had placed him in power and they could remove him as well, technically.

This vote would cement his power base or break him. Nearly two hours before, when he'd begun his explanation, he'd felt a curious thrill run through him as he observed the shocked looks on his colleague's faces as they realised the scope and audacity of his plan. Only two others in the room had known what was coming, Namur the Interior Minister, a poisonous but useful little man, and General Guerrier the head of the armed forces.

Farache had nearly laughed out loud at the reaction to Namur's admission that he'd been responsible for nearly all the terrorist activity of the last two years. He'd had to bite his lip hard to prevent the laughter bubbling up when the dead-pan Namur had gone on to describe forthcoming atrocities and the fact that these would provide most of the justification for the ensuing invasion.

He waited calmly for the last, but inevitable, question, wondering who would ask it. His eyes roamed the assembled faces looking for clues. Surprise, surprise! Louis D'Orville, Minister of Agriculture and Natural Resources. The token liberal in his cabinet had found his voice.

"How will America react Mr President?" D'Orville asked, hesitantly, almost timidly.

Elated, Farache controlled the urge to jump in immediately with the answer, instead he stood and leaned forward, fists on the table top. Quite theatrically he gazed around the table waiting for each set of eyes to drop before passing on.

"What business is it of the Americans? Are we not a sovereign nation? And anyway how can they complain at our actions in retaliation for these acts of state sponsored terrorism?"

He was on his soap box now and the ministers relaxed a little, they knew he didn't want input, just the occasional nod while he wandered the room justifying his actions against the backdrop of global events.

"What about the Iraqi invasion in 2003? 'A strike at the roots of terrorism' they called it and yet Hussain saw the terrorists as more a threat to himself than America. There wasn't any correlation or connection to the kind of terrorism they were seeking to eradicate but they really just wanted rid of Saddam. And what about Afghanistan to topple the Taliban and kill Bin Laden? Another strike at terrorists?"

He held his hand up and counted off on his chubby fingers, the gold from his many rings flashing.

"We had Afghanistan, a country destroyed over a decade and more because America wanted to stop AQ, but did they? Then came their interference in Egypt because Mubarak had disagreed with them. Next Libya, because they hated Gadhafi, no 'boots on the ground' though, because Obama was starting to tread carefully, but plenty of help from the French and British for a change. What a balls up! In Syria they focussed on Assad instead of what was bubbling beneath the surface and wham bam we had ISIL well-armed too, courtesy of the CIA, and well-motivated by twisted religious zealotry and a hatred of America. Need I say more?"

They all nodded sagely, they'd heard it so many times before.

"All to strike at terrorism. How can they deny us our right to strike at terrorism too?"

He aimed his pacing back to the head of the table, whilst the lecture continued. He didn't wait for answers and no one would have dared offer one anyway.

"American foreign policy has brought disaster to everything they stick their nose in. Look at Ukraine, how much do they appreciate US dollars now? The Yankees spent millions buying a revolution with their EU friends –who are actually opponents really, and how did that turn out? The fool they put in power allies with militias which are far right of Attila the Hun! The current US president is a pussy."

This drew laughs for obvious reasons.

"America, having caused most of the mayhem in the last two decades now wants the world to go away. And the American people are ashamed of their government and no longer automatically worship their armed services."

He paused and stared around the table.

"America has 'boots on the ground' to use their term, in Afghanistan, Iraq, Ukraine, the Baltic States, Libya and Syria. They won't want to get involved in the Caribbean, they'll leave it to the ACS or CARICOM or the OEC."

He paused again and took a sip of water in order to let that sink in.

"We use the same reasons gentlemen, the same ones that America used to launch its attacks and invasions."

He banged his fist hard on the table startling everyone.

"We use the Israeli excuse too. 'We reserve the right to retaliate in the face of terrorism -and will do so'. Besides, all eyes are on the Middle East not this backwater. The Caymanians must not think themselves immune from our national wrath, just because they are at the other end of the Caribbean."

He continued calmly.

"We have very carefully cultured an atmosphere of injured innocence on the world stage after the recent outrages; we *will* be condemned overtly. However we will be covertly understood and sympathised with. No one will lift a finger to interfere. We leave when our man is in power and pluck the puppet strings as we want thereafter. That is what matters in this world, power. Now, any other questions?"

D'Orville found his voice again.

"...and Britain, how will she react?"

Farache let his temper have free reign this time. His fist smashed down on the table once again.

"Britain? Britain?" He screamed.

"They will do nothing. They never do. Why should they? The Caymans are no longer their responsibility."

He shrugged and continued in a more normal tone.

"Besides, here in the Caribbean, they have little enough to do anything with. They've pulled out of Belize, and don't even have a West Indies guard ship anymore when they used to have an entire squadron and troops! Britain? Pah! They're not even worth considering nowadays, our Navy is just about as big as theirs and with a bigger punch. They grow potatoes on the flight decks of those miserable half-carriers because the Americans can't get their hyper-complicated planes to work and when they do they get beaten in a dogfight by a 40 year old relic!"

"No my friends, you watch. The US and EU will mutter but do nothing, Britain will talk big and do nothing, and the East? It only cares about itself and making more money."

The vote, such as it was, approved the motion unanimously.

Monday 7th May 2018

HQ, US National Security Agency, Fort Mead, USA

Nathan King sat in the sterile box of a meeting room and reviewed the forensic report in front of him, whilst he waited patiently for the two other members of this ad hoc committee to arrive. The agenda he'd quickly sent out had just one word on it: 'Haiti'.

It wasn't his first visit to the Fort Meade complex by a long shot; he smiled to himself as he remembered that first visit some twenty years before. Determined not to be impressed by anything a sister agency had, the young fresh faced DEA agent had still been amazed by both the security and the size of the complex that made up the Headquarters of the National Security Agency. The identity checks at all the security gates, was it three or four? Couple that with the size of the place and it had struck him dumb for most of his first visit. He no longer even noticed any of this, just took it for granted. His young self was a far cry from grizzled and cynical, veteran DEA agent that sat there today.

The door opened and in walked the other two members of this unofficial group. Sometimes protagonists, when it came to budgets, and most times friends when it was anything else. Vernon Weathers the NSA man, this was his home turf, and Miles Carlson of the CIA shook hands with Nate. All were old friends.

The three were on a par in their respective agencies, just below director level. Though it was plain to see that Vern had weathered the trials of life less well than the other two. Poor Vern, so proud of his almost bleach blond mane years ago, was now reduced to the image of a friendly friar Tuck, complete with the belly and jovial appearance. His analytical mind had survived the years intact though.

Miles' limp was better than usual Nate noted, originally the result of a disagreement with a truck fender in Jakarta whilst on duty, so the story went, but you never really knew with the CIA types he confessed to himself. Still it had landed Miles a forced desk job at Langley which he'd initially hated but then started to appreciate. He was to all intents and purposes a 'reader between the lines' now, thought Nate. Miles picked up the raw data and looked at what was not said, asked the right questions and drew connections where none had been seen before. And he was damned good at it.

Nate exchanged the usual inquiries about wives, sons and daughters, and in Vern's case a granddaughter, with his old friends and after a cup of coffee and inconsequential agency chat, the trio got down to business.

The purpose of these periodic but 'nearly off the books' meetings that Nate had initiated some years before, was to use each other as a sounding board for theories. They had all met initially when representing their agencies on a tough investigation which had involved the Middle East, drugs and human trafficking. It had been a grisly affair and had bound the three by mutual experience and a developing friendship.

The worst part about it had been discovering that each had withheld information from the other that could have given a different outcome. They had resolved afterwards to share ideas on a regular basis. Each was a master of his own sphere of business, so much so that it sometimes severely limited 'idea generation' from their subordinates and they needed other jaded eyes to see the crap that had been missed. They'd discovered, quite by accident that fresh approaches to problems could often be obtained by bouncing these theories off a non-partisan but equally 'grizzled' peer.

"You heard about the big 'bust' off the 'Keys' the other day Miles, Vern?" They nodded in unison. Both had noted the capture of the two motor cruisers, near the Florida Keys, loaded with around two hundred kilos of 'coke' as well as weapons and both had wondered whether Nate had been involved.

"Well I have the forensic report here. I don't need to tell you how thoroughly those boats were examined, suffice to say that you'd need to be a damn fine model maker to fit them back together."

He let them digest the news and read the summary he'd prepared.

"Right, now here's what we found." He began to quote parts of the report. "A small light bulb, located in the master cabin was found to have a thumb and index finger print burned onto it. The bulb had been located at the back of a drawer and was found to be inoperative." He looked up at them to explain.

"We reckon that the 'prints' owner tried to change the bulb while it was still too hot and burnt himself, shame eh?. We ran the print through the computers and guess whose name popped out?"

He didn't wait for the inevitable response of 'Ronald Reagan, ..er...Joseph Stalin' etc.

"Eduardo Andino."

Nate looked up triumphantly. The other two didn't comment, knowing there was more to come. He read on.

"An examination of the garbage disposal system revealed the presence of a Gold plated teaspoon (badly twisted) with a crest or insignia of some kind at the top of the handle."

He showed them the photos of the spoon.

"That spoon gentlemen."

He paused theatrically.

"Came from the cutlery set of a certain President General Farache of Haiti! It has his Presidential seal embossed on it."

Miles Carlson's eyebrows shot up to an impossible height and then came down in a deep furrow as he digested the import of the information. This was very definitely interesting stuff and could be the answer to a question that had been niggling at him and his staff for some months.

"So how do you put this together Nate?" He asked, making an attempt to overcome the eagerness in his voice and failing miserably.

Nate noticed his friend's interest and his pulse quickened too. Perhaps some of the answers *he* sought would come his way today.

"Basically this. About two years ago we lost track of Andino when he made a rare exit from Colombia, he was away for 3 days, you supplied us with information that he'd been identified on a boat off Cuba." He nodded at Miles.

"We wanted to know what he'd been up to for those three days. At the time there was something tugging at the back of my mind about this but it wouldn't surface. It occurred to me moments after I received this report."

Nate straightened up in his seat and carried on.

"The memory was about Farache, I checked the logs, coincidentally on that same weekend he'd cried off from a public appearance, something he never does, due to a head cold and had spent the weekend at the Presidential retreat on the island of Gonave."

He paused and sipped his coffee, now going cold.

"That was also odd, slash unusual, because the last time he tried to spend a weekend away was four years ago and no sooner had he left Port Au Prince than there was a coup attempt by members of former president Jean-Bertrand Aristide's party Fanmi Lavalas, which was ruthlessly supressed. The guy clings to power like dog-shit to your shoe."

He looked at each of them wondering if the answers he sought would emerge.

"Now I think that Andino and Farache met that weekend to cook up a deal of some kind. The spoon was neat, it doesn't put Farache on the boat but I figure it puts the boat near to Farache. I speculate that one of Andino's bodyguards or flunkies pocketed it, thinking it was solid Gold when they were being fed or something in one of Farache's kitchens at Gonave."

He tried the coffee again, regretting it immediately, the damned stuff was barely drinkable when hot.

"He must have been real disappointed to discover that it's only plated. That's why it probably ended up as a teaspoon on the boat. My problem is what the hell did those two bastards cook up between them?"

Nate sat back, glad he'd got the problem off his chest, it had been niggling for far too long. Vern picked up the phone and ordered another jug of coffee and some cream. He would have preferred Darjeeling but that was asking a bit much of even the NSA.

Miles picked up the baton. He paused considering his next words very carefully.

"Nate, we're going to have to take this a bit slowly and carefully because what you've just told me answers a whole load of questions that CIA had about Farache too. The problem with that is that I don't like the picture that's starting to form."

He pushed his own coffee cup away having seen Nate's reaction.

"I think I can confirm or at least add to the circumstantial evidence anyway. A bit of Background might help here, this has a real crossover to you Nate." He pointed at his friend.

"OK. We thought he'd perhaps gone to Bolivia to see some of his suppliers. Most people think the Coca is Columbian in origin but in Bolivia over 70% of all arable land is given over to growing Coca and it is perfectly legal to possess Coca leaves and grow the trees! Export of the stuff is illegal though, go figure."

He continued the informative story.

"The green paste of Coca leaf pulp is shipped into Columbia by the ton for processing into cocaine and Andino has a big say in the how and where."

He typed furiously on his laptop for a few seconds then spun it round so the others could the images.

"Look at these. Some recent sat shots and a thermal image showing a Ho Chi Min style supply route at night in the jungle."

The pair studied the images of what appeared to be a chain of fairy lights. Miles continued.

"That is the only illegal part as far as Bolivia is concerned, how the hell they square that hole is a mystery to me and no doubt you too Nate. Anyway there we are pouring millions of dollars of aid into Bolivia in order to educate the people into growing something else, whilst thousands die in our own country because education is a slow process and the cartels would get a little pissed with any farmer that said he was growing coffee or corn instead! The naivety of the 'do gooders' is just staggering at times."

Miles looked like he'd eaten something bad.

"But we got a lucky break. Whilst we were peering up the ass of everything crossing the Bolivia-Columbian border in each direction, a report came in from Cuba."

Again he pulled up some images, photos this time, of an olive skinned, handsome, rakish man.

"One of those flukes that occur all too rarely in my humble opinion, placed a Cuban intelligence officer, who now supplements his income by moonlighting for the CIA, in just the right spot. He'd gone down to the coast for the weekend, a rare occurrence in itself because this man apparently spends most of his time climbing in and out of women's beds, seldom his own wife's. He had just spent a quiet weekend relaxing and drinking at a place called Santiago de Cuba on the south coast, when to his immense surprise he spotted Andino."

More images were brought up showing half a dozen views from an oblique angle, very good quality with a date time stamp of 6th February 2016 in the corner.

"He had apparently arrived on a large oceangoing cruiser which had dropped its hook nearby. The intelligence officer, bit of a boat buff it seems, casually scanned this impressive cruiser with a pair of high power binoculars and spotted Andino. Then of course he sat up and took serious notice, broke out his best spy camera, his iPhone and happily snapped away as Andino was met on the jetty by a well-dressed very black man with an apparent military bearing, but who showed no deference to Andino."

More images appeared on the screen and Vern and Nate pored over them as they appeared.

"After a wait of about ten minutes he saw a military style rigid inflatable come bouncing into the harbour and pick up the black man, Andino and their BGs. He then watched the inflatable rendezvous with a small warship of some kind a mile or so offshore which everyone transferred on to and which promptly turned about and disappeared."

A last set of grainy images showed the ship.

"The warship hadn't worn a flag and our man was unable to identify it from a copy of Jane's. However gentlemen, according to my Pentagon navy pals that is a type 37 *Houjian* class corvette formerly of the People's Liberation Army Navy, or PLAN if you want a smaller mouthful. Guess which nation is the only one in this hemisphere which owns any? You got it, Haiti."

Vern flicked back through the images while he started on his ten cents worth.

"It's surely no coincidence at around that time Miles, Nate, that Haiti suddenly got rich. By rich I mean like lottery winners or something. They started an arms spending spree that briefly hit the news a couple of years ago because some of it came from Ukraine, which is of course almost totally bankrupt because of that idiot that State insisted on installing as their president after they'd caused the Goddamned revolution in the first place."

His disgust at his own nation's foreign policy makers dripped from every word.

"The fact is, as you know, you can buy almost anything if you have the will and the money. Enough in this case for Haiti to buy itself a sizeable navy, a small air force and to triple its army."

He paused to let that nugget sink in.

"From what we know and have seen since then, these guys have been recruiting and training like it's the day before the Third World War in which *they* are going to play a leading role; no expense spared on the shooting ranges ashore and afloat."

The others looked interested but not alarmed and Nate was beginning to think he's missed the catch somehow. Vern noted the looks and continued.

"I mean we're talking some seriously big bucks here gents. Our intercepts in these republics and bank enquiries confirm that Farache paid nigh on seven hundred million dollars for his navy, another seventy five for the air force and another hundred and fifty for a box of gadgets the army wanted, like multi-barrel rocket launchers and light armoured vehicles as well as ordinary artillery pieces and a shed load of small arms and ammunition. In addition, technical aid and logistical support worth another fifty million from both Ukraine and the PRC."

The last statement raised already high eyebrows further still but they were not ex-navy guys like him so he tried a different tack.

"Put it like this, with what he's got he could wipe the floor with any two, even three South American navies except in submarines. He bought a fucking 'off the shelf' missile cruiser from Ukraine for Christ's sake! It started life as a *Slava* class back in the soviet days but was laid up uncompleted in Ukraine. They had started to work on it with Russian help when it all went down the spout after the revolution and Russia took back the Crimea.

The others were starting to take more notice now.

"Then he bought some more stuff from China, frigates, corvettes, landing ships etcetera which whilst not top of the league, is nowhere near the bottom, it will all be in the notes I'll send you."

They were interrupted by a knock, the door opened and in came the new coffee and out went the old. No one spoke while the steward was in the room but Vern started up again the moment the door closed.

"I started to realise this was no haphazard purchasing spree and it began to dawn on me that this was a shopping list for a tailor made force. A total of twenty two ships ranging from a cruiser to assault ships, corvettes and destroyers with their own replenishment vessels. Enough BMP armoured personnel carriers for two well-equipped motor rifle battalions and support equipment for all."

It was his turn to type furiously and spin his laptop round. He put a it showed a Pentagon headed report from eighteen months previously.

"My tame commander put this together for me because I was curious at the time but with nothing else on the horizon and no apparent threat, it got shelved with all the other stuff we turn up. Anyway, he has enough shipping to escort and transport a combined arms brigade anywhere it wants to go, and then support its operations my guy said. And, last but not least on this shopping list, and missed initially just because of the time gap, were a half squadron of Ukrainian Mig 29's and a half squadron of Chinese, slash Pakistani, JF-17s, the air cover and support of the afore mentioned combined arms brigade. Given what we now know, I would say Haiti is severely pissed off with somebody and now has the gear to do something about it!"

They looked up expectantly.

"My question of course *was* where the fuck did a bankrupt country like Haiti get the money in the first place and you gentlemen have provided the answer I believe."

Miles continued as if there'd been no break.

"Now I admit that we haven't got many sources in Haiti itself but we do have one good one in the naval supply set up. Just for a bit of background, he started taking money from us just after

Farache ordered his navy and since then of course the navy infrastructure has grown out of all proportion because of its expansion. This guy, who thought he was in a dead-end job has now been promoted right up the line. Of course now he started getting a little reluctant to play and we had to remind him of his loyalties."

He smiled without a trace of humour in his expression. The others nodded, knowing the leverage Miles had, once the first pay check was taken.

"Just a week ago he was ordered to prepare stores and equipment for the whole fleet for, quote, 'an extended period of operations' to be ready for Tuesday the 22nd of this month. Security is very tight and he's got no idea what Farache has got planned."

As he paused to draw breath Nate jumped in.

"Shit I thought they were cooking up some super trafficking route or something, the Haitian military are already well up on our shit list of legalised traffickers. So why the hell would Andino drop a billion bucks or so on Farache, he ain't no charity worker now is he?"

Miles Carlson sat looking at both his friends. "That's what I want to know, we figure Farache is going to start a war with someone and we think it's going to be the Dominicans next door; given all the recent shit about Haitians having to register if they want to work in the Dominican republic and the history of cross border clashes, some of them quite heavy. The guys in Santiago must be sweating a bit in case he comes their way, they can't help but have noticed the build-up. But I can't for the life of me work out why Andino should cough all that money for Farache to invade the Dominican Republic. Where's his payoff?"

Vernon Weathers sat up quickly, you could almost see the light bulb light up thought Miles.

"Try thinking about it from a different angle guys." He addressed them both.

"Firstly, we have detected a significant increase in the Haitian naval signal traffic, possibly suggesting the start of a major operation sometime soon, so that confirms your man in Haiti's story. But it was a bit flimsy to go anywhere with on its own. Secondly, just ask yourselves this. What has the cartel lost in the last few years that's worth laying out a billion to replace?" He asked with a knowing smile.

Nate King shot up out of his chair catching his knee on the edge of the coffee table, spilling cups, saucers and coffee all over.

"Shit it's... fuck!" He frantically brushed scolding coffee off his pants leg.

"It's not Dominican Republic, it's the Caymans! Remember all that shit two years ago when we bust the huge laundering racket with the help of the new government? Well that cost the cartel a whole lot more than a billion at the time and in future revenue who knows? What if Andino's persuaded Farache to clobber the Caymans? His payoff would be re-opening the laundering facility. It'd be worth fucking tens of billions to Andino and his boys! His influence in the other cartels would rocket too, he'd be able to charge a fee for laundering services."

Miles joined in.

"Yeah that might figure, Farache has been verbally abusing the Caymans *coincidentally* ever since their independence. Maybe he's just set us up to think that the Dominican Rep was the target, while all the time setting the international stage for the invasion of the Caymans! Vern you're a fucking genius." Said Miles, thumping his friend on the back.

Vern dabbed at the splashes of coffee on his trousers and spoke without looking up.

"All we have to do now is to get someone else to believe it and that won't be easy. You couldn't go to the President with what we've got here, it's all circumstantial, supposition and conjecture."

Nate sat down with a thump.

"Damn, you're right, I was getting a little carried away here. Even if we got it to the president's National Security Adviser and they believed us, there's not a damn thing that would stand in public. The bastards have worked it so that we have to react to an accomplished fact once they've invaded."

Conversation stopped for a few moments while they each considered the problems.

"They're nice people down there in the Caymans." Mused Vern quietly. "Sally and I had a great holiday there when it was a British dependency, pity we couldn't unofficially warn them."

"Hey Miles do you still have any contact with that 'Limey' air force general or whatever he was, the one that you got friendly with when you were working in London? Isn't he their Chief of Defence or something now?"

Nate had a hopeful expression on his face as he waited for Miles's reply.

"Yeah actually I do, he's an Air Chief Marshal, actually Chief of the Defence Staff, that's like our Chairman of the Joint Chiefs; as a matter of fact his wife and Betty got along real well and the kids still swap countries for holidays sometimes. You figure I should drop the hint to him? That might not be a bad idea at all. Perhaps he can do some discrete pre-positioning with the little they have left nowadays or something. Damn it, I will. Meanwhile guys I think we should get our people to put that area under the microscope."

He gave Vern a lopsided grin.

"I know it's not specifically in your ball park but what about increased satellite coverage?"

Vern shook his head. "That takes a damn sight more clout than I've got Miles, I reckon that we need to put this in front of our bosses soonest without mentioning that Brit connection of yours Miles, agreed?"

The other two nodded wondering whether anything would be done before the shit hit the fan, if indeed it did.

As they left, Vern compared the process they'd just gone through to working on a massive picture puzzle with thousands of helpers. Suddenly a piece that you thought belonged over on one side was found to fit in a little patch on the other and it was Eureka time! Then someone would dump another thousand pieces on the table and you'd have to decide whether they even belonged in the same damned puzzle.

Tuesday 8th May 2018

Extracts from a CNN Evening News Broadcast

Reports of further serious clashes along the southern part of the border between the Caribbean countries of Haiti and its neighbour the Dominican Republic, have been confirmed by both governments.

A Haitian military spokesman stated that units of the re-formed elite anti-terrorist unit the 'Leopards', had been fired upon by Dominican border units whilst pursuing a terrorist group thought to be responsible for bombings in the northern city of Cap Haitian yesterday. The spokesman added that Haitian units had returned fire and there were a number of casualties on both sides in a fire-fight reportedly lasting three hours.

He confirmed rumours that more Haitian units had been deployed in the border areas. However the Dominican spokesman refuted the allegations stating that an unprovoked Haitian attack on a Dominican border post had been driven off when reinforcements arrived. He also stated that this was the second incident of its kind this week and that the Dominican Republic would not be pressurized into giving up the disputed territory.

After the break, a report from the Cayman Islands looks into the surprising and embarrassing admission and apology yesterday from Caymans Prime Minister Andrew McTeal, that allegations made by Haitian President General Farache, of Cayman support for Haitian terrorists did have some truth in them. This admission is certain to spark off more lively rhetoric from Haitian President Farache. Meanwhile nearer home a Boston man…..

Evening Tuesday 8th May 2018

Prime Minister's Study Government House, Georgetown, Grand Cayman

Andrew McTeal used the remote to set 'record' for the rest of the bulletin and then switched off the TV. He turned to face his colleagues; the oak panelled room was silent except for the whap, whap of the ceiling fan and the irritating tap, tap, tap of Georges Caram's fountain pen against his pearl white teeth.

McTeal suppressed a sudden urge to shove the pen down Caram's throat, sideways. As Minister of Finance he was responsible for the events that led to McTeal's embarrassing admission and apology on the news.

He looked across at Caram's unhappy face, pale in the glow of the standard lamp. At thirty eight he was young for the job, but brilliant, with his classic Latin features and the 'little boy lost' look, women seemed to find him almost irresistible.

Here was the architect of the 'Great money bust', as the press had called it, now dispirited by the knowledge that his own ministry was technically culpable for this fiasco. McTeal clamped down on the sympathy that welled up briefly.

"Georges, have you anything for us yet? Any indication of which one of your imbeciles allowed this transfer, without a background check?"

Caram shifted uncomfortably sitting on the edge of his old leather Chesterfield armchair. He tugged an envelope out of his inside jacket pocket.

"Only my resignation Prime Minister, I have nothing else to offer at this time other than abject apology."

He trailed off uncertainly as he saw McTeal's face harden. McTeal took the envelope and threw it onto his already cluttered desk.

"So things get a bit rough and you want to bailout eh Georges? Well it's different at thirty thousand feet when the flack starts rolling in. Different to just posing for the cameras and playing with spreadsheets."

Fists on hips, jacket thrust aside in his classic QC stance, he looked down on the sitting man.

"I won't let you get out of it that easily. I may well accept that." He wafted a hand at the letter on his desk. "At some later date, but for now, you got us into this mess so stop feeling sorry for yourself and start thinking of ways to help get us out."

With a snort he turned away from the unfortunate Finance Minister and surveyed his other guests.

His roving eyes came to rest on the calm countenance of his Foreign Minister, Erskine Buerke.

"Reactions Erskine?"

Buerke looked relaxed and exuded a charming assurance that wasn't quite arrogance. McTeal's mind raced while he waited for the inevitably well considered answer. He thinks this should be his study I can see it in his eyes. He gave a mental shrug, can't really fault someone for having ambitions can I?

Buerke ignored the Prime Minister's intense scrutiny and concentrated on appearing calm and collected. It won't be long now before I sit behind that desk, he mused as he prepared to deliver his pre-prepared input.

"The usual public condemnations Prime Minister, but I've spoken to Washington and London and they are both now aware that we were set up as it were."

He paused in his carefully rehearsed speech.

"I must add however, that we should be mindful that this was no spontaneous outraged release of information from the Haitians. It had a definite purpose apart from our embarrassment in the eyes of the international community and just as our application to join the UN is due to be tabled too. I detect something rather more sinister."

"Can't you be more specific Erskine?" Asked McTeal.

Buerke smiled his most winning smile.

"Unfortunately no Prime Minister, it's just a feeling that I have."

McTeal suppressed his irritation at Buerke's remarks. It's almost as if he's damn well enjoying it, he thought, as he turned his attention to the other person seated on the two-seater couch with Buerke.

Now this man would remain silent until prodded. He was sitting, as McTeal fully expected, in the corner of the couch as far away from the lamplight as possible. His coal black face was nearly invisible, a man of few words, he shunned the light as he shunned publicity.

"Any comment Sandy?" He prodded.

Sandiford Roche, Minister without Portfolio, eased himself reluctantly into the light. To say that he had no portfolio was not strictly true, he had many small ones along with McTeal's total confidence and trust. He supervised the internal affairs of the country, from the police and the small anti-terrorist unit, to the tourist board and the Department of Public Works.

"I'm looking into it Prime Minister, I'll let you know the moment I have something worthwhile." Roche smiled.

McTeal bid them goodnight as they left and went back into his study after casually chatting to the guards at the front entrance. He liked to gauge things by talking to ordinary people. Whilst the MPP weren't quite in the category of ordinary they were the nearest apart from his butler staff and the maids.

Back in his study he headed for the drinks cabinet and poured himself a decent measure of Dalwhinnie. He knew Jake König would prefer the Lagavulin next to it, but liked the Dalwhinnie because he felt it offered a balance between the smooth subtle flavours of the east coast whiskies like the Speyside distilleries, and the more powerful phenolic malts of say, Isla. The fact that the Dalwhinnie distillery sat about halfway between the two sides supported his case for balance.

He briefly considered König's recent escapade in the Mediterranean. His new ship had made a timely arrival on the scene and from McTeal's legal perspective had clearly answered a distress call, taken what he saw as appropriate action, and successfully brought an end to a potentially horrific episode. Erskine Buerke however, had been all for severing ties with König industries, claiming they were mavericks and undisciplined.

Having read all the reports, McTeal saw it differently. Looking at the operation as planned and executed, it was a marvel of coordination with luck playing a part only at the beginning as far as he could see. Everything else had interlocked in a frighteningly efficient manner resulting they thought, in the deaths of about thirty of the worst kind of criminals. He wondered at Erskine's opposition. He'd have to give that some more thought.

Friday May 11th 2018

St George's Bermuda

Now, with the old Gate's Fort to starboard and Higgs Island to port, *Bismarck* glided slowly into the narrow channel they appropriately called 'New' cut, which led to the picturesque St George's harbour and town.

The glittering turquoise sea formed a perfect foreground to the island spread out before them. The scene was like something out of a Hollywood movie as the sun, as if on cue, dipped down behind the buildings ahead and everything turned gold rimmed or blackest shadow.

Captain Reiner Krull checked the bearings for the umpteenth time as he carefully conned his three and a half thousand ton charge through a waterway crowded with motor cruisers and sailing vessels. Many were desperate to get a better view of their 'nouveau celebrity' guest, and all of whom seemed hell bent on ramming him or committing 'suicide-by-boat'. He'd successfully avoided killing, sinking or tipping into the water any of the 'Lemmings' in small craft for the last five days and hopefully this would be the last time.

Such was their concentration that neither Reiner nor his mooring parties were other than peripherally aware of the beauty of the scenery that slid by the Atlantic grey flanks of their ship. Only a passing note had been taken the first day when the lush green islands had come into proper view and by the time the pastel pink beaches could be made out everyone on duty was too busy to notice, all except the 'goofers' down aft. These were off duty crew standing in the shadow of turret 'Caesar' as they ogled at the dazzlingly white limestone roofs which topped the pastel shaded houses. These, now in shadow, slid by to starboard. There had been abundant speculation on the nature of the females who may be persuaded to share an evening of good food and much beer and whatever else was on offer.

At last, satisfied with their GPS position, Reiner gave the order to stop engines and after a pause, to let go the bow anchor. Then as the way came off her, he ordered the aft anchor let go as well.

They were perfectly lined up in their previously arranged slot three hundred yards off Ordnance Island, a one-time arsenal and now the cruise ship terminal, if such a small jetty could be so called.

The First Lieutenant, Lt Cdr Simon McClelland, quietly gave orders that sent the crew moving purposefully about, rigging white canvas awnings over the entry port and the quarterdeck in order to grant shade to those who would be coming and going tomorrow.

In addition there would be roving deck patrols deployed as it seemed clear their notoriety had not yet diminished despite the Atlantic crossing and a week of day-running exercises from here. The patrols were armed, the fact of which the Governor had initially been against but had been persuaded by his Police Chief to allow, as there had been threats from various Muslim groups. All vessels operating in the area had been warned that one hundred yards, marked by a number of buoys, was the closest any craft was allowed to come.

Bermudans still liked to turn out and ogle at her as did the increasing number of tourists and of course the media. These had spent all week stalking members of the crew whenever they'd been ashore for a wander. The last five days of being politely told to 'piss off' had not really dimmed the media interest in them since the cruise ship incident off Malta, it was only to be expected he supposed. He doubted any of the crew would have spoken to them anyway, most of the company treated 'journos' like plague carriers for good reason and quite naturally. He also knew unofficially that Kipper had cleared the lower deck and made it plain that speaking to the press was a P45 offence.

The speculative, and in some cases completely untrue narratives, that had appeared in European papers had diminished but there were still a few miles to go for the American press yet.

As the ship stilled and non-duty crew went below for showers and to wait to see if shore leave would be granted, Reiner took a last look around and handed over to the Officer of the Watch, Lt Ian Halshaw before going below to wait for the port immigration officials and customs for the fifth time. He also expected a visit from someone in the Governor's office at some point and quite probably the Island's government as well, regarding arrangements for the evening's entertainment.

Down in the wardroom Reiner felt the tension drain away as he sipped an ice cold very weak gin and lime with soda water and reflected on the reasons Jake might have had for berthing the ship in St George's Town rather than going into the main harbour at Hamilton. He thought it probably had something to do with trying to keep them out of the limelight after the ship's first taste of action near Malta but there could be other reasons like proximity to the airport or the amazing setting that the ship sat in.

St George's Town itself was at the Northern end of the island group and was the oldest settled part of the British Overseas Territory which was only thirty three square miles in total. It was also about as far away from the capital as it was possible to get and yet still be in Bermuda.

Only Simon and Ian had visited Bermuda before, both when in the RN and some years ago. Simon's lurid tales of wild parties and never ending supplies of rum and willing females had entertained them for the first day and many crewmen had ventured beyond St George's, but liberty boats stopped running at 02.00 so no all-night flings.

For Ian though it had been a bit of a 'Roots' event since his ancestry included great, great grandparents who had been slaves until all had been granted freedom on these very islands.

Reiner tuned them out as he checked his watch, only another hour until Jake landed at Wade international airport. They'd see his plane land or at least hear it because the airfield was on the south side of the harbour. He got up and placed the glass on the bar nodding to all before exiting.

Simon McClelland watched the Captain head off to his cabin, he seemed to be deep in thought. Simon then ordered a 'dark and stormy', a local favourite whilst he contemplated the evening ahead. The slowly turning deckhead fans stirred the air and the aircon kept the overall temperature at a decent low, it wouldn't do to be sweaty when he met the boss and family.

He considered the skipper. Everyone appeared to like and respect Reiner even though most of them had felt the quiet, but sharp edge of his tongue during the last week of exercises. Simon thought Reiner had 'the glow'. He had been privileged to meet few natural leaders in his time, he didn't see himself in that category either but he'd met a couple, most famously the late lamented Commander Frank Trickey.

Reiner fitted the bill too. It was almost as if these people had the 'Reddy-Brek' glow. There was just something about them that gave you confidence and made you want to do well for them. Jake was another. I suppose, he thought, we should consider ourselves exceedingly lucky to have just one such character but two was being greedy.

Simon looked over at Ian Halshaw, the Weapons Electrical officer, as he joked with Ivan Scotnikov about today's electrical mishap. Ian was a quietly spoken guy with skin the colour of burned mahogany and he had been the one to take a large share of the quiet wrath that had poured from the Captain during the daily 'wars' they'd been having. But it seemed to wash straight over him and he kept his wicked sense of humour throughout. It did help that he was a total geek with anything that an electric current passed through.

As with all new ships there are glitches in the systems and unlike his title suggested, Ian and his small gang of 'Greenies' were responsible for absolutely anything electronic on the ship outside of the engine room, not just weapons. Simon checked his watch, the Boss would be landing soon and he'd better be there to meet him. He finished his drink and made his way up to the midships entry port collecting Pete Jervis, one of the stewards, to help with everybody's luggage.

As he arrived on deck he could hear raised voices. Tied up at the base of the steps leading to the main deck and next to the sea boat was a Bermudan harbour police boat.

Standing at the head of the steps were a customs officer, a police inspector and a constable, the former haranguing the DSR, Petty Officer Rautsch. Behind Rautsch and looking menacing was one of the security guys left on board. He looked ready to pounce and the policeman was clearly aware of his direct gaze. Rautsch, a German born marine engineer, saw Simon approaching and turned towards him with a look of immense relief.

As Simon covered the last half dozen steps, Rautsch snapped to attention and barked out a report in his best rapid Teutonic manner, unfortunately in his agitation he'd spoken German.

It was way past Simon's translational ability but not wishing either to get involved or embarrass them both by asking for a translation, he listened to the spate of staccato German, at the end of which he nodded, smiled at the visitors, then walked across to the communicator on the bulkhead since he wasn't wearing his headset.

He pressed 01 on the panel and waited for a reply.

"It's Simon Sir, I believe you're wanted at the gangway by the Duty Senior, it's about customs I think, oh and there's a police inspector too."

He turned, nodded to the visitors and switched on his plumiest Dartmouth voice.

"Would you mind awfully if we pop over to the airport and pick up the owner and his family? The Captain will be up to see you in a tick."

The locals, evidently surprised at the language switch and politeness of the officer in the immaculate white tropical uniform with two thick and one thin gold ring at the cuffs, looked at each other and nodded their assent. Simon smiled at them again and headed for the entryport.

"Cheerio then. Come along Jervis don't dawdle or we'll be late for the big boss."

He added over his shoulder as he descended.

The large and overtly menacing security type entered the boat as well.

"Ah, you're with us are you?" Said Simon noticing him.

"Paulo Sir. Boss Fraser sent me." Responded the man with a strong Italian lilt to his English. His manner changed from menacing to affable as he broke into an 'ultrabrite' smile.

"Cannot be too careful Sir, now we're famous."

"Quite." Was Simon's response to that.

Their arrival at the steps near the pilot boat moorings at Ordnance Island was followed by the usual camera flashes and the odd shouted question.

Paulo went up the steps like a rat up a drain pipe and took up position at the top, with 'menacing scowl' switched on again.

Simon shook his head, ignored the press and oglers and made his way up the steps to the top of the jetty and over to where a pair of mid-sized chauffeur driven Mercedes were waiting along with a utility van. Large cars were not permitted on Bermuda and only residents could drive them at the heart stopping island top speed of 20mph.

Jervis jumped in the utility vehicle with Paulo and Simon got in with the driver of the lead Mercedes and they set off in convoy for the airport.

Evening, May 11th 2018

König Industries G450 Gulfstream, on finals,
Wade International Airport, Bermuda

The jet banked steeply, as if the pilot were trying to impress or had forgotten that this was a Gulfstream and not the Tornado GR four that he used to fly. He turned on finals towards Wade international, formerly Kindley field and previously home of the US Naval Air Station Bermuda, now the island's civil airport.

Out of the corner of his eye Jake had just caught sight of what he thought must be *Bismarck* lying at anchor in St George's harbour, he would be pleased to set foot aboard her again. He turned to his left to catch the expression on his family's faces as the aircraft slowed and straightened for landing. His wife Sophie, looked as serene as usual, very little could ruffle her calm.

His teen children, Helen eighteen and James nineteen, by contrast, were straining against their seatbelts as they tried to get a look at this new playground called Bermuda. Behind them Reiner's children, Elsa sixteen and Hans eighteen, were chattering away too as the jet flared just before touchdown.

He had been more than happy to bring them along since Reiner's, wife, Trudi had agreed to stay in Paris helping to organise and coordinate the rest of the ship's wives and sweethearts as they gathered for their charter flight to Bermuda before continuing to the Caymans.

The rest of the crew did not yet know that he'd booked for everyone to stay at the Rosewood Hotel, Tucker's Point, a fantastic golf resort hotel and beach club just a few short miles away, once the final exercises were complete on Monday.

Trudi obviously took her husband's new career very seriously and had taken a three month leave of absence from her own job as an ENT consultant in one of Hamburg's largest hospitals in order to help out during the establishment phase in the Caymans.

Jake settled back in his seat as the wheels touched with a brief muted screech, and reviewed the events of the thirteen days since he left *Bismarck* in Gibraltar harbour.

A seemingly endless series of business meetings, some concerned with *Bismarck* others concerned with general organisation of his network of companies worldwide had occupied the useful time; the press, media and his lawyers had occupied the rest, which had sadly been the majority.

He had stuck to his brief about *Bismarck* and its role as a 'Merchant Protector'. He had ignored any questions or negative insinuations of any kind and had repeated endlessly that it was the duty of any mariner to offer assistance to other mariners in distress *AND* that to fail to do so was a criminal offence in many countries.

On television Jake managed to get the point across that his Merchant Protector had received a valid distress signal from the *Kristianstaadt* so what was he supposed to do? Wait the hours and hours before any national naval vessel was available to assist or carry out reconnaissance and take action when they thought appropriate?

In addition he'd managed to get hold of a couple of the passengers who were still looking up old friends and relatives in Europe before flying back to Australia as well as Jeff Bannister the first officer, now on leave.

The TV interview of the old couple was a real PR bonus as they sat holding hands describing the heart rending fear they'd experienced when the terrorists had shot their way on board and then the overwhelming joy as *Bismarck* had destroyed the terrorist vessel.

Add to that Jeff Bannister's story, one full of self-effacing humility but clearly he was the real hero of the hour. It diverted almost all of the attention from *Bismarck's* explosive intervention in the grand finale, which was of course what Jake wanted. He even started the Twitter feed suggesting that Bannister should get the George Cross for his bravery during the attack –and quite rightly too.

Photographs and even short films of the terrorist boat's final moments had been taken by a number of passengers from their balcony and were shown live. On some of the better ones the leader was clearly holding a box in his hand just before he disintegrated.

Better still, when asked what they thought of *Bismarck's* intervention the old couple went into overdrive with many tears of gratitude and sniffles, then a final voice call from Australia with their son saying much the same thing, calling anyone who thought the intervention wrong, utterly stupid. Perfect, thought Jake.

He'd said 'Merchant Protector' so often that the press now at least called his ship a 'Merchant Protector' vessel and 'talking heads' could be heard pontificating on the concept of Merchant Protectors.

That was good, that was really positive.   Then he commissioned a number of surveys in various European capitals and in a number of rural areas. Curiously, or perhaps not, across Europe the 'Luvvies', or liberal progressives, seemed to be concentrated in the cities, it shouldn't be a surprise really he supposed, city dwellers often considered themselves to be superior to others.   Rural people were more practical and pragmatic than capital dwellers many of whom seemed to be detached from reality most of the time. Still, even in the capitals his actions were well received by a majority, in the rural and extra urban areas, very well received with a large majority.

So the results had been carefully leaked in the appropriate places and sure enough they appeared in the European press, including surprisingly, the British Guardian which had done an article and not managed to call him a fascist once.

All of this activity had come at a time when he was shifting day to day control of König Industries to three of his longest serving executive board members and closest associates, while he concentrated on his newest project.

The three he had chosen were utterly reliable and had proven their loyalty and business acumen on occasions too numerous to mention, they'd also been with him from the start back in 1997 when he succeeded his father as the major shareholder and chairman, but was still in the navy.

They understood the way he worked and would expect them to operate in his absence. To say they were initially puzzled by the relocation to the Caymans was an understatement, at least until he explained the legal side of things and the EU effect. But to give them their due, they'd immediately grasped the commercial potential of the 'Merchant Protector' project and had suggested several useful ways to take it forward.

One of the most annoying meetings had been at the Foreign Office in London, where he'd gone to ensure there would be no problems regarding using Bermuda briefly as a location for the intensive trials he intended to put *Bismarck* through, prior to its acceptance as an auxiliary by the Cayman government and before its initial deployment for König Marine on contract.

The first civil servant he met had been so arrogant and dismissive that Jake had been sorely tempted to punch him. As it was he just stood up whilst the chinless wonder was in mid flow, looked him straight in the eye and said.

"I can see I'm going to have to go further up the ladder if I'm going to hear anything at all sensible. Good day."

He walked out feeling a large measure of satisfaction at the expression of utter confusion and astonishment on the man's face. It had taken another two days to sort out the mess, thanks mostly to Sir Bernard Law, one of the trio who would be taking a more prominent role in the decision making of König Industries.

Of course, the old school tie brigade still ran the country, but Bernard hadn't become one of Jake's deputies for that reason, he got there by having a scalpel like business mind, tempered unusually, with an innate sense of fairness.

Bernard's insistence on the incentivising of all company employees through profit sharing and maintaining one of the few final salary schemes for the company pension, had made him popular with the ordinary workers and managers up to the top tier and recruitment was never an issue, however he had made enemies on the board when his actions had directly affected their income.

Jake hated naked greed and had sided with Bernard each time by commissioning his own report on the likely effect of these actions on long term profitability which showed that willing workers were much more productive than ignored or mistreated workers –obviously, Jake had added.

But Bernard had the top tier credentials and a bit of blue blood to boot, so having gone to school with the man who daily briefed the Foreign Secretary and organised his diary, he was particularly useful at times like these.

Jake's meeting with the Foreign Secretary had been brief and gratifying. Gratifying because it was nice to know that there was someone in the job who had a grasp of global affairs without referring to masses of position papers. Brief, because the man saw no problems with the request and would pen a memo to that effect, for Bernard's friend to circulate as appropriate. The Foreign Secretary had finished the meeting with his own questions regarding the action off Malta and having listened carefully, had offered his approbation but added for heaven's sake to be careful. Privately, he continued, the government had no objection to anyone knocking off terrorists or pirates but sadly they had to be heard making the right noises so Jake should not expect any overt assistance at any time. However, he added significantly, wherever possible HMG would attempt to be a bump in the road for anything coming from the supra-nationals –he meant of course the UN, IMO, the EU and others.

They would of course have to apply to the Bermudan government but having the Foreign Secretary's advanced approval made that proposition so much less fraught.

Meetings with Saab radar division had been fruitful and Jake had personally handed the MD the data store dump from *Bismarck's* action off Malta so they could analyse it. Also, they'd also agreed to foot one third of the bill for the very expensive drones needed to test their new radar, ammunition and the new gunfire control system that Jake was proving for them.

He had left the Saab meeting feeling both a good deal of satisfaction over the shared costs, and also a need, almost a longing, to get back to his new ship.

Out of the plane's window he could see Simon McClelland and Jervis standing near the terminal building next to a pair of Mercedes and a panel van.

Seeing them both forced his mind back to the last time he saw them at Gibraltar and then to his conversations with Roby, and they had the knock on effect of bringing back the old ache of his own wartime service where he felt that somehow he could have done better.

Few people in Britain realised that the Falklands campaign was won, not only by the great skill and daring shown by the servicemen, but by the fortuitous incompetence of the Argentine armourers who adjusted the fuse settings on the bombs. Many that struck ships just did not explode because the fuse mechanisms had not had time to arm before they hit. Had all the bombs exploded that actually hit, then it is likely that, having lost another ten or so ships, the public outcry would have forced Mrs Thatcher to sue for some sort of compromise settlement.

It seemed men always had to die or suffer before things were changed in the Navy. The classic example was the Action Working Dress, the bureaucratic name for the clothes that sailors worked and fought in but were just called number 8's by them. In 1982 these clothes were made of synthetic fibres originally brought into the service for use on submarines, because they were easy to launder.

Someone in Whitehall had had the bright idea of issuing them to the rest of the fleet because they were cheaper, despite sensible protest that these clothes were flammable!

Things quieten down, as they do, until years later our ships started getting hit and sinking near the Falklands and the casualties started to come home. Then, when it came out that these uniforms actually caught fire and melted onto the skin of the sailors, there'd been holy hell to pay in the newspapers and parliament.

Jake would never forget being cornered by his mother when he was at home on leave after the war, the scars still fresh and pink on his arms and legs. She had been furious over an article in the paper about the flammability of 'our sailors clothes' and had demanded of Jake that he refute such an irresponsible allegation.

He couldn't, he just shook his head sadly and held up his arms, the livid flesh visible below the level of his short sleeved sports shirt where his own number 8 shirt had melted on to him.

His mother had given a cry of anguish, 'it's too much' she'd said and set to with her typewriter adding her voice to the many who'd clamoured for change. It came, but as usual it was too late for some. Jake sighed to himself as he unbuckled the seatbelt and made ready to exit the plane.

Standing at the hatch waiting for the steps Jake did a double take. Instead of just Simon McClelland, Jervis and a security guy waiting by the cars, there was now an additional figure. Andy Evans his Security Chief stepped out of the shadows cast by the floodlighting. Two more figures materialised a little further away facing outward discretely guarding them all.

Jake stepped down and Andy immediately walked forward to greet him, eyes still scanning everywhere.

"Hello boss, nice flight?"

"No Problems. How's it going Andy?"

Evans grinned and shook hands.

"You pick some ace places to do business Jake. Got to hand it to you, Bermuda is one of the best."

It was worth a million to see the look on Simon's face as he realised Evans had approached without him even being aware. Jervis too looked a little taken aback as he checked out the chunky buzz-cut duo standing a few yards away. Paulo was unfazed, he'd been in radio contact as soon as Andy and his small team entered the airport –obviously, his look said.

A brief chat to the customs and immigration officers, handshakes with big smiles and Evans watched Jake work his magic on these two guys who had started off pissed at having to come out and check over another wealthy visitor and would now trip over themselves to help him. A passport check, smiles, nods and a hand shake, then on their way.

Jake told the lead driver to take them all to the Rosewood at Tucker's point first to drop off the families and all their luggage which annoyed James who wanted to go to the ship immediately. Then he, Simon and Jervis, minus the two security guys who'd arrived with Andy, would head off to the ship once they were settled.

Jake relaxed into the back seat of the car as it sedately cruised out of the airport and on to the causeway which joined St David's Island to the rest of Bermuda. Sophie was quiet, looking out of the car windows at the shimmer of the moonlight on the water of Castle Harbour, and Jake wished he could hold her hand but Helen was in the middle seat. As he studied his daughter from the corner of his eye, Jake once again marvelled at her likeness to her mother.

He knew Sophie had not yet adjusted to their newfound 'celebrity' status, which was something she'd never courted and never wanted despite how wealthy they'd become. James was in the next car with Reiner's kids accompanied by Simon and Paulo. Bringing up the rear in the utility was Jervis with the extra security guys.

Andy Evans appeared quite relaxed as he spoke over his shoulder from the front passenger seat but his eyes darted everywhere. He also looked as fit as the day Jake first met him some twenty years ago. God, has it been that long, he thought.

He remembered when they'd first met at Devonport Dockyard back 98'. Jake was Duty Lieutenant Commander (DLC) of the old Type 42 *Manchester* and the ship had just finished a gruelling two week work-up. For reasons that only became apparent later they had been berthed right at the end of frigate alley. He'd been standing on the flight deck at the brow talking to the duty PO when they both heard an odd sound from the direction of the jetty, a kind of muffled rhythmic thumping sound. They looked along the jetty as far as they could see, a moving dark 'blob' appeared in and out of the lights along the pier, the sound was definitely emanating from it.

It suddenly dawned on Jake that it was a group of dark clad men he was watching and that the noise came from their rubber soled boots rhythmically slamming into the ground as they ran.

He recalled the twirl of thoughts that rushed through his mind, was this an unscheduled drill of some kind? It would be just like FOST staff to put on something like this especially because they knew he was on board and since he'd only left FOST three months before and most of all because *Manchester* had just come through with flying colours.

His new Captain had had a 'friendly' chat before their FOST visit and basically said that if the ship came through with good marks he'd be a shoo in for his third ring, given the report that he *would* be writing. He hadn't needed to say what would be written if the ship didn't do well.

So yeah, just when they thought it was all over and relaxed a bit. Perfect timing. Now what the hell should he do, the skipper was conveniently ashore having dinner with the Port Admiral as he recalled?

"Quartermaster, pipe for the duty watch and then...." He turned back to observe, the darkly clad figures were about one hundred and fifty yards away still. Should he rig hoses? The repel boarders

drill?

"....then rig fire hoses fore and aft on the seaward side and out of sight. Open the armoury and have a couple of unloaded weapons issued, get yourself and myself a 9 mil and webbing belt."

"Sir." Barked the duty PO and pointing to the first two ratings that appeared. "You two, with me now."

The Quartermaster starting speaking on the main broadcast drowning out thought word and deed and then took charge of the rest of the duty watch as it emerged on to the flight deck.

The duty PO returned with the weapon holstered for Jake and wearing his own already.

"You go up to the fo'c'sle with them PO and keep in line of sight with me. If anyone tries to board wash 'em off." He turned to address everyone else.

"Double time people, our visitors aren't far away now."

What an anti-climax. The usual cock-up. Message not passed on. A signal telling *Manchester* to expect twenty two Marine SBS trainees embarking overnight, to sail with the ship next day, had not, even left the Comcen.

Jake had sat in the wardroom half an hour later drinking a cup of coffee with the marine Lieutenant who was their OC. He'd told him the cock-up story and informed him of the reception committee that had been waiting for him and his men, Andy Evans had thought it was hilarious.

He'd seemed to be one of those characters who took everything in their stride, who just said 'shit happens' when the wheels fell off, and got on with it. Jake took an instant liking to him. The marines were to practice an opposed night landing from *Manchester* into Cawsand bay, their kit was sitting in a chacon on the jetty.

Jake remembered with clarity meeting someone alarmingly just like him years before on board the hospital ship *SS Uganda* back in 82'.

Jake's burns although painful had not been too deep and after two weeks of treatment which involved his arms being lathered in Flamazine cream and wearing bags on his hands also covered in the cream, he was waiting for transfer to an 'ambulance ship'. This was what the survey ships *Herald*, *Hydra* and *Hecla* had been re-tasked for then onward transfer to Montevideo, thence home by RAF VCIO.

He was, it has to be said, gloomy and introspective. People already left him alone having found out that he'd a short fuse and a sharp tongue. He was in 'Seaview' ward at the stern of the ship, sitting on the counter of what had originally been a canteen but was now a pharmacy, talking to two of the navy pharmacists that ran it and having one of their 'Yorkie' brews, tea that you could stand the spoon in unaided, when someone bumped into him jarring his shoulder.

Arcs of pain shot through him and he took a deep breath biting hard on the agony. He spun round ready for an angry outburst, his face already twisting in anger and his mind running through a full repertoire of scathing comments but the words caught in his throat.

"Sorry Sirs didn't see yew, I ain't got used to these extra legs yet." The lad said with a thick Brummy accent as he looked down at his crutches. "I keep looking down to make sure I don't stick one in an 'ole again."

He laughed cheerfully as he hopped on his right foot, the other was missing up to just below the knee and his right eye was bandaged. A chest bandage which was already staining red with a pinned label of Mne 'Paul Carson' completed the bandaging ensemble, and perched on his head was the ubiquitous green beret of a bootneck.

"Caught it in the shoulder." He said, indicating the bandages. And then as if realising that didn't explain the rest of the damage.

"Fooking Skyhawk strafed us and I caught a ricochet off a fooking boulder. It spun me round and I stood on a fooking land mine. Whar a fooking pillock eh?" He laughed again and headed further into the ward looking for his bed.

Then over his shoulder he added.

"I'm seriously chuffed gents. I just found a mate in 42' who's got the same sized feet as me and he's lost 'is left foot. We're going down town when we get home and buying a pair of shoes together. Brill eh? I'd 'ate to chuck one away each bloody time."

The young marine had been a life saver for Jake. His innate and irrepressible humour coupled with a typical marine 'can do' attitude, despite horrific injuries completely overwhelmed Jake's

157

self-absorbed depression and made him see how selfish and foolish he was being.

Pete and John behind the counter remarked on the change that had occurred over the next couple of days before they said goodbye to him when it was Jake's turn to go home.

Such a demonstration that there was always someone worse off than you had had the necessary effect. They were so alike, the 'Andys' of this world.

Andy nudged Jake. "You-hoo, earth calling Jake. Seems I've been talking to myself for the last five minutes or so. I said, is there anything for me and the boys to do or do you want us to go straight down to Little Cayman?"

Jake returned to the present and thought for a moment.

"No Andy, after our sudden celebrity status I need to Skype the PM on Grand Cayman which I need to do from the ship; I expect Andrew could be subjected to all sorts of subtle and not so subtle pressures too, poor bastard. However I will be staying with Sophie at the hotel overnight, so I want a team watching the place whilst all of us are there in case any unwelcome visitors arrive."

Jake fixed him with one of his no nonsense stares.

"I also want you to renew your acquaintance with the MPP chief on the islands when you get there, you two need to be thick as thieves and have rock solid communications."

He didn't have to add that you can't be too careful, Andy Evans had managed over the years, throughout Jake's meteoric rise in the business community, to get him into what Andy called 'a security conscious state'. Now it was second nature.

Later as they shared the boat over to *Bismarck,* Simon briefed Jake about the repeated Customs and Police visitors. Jake was unconcerned, they were technically correct and had the right to search the ship keel to topmast if they desired every time *Bismarck* left Bermudan territorial waters and returned.

That they had chosen so to do was probably because noses had been bent out of joint by being told by the UK foreign office, however delicately, to please cooperate.

He would have to organise a visit to see the Island's Governor tomorrow evening if possible; he suspected that this repeated customs visit was his way of showing annoyance at Foreign Office interference and telling Jake who was local boss.

Still, he mused, I couldn't have done with a flat refusal for an anchorage, so I had no choice. There was also the matter of what would be landing at Wade International in a couple of days.

Most people did not realise that whilst Bermuda had the third oldest continuous parliament in the world, the Sovereign appointed Governor still controlled the police, internal security, foreign affairs and defence, making Jake's ship and its visit definitely within his purview.

Jake settled into his chair as he waited for his Skype call to go through, knowing that the next two days would be hard work, but he knew that it was vital to test certain systems before arrival in the Caymans.

The real trials on the new munitions and fire control systems would only start once they got down to Grand Cayman but there was still the cooling by pre-wetting system and infra-red testing afterwards, as well as the effectiveness of their radar absorbent composite paint. The drones would be busy.

Still, it was always good to have a ship worked up to speed. He would always remember the somewhat acerbic conversation with his opposite number from the *Glasgow*, after the *Sheffield* incident.

There had been a Warfare Officers briefing on the flagship and he had attended as junior to *Coventry's* PWO. Over a coffee the man had introduced himself, he'd been almost apologetic for asking what had happened, Jake thought.

He recalled that it was almost as if someone had flicked a switch. The compartment went quiet as everyone wanted to hear his answer.

'I almost wish they'd fired at us.' The silly man had said. 'I've never seen a more completely worked-up ships company than ours. Sorry, I didn't mean to infer anything, it's just that I have bags of confidence in them.' Jake had been pleased with his restrained reply, as he recalled.

He'd kicked off with. 'That has got to be one of the most foolish comments I have ever heard.' He felt an arm on his sleeve as his new boss gently restrained him. But he was not going to let that one settle.

'Actually I wasn't on watch when it happened, I was laid on my bunk reading so I haven't really got a clue what actually happened. Action stations sounded and about ten seconds later we were hit I think, but I can tell you that our ship's company was on top line. Yes, clearly either someone or something fucked up to let us take the hit, but the real problem was one of design."

They looked askance. He took a deep breath and went on.

'Ships have to be able to take damage. Some plonker decided we only needed a single saltwater main running fore and aft so when the missile flukily cut that in two, we were pretty well stuffed. No redundancy. By the time we got alternate pumps rigged, the fire from the burning missile fuel had taken hold and that was that, it didn't even bloody explode.'

The conversational buzz restarted and everyone studiously avoided looking in their direction. But Jake knew that the idiot *had* meant to infer something really, and had never forgotten it.

Glasgow didn't have much luck herself he recalled, the day after that meeting she'd been paired with a Seawolf armed type 22 to patrol Middle Bay.

The 22 had saved her bacon by taking out three Skyhawks when *Glasgow*'s Sea Dart had failed at the crunch moment. As they were pulling back the next wave came in and the Type 22's Seawolf became confused unable to lock on to the low flying target and reset itself. The Argentines managed to get a bomb into *Glasgow* which luckily passed straight through the engine room without exploding, but she was sent home leaving Jake's new ship, *Coventry*, all on its own as the fleet long range AA defence.

*

The following morning back on *Bismarck,* Reiner was reading the overnight signal traffic. The day watch was having breakfast whilst the night watch was writing up its logs and making notes for their opposites, when the whole of St George's harbour shook and echoed to the deep basso profundo sound of a big ship's foghorn.

Again and again it sounded, until people were driven to the upper decks to see what the hell was going on. Coming into the cruise ship berth was a monster, the new Holland America Line *Leerdam* to be precise; all ninety nine thousand tons of her, and lining the sides were hundreds, no thousands, of people, ship's company and passengers alike.

Jake stood next to Reiner as they looked over the short stretch of water to the massive vessel. More incredibly to the stunned sailors looking out over *Bismarck's* sides, they were waving and cheering in between the massive reverberations of the horn.

Clearly the *Leerdam's* crew had identified the mysterious, old fashioned looking, warship as the one which had gone to the rescue of the cruiseliner *Kristianstaadt* in the Mediterranean, and even more clearly, both passengers and crew were saying thank you in the best and most emphatic way they could.

Bismarck was tiny compared to this leviathan, but whilst this ship was itself bigger than the *Kristianstaadt*, it brought home to the watching sailors just how many lives had been on the line just a week ago.

Quietly they watched, occasionally waving in sort of shy acknowledgement, as the giant reversed course in its own length and then slid sideways into its berth, still occasionally sounding that incredible foghorn. A great way to start another day of exercises, and wake up every one for forty miles around, thought Jake as he gave a last wave and returned below.

Monday May 14th 2018

Off Eastern Bermuda

Senior Lieutenant Yuri Nekrasov again scanned the instruments of his Tupelev TU-22M3 long range maritime strike bomber (NATO 'Backfire C') one more time. He nodded to Sergei Obyekov, his co-pilot who was checking the engineer's panel.

"Just about time Sergei."

The two massive Kusnetsov NK25 Turbofans were purring along steadily and with wings at max spread they pushed the supersonic bomber at a sedate, fuel conserving cruising speed of five hundred and sixty mph.

He flicked a switch to connect him to the communal intercom.

"All ready in the back you two?"

He waited for the answer, eyes automatically scanning instruments and having received a chorus of 'Rogers' he flicked back to the 'buddy' circuit with his co-pilot.

"OK old friend let's set it up."

Sergei began the arming checklist, but part of his mind still bothered about the absence of a venerable Tu-95D reconnaissance plane out in front guiding them or a submarine, as would be normal. They hadn't enough fuel for a prolonged search, so the estimated position had better be accurate.

The checklist complete and unflawed they settled again. Both were fully accustomed to the frightening sight of the sea flashing by a hundred feet below at over 560 miles an hour as they roared in towards their boost point. Then, they would pop-up on re-heat to 10,000 feet and activate their forward and down looking Leninets PN-AD radar prior to activating the attack system, if they had a target. With any luck they should pick up the contact and be able to launch immediately.

"Increase to full military power and sweep those wings Sergei." Said Nekrasov, as he scanned again and prepared to take them up.

"All right everyone listen up. On my mark." Sergei intoned, the tension just discernible in his voice.

"3..2..1. Burners on, climb now." He almost shouted over the open intercom.

His back was pressed against the seat as Yuri pulled back on the yoke, launching them towards 10000 feet as quickly as possible. Even on burners, being heavily loaded it would take nearly three minutes to climb the two miles to ten thousand feet. "5000.....5500.....6000 . . . ."

The count was interrupted by a quiet voice over the intercom.

"Markov here Captain, I have Sierra band radar transmissions on ESM at 220 degrees, we are not detected yet I think, frequency is shifting throughout the spectrum and the pulse repetition is very high. Range guess, 150 miles."

"Roger Markov, keep listening." He looked over at his co-pilot.

"A bit further out than we thought Sergei, eh?"

Sergei was not taken in by his friends' relaxed air. This would be the first real attack for both of them.

"9000...9500....10000. Burner off, speed 1300 knots, standby to activate the attack system on contact. Weapons pre-set to command guidance! Radar active now!"

There followed a heavy, tense silence for about five seconds.

"Sorokin here. Small surface contact at 223, range 105 miles." Chimed in the fourth member of the Backfire's crew.

"It is the emitter Sir." Said Markov. "They have us. They're tracking. Holy shit the S-band has switched to an even higher PRF Sir, fuck me it must be one per second on sector scan now. They'll be able to be able to draw a pimple by pimple picture of us; I can feel my balls shrivelling at this range with the power output from that thing!"

"Calm down Markov, keep the reports coming, remember your training."

"Yes Sir." Replied a chastened Markov. "There is second transmitter, same type this one on the lower PRF and it appears on a full scan Sir."

"Roger, that Markov. Do we have a lock?" Asked Sergei.

"Locked and fed into the weapons Sir along with the INS data."

"Roger that. Releasing centreline missile now!" Intoned the now calm voice of Sergei Obyekov.

Nekrasov was ready for the sudden lightening of the load as Sergei released the thirty seven foot, 5000kg monster from its recessed position, snug beneath the belly of the *Backfire*. He regained his trim almost immediately and turned slightly west towards the next drop point.

"Command guidance accepted Sir."

Reported Sorokin quietly, with awe in his voice.

"Taking it eastwards." Said Sorokin as he took control of the missile also a little in awe at what they were doing.

In his five years of flying he'd never 'dropped' for a live target either.   He hadn't thought that he would ever have to since the men in the Kremlin weren't communist any more and everyone just wanted to earn some money instead of changing the world.

Nekrasov straightened the aircraft on its new course.

"Port pylon first if you please Sergei, anytime now."

Sergei reached over to the panel and selected the portside underwing missile release.   The two underwing missiles were located close to the fuselage at strong points to minimise the destabilisation effect of the weight change on release.   Even so the aircraft lurched slightly to starboard as the heavy missile dropped away before igniting.

"Coming left, ready for the starboard launch."

"Command guidance accepted on two. Said Markov.

"I have it. Steering twenty degrees to the west."

Intoned Sorokin, now clearly concentrating on steering the monsters to attack from different directions before he let them go on their terminal homing settings.   No trace of excitement now.

"Ready for starboard release. Now."

Said Sergei, with a little relief evident in his tone.

Suddenly the aircraft was responsive again as the last missile dropped away on its one minute forty second, one hundred mile journey.

"Command guidance accepted on three. Taking her up now. All birds are tracking nicely."

Sorokin was now the most important man in the crew, the others mere chauffeurs as he guided the missiles toward their target from separate directions.

At this point they would normally let the missiles use their own radar and would dive back towards the sea and safety. Instead Nekrasov relaxed slightly and throttled back to loiter, beginning a forty degree zigzag that would keep the missiles on radar but reduce the aircraft's approach rate as they watched them into target. Crazy world, he thought, pity the poor devils on the receiving end.

15.45 Monday 14th May 2018

Bismarck exercising off Bermuda

Chief Petty Officer OPs, 'Taff' Elias was tired. His head and eyes ached from hours of exercises and staring at the array of screens in front of him. There were three identical work stations, for want of a better word, in the operations room, each could be used for general operations or tasked for a specific one.

When Taff had first seen his new OPs room he had been more than a little surprised and mystified. Instead of wall to wall machines and displays, as in other OPs rooms he'd worked in, this one was relatively empty.

The clutter had been replaced by the three stations or focus points, one each on the port and starboard sides, angled outward slightly, and one in the centre a little forward of the other two. They all faced approximately forward and together they formed an arc across the almost square compartment.

Behind them was the overall command area with its holographic representation of the battle area and the Captain's position with its associated chair and screens. He faced the port bow with the holographic display to his right so his screens did not obstruct his 'God' view of the battle arena, which could be adjusted to any size out to five hundred miles.

They looked like a cross between an aircraft simulator, and an expensive arcade game, with multiple 'touch' LED screens angled and centred around a larger main display and there was even a quick release lap strap for each of the special contouring chairs with attached footrests to keep you comfortable!

Now that he had become used to them his earlier reluctance had turned first to respect, then admiration for the mind that had devised the system.

On taking over a watch you sat yourself into the automatic contouring chair, a little like a dentist's chair with neck, head and leg support. Like a dentist's you pulled a hinged tray around in front, this was the work console and it fastened just like the lock-bar on a theme park ride; after that you logged on to the system and got your permissions. You then had in front of you a 21 inch central LED screen with three 14 inch screens in a horizontal line above it. Ranged down the sides were a series of selector keys, track balls, mice and stylus pointers. Directly in front was the small desk area with embedded shaped keyboard and wrist rests on the tray.

It had been decided that only one person need be locked in place on duty routinely with another OPs room staff member merely present, running maintenance, calibration checks and making the tea/coffee etc. and swapping every so often. If the person manning the station needed to leave the chair for any reason, the number two had to be in place before he unlocked so there was continuous monitoring.

The screens could display all of the information necessary to monitor the ship's situation and the keyboard and stylus pointer were alternate input options for the operation of the touch screens. All methods could access the commands required to fight the ship, steer it or set sensors and defensive measures.

Most of the ship's systems were automatic, so most of the time a watch would be spent supervising the ship, watching out for itself. It was theoretically possible for one man to run and fight the whole ship from any of the work stations, but in reality for a solely surface threat, the Gunnery Officer dealt with the main and secondary armament with the OPs team designating the targets and maintaining the overall picture.

There was a similar setup in the Main Gunnery Control Centre (MGCC) above the bridge where Lt Julius Kopf sat with his number two. In effect it was a standby OPs room in case the main one was knocked out. The MGCC need only be manned at action stations but Kopf and his partner in crime spent most of their time up there. In harbour with a good internet signal, the thud of gunfire could be heard as they played World of Warships on their consoles.

With a solely airborne threat the OPs room had overall control of all gunnery systems and the Gunnery Officer and his mate monitored ammunition expenditure and re-supply. In a combined action they split to their surface and air roles with a fully manned OPs room picking up all the extras.

If action stations sounded, the OPs team was boosted by Simon McClelland who acted as Principal Warfare Officer as well as First Lieutenant and took a spare station. The Captain manned the command area with the holographic display. If required the spare OPs number could pick up the last work station and another crewman would be drafted in as runner.

Taff was near the end of his watch now, in about fifteen minutes Inonu Kyne San, his Sierra Leone descended opposite number would come and relieve him. He sighed; he'd have to chase down Brendan the mad medic for some more headache pills before crashing out in his pit.

Everything was pretty quiet at the moment, the last of the work up exercises had just wound up and after the 'wash up' they'd be turning back towards Bermuda and a day off.

He heard a 'chirp' from the ESM array and turned back to his displays. He pulled the Air picture on to his third screen displacing the stores list he'd been looking at, and re-ran the last minute on his ESM picture at speed. A weak radar transmission to the north, possible K-band had registered briefly.

He boosted ESM up onto one of his smaller screens whilst bringing the Air picture to the main screen. He yawned mightily as he studied the Air picture for a moment. Commercial traffic to the north, plenty of transponders. He eliminated commercial transponders from the clutter to see if there was anything left that might have briefly activated what could only be a military radar. Nothing.

The main radar antenna above the MGCC was on an intermittent setting at present, which meant that it became active for short bursts on a semi-random timer basis, with this one on standard settings, ten seconds active would give five full rotations with simultaneous band changes top to bottom of the range then the whole picture, surface and air, would be updated and displayed before him.

Gone was the glowing line sweeping around a dark screen that most people associated with radar from Hollywood films, instead, the computer translated the information into a different kind of picture, with a set of standardised symbols representing ships, aircraft and submarines. It also colour coded as to where they were friendly, unknown or hostile, the only change you actually saw on this one was when it refreshed briefly every few seconds. When it was fully active the updates were seamless and immediate.

He returned his attention to the central screen display momentarily. Another 'chirp' and a flashing screen border dragged his eyes back upwards to the ESM picture, a second racket, or unknown transmitter had appeared. At this point he switched on his personal audio notifications, these would inform him of anything important while his attention was possibly elsewhere; he'd customised it to use various famous voices programmed into the system.

Contemplating the intermittent ESM contact, he wondered if US *Orions* still flew out of Bermuda's airfield, it had been a US airbase for years, perhaps they still call in occasionally? That could account for it, he thought to himself as he studied the air picture again.

Directly in front of him a yellow V shaped icon appeared with a vector line pointing towards *Bismarck*, at the same time the disembodied voice of Joanna Lumley informed him that there was a new radar contact.

"Taff there's a Bogey at 005 degrees, range 105 miles and low."

He immediately commenced the standard procedures for a possible hostile contact, might as well play the game, he thought to himself as he activated the forward and after radar antennae.

Setting the forward unit to high pulse repetition frequency (PRF) with sector search centred on the contact, and the after unit to air search standard, full sweep, he brought his detection systems to life.

The computer, at this point, was automatically sifting the database looking for a match with the contact based on all recorded tracks they'd come across up to now. This was mainly civilian traffic encountered on the way across the Med and down to here; so not that much. There had been some military traffic near Sevastopol and passing through the Bosporus but not a great deal, so he wasn't expecting a match.

It now 'pinged' to indicate the search had finished but before he could say 'what is it Joanna', expecting the beautiful voice to say 'I have no matches Taff', Elias's work station went berserk. His ESM screen lit up and Judi Dench informed him in an angry voice that they were now being scanned by an active radar, type, Nato code 'Downbeat' which had locked onto them. This started a chain reaction.

The Combat Management System (CMS) was programmed to recognise certain threat profiles and take pre-set actions if they occurred. Consequently, having decided that a 'Downbeat' (Leninets PN-AD) radar in these circumstances posed a threat, Tom Jones in a loud and irritated voice, prompted Taff to sound the Air Action Stations alarm. He then informed Taff that he had activated the automatic fire control systems.

As Taff debated whether or not to sound actions stations, another beep sounded and Joanna in a sexy voice said '*Vampire, Vampire, Vampire*'. The central screen border began to flash red with the word 'Vampire' in black along the top border.

"Fuck." Said Taff and nearly wet himself as he punched the Air Action Stations alarm then sat back as the world went crazy around him.

Vampire was the code for 'hostile' missile detected'. Taff felt the hairs rise on the back of his neck and a chill in the pit of his stomach as his tired brain absorbed the shock. Something had most definitely detached from the contact, but before he could think further, two more events intruded.

The computer had now recognised the first contact's image and his top left LED screen was showing a rotating aircraft outline and Judi Dench was saying 'It's a 'Tupelev TU-22M3' Nato codename 'Backfire C, Taff', its role is maritime strike.

Then when he said 'Judi stop' into his mike she went on to her next nugget of information. She listed its weapon loads and flying data and had started to repeat it all when he said 'Judi stop' and she shut up.

Barely had he time to absorb the information when a double 'beep' dragged his eyes back to the central screen who's border now flashed the message 'Vampire x 2' and Judi started up again.

"Taff, another Vampire detached from that TU-22M3 I told you about."

"Fuck a Stoat." He cursed out loud.

"John boy, some bastard's attacking us." He heard the clunk as Urwin locked into his station. Taff's fingers tripped across the buttons of the right-hand panel as he confirmed the ship's defences were on 'auto' and told Judi to shut up again.

"John you have ESM and ECM. Watch over the AKs as they wind up and switch the autoloader to active." He quickly issued orders.

The right ear piece of his headset was filled with repeated requests for information from the bridge and the Captain. Drawing a deep breath he responded.

He spoke into the mike. "Link Captain and Bridge." The mike clicked in response as the connection was made.

"We have two (another beep) correction three, fast moving Vampires incoming from a Backfire C. Vampires are designated contacts Vampire two, Vampire three and Vampire four. Pushing now to bridge repeaters." He took another breath as he touched each in turn giving the data.

"Vampire two bearing 048 range 81 miles course is 184, altitude 15000, climbing; speed is Mach 2.7. Vampire three bearing 040 range 84 miles course is 247 altitude is 12000, climbing; speed is Mach 2.6. Vampire four bearing 044 range 90 miles course is 220 altitude is 11000, climbing; speed Mach 2.5. No emissions, repeat no emissions. Suspect command guidance. Computer indicates profile match with the Raduga Kh-22 missiles, aka Nato AS-4 Kitchen. Time to first engagement zone ninety seconds on contact Vampire two. Systems are on auto."

He looked to the holographic display and noted the missile tracks and their projected paths had now appeared.

Lieutenant Julius Kopf had the watch, the Captain had just left the bridge to return to his quarters when the alarms went. It was down to him now, no time to wonder who? Why? Or even how? Just time to do, hopefully.

He studied the bridge repeater screen. Three missiles on command guidance, moving on three different bearings, a fan attack then with a near simultaneous arrival. He adjusted the earpiece of his headset while his brain went into overdrive, then glanced at the bridge repeater again and snapped out a request.

"Wind?"

"Negligible Sir." Came the reply from Buller at the con.

'Sheisse' thought Kopf, the chaff won't be as effective, some drift was useful to fill out the bloom of aluminium foil. Still, better to do something rather than do nothing.

The damned things were on command guidance but at some point they would be let loose and then they could be decoyed. Better to be slightly oblique to as many of them as possible he decided, so the maximum number of weapons could bear.

"Emergency port helm, steer 220, sound the brace alarm. When we get to two five zero go to full ahead and leave the port wheel on." He ordered.

"Aye Sir. Emergency port helm on." Replied Buller at the helm.

Kopf spoke into his mike. "Shipwide." Then the connection click.

"Do you hear there, we have incoming missiles. This is not an exercise, repeat this is not an exercise."

As the ship wide announcement blasted out, Buller belted himself into the chair and completed the procedure for an emergency port turn, the Steerpods could rotate to 90 degrees or more but at speed it wasn't as effective as turning them to forty five degrees initially then increasing up to sixty degrees. The pods themselves were computer controlled and although Buller moved the control stick all the way to the left and held it there, the pods would only go as far as the computer calculated their maximum effect. If the brace warning hadn't been given people and things tended to fall over and fall off.

Kopf next spoke to OPs.

"Ready the chaff launchers. Port and aft patterns but hold for now."

That would make them appear much longer to two of the missiles and give *Bismarck* a chance to turn to port behind one of the blooms.

Now, better turn to run directly away from the one coming straight at us, which would leave one coming in on each quarter the best point of defence for this ship.

"Now at 220 Sir, helm midships." Buller reported, and another ten seconds had passed.

Lieutenant Commander Simon McClelland had just taken his seat in the OPs room, luckily he'd been on his way there when the action stations alarm sounded. He was busy organising his displays as Kopf's voice came through with the course and speed change and the chaff seeding order.

He felt the ship heel right over as the powerful gas turbines carried out their instructions and wound up to full power. Few people ashore could understand the electrical power that engines like these could generate. They could take *Bismarck's* 3500 tons from standing start to thirty five knots in almost the same number of seconds, you really could feel the acceleration.

McClelland's mind became like ice, as he absorbed the information, he was in his element now. Gone was the chirpy, easy going character that most knew, in its place was a mind as cool and as calculating as the machines it controlled. He assessed the situation in a two second glance. He was now in command of the ship and informed the bridge accordingly.

Kopf's decision on the course was spot on but he ordered eight knots off the top speed, they were not going to outrun a Mach 3+ missile and although *Bismarck* was a very stable platform, the eight knot lower speed would reduce any vibration and movement further and ensure the stabilisers were at maximum efficiency, accuracy was what would count now.

He spoke to Taff and Big John.

"Elias, you take the 76's and Urwin you take the 630's. And Taff, for fuck's sake turn the voice to the default please it spooks the shit out of me hearing those voices in here and spoils my appreciation of those two fine ladies." He added, doling out the weapons systems. He retained the overall radar picture himself.

Bismarck's two antennae were the Saab Sea Giraffe AMB or agile multi-beam radar. The system could track up to 1000 targets simultaneously in its various modes, using the full range of S-band. It managed an astonishing one full rotation per second when at peak, so the picture refresh rate was near real time. Not only did they have the Saab radar but the Saab CMS had come with the package enabling them to tailor it to their needs.

Right now Elias was checking the 76mm systems, effectively one in each quadrant but with a major overlap in their firing arcs, he instructed the system to load the new test munitions, Proximity fused, pre-Fragmented, Directional, High Explosive Canister (PFDHEC) or 'PC' for short.

This new ammunition was ideally to be fired only at targets that could be engaged head on which would be the case when all the missiles got within range but it wouldn't be automatically the case for aircraft.   Inside each shell 1.5kg of sharp edged Tungsten alloy cubes was packed around an explosive charge with a laser proximity fuse to explode it at a range of 10 yards from its target. Instead of the spherical explosion of a normal shell, this one exploded like the charge from a shotgun, forward and spreading out in a cone shape.

Elias completed the checks and ordered them to load HE until the round 15 stage then 'PC' to give the fire control system time to adjust, at 85 rounds per minute per barrel that wouldn't take long to reach.

If the missiles managed to get through to three miles, then the pairs of AK630M2 30mm Gatling guns, again in each quadrant, would join in and he pre-set them to 2000 rounds per minute per Gatling, a staggering 4000 rounds per minute per double mounting.

They could actually fire much faster but the ready use ammunition could only hold 4000 rounds of these heavy slugs. He didn't bother with the eight big AK130 guns because they hadn't any proximity fused rounds for them in the magazines at the moment.

McClelland busied himself organising the chaff patterns and jamming frequencies he would use when the missiles switched on their active homers for the final approach.

The computer had supplied the identification of the in-flight missiles, AS-4 Kitchens were a truly massive missile at 5800kg or 12,000lbs, looking rather like 'Thunderbird 1'. They'd always been jokingly referred to as the 'kitchen sink', it had seemed funny before but not now when three of them were targeted at *Bismarck*. Curiously, they had a much greater range than they'd been fired from, that was something to think about later.   His analytical mind went to work as the seconds ticked away.

Lt Cdr Scotnikov had been as surprised as anyone else when the action stations alarm had sounded without the usual precautionary 'for exercise'. He had been a little annoyed that

Kopf hadn't followed exercise protocol and had made a mental note to speak to the First Lieutenant about it since he'd been calibrating one of the Steerpod motors, a delicate operation at the best of times. Around the ship Kopf's quick broadcast after the action stations alarms, had galvanised any who'd thought it was just another exercise.

As Kopf finished his short announcement, Scotnikov was already speeding towards the engine room as fast as he could. Elsewhere, men rushed to their action stations wondering what in hell's name was going on. From the damage control teams to the medical staff, and first aid party, everyone switched onto 'auto' and left the worrying to some distant part of the mind.

As Bren the Medical Chief legged it forward to take charge of the first aid party mustering under the bridge, he analysed his thoughts. Training, he decided, was what kept you moving, stopped you freezing like a rabbit in the headlight's glare. You seemed to operate on two distinct and totally different levels simultaneously. While one part of you was screaming silently in disbelief, the other part just carried on.

The Doctor was less sanguine, the incident with the cruise liner hadn't really put him in danger, but now Lawrence Cribb Surgeon Lieutenant, wondered whether he had made a wise choice joining König Industries and volunteering for this new project.

Throughout the ship the fear and tension mounted as the seconds ticked away. Who the hell was attacking them and why for Christ's sake? The real problem for most of them, was not being able to do anything. It was a case of waiting to see what happened. Everything was in the hands of a few men and some very complex equipment.

Jake had returned to the bridge, he sat in the command chair, outwardly calm whilst monitoring events on the chair arm displays. He didn't want to cramp Reiner's style by being in the OPs room as well this time, besides if they took a hit it was best if the two commanders were not together.

The seconds ticked down. Privately he relived the awful last seconds before the hit on the *Sheffield*, then his terrifying impotence on *Coventry* as he realised he'd not even get to his action station before it was all over one way or another.

McClelland looked away from his viewing screens briefly and across to Reiner, now in the command chair. Damn it! Has the man no nerves? He thought. Reiner appeared engrossed in tweaking his displays without the slightest hint of nerves. A drop of perspiration trickled down Simon's forehead as he returned his attention to the rapidly approaching threat, he cuffed it away with an apparently casual swipe before anyone noticed.

On the bridge the lookouts and helmsman sneaked looks at Jake, they noted the apparent lack of concern and took some comfort as all men do in time of crisis. A tinny voice sounded out loud on the bridge speakers and softly in the right ears of those who wore headsets.

"Twenty seconds to first engagement zone."

Four more seconds passed and the starboard 76's began firing to meet the missile coming in from the west at extreme range, thumping out shells with a double crunch at a rate of more than one per second.

Jake was peering to starboard through his viewer, watching for a sight of the nearest missile, using the target data from the OPs room to line up. He jumped slightly when the remaining 76mm turrets burst into rapid and violent life on the port side as the next missile came into extreme range.

The last missile had climbed to above 60,000 feet, the maximum vertical detection range, and would be nosing over even now to finish in a Mach 5 terminal dive.

There was something truly unnerving about a five ton missile screaming down at you, traveling at 3800 miles per hour or more, if you thought in kilometres per hour it was worse at over 6000!

The noise level throughout the ship, despite the heavy soundproofing, rose to an unbelievable staccato thunder. Jake had just focused on his missile, amid a forest of black harmless looking puff-balls, when it exploded with a titanic yellow flash that made him cringe instinctively even though it was still miles away.

"*Vampire* two is splashed, *Vampire* three is active and *Vampire* four has been reacquired in its terminal dive and is active."

Intoned the calm voice of the CHOPs, telling them the remaining two missiles had switched on their own radar and were now in their terminal phase, independent of the bomber.

"Launching programmed chaff patterns NOW."

Said Elias.

Another set of thuds as the aft launcher joined the port launcher in thumping out nine canisters of chaff each.

Jake was looking to port through his viewer when round number 15 was fired by the port quarter turret. The result was spectacular, to say the least, as the shell detonated 10 yards in front of its target.

The cubes of Tungsten were propelled forward and out from the exploding shell at nearly three thousand miles an hour, almost instantly encountering the missile's head and because they were slightly off angle, the upper body too.

They passed unchanged through the metal skin, almost without pause, hundreds of them practically dissolving the missile's body, until they reached the liquid rocket fuel tanks. At that point the missile simply disintegrated.

Astern, the high missile had closed to the three mile point as it dived steeply towards the ship. With a sound like tearing linen, all four AK630 mounts began firing and streams of bright green tracer rose up to meet it. The fire control system measured the 'miss distance' of each round from each gun and made minute adjustments to correct the aim.

"Port thirty."

Ordered Simon, as he turned the ship behind the chaff clouds hoping to make the missile's target appear much bigger. If he could do that it would hopefully miss when its on-board seeker halved the length of the radar image and then aimed for the middle of the target.

"ECM active Urwin." He ordered, and Big John switched on the jamming suite which should fool the missile's radar return by filling its sensors with 'white noise', as lasers seared any TV seeker and directional microwave emitters fired so much energy up on a narrow beam that it would fry any infrared detectors.

Everyone seemed to hold their breath praying for a hit as the arcs of green light lanced upward towards the falling missile. There were now eight 76mm and eight Gatling guns firing at that missile and Jake sat wondering how on earth it had survived so far and what damage the bloody thing would do if it did hit. Just seconds only now before impact.

Then it exploded in another of those blinding yellow flashes that seared the eyeballs. The guns ceased their clatter and returned to their rest positions with streamers of smoke drifting clear of the barrels and sooty muzzles.

Silence reigned momentarily, broken first by the inimitable Kipper Herring whose voice came clearly over the main broadcast from the damage control centre down aft, he'd obviously left his mike open and had been watching through the viewer down there.

"Bugger this for a game of sailors I reckon I'll just have to nip down to me cabin and change me 'shreddies' now." He said, referring to the matelot's term for underpants.

Gales of relieved laughter swept through the ship as they realised it was all over, for now at least. Jake smiled to himself, they'd been tested in the most realistic way and come through with flying colours.

He would wait until they were back alongside before confessing that it was he who had contracted the *Backfire* to shoot at them and that there were no warheads on the missiles; in addition they had been instructed to detonate if they got to two hundred yards from the ship.

Jake had set it all up before leaving Russia with Leonid Gasparin, a contact from the Titanium purchase years ago; he was now the Admiral in command of the Russian Northern fleet to whom the Backfire and its crew belonged.

He'd paid out a small fortune for this test and called in many favours to get clearance, because the *Backfire* would be landing at Wade International in Bermuda very soon and that would cause a bit of a stir.

As soon as it was on the ground it would be guarded by his own security team and members of the Bermuda regiment, since government house had vetoed the Russians bringing their own security team.

Evening, Monday 14th May 2018

Bismarck, St George's Harbour, Bermuda

Jake put his pen down, yawned mightily and leaned back in his chair massaging his eyes. He checked his watch again, 19:00; at this rate he was going to be very late meeting Sophie for dinner and thereby on the receiving end of some serious 'looks'.

He checked the completed report on his desk one last time and glanced at the pile of duplicate statements next to it. Damn all bullies and thugs worldwide, he thought to himself.

The police had left only half an hour ago, at least they hadn't insisted on arresting any of his men until they'd read the statements and conferred with Government House. He stood up angrily and went to his drinks cabinet, pouring himself a small Lagavulin he reviewed the events as he knew them, and the actions taken.

It had all started after the pep talk and confession he'd made on the quarterdeck, after returning from the supposed hostile missile attack. He *had* been a little worried at the reaction of the crew, he hadn't even told Reiner about the upcoming attack let alone the rest of the crew.

They had performed superbly though, the radar, fire control and gunnery systems seemed excellent. Then it was confession time. He'd wondered at the best way of putting it and decided to come clean on their return to harbour.

The speculation on the identity of their assailant and the reasons why, had been rife as soon as the shock had worn off, not surprising really, you didn't get three massive missiles fired at you without warning every day of the week –thank God!

Jake had asked Reiner to muster everyone on the quarterdeck once the awnings were set up. Then he'd walked out there, every man's eyes on him. With his back to turret 'Dora', the aftermost of the main gun turrets, he had addressed the crew.

"Your work–up and training is now over, clearly this ship's company is a great team and I congratulate you and your Captain."

There were a few cheers from the back so he held up a hand to still them.

"I know speculation has been rife since the attack this afternoon so I will first dispel the wonderful theories that you will have come up with. No doubt me bonking Mr Putin's wife came near the top of the causes list."

He waited for the laughter to subside before continuing.

"The *Backfire* that attacked us, did so on my instructions."

He waited for the clamour to die down. The actual cost of 'borrowing' a Backfire and three missiles had been £175,000 plus fuel, all quite easily arranged in the modern Russian republic if you knew who to see, with £10,000 for each crewmember and the admiral.

"The missiles it fired did not have warheads and were proximity fused for 200 yards should we fail to knock them down. I realise that even without warheads those things are dangerous so I owe you all an apology for that. Now I would like to tell you why I did it."

He took another breath as he mentally framed the words he needed.

"In all the navies that we served can anyone remember being really frightened on an exercise?

He looked around the faces for any indication and got a series of negative head shakes.

"Did anyone ever convince you that you were in danger from the Blue force or the Orange force or whatever? Did any of them have a 100% feeling of realism?"

He went on remorselessly.

"For most of us the worst that failure would have brought is a bad report or a reprimand. There is truly only one circumstance in which a fighting man can be judged and that, as you must know, is in action."

He held his arms out to them all.

"So I apologise to all of you unreservedly for making you fear for your lives and especially to Kipper for his ruined shreddies."

He waited for the spontaneous burst of laughter to die down and watched Kipper grinning with indignant embarrassment.

"Seriously gentlemen, we all know that ships, even the most modern, are vulnerable to surprise missile attack from just over the horizon. That doesn't mean to say that it's impossible to defend against one, it just means that those in OPs must always be conscious of the threat and ready to act. They are our eyes and ears when we are at sea. Your Captain and I will never criticise a false alarm." He paused to let that sink in. Jake never wanted anyone to be reluctant to press the action stations alarm.

"I would like to congratulate the OPs team and Gunnery department for their splendid effort this afternoon, a case of beer

each for the lads and a bottle of port for Reiner, Simon and Julius
–whether they like port or not."

There were a laughs and a few 'hear, hears' and some gentle
barracking. Jake waited until it had diminished.

"In addition, I have booked the entire company into the
Rosewood Resort Hotel just down the road at Tucker's Point;
wives and children are already there."

More whoops and cheers.

"We shall have a couple of days of sun and sea before we set
off to the Caymans later in the week. There will be a formal
dinner tomorrow night with a free bar and we will have some
surprise guests to greet." He waited again for the murmuring to
still.

"Additionally all of the OPs team and spouses are dining out
tonight with my wife and I at the Tempest Bistro in St George's.
Lastly, your Captain has granted free gangway for single men in
thirty minutes, for the rest of you, there will be a bus, I couldn't
let you go or your wives and partners would kill me!"

Well that bit had gone OK, he thought to himself. After the
presentation he'd asked Reiner to give both watches leave and
had Andy Evans and his people prepare to assume responsibility
for the ship when everyone who wanted to, had gone ashore.

The next thing had been when Reiner had paid him a visit
just after six that evening. He'd been cagey and had gone
through a list of routine stuff that Jake damn well knew he didn't
need to bother him with and being pressed for time he was more
abrupt than usual.

"Come on Reiner spit it out, what is it that you don't want to
tell me but must?"

Reiner had the decency to colour slightly before he began his
explanation.

"There is something else Jake, you're quite right."

"Ok, now what? Saving the worst till last eh? Come on you
know I've got a thousand things to do before we meet up with
Trudi and Sophie tonight, what's the problem Reiner?"

"OK. Last night I received a message from the German
Consul here. I did verify the origin of the message. He asked
me to meet someone this morning and it would be to our benefit
to listen to what the gentleman had to say. It was all very 'Cloak
and Dagger' -this is the correct euphemism?"

Jake nodded, intrigued.

"I met him at 6 o'clock this morning, we went for a walk
through Somers Gardens not far from here. He didn't introduce

himself or state who he worked for but I'd guess he was CIA or DIA, something like that."

"Hold on. The German Consul asked you to meet someone at six in the morning and you've waited until now to 'bother' to tell me Reiner? Sorry but I'm utterly confused now."

"Sorry Jake I did try first thing this morning if you recall but you had a call booked with the Bermuda Governor. Then of course we sailed and I was conducting the exercises you asked for and then someone tried to sink us." He added with a single raised eyebrow. "So really I didn't have an opportunity until now."

He paused there waiting for a comment from Jake but none was forthcoming. Reiner continued.

"He said to tell you and Mr McTeal that there was trouble brewing in the Caribbean and that he and his colleagues were pretty sure that the trouble was heading towards the Caymans."

He paused again and looked directly at Jake.

"He said that this contact was not official and that the whole mess appeared to be a drug related problem. He also said that for various reasons, America was unlikely to be able to offer assistance in the event of trouble so Mr McTeal had better be getting on the phone to the British if he could, asking for some kind of token force or gesture that might deter any aggressors. That's about it, except for one thing. "

Reiner observed the effect of his last words carefully, he was aware that one of Jake had a particular loathing to anything 'drug related'. In Jake's scheme of things he knew, those involved in the drugs trade hovered somewhere between pond slime and what usually got-flushed down a toilet. He also knew why Jake had a particular loathing for them.

Sophie's younger sister had died in New York three years ago after a party in which she had been slipped a drugged drink and subsequently raped and beaten by five men who were out of their brains on 'coke or crystal meth' as they said in the witness box. The trial had failed because of an irregularity with search procedures or something.

Subsequently, all five had disappeared and a veritable queue of pushers and suppliers had suddenly gone out of business permanently.

It was just coincidence perhaps that Andy Evans and several of his men had been loaned to the New York offices of König International for several months around that time. Reiner knew it was wrong but felt that he would have done the same if he'd had it within his power.

Jake sat quietly for a moment, his coffee untouched and cold on the desk before him. He was making a visible effort to separate the emotional reaction from his thinking.

"He didn't give any clues as to who was making the trouble? Or how the drugs thing was involved?"

Reiner just shook his head slowly.

"Hell Reiner we could be heading straight into a war zone or it could be nothing more than a rumour. If however this is a threat to peace in the region, and in particular to the Caymans..."

He sat lost for words for a second or two.

"The Islands have no defences to speak of. They haven't even got an army really."

He put his head in his hands for a moment and concentrated.

"Ok, let's tackle this logically. First we must warn Andrew down in the Islands, I'm sure he knows someone in London who could pull some strings and get approval for some kind of exercise or something. Belize would be happy to allow base facilities I'm sure, they welcome an occasional friendly visit now we've pulled out. Did this chap give you any idea of a time scale or even the level of threat?"

"Sorry Jake I forgot to say the last part, they think that it will start before the end of May and, we should think sooner rather than later. Also, it's not just a bunch of gun happy Colombians."

"Oh for fuck's sake, that gives us no time at all; another month or three and we could have had two ships down here."

Jake was talking more or less to himself as he searched his mind for practical things to do whilst pacing up and down by his chair. But now Reiner was puzzled.

"Jake, what did you mean in another few months we would have had two ships. What and where is the second?"

Jake stopped in mid pace and turned back to face Reiner a look of surprise on his face.

"Sorry Reiner, I shouldn't have let it slip. The second ship is nearly complete, she's due to join us down here in Septemberish, I will command her, at least for a start."

Reiner's look of mystification deepened.

"Second ship Jake? You never told me there would be a second ship, in fact you said there wouldn't be. What on earth have you built this time?"

Jake smiled at his friend's puzzlement.

"Sorry old friend. I just knew I was going to get so much shit thrown at me for building a German battleship, really, and I was correct; even people I thought were sensible have put a question mark over me since *Bismarck* sailed. That is despite them knowing my father fled Germany in 36' because he didn't like what Adolf was up to. So I decided to balance things up. Sorry Reiner, bit of a bombshell to drop on you. I had in mind a surprise return to the Caymans after mysteriously disappearing in September."

He moved back to the coffee pot on the sideboard and poured two cups.

"I always thought the Germans built the best looking ships, I mean just look at *Bismarck* or Scharnhorst. But of course the British did build one in particular which rivalled them aesthetically and it was the darling of the RN until this ship's namesake," He said, pointing at the deck. "...put her on the sea bed. So I had them design and start on *Hood*. She is six months behind *Bismarck* but everything is going fine and all the things we learned building *Bismarck* have been applied which is why it will be so much quicker."

Reiner was speechless for a moment, his mouth opened and closed but no sound came out. Finally he managed to speak.

"Jake I, I..." He petered out.

"No, this is it, definitely the last one that could be called a blast from the past anyway....honest."

Jake added with a big smile.

"Well now you know I'll put you down for helping to pick the crew as well?"

Reiner shook his head slowly.

"Jonathan Henry König, when were you going to tell me this trivial piece of information?"

Jake shrugged.

"Sorry Reiner, as I said I had kind of planned a surprise arrival when it's completed. I envisioned *Hood* sailing into the harbour at Little Cayman unannounced."

Jake sipped his coffee.

"Anyway I wish the chap you spoke to had given you more information. We can't ignore the threat but really we have no idea how serious it is or where it originates."

Reiner shrugged. "I thought he might have a spy pen or something to stick in me if I picked him up and tried to shake the answers out of him. Anyway, wonder who the 'bad' guys are? I hope to hell that this is nothing more than a bad case of CIA Paranoia. Can we get Andy Evans to use some of his contacts and see if he can find out what if anything's brewing down there?"

"Consider it done." Replied Jake.

Jake closed the reports and considered; a punch up on the jetty between a few of the crew and some stroppy ignorant Americans on a stag run should not be allowed to spoil an almost perfect week. He sat back staring at the pictures of his wife and children on the desk.

This little fracas, he considered, could be a very damaging incident if the press did their usual trick of embellishment and pot stirring.

I'll have to pay a visit to the Governor again now, he groaned mentally. He quickly checked his watch, damn! He was really late now. Dismissing thoughts of the battle on the jetty, he quickly grabbed his wallet and headed for shore.

The security guard at the gangway looked puzzled as Jake went by chuckling. He was already anticipating the shock the OPs room boys were going to get when they found that they were having dinner with the crew of the *Backfire* that had launched the missiles at them. He made a mental note to thank the Governor's secretary for smoothing the way with the Americans.

They hadn't been too keen, by all accounts, to have a 'Rooshian' *Backfire* bomber dropping in for a couple of days - albeit now unarmed. Fortunately, it transpired, Jake had coordinated things so that the *Backfire* could launch its attack on its outward leg and then proceed to land at Wade International with empty weapon pylons.

The Russian pilots had not been too pleased either at the route from Murmansk to Nuuk in Greenland for a re-fuel, then down the Atlantic to Bermuda, which had left them not enough fuel to make it back to Nuuk if there were problems in Bermuda. Jake didn't blame him one bit.

Morning, Wednesday 16th May 2018

DEA Headquarters, Washington DC

"I've already explained Nate. The president took Hoskin's word for it. The bastard just set me up to look stupid, he'd gotten some staffer to do him a paper on 'why nothing was likely to happen and if it did, why it was likely to be Dominican Republic that took the fall'. I didn't even get my toe in the door before Hoskin stood on it."

Nathan King felt sorry for his NSA friend and counterpart, it was impossible sometimes to get the people at the 'big house' to listen. He'd run into the same kind of official blindness over the so called Syrian moderates; what the hell is a moderate zealot anyway?

"Did you have any luck with the satellite coverage over the Caribbean Vern?"

Vernon Weathers perked up a bit.

"Yeah that was OK. There was obviously sufficient evidence that 'something' was going on, so Hoskin agreed increased coverage over the whole area till June just to cover his ass. How about the DEA side of things, Nate?"

King shrugged a negative and turned towards Miles Carlson.

"How about the CIA's unofficial little trip to Bermuda Miles?"

Carlson stood and started his habitual pacing, immediately encountering problems with the size of the small windowless conference room. He contented himself with repeatedly taking one step forward and one step back as he spoke, resembling King thought, someone who wanted to go to the John badly.

"Well, you've read the factual report, now here are my impressions. König. I had a tour of his 'pocket battleship' with the American consul earlier in the week after one of their little receptions and believe me it's impressive. I didn't get near any sensitive gear though but the 'specs' we obtained cover that stuff anyway. It's a truer 'pocket battleship' than the ones that the Brits labelled so in War Two, you know the Graf Spee etc."

He waited for the nods to see everyone reading from the same page.

"His people are every bit as impressive as their files led us to believe. The guy I met with, this Captain Krull, kept on pushing for more information to give his boss, he was pushing in all the right directions. I gave them as much as we agreed but I reckon I'm going to have to go down to the Caymans and meet with McTeal and König soon. Krull struck me as one sharp tack and since it was he who planned and executed that rescue in the Med not long ago, all in the space of about twenty minutes, he's no slouch when it comes to taking action."

He stopped pacing just for a second and actually sat down, to King's surprise.

"In summary gentlemen, the vessel and its crew are top quality; of course it's got no missile armament, but if anything got within range of its guns…."

He made a cutting motion across his throat. There was a pause for a moment while he considered his next comments.

"There could be another fly in the ointment."

The others looked up and waited.

"König's wife, a very nice lady by all accounts, plans a visit to Haiti over the next few days."

There was a sudden palpable increase of tension in the room. Carlson held up his hands defensively.

"Hey, what are we supposed to say or do? I couldn't drop into the conversation 'oh by the way your wife is heading off to Haiti and you'll be shooting at Haitians before she leaves' now could I?"

He picked up his plastic coffee cup and reflected that things were even tighter at DEA than in his part of the world, if the coffee for senior officers was always this bad, and he then continued.

"She's going to stay with some aristocratic family at Petionville near Port Au Prince. She's long-time friends with the lady of the house, a Mrs Francesca D'Orville wife of the Minister of Agriculture and Natural Resources or some such. Farache wants everyone to believe it's all quietened down now and that he's not the bad-ass everyone thought he was, which is why we think he included the good lady's husband in his cabinet."

Vernon Weathers put his head in his hands, his normal taciturn persona out of the window now.

"Oh for Christ's sake Miles, are you telling me that König's wife is going to be 'guesting' at the house of one of Farache's ministers whilst he goes toe to toe with Farache's navy? You fucking well couldn't make this shit up could you?"

Nate tried to remember the last time he'd heard Vern swear but gave up after a few seconds.

Miles continued.

"Look, with any luck she'll be in and out before Farache starts playing fucking Napoleon and König will be free to play it how he wants.″

There was a moment of silence as the other two absorbed the information, three very canny and intelligent men quickly crunched through the permutations and possibilities of this unexpected twist. Nathan King was the first to break the silence.

"Suppose she's still there when the shit hits the fan? How the hell is that going to affect König's resolve to defend the Caymans?"

Vern chipped in his ten cents worth.

"Suppose the Haitians get wind of König helping the Caymanians? They're not stupid, they'll know who she is the moment she steps off the plane, hell they'll probably know in advance from the pilot's flight plan. Miles, you've met him. How do you think König would react if they took his wife hostage for his good behaviour?"

Miles stood up again causing a brief smile to flicker on Nate's face as he then sat again, clearly unhappy with the available pacing room.

"It's a hard question Nate. I figure he's not the sort to piss around with diplomacy when direct action is possible. You both know that had it not been his warship that was in the right place at the right time then that cruise liner would be on the bottom and the 'Raggies' would be celebrating another 9/11. A ship from any 'Navy' would have backed off and waited for approval. Just shows you what we've become. Micromanagers rule the waves now not Captains."

He drew a breath then let it out slowly as he formulated his reply.

"After looking him in the eye and listening to him fence with the consul that night on his ship, and after what I've read about him -yeah we have quite a thick file including the business in New York with the druggies- I wouldn't like to cross him in any way, shape or form. He's got a lot of worldwide high-up contacts and clout. But I wouldn't put it past him to do something himself since he has what amounts to a well-armed private army too."

Miles picked up and put down his coffee cup again, 'done that' he thought to himself before continuing.

"As to whether it would stop him helping McTeal, I know the answer now. No. He's one of those honourable types, he'd do what he had to do for the Caymans and then go and rip Farache a new hole to shit through if his wife was harmed."

Friday Evening 18th MAY 2018

Bismarck, Windward Passage, Caribbean Sea

Captain Reiner Krull had felt a chill of apprehension that morning as he'd taken his bridge watch. He'd struggled to pin down the source of his misgiving whilst doing all his usual systems checks and reading the logs, but as usual, the act of trying to corner it, pushed the answer further away. He knew it would come to him when he least expected it.

It was now 23:30 and he was back in the OPs room again. Lt Cdr Simon McClelland had buzzed him to mention an oddity. Duty OPs had noted a brief 'racket' a little while ago which was curious for a couple of reasons.

A racket was simply a transmission of any kind and could be classified by type, but if it were brief the location could only be narrowed down to a rough bearing, to get a good bearing it needed to be repeated or continuous. Range was guesswork though, based on the strength of the signal, atmospherics at the time, experience of the interpreter, if the source was identifiable and past records.

Like now, for instance.

"It's the second time we've picked up this particular racket and I have to say it makes me nervous whenever I pick up a missile fire control radar boss."

Reiner's eyebrows rose a little which was likely the only indication Simon would get that the Captain was in any way concerned.

"What have you identified Simon?"

"Well the first was a 'Palm Frond' –shall I use NATO code sir or manufacturers names?"

NATO codified all identified missiles, radar, ECM, EW, ECCM and practically anything that flew and emitted signals, so Reiner knew it was either Chinese, Russian or North Korean in origin. The NATO codes were of course different to what the manufacturers named the emitter.

"NATO will be fine thank you." Returned Reiner.

"Well the first was Palm Frond, Russian origin navigation radar, no clues as to the owner since most Russian ships use the same or very similar."

He checked the logs.

"That was about half an hour ago and we've had it almost clockwork since then every five minutes with an increasing strength so clearly we're approaching them. The bearing has remained fairly consistent so I suspect we are on converging courses."

"What is our emission status?" Asked Reiner wondering what they themselves were punting out into the atmosphere.

"Just the Nav' end of the Giraffe's spectrum a bit like them Sir every five minutes or so but more random." He said referring to the ability of the Sea Giraffe system to operate in a wide variety of modes dependent on the task at hand. Just using the Nav mode was a bit like using the latest i7 processor as a simple calculator, given the system's overall capability.

He checked Reiner's face to see if he wanted anything else and then returned his attention to the logs when he saw he didn't.

"About fifteen minutes ago we got a brief racket which the computer classifies as 'Top Steer' air and surface search, which narrows it down a bit to the larger Russian ships and excludes Sovremenny and Udaloy destroyers. Then we had 'Front Door' missile fire control radar which came on and went off twice, the last time a minute or so before I called you Sir. As far as I can tell the only ships still afloat operating that one are *Slava* class cruisers using the SSN12 Sandbox missile."

Reiner thought for a moment.

"Was there any indication that either the 'Top Steer' or 'Front Door' found us and what's your best guess at range?"

"I don't think they had us Sir. The racket gave us two sweeps and stopped; I'd guess they were about twenty five miles away at least so we'd really be on the edge of detection were we not semi-stealthy. I think it was maybe a test given the other systems going on and off too."

Reiner sat in his OPs chair but didn't buckle up or activate his own systems.

"Right, after our recent warnings of 'trouble to come' we need to play this carefully. Cease Nav radar transmissions and switch to Infra-Red for navigation. In fact let's go EMCON silent." He said switching the ship to a total blackout of emissions status.

"Can we get an Arado up do you suppose?"

Simon knew he was really talking to himself and so didn't jump in.

"Yes let's get one up with a recon package on and keep an IR sensor trained along their last bearing."

Because they were in silent hours Simon just spoke into his mike to get Kempfe on the comms unit rather than use the Tannoy.

"Kempfe." Click.

"Chief, we need one of your drones up with a recon package, could you get cracking please we really need some info pretty quickly."

"Aye Sir." Came the immediate response from Kempfe who rolled himself upright and put on his own mike.

"Abbate." A click then. "Luigi you lazy Italian salami eater, get out of that rack and get to work. We need one of your little girls up friend, rapidamente!" He was quite proud of his ability to use English, German and Italian slang phrases now. What a mixture he chuckled as he dressed and headed for the drone control centre near the catapult platform.

Back on the bridge Reiner was rapidly updating his knowledge of Caribbean national navies from his datapad and having just read what Haiti had purchased two years ago he thought he could guess what was emitting and who owned it.

"Simon have you managed to work through the digest of Caribbean armed forces yet?" He asked knowing the answer.

"No Sir, I've barely touched it, I think I got as far as Dominican Republic." Simon knew he was about to discover that he should have prioritised his time differently.

"Had you done so you would have discovered that Haiti has been buying vessels formerly owned by both the People's Republic of China and Ukraine. Further it seems that the larger units are all of Russian design and build."

He switched the datapad off and looked out over the dark sea, not even a twinkle of light with it overcast like this, he noted.

"I believe we have a *Slava* class missile cruiser ahead, in fact specifically, the former *Ukrayina*, the one that didn't get completed until very recently and then sold to Haiti. Whether he is alone or not remains to be seen. Hopefully the overcast will not be too low for the drone, and not too turbulent either."

"Shall I alter course then sir?"

"No. We'll wait for the drone to give us more accurate information and then position ourselves about two miles off to his port side. It should be far enough away that only the most observant watchkeepers will have any chance of seeing us BUT it will be interesting to note if any of their radar come on, whether Werner Nickel's radar absorbing paint is really any good. It should not be many minutes I would think."

"Aye Sir." Simon automatically answered as he used a night viewer to check all round again whilst trying to estimate how far he was actually seeing into the night, the range indicator wasn't so accurate when it only had wave tops to point at.

The Arado 196 drone purred away into the night its spent bio-degradable boost rockets would fall away when it attained acceptable altitude and flying speed.

Kempfe ran the diagnostics on the on-board sensors while Abbate steered the drone and monitored its avionics.

"Bridge." Kempfe spoke quietly into his mike. Click and then connection.

"Bridge aye." Came the answer from the now recovered Erich Stroder. Recovered was a bit of a stretch really since he was still black and blue around the head with half a dozen stitches still to be taken out after his fracas on the jetty the other day.

"Drone control. Cyclops 1 is up and we are receiving sensor data now. Vessel bearing 198 degrees, range 8.6 miles, course is 22 degrees, speed 17 knots."

"Bridge, acknowledged. OPs did you copy?"

"OPs aye." Came the voice of Inonu Kyne San stifling a yawn and thinking about his watch ending in less than half an hour.

All Drone control communications were supposed to be routed through OPs as well but Erich thought it best to be sure.

Inonu gave up on wishing his watch was over as the presence of a ten thousand ton plus missile cruiser started to pique his natural interest in such things. He did a quick check of the same digest Reiner used noting that the cruiser carried an IR surveillance set NATO coded Tea 'Plinth' or later version thereof, it said. Who dreams these fucking names up he wondered as he checked out what was known about it. He was pondering whether the character out front was likely to be using it if he was testing everything else, in which case it could detect *Bismarck* without them even being aware.

He spoke into the mike. "Bridge."

Click then connection.

"Bridge OPs here. Do we want to activate the pre-wetting system in case this fellow out front is playing with his IR gear, and maybe get the engine room to boost the funnel cooling system for a while?"

Erich took the call.

"Bridge aye. Wait one."

Reiner looked at Simon and nodded.

"Good idea."

"OPs, yes please; make it so." Answered Simon.

He looked towards the bows as the pre-wetting system engaged. Vertical sprays of water drenched the ship bow to stern as the pumped seawater made her external temperature as close to sea temperature as possible.

The idea of pre-wetting had originally been to wash away radioactive or biological waste products from the decks and superstructures in time of war but nowadays was likely to be more use hiding a ship from heat sensors as anything else. *Bismarck's* were designed for that second purpose entirely.

In addition the duty engineer Trev Kent started the boost to the exhaust gas cooling system located in the funnel. Clever bit of kit this thought Trev Kent, as he engaged the system. Exhaust from the gas turbines would now be cycled through copper veined cooling fins in the lower funnel itself a number of times before being fed further up into similar fins, which circulated refrigerated liquid through them before finally being allowed to exhaust into the night sky. The captured heat was used to heat the water the crew showered in by used of a simple heat exchanger system. With the boost on, by the time anyone would be able to detect the cooled gases they'd be literally yards away.

The tension climbed by degrees over the next few minutes as the big cruiser –now identified as *General Farache*- ploughed through the gentle swells on a course only a degree or so off the reciprocal of their own.

Erich manoeuvred *Bismarck* to a point some two miles to its port side and speed was dropped to ten knots so as not to give the cooling systems too much work to do, and to reduce the bow wave. Then they all waited to see if anything changed and the *General Farache* became aware of their presence.

Meanwhile Kempfe, using Cyclops 1's thermal imager, was recording the ship from every angle for their computer records. The drone based unit wasn't as good as the best ground or ship based thermal imagers because it used an uncooled microbolometer, whereas the ones on *Bismarck* and the *General Farache* were actively cooled to increase sensitivity, they also weighed about forty times as much as the one in the drone.

He'd now craftily positioned the drone about two hundred yards astern and two hundred yards above the ship and concentrated now on listening to any and all emissions. The relayed data would be stored in *Bismarck's* database and hopefully never needed again.

Sure enough like clockwork, up sparked the 'Front Door' targeting radar for a couple of sweeps and then the 'Top Steer' and finally the 'Palm frond'. Never a good idea to be so predictable on a warship thought Kempfe. He sincerely hoped they wouldn't put their helo up as well since that was the other potential piece of the SSN12 operation. The helo could discretely view the target and transmit the information directly to the incoming missile warhead thus saving on final manoeuvring.

"Exzellent." Murmured Reiner noting that even at this range the radar absorption paint and the high carbon material in the upperworks made them quite invisible to the cruiser as it activated both search and targeting radars briefly.

Fifteen minutes later with the *General Farache* now having passed without becoming aware of them, Reiner ordered the drone recovered and they secured all cooling systems.

"Right, I'm retiring Simon, keep the Nav radar off for another twenty minutes before re-commencing sweeps and call me if he changes course or any of his friends turn up."

"Aye Sir." Said a relieved Simon, now biding his time before Julius arrived to relieve him in just a couple of minutes. He's going to be seriously pissed off that he didn't get a chance to play with his guns and point them at a missile cruiser, thought Simon with a grin on his face.

Reiner wandered back through the wardroom and picked up a glass of juice before turning in again. He knew he'd be awake for a while before sleep returned.

It was now 19th May 2018 and as he glanced down at an open book on a table he noted it was a copy of Robert Ballard's 'The Discovery of the *Bismarck*'. It had been left open at a page which described preparations for *Bismarck's* maiden operation.

On the 18th May 1941 the great battleship had signalled its readiness to proceed to sea and commence operation 'Rheinubung', it's one and only mission and sailed in the early hours of the following morning. Reiner was not a superstitious man but today, the 19th of May, his *Bismarck* would commence its first operation around the Cayman Islands, exactly 77 years later. Now he knew what had niggled him earlier.

*

Janjak Pantal, junior radar operator on the missile cruiser *General Farache*, flagship of the Haitian navy, did a double-take staring at the radar display. Had he imagined that brief return almost on the port beam?

He activated the 'Top Steer' again for its routine two sweeps. There looked to be something at about two miles range but it was faint and in several bits so it seemed. Perhaps a little debris on the surface? Should I report it?

Easy to answer that he thought. The last time he had had a contact during an exercise was when they were playing against one of their own earlier this year. He'd been so intent on refining what he thought was something, that he'd missed the cheeky corvette as it appeared from behind an island at their quarter position and shot an 'electronic' missile at them. It would be a long time before he exercised his initiative again after the subsequent bollocking his boss gave him when he returned from the bridge wiping the spittle from his face, having himself been dressed down by the Admiral in person.

Toussaint L'Ouverture International Airport, Haiti

Winston Parfty stepped down to the tarmac, looked all around and listened to the ticking of the engines as they cooled. The continuous chirping of the cicadas was apparent even here on the airfield.

Heat from the midday sun bounced back off the concrete as he stood waiting patiently for his charge and a sheen of perspiration stood out on his forehead as his body adjusted from the quiet air-conditioned 'coolth' of the Lear Executive, to the oppressive damp heat of Haiti. The bright glare made him grateful he'd remembered his RayBans.

This place is a dump, he thought to himself as he took in the newish but already slightly dilapidated looking airport facilities. Lots of whitewash over the cracks he noted. He wondered if the cracks were from impacting rounds or just the building settling, it was just a bit too far to be sure either way.

He turned back towards the aircraft as his friend and colleague Tetsunari Amada filled the dark opening of the doorway. Tetsunari stepped onto the tarmac on the opposite side to Winston and glanced warily around.

His impassive Japanese features hardened slightly as he took in the lounging blue uniformed guards near the entrance to the terminal buildings.

They stood nonchalantly cradling their automatic carbines as they disinterestedly observed the two men disembark. Tetsunari noted a sudden change in their alertness and guessed that Mrs König had come into view.

Sophie stood quietly in the doorway for a few seconds looking down at Winston and Tetsunari. What a combination, she thought for the umpteenth time, my two guardians, as different as, as, whatever.

A more incongruous pair she could never have imagined; they'd been her guardians now for two and a half years but she still marvelled occasionally at the situation which put a tall and wiry, black, south Londoner and a small, broadly built Japanese together.

Winston was the easiest to work out. He had worked with Andy Evans in the SBS for a couple of years, and as Andy had said, anyone who could make it in the Marines nicknamed 'Pufti' had to be as tough as nails and a born survivor.

Sophie noted Andy hadn't mentioned Winston's colour when describing him and puzzled about that. She knew he genuinely held Winston in high regard as well as almost fathering him when his mum had passed away last year. She remembered clearly the one time that she and Winston had discussed race, it had been after another one of those tabloid exclusives about racial persecution and bullying in the armed services.

Winston had looked mildly surprised when she had asked if he'd ever encountered racism in the Marines.

"Nah, never had issues with that crap. Don't know about 'Pongos' though." He said using the Navy's derogatory term for the Army.

"Bootnecks is all about skills and thinking it through. We all wear the Green Beret so we've proved we can push the edges. You don't get it unless you can shoot straight, march forever and keep going when smart people would quit."

He smiled at her.

"So we're all the same from the start. Respect it's about I suppose. Booties respect each other for a start because there's no easy way to get that Green Beret and 'cos there's no piece of paper that will make you tough."

He'd said, pointing to the paper.

"You don't want to believe that, it's just journo bullshit Ma'am." Then on a last note he added.

"If you're black and you've got a chip on your shoulder you'd have problems, but you wouldn't pass through the selection and training. The instructors," he said, clearly giving it serious consideration, "were there to weed out people who wouldn't make good marines no matter what colour their skin was."

Then he laughed out loud as a memory surfaced.

"As one said to me in the morning after a night exercise, 'Winston, he says, you're a lucky bastard -pardon my French Miss- you've got built in war paint' he says talking about the cammo cream. It takes me ages to put this shit on and then get it off'. So no Miss, I didn't have no problems."

That had been the last said on the subject.

Tetsunari however, was a whole different book. Jake had explained how he'd met him on one of his trips to Japan and that he was a bit of an enigma even as Japanese go.

Apparently they'd met in a martial arts 'Dojo' when Jake was practicing his Ju-jitsu during a break in his business discussions. Jake had accepted a Japanese training partner who was waiting to start, pretty normal for Ju-jitsu where you needed a training partner, except that the Japanese he normally met in such places studiously ignored him because he was a 'Gaijin' or foreigner, and he usually had to pay an instructor in Japan.

This particular fellow had decided, it seemed, to teach the Gaijin how Ju-jitsu should be properly practiced. He had set out to hurt and humiliate Jake, but had come up against someone who had been taught by the best over many years.

The 'training' session had taken on a ferocious quality almost immediately, as Jake's partner fought to pin him and over applied pressure even when Jake had tapped the mat to signal a break.

Jake had not reciprocated when it was his turn, sticking to the custom of release as soon as a partner tapped but had easily locked and thrown his partner.

Unfortunately this partner was quickly becoming an 'opponent' and was having none of it, applying more and more pressure during the joint locks and, egged on by a couple of friends, was in real danger of doing serious injury in an apparent attempt to teach Jake a lesson.

Before it had got completely out of hand, Tetsunari had arrived out of nowhere, which Jake said was pretty good going on its own. He had stepped in front of Jake, slapped his surprised partner backhand across the face, not hard, and using the shock as cover, established a series of holds which placed his opponent on the mat flipping forwards and backwards like a landed fish writhing in humiliation and pain before he would consent to tap the mat.

His foolish reluctance to tap had left him with a ligament tear. Tetsunari had hissed to the fallen man that the Dojo was a place of honour and not a place for brawling. Jake spoke good Japanese and had understood every word.

He hadn't spoken to Tetsunari but had just bowed and left to resume his business. Later when he'd told his Japanese business partner Saigo Shiota about the incident, the man had been horrified at the insult and had made his own inquiries meaning to punish someone. Jake was, after all his guest.

Nothing more was said about it until two days later when the subject came up in the usual roundabout way over tea. Saigo had been reluctant to reveal what he had discovered about the incident in the Dojo because it would burden his friend and guest. Tetsunari, it seemed, had not been training but was employed as an instructor at the Dojo and had been summarily dismissed by his employer.

Jake's opponent had been well connected and very wealthy. Delicately Jake asked, realising Saigo's awkward position, if his unfortunate ally could be located; if so he would like to meet with him. The meeting had been arranged for several days later and since Jake's Japanese was nearly flawless he'd no need of an interpreter.

Jake explained over tea and after the usual courtesies that he would like to recruit Tetsunari into his security company in order for him to teach his superb techniques. Tetsunari had been surprisingly reluctant initially but finally agreed. Jake knew Tetsunari would have declined if anything about the 'incident' had come up, or if Jake had in any way indicated that it was out of pity or gratitude that the offer was made. He had subsequently found out that Tetsunari had good military service behind him in the Japanese Marines which was an added bonus.

Tetsunari still taught classes once a quarter to Jake's security people the world over, attendance at these master classes and competition for places was intense.

The biggest enigma to Sophie was how could two such totally contrasting people become such good friends? She had never detected any tension between the two, you'd never know with Tetsunari but she thought she'd spot it in Winston if there was any.

After the usual customs formalities a limousine appeared to carry them into the hilly district of Petionville. Sophie was really looking forward to meeting Francesca again, they hadn't seen each other since her wedding in Paris two years ago, so there was a lot of catching up to be done.

Back in the airport terminal Major Raoul Mercier observed the departing limousine from behind mirrored aviator glasses. The two customs officers who'd dealt with the König party stood nervously to one side of him. They didn't like the Interior Ministry people at the best of times but this particular man was one who they would travel a long way to avoid. Mercier turned to face them as the car passed out of sight down the road.

He didn't speak for several seconds, enjoying the fear he created with his presence, knowing that it was heightened by his silent scrutiny. Finally, he grunted a dismissal and the two customs officers fled back to their posts, thankful that they'd apparently done nothing to anger the man from the most feared Ministry in Haiti.

Then having ensconced themselves in their office, the two men collapsed into the available chairs and one produced a half bottle of corn spirit. Several 'chugs' later, heart rate slowing, Victor, the younger of the two, managed to speak.

"Was that really him?"

Francois replied with a nod and after wiping his mouth on the sleeve of his uniform jacket, elaborated for the benefit of his younger colleague.

"Yes that was him alright, they say that he has personally tortured and killed hundreds of anti-Farache dissidents." He shuddered. "Just looking at him makes my flesh creep; it's like looking at the grim reaper himself." He belched loudly and reached for the bottle again. "I sure pity that 'whitey' bitch if the 'Mad Major' has any interest in her." Victor nodded sagely in agreement and crossed himself before reaching for the bottle again.

*

The stretch limousine ploughed through the urban decay that is endemic to Haitian cities. Winston studied the terrain. Not just the neglect that marks any big Western city's slums, he thought, but the kind of downtrodden misery found usually in places like Beirut. The people seemed in a state of decline too, as if the despair caused by their crumbling surroundings had infected them.

"Spot him did you?" He said to Tetsunari in a low voice as the car bumped and bounced along the poor surface towards the villa in the hills.

Tetsunari's smooth head rotated towards him like a gun turret, Winston irreverently thought. It seemed to come straight out of his shoulders. He would have been nicknamed 'No neck' in the Corps, decided Winston. No, actually, he'd have been have been christened 'Odd Job' out of that Bond film.

He smiled at Tetsunari in genuine friendship. Tetsunari's placid features revealed nothing of his inner self, but his eyes bored into Winston's.

Tetsunari had noted the low level of Winston's voice and reciprocated.

"Tall, well-built black man with the blue, well cut uniform; red piping, a major's crown badge and a scar on his right cheek. Stood well behind the counter to the left of the 'Welcome to Haiti' sign?"

"All right smartarse." Winston conceded.

He paused searching for words.

"He looked a bad'un to me. I didn't like the interest he showed in Mrs K either."

Tetsunari ruminated for a few seconds before replying.

"Yes, he has the mark of death on him. I too noticed his interest and also the nervousness of the customs officials. I do not like this place Vinston." He said massacring the 'W'. "People

198

walk in fear. Their faces betray it and their movements are defensive."

Winston nodded in agreement.

"We're a bit out on a limb here 'Tettas', I'll go for a walk-about this afternoon when we're settled in."

Tetsunari looked directly at Winston while he mentally translated what 'out on a limb' meant and then 'walk-about', from the colloquial English his friend was fond of, then nodded.

"I will communicate with Mr Evans using the sat-phone I think. I will walk around the gardens as a security check but also to ensure privacy. I would not be surprised if people were listening in the house."

Winston nodded, his brow creased with a frown as he maintained his external scan but his brain was working furiously through options.

Sophie had heard the low voices as she had been taking in the scenery. Now she turned back to face them, as they sat opposite her. Checking Winston's face first, as his was the only one she could read, she detected a tension in it.

"What are you two whispering about now?" She said noting the frown Winston was wearing and had been since they'd arrived.

"Nothing much Mrs K. I was just saying to Tettas that this whole place seems a bit like Beirut."

"Oh." She turned back to the scenery. "Yes it does rather doesn't it? More so near the airport than here. Francesca tells me things are getting better now though. Lots of new building and such-like going on. Can't be far away now, Francesca said it was about half an hour from the airport."

The scenery had changed markedly over the last ten minutes or so since leaving the built up areas and now they were in a hilly forested region where white painted villas of the rich perched on the hillsides.

They turned in through a set of ornate iron gates, noting the two uniformed guards. At the end of the driveway stood a red tile roofed and impressive looking, modern, two storey villa. The gardens appeared to be well tended and the white painted brick glowed in the bright sunlight as they swung around a shrub clad roundabout and stopped outside the impressive main entrance.

Along the front of the house ran a wide, Spanish style arched veranda and standing on the bottom of the six steps leading to it was Francesca D'Orville and her husband Louis. Francesca's greetings were profuse and Sophie's first impression of Louis was of an educated, sincere person, a relief, since she would need his active assistance with her forthcoming project.

Winston and Tetsunari stood back a little on either side of her, eyes roving, never relaxing.

19.50hrs Sunday 20th May 2018

George Town, Grand Cayman

"Starboard fifteen." Ordered Reiner as *Bismarck*, bathed in the last of the ruddy glow of the setting sun, threaded her way through the giant cruiseliners anchored offshore, and pointed her bows finally towards the harbour wall. Buller moved the Steerpod control so that the two units angled slightly left in order to push the bow to the right.

"Steady on that." Instructed Reiner as the pods were centred then a slight touch the other way to counter the swing as Reiner expertly lined her up so that the bow would close the jetty at an acute angle and allow the bow line to be taken first so that the pods could swing the stern gently round.

The lights along the front, from North West point along Seven mile beach to George Town, looked like strings of pearls against the already black eastern sky.

On her decks, seamen moved purposefully amongst the cables and shackles, preparing for her berthing. Erich Stroder stood in front of turret Anton leaning against the still warm metal as he tried in vain to argue his case but Pete Nuttall the 'Buffer', or Petty Officer seaman, also in charge of the fo'c'sle berthing party, was having none of it. He had definitely seen Stroder's hand appear from under the nurse's dress, despite Stroder's denials.

"...and all that time I thought you was at death's door, you were poking nurses you shamming bastard. Go on, get off my fo'c'sle you randy little tyke, those 'Lindt' chocolates cost a fortune in Bermuda."

Stroder shrugged and began to move back along the deck a big grin on his face. The bruises were starting to fade now but the ugly gashes along his cheek still had stitches in them.

Well, it could have been worse, the doctors said he'd been lucky to get away with a concussion, and the Commodore had offered to get his scars seen to if they didn't heal properly.

He smiled secretly to himself as he paused at the armoured hatch opening into the base of the bridge superstructure, the Buffer didn't miss much. But it was a good job he hadn't come into the room ten minutes sooner.

He turned to look forward at the lights of the approaching town, and then stepped inside.

"Standby stern lines." Reiner gave the order as the ship angled in towards the harbour. He cast a glance down at the fo'c's'le party and saw Stroder walking nonchalantly back towards the superstructure. He briefly wondered what had taken him up there.

Reiner was relieved that Stroder's injuries hadn't been worse and that they'd been able to sail with him rather than leave him behind. That was awful, being left behind. It had happened to Reiner once when he'd been left at Göteborg with a suspected appendicitis. He turned as Jake approached.

"Not long now Reiner eh?" Jake grabbed a spare viewer and focussed on the shoreline in particular the reception party.

"Just one hundred metres."

Reiner replied automatically, even though he knew Jake could see the range readout on the viewer screen that he was looking through. Something's bothering him thought Reiner.

Jake couldn't concentrate on what he was seeing; his mind was on the upcoming meeting with Andrew McTeal and his ministers.

After the conference call yesterday a meeting had been agreed for as soon as possible after their arrival. The call itself had been quite tense; McTeal had been shocked by the news and had pressed for details, the others had been angry and not a little outraged that something may be going on.

The foreign minister Erskine Buerke's attitude, however, had been a little surprising, the man had been almost, 'hostile' was the word he was looking for. His reaction to Jake's revelations weren't quite what was expected. It didn't seem to be the news itself that was the 'problem', it was as if the manner of its delivery was the issue. Why though? Was it possible that the news wasn't actually news to Buerke? Then later, like a Chameleon, he'd slowly blended his opinion with the others around the table and was advocating a strong reaction by the end of the call.

Weird. Maybe it was just that he was a politician hedging his bets. If it blew over he could say that he'd been sceptical but if something happened he could point to the record and say he had advocated a strong response. Crafty bugger.

Jake moved away from the viewer, his mind still turning over and sifting facts and impressions. He decided that he needed a one-on-one talk with Sandiford Roche soonest; McTeal's Minister of odd jobs was incorruptible. Best wait until after the cabinet meeting, just to get a better feel for things.

*

Prime Minister Andrew McTeal adjusted the focus on the powerful binoculars borrowed from one of his MPP guards, and the object of his curiosity leapt into clarity. A magnificent sight, he thought as he observed *Bismarck* commence the turn that would bring her sideways into the enclosed part of the harbour. It fairly emanated 'threat' he fancied, or was he just more aware of its capabilities than most watchers. It did bristle with guns and had a pleasing sheer from the high flared bows, menacing yet aesthetically pleasing to the eye, he decided.

He'd got his driver to drop him at Rackam's Bar on North Church Street. Without a lot of fuss his security people had taken a table on the seaward side right next to the water. He watched as the ship glided past the four huge cruiseliners anchored off and noted that one after the other they all saluted *Bismarck* as she passed, what had been said about their reception at Bermuda was clearly no exaggeration. It seemed mariners of all stripe supported their action in the Mediterranean -as did he.

People in the bar were now wandering over to the waterside to see what the fuss was about as the deep basso profundo fog horns reverberated several times each. *Bismarck* changed shape, burnished copper light reflecting from the seaward side of her upperworks and jet black on the other.

Yes, he thought, an appropriate contrast, as is the ship itself. A shining, pretty bauble from one perspective, but a lurking deadly machine from another.

Smiling at his own philosophising he lowered the binoculars and indicated that he wanted to leave. A cabinet meeting was now scheduled for eight o'clock. That gave him time to do some thinking and also time for a quiet word with Jake.

Other less friendly eyes monitored the approach of the ship as it made its way toward the harbour.

Armand Bennot decided he would have a wander down to the dock and see if he could get close enough for a good look at the ship. He hadn't been able to make out the flag flying at the stern and he didn't recognise the class by its silhouette.

He'd been told to report any unusual or significant events to his masters, he didn't know why. Anything military however was for sure unusual out here in this backwater. Picking up his fishing rod and the old tattered bag of tackle, he looked down and checked his appearance. Good, the old patched denims, dirty plimsolls and sleeveless, tatty denim jacket made him look the part. Well the part he wanted them to think he was playing. Dressed like this, blending in with the other old boys down on the dockside wouldn't be a problem. He grinned suddenly, showing brilliant white teeth against his walnut coloured, age lined face;

this spying lark wasn't too difficult if you could just fade into the background, and the money was damned welcome!

*

Jake had left the bridge before the final docking manoeuvres began, he didn't want Reiner to think he didn't trust his judgement. Besides, he'd always hated it when the 'Old Man' had stood behind him as he conned a ship through a tricky manoeuvre. Down in his stateroom Jake spoke into his mike.

"Evans." Click.

"Yes bossman, what can I do for you?"

"Andy, pop up to my cabin will you please and bring Simon with you."

"On my way Jake." Was the brief reply.

A minute later a knock announced their arrival.

"Come in and grab a seat you two."

Jake ushered them into his office-cabin.

"Simon, you're the DCO tonight, which is why you're here."

As the Duty Commanding Officer, Simon was literally in command of the ship in Jake and Reiner's absence. In normal times this was no real burden but Simon sensed these were no ordinary times, so he took particular notice of not just what Jake said, but how he said it as well. He glanced across to check Andy Evans's face for clues. Needn't have bothered he thought, Andy's expression would be the same if he had one foot on a mine and the other in a shark's mouth.

Jake knew he had to be careful, he knew he *couldn't* alarm Andy but he didn't want to alarm Simon, he just needed to make him aware.

"Right. Things don't add up. I don't know what is going on and I'm not sure anyone around here does either. This is a friendly port but..."

He let that linger just for a few seconds.

"I want you Andy, to put two of your men on watch with the normal duty staff. One to stay on the ship and one to wander around the dockside, just tell them to treat it like it was a real 'Bikini Amber' back in the UK. OK? I'll have the local police maintain a ten metre cordon."

"OK boss, no problem. I'll be coming with you when you go for your meeting with Mr McTeal."

"That won't be necessary Andy, they're sending an official car for me as we arrive."

"That wasn't a request boss; it was as statement of fact. My antenna is twitching, I'm going. Besides I need to talk to Steve Robinson, the Ministerial Protection Police boss."

204

Jake looked at him for a second, long ago he decided never if possible, to argue with Andy on matters of security.

"Fine, if you 'feel the need' as they say."

He turned towards Simon.

"If for any reason you believe the ship is in danger, don't hesitate; take her out and bimble up and down offshore until we sort out any problems. You are authorized to take any, and I mean *any*, action you think fit to protect the ship and its crew. That clear Simon?"

"Yes sir. Shall I stop leave or just brief the libertymen to be careful what they say and to whom they say it?"

Jake considered for a moment, he didn't want to do anything that would show a 'watcher' that they were more alert than usual.

"Just do the usual briefing but make sure they know you're serious. Also, have a quiet word with Kipper to make sure the Senior Rates know to be extra careful."

A gentle nudge against the fenders told them all that they had arrived.

"Right gentlemen let's get on, I'll be up in a minute Andy, I'll see you by the midships gangway."

His ear piece chimed. It was Reiner telling him that the ship was secure alongside and that an official car was waiting down on the jetty. I need my boardroom brain now, thought Jake as he gathered a few papers to put in his portfolio. He was piped off the ship by Kipper.

Jake and Reiner climbed in the car and were surprised to discover that Andrew McTeal had come in person. Jake took the seat next to him and Reiner the jump seat opposite. There was quite a crowd on the waterfront, most just ogling the brightly lit unusual ship. A few of the more observant had spotted the Prime Minister, including a certain Armand Bennot who now had more to report. The car drove away rapidly from the busy dockside with 'outriders' to front and rear as well as a backup squad in a panel van.

*

The meeting wasn't going well. Jake was simmering in the background, an invited guest but not a debater. It had now degenerated into a 'point scoring' game or a dismissive eloquence contest, he wasn't sure which, and had strayed away totally from the shadowy threat hovering in the background.

Jake had delivered his warning and had brought Reiner in as the first hand witness. Reiner had not coped well with the questioning that had followed. At some point he had realised that

205

his integrity was being questioned by Erskine Buerke and that was the end of his usefulness. First he'd coloured up evidently angry and unused to being questioned in this peremptory manner. After that he retreated, tortoise-like, into monosyllabic replies until dismissed. Reiner had left seething with indignation, glancing at Jake and receiving a sympathetic nod on his way out.

Everything seemed to centre on two omissions, the first being the identity of the 'intelligence' agent in Bermuda, the second being the identity of the 'supposed' aggressor.

Damn the man in Bermuda, Jake thought savagely, these fools are going to ignore the threat. They weren't even prepared to make discreet enquiries of Britain about her position if events proved the informer correct.

Erskine Buerke was the self-appointed leader of the sceptics, he was the one that had cleverly teased Reiner's neck out of the shell only to savagely attack as soon as it was visible. Buerke had culminated his dismissal case with speculation about who this imaginary opponent might be.

Finally, crushingly, it seemed to Jake, he'd asked how in heaven's name could 'whoever it was' expect to get away with it in the 21st century? There followed a general murmur of agreement.

Thank God for the pre-meeting chat with Andrew. Then, the problem had been discussed without fire, just cold hard logic. Andrew had resolved that no matter what happened in the cabinet meeting he would speak to the British Prime Minister and ask for enquiries to be made.

The dual purpose being to alert the British at the top thus ensuring enquiries would be seriously undertaken and secondly to see if the security services there were monitoring anything interesting in the Caribbean.

Jake had made only one proviso, that the assumed link with American intelligence not be mentioned. He didn't want to discourage the source from trying again.

He resolved that if 'Mr Mysterious' put in another appearance, then he wouldn't slip out of Jake's hands without divulging 'all' of the relevant information. If the source proved reluctant then he'd have to be introduced to Andy and Arkady if necessary; it was just too important to piss around with the niceties of diplomacy.

The meeting drew to a close with an apparent majority in favour of a 'wait and see' approach. Buerke's attitude still rankled with Jake. He was aware that Buerke had opposed the

'*Bismarck*' arrangements from the start, but was there another reason for his opposition?

The two situations were not obviously linked, one being a commercial venture and the other at best a hoax threat, at worst the real thing. But at their heart, both the presence of *Bismarck* and tonight's discussion topics dealt with the ability of this country to respond to foreign aggression.

Jake waited until Buerke had left before approaching Sandiford Roche. The large, high ceilinged cabinet room was emptying rapidly giving it an increasingly echoic nature as Jake sat down in the ornately carved chair next to Roche.

"Mr König, I somehow expected you would want a word with me."

Roche continued shuffling through the papers in the portfolio on his lap and didn't look directly at Jake and Andrew had gone straight to his private office for a call.

"What can I do for you? The meeting is closed and I have an urgent appointment."

Jake speculated on what kind of urgent appointment awaited McTeal's 'special' minister at 10pm on a Sunday evening, but said nothing. Roche turned to observe him, his amber eyes sparkled in the now subdued lighting.

"You did wish to speak to me, didn't you Mr König?"

There was something in his tone which suggested that he already knew what was on Jake's mind. Again Jake said nothing, simply returning Roche's gaze.

"Come Mr König, you're not normally reticent. Let me put you at ease by suggesting that you were about to voice misgivings about a colleague of mine."

He smiled at Jake's expression of surprise.

OK, asshole, thought Jake, play your games. He was far from reassured by the minister's words, but he was now committed. Or was he?

"I just wanted to comment on your lack of involvement in the proceedings tonight."

In fact Roche had only spoken once during the entire meeting.

"I'd have thought that this business fell well within the purview of your invisible portfolio. I confess I'm curious."

Roche cocked his head slightly to one side, giving him an almost boyish look as he replied but his words belied the image.

"I will answer your unasked question and ignore your curiosity Mr König. Yes I am concerned that a certain member of the cabinet was more than 'necessarily' against any action which would enable this country to prepare itself to deter a potential aggressor. Does that satisfy you? I hope for his sake that my concerns are misplaced."

Jake now returned the smile.

"I'm glad we understand each other Minister, I will inform you directly if I have any other misgivings."

He stood up to leave and turned back.

"I understand you wish to inspect the facilities being constructed on Little Cayman. We will be sailing sometime on the 23rd; perhaps I can offer you passage since our first stop will be the Little Cayman site?"

Roche looked up. "I would value the opportunity to sail in your ship Mr König, please inform me when your sailing time is fixed."

Jake nodded and left Roche sitting at the now empty table, a deep frown creasing his features as he stared at the far wall.

He saw Reiner waiting outside, obviously still seething from his cross examination. The night air was warm but Jake still felt an unsettling chill. He sensed he was being manipulated by invisible puppeteers, that events were coming to a head and everyone seemed reluctant to look down the dark corridor of the future.

Mentally shrugging he joined Reiner and deciding to pre-empt his indignant friend, he held up a hand to forestall any outburst.

"Don't go off half cocked. I know that wasn't very pleasant but the whole evening wasn't wasted, come on let's get back to the ship and I'll tell you what happened after you left."

Morning Monday 21st May 2018

Petionville, Port Au Prince, Haiti

Sophie was pleased with Francesca's choice of a husband; she really needed someone to take care of her. The contrast between the two women would be absolute were it not for the fact that both would be considered strikingly pretty.

Sophie, auburn haired, pale complexioned, tall, slim and totally self-confident as opposed to the small, raven haired, equally pretty but exotically olive complexioned and insecure, Francesca.

They had gone to school together, a private school sure, but a good school all the same. Sophie had been Francesca's mentor, saviour on occasion, and confidante. The problem had been that Francesca, a foreign diplomat's daughter, was 'different`, and she also lacked the confidence to make the most of it; so she was an easy mark for bullies, that was until Sophie took charge.

Overnight Francesca's lonely world had changed and she blossomed under Sophie's umbrella of benevolent friendship. It was a debt that Francesca knew she could never repay, but she would never stop trying though.

It was for this reason that she had been so unusually insistent with her husband when Sophie had written outlining her proposal. Francesca's husband had been very reluctant to discuss a ministerial topic with his wife but she had persevered and finally he'd agreed to listen to Sophie's idea.

As Minister of Agriculture and Natural Resources Louis's position was not a senior appointment within the Farache regime. Farache disgusted him, he was an arrogant, pompous ass and his latest schemes couldn't bring anything but disaster to Haiti. He knew he should have objected but that wouldn't have stopped Farache, it would just mean that he would be replaced and very likely disappear.

He tried to justify his lack of opposition by telling himself it was best to work from within to try to be the voice of moderation whenever the opportunity presented itself. He was also puzzled and disturbed by the recent abundance of money for projects which had previously been pipe dreams.

Last year he'd tried to prize some information out of the Finance Minister, an action which had nearly ended his ministerial career on the spot. The man had clammed up and Louis had been visited shortly afterwards by his colleague the Interior Minister.

The message had been received loud and clear, but he hadn't stopped wondering.   Privately he longed for a return to democracy, true democracy, the brief taste during President Aristide's fleeting reign had whetted his appetite.

Louis also had his doubts about some of the things that Aristide had allowed to happen in his name but the transition from a century or so of ruthless dictatorship to democracy was bound to be fraught with difficulties.   What this friend of Francesca's suggested was a first step along the path towards getting Haiti off the list of the world's poorest nations.

She ran a small division of her husband's corporation which specialised in bringing industry into areas where it had died away or had never been.   The benefit to the company was not immediate; the contracts always specified that the parent company would not take profit until a certain level of local profitability had been achieved.   They saw it as a long term investment not a short term 'rape and escape' move.

He was wholly convinced of Mrs König's personal sincerity and by reputation, of her husband's integrity, no doubts at all there.   The trick, as she'd stated, was to keep a certain kind of local person away from the neonatal industry. For that she would need ministerial support.

Yes, he admitted to himself, she had a good point, there was far too much corruption and 'protection' money paid out by businessmen at present.   It sapped the will to succeed and encouraged the idea that certain types of crime were OK.

Anyway he would certainly look into it, if there was any way that it was feasible then he would push for it. A sudden thought struck him; perhaps he wouldn't be around after next week. He hadn't liked the way Farache had studied him during the last full cabinet meeting.

Monday 21st May 2018

HQ, US National Security Agency, Fort Meade

Vernon Weathers re-read the satellite evaluation to see if he'd missed anything on his first fast pass through. It's already started, he thought, picking up the phone and asking for a secure line.

He punched in the two numbers he needed for his conference call and waited for the three way link.

"Miles, Nate, I just got the latest sat-eval. I'll read it to you both, OK. Here we go.

SAT RECON EVAL. CARIH/HAITI/PORT AREAS. 211830ZMAY.
1. CONCENTRATION OF NAVAL UNITS ON JACMEL.
17 VESSELS. ID LIST FOLLOWS. ANNEX A
2. ADDITIONAL 7730W.l830N. 1DDG.2FFG. COURSE 272 SPEED 15.
3. APPROACH RDS JACMEL SHOW. ARMOURED REC UNITS
INF ASSAULT EQUIP INF UNITS. EST REINF COMBINED ARMS
BDE. BREAKDOWN FOLLOWS.

Did you get that, both of you?" Vern sat back in his Chair and picked up the attached lists. Miles Carlson down at Langley was first to reply.
"For your benefit Nate, 'cos I know you DEA types aren't into this military bullshit, I'll read back my translation to Vern. OK? Number one's obvious, right? Number two, a position ref, I guess somewhere between Haiti and the Caymans, am I right?"

"Go to the top of the class big boy." Chuckled Vern.

"It's about halfway and the stated course is towards the main island, Grand Cayman."

Miles continued.

"Right, fine. We've got one missile destroyer and two missile frigates or something going towards the Caymans. Now have we got a case for the National Security Council or not Vern?"

Miles Carlson had been an army man before the CIA so he could guess some of the shorthand but not its strategic meaning.

"No I don't think so Miles, you know what our president thinks about poking our military nose in things nowadays, even when it isn't guesswork. Like, we won't be allowed to do anything until those SOB's are running their flag up on Grand Cayman."

He snorted and climbed on his favourite soapbox.

"Whitehouse foreign policy experts, an oxymoron if ever there was one, have had their collective fingers fried once too often over the past two years for them to take any notice now."

He could almost see his DEA friend bridling at that and knew he'd be next to comment.

"Time out Vern. That's a little unfair, I admit they've become a bit ostrich-like where foreign policy is concerned but this is right on the doorstep for Christ's sake, they can't ignore it."

"Watch 'em." Was Vern's only comment.

Nate was no great lover of politicians, period. But he thought that the newest member of the gang had brought a little more naïve but honest intent to the White House. But there was no way they could keep everyone happy, which is what they invariably tried to do.

Miles butted in.

"I think Vern is right Nate. They will continue to ignore it until Farache walks into the UN and rips the Caymans flag out of the 'proposed member's booklet' and even then they'll just try and reach an accommodation.

He sighed audibly.

"All we've got really is a bunch of ships sitting around a harbour with a load of 'grunts' heading towards them. We have another three ships sailing in the Caribbean which is of course international water, and they can be going anywhere."

He recalled the comments made by Sir John Knott and wrongly attributed to Margaret Thatcher, after the Belgrano sinking back in 82'. Nott had said "I remain astonished that anyone should consider the momentary compass bearing of Belgrano's passage to be of any consequence whatever. Any ship can turn in an instant". So in reality their current direction of travel could not condemn them, Nott was absolutely correct.

Miles had his own idea of what to do about the situation; they had already stepped out of line on this one, so what had they got to lose now?

"What I think we should do is sit on it until the main force moves, we can't go raise the alarm now just for three ships. We don't have a clue what they're up to anyway. Either of you got any problems with that?"

No, they hadn't. They agreed to meet as soon as the main force moved.

Tuesday 22nd May 2018

Bismarck, off Grand Cayman

Lt Ian Halshaw stepped back quickly as the Arado 196 drone seaplane accelerated past him along the catapult launching platform. The small launching trolley hissing by noisily leaking compressed air as it gave the aircraft the speed required to keep it flying until the small booster rocket underneath took over to lift it to its operating altitude, before then dropping away.

Just as suddenly as it began, the harsh noise ceased. All that remained was the gentle whine of the electric motor reeling in the launch trolley ready for the next plane. He wiped his forehead on the sleeve of his white overalls and turned towards Ian Waylen. Waylen was the electrical mechanic manning the launch console and was now using the derrick to lift the next Arado on to the trolley ready for take-off.

As yet its wings were still folded and it had not ordnance or recon pods attached. Luigi Abbate was ready with the required attachments for it and waited while Waylen began unfolding the wings. As each wing was locked in place Luigi approached and began plugging in or fixing on whatever was required.

"I must admit Waylen, it all seems fairly primitive compared to the rest of the ship." Said Halshaw.

He waved his arms to take in the expanse of the launching area and the catapult track that extended out over the ship's side; it ran literally from one side of the ship to the other and beyond.

Waylen nodded in agreement and smilingly pointed to the diminishing Arado.

"I can see your point boss but there's nothing primitive about that little beauty though, is there?"

Halshaw watched the shape of the diminishing aircraft for a few seconds, no he thought, nothing primitive about that bugger.

It had kept him and his small staff of electrical engineers busy for the past week trying to locate the 'glitch' that had prevented them exercising this part of the ship's armoury during the trials off Bermuda. The problem, when it had eventually been traced, had been within a 'co-processor' chip in each of the four Arado's. The faulty, silicon artificial brains had eluded the diagnostic tests for ages.

Then, by the time the problem had been located, the trials had finished, the whole ship tested but for this small extension of his department. It annoyed him to say the least. But he felt the warm glow of achievement now as he watched the drone, go through its paces.

On the bridge all eyes were glued to viewers as the Arado performed it's tricks. The thought at the back of everyone's mind had been 'Thank the lord it hadn't failed when first used in the Med!'

It was closing in now on the small plastic container filled with hot water, that had been dropped over the side on four hundred yards of line a few minutes ago.

Using the sensitive infra-red scanning cameras to locate it the picture was then relayed directly to the viewers on the ship. Now it had a lock on the target and the laser designator switched itself on automatically, centring its cross hairs over the plastic container.

Jake smiled to himself and turned away from the viewer.
"Excellent." He said to no one in particular.

The four Arado's were his favourite 'toys'. They gave the ship a reach it could not possibly obtain any other way short of having its own personal satellite to relay information. Now that's a thought Jake ruminated.

The obvious visual difference between the old *Bismarck's* manned Arados and this set, apart from their size, was the propulsion system. From propellers to ramjets; the current engines used a mostly porcelain and carbon fibre structure so were invisible to radar as well as being incredibly fuel efficient.

The only propellers on these were tiny and used its forward momentum to trickle charge and store electricity in some pretty cool lightweight carbon cells which were built in to the fuselage. Add to them the thin film solar collectors built into the upper surfaces and these planes could keep a reconnaissance going for hours.

Jake had been as proud as a new father as he'd inspected the first one back in Sevastopol, only four yards long with a wingspan of six, they looked just too small for manned flight yet too big for unmanned.

Bismarck's four drones were normally folded away in what should have been the steam pinnace sheds, on either side of the funnel. The original *Bismarck's* hanger had been immediately aft of the catapult but on this ship that area was part offices and part Jake's cabin.

Simon McClelland's voice came through the left earpiece of Jake's headset and he immediately said 'Share Captain' so it fed into Reiner's at the same time. Simon had spent the last twenty minutes searching for a radar return, however small from the drone.

"No radar targets at all boss on any frequency, we can't see it at all.   I've been through all of the bands twice and very carefully, but ESM is of course tracking the bearing of the emissions when she's out of visual and unable to use laser. Mind you, I do have the advantage of having pre-set all of the frequencies.   So I'm pretty certain that its frequency agility processor will hop faster than anyone could either jam or get a lock on. The only way to beat it would be to know the algorithm that the computer shared with the plane before it took off."

"Thanks Simon, so the data-link is working in both modes OK? Are you getting good targeting information?"

"Yes boss I did all that on the earlier runs when we tracked the ship's boats. It works perfectly, really."

"Excellent."   Jake said again turning to Reiner who was smiling and nodding agreement.

He was immensely pleased, the Arado was invisible to the ship's hi-tech radar and it would be difficult for an enemy to locate and pin down the brief, frequency agile, data-link transmissions.   He knew that all ears on the bridge were discreetly and not so discreetly monitoring his conversation, especially the next bit.

"Right, OK Simon. That's my testing set complete. Over to you Captain Krull." He gave a mock bow to Reiner who returned it and then spoke to Simon.

"Recall and recover the drone, let's secure down to cruising stations, we'll head back to George Town now Simon." Said Reiner.

"Roger that boss."   Came the joyful reply.   Simon was obviously looking forward to another night on the town, Reiner thought.

He spoke into his mike "Guns." A click then connection.

"Julius can you climb out of your eagle's nest and take over the watch for a while please, I'm leaving the bridge with the Commodore."

Acknowledging the order he climbed down into the main bridge to take over.   He was so often up above in the Main Gunnery Control Centre or MGCC that people simply forget he was there. Julius and his assistant, Carl Heinz Dettweiler, were forever running simulation gunnery engagements and walking the upperdecks could be hazardous if you didn't keep alert.

A notice on each turret proclaimed that it could train and fire without warning.   But it wasn't so much the chance of being blasted to pieces that made upperdeck walkers wary, it was much more likely that you'd end up 'wearing' a couple of large sized gun barrels as they swung quickly to point at their imaginary targets.

The ship's computer system provided a full range of simulations dealing with all kinds of scenarios, Kopf and his assistant made full and frequent use of them. The MGCC was located almost in the same place as on the original *Bismarck* and for the same reasons, it was important to have a clear view of targets especially if your radar had been knocked out. Their 'eyrie', the MGCC was the highest manned position on Jake's *Bismarck* and because of its importance it was also heavily armoured.

*

Down in the wardroom Jake was chairing the meeting; they all sat around the large dining table on the port side sipping tea and coffee as they discussed the plans spread out before them. A large scale model of the northern end of Little Cayman was the centrepiece of the table.

An integral part of *Bismarck's* commercial viability and its potential military capability depended on the construction of base facilities at the north Eastern tip of Little Cayman.

Jake wanted as much as possible of his organisation out of the direct reach of the European Union as well as the United States. He was still anticipating trouble from having effectively constructed and armed a private warship.

He knew he could not use the Cayman naval ensign when his vessels were on their commercial operations but that gave rise to another potential problem.

A 'belligerent' national warship *theoretically* had the right to stop and search them. As they *theoretically* could any merchant vessel on the high seas whether neutral or enemy. Belligerent was the key word.

Since America had declared war on 'terror' did they now think they had a right to stop and search any ship? Would other national navies take a chance? Perhaps a quiet agreement behind closed doors for NATO ships to do so? He did not think for one moment the Russians or Chinese would be bothered.

What would constitute valid grounds or suspicions that they could justify in court? Which court?

Such activity by Britain had in the distant past led to war. What was a distinct possibility however was some enterprising soul putting it to the test and them ending up with a stark choice of compliance or refusal, and damn the consequences.

The new facility at Little Cayman was ideal. Jake's own house was situated about a hundred yards inland from East Point and he'd often looked out over the arc of the sickle shaped reef thinking what a perfect harbour it made.

The reef stretched from Snipe Point to his left curving around almost to his front. Not wishing to upset the natural balance of the area too much, Jake had ordered extensive environmental surveys before adapting the reef to his own uses.

Holes had carefully and slowly been drilled through areas of the reef which were actually dead, then piles had been sunk to support the harbour structure itself thus not doing much more than shading areas.

To mitigate that even, reflective materials had been underpinned to ensure light reached all areas it used to. Additional work had been done to aid reef development all around the island since much damage had been done over the years before people had understood how important it was to preserve them.

The construction of the harbour walls, which were 'Y' shaped in cross section, and the docking facilities, was all but complete now and all of the construction had been done in local materials. The seaward sides of the harbour were rugged and blended in well with the low cliffs in the background.

Those that sat around the table were impressed with the lengths that Jake had gone to in order to disguise the facilities. Much of the construction had been, of necessity, underground. This was partly due constraints imposed by the island's size, it was only ten miles long and a maximum of one and three quarters wide, and partly for security reasons. The apartments had been built behind the tree line on the wooded Weary Hill, up behind Jake's house and for every tree removed, two had been planted elsewhere.

They would be sailing to the island early on the 24th but the families would flying into Grand Cayman tomorrow and on smaller charter planes direct to the strip on Little Cayman, the same day.

It was a big deal for the families moving out here, so Jake wanted to be sure that everything had been done to assist with the settling in process. The meeting continued for another half an hour before Jake called a halt to it.

"Right everyone, just one more thing before we break up."

He waited until he had everyone's attention.

"About an hour ago we received a communication from the Prime Minister's office. It is possible that we have identified our opposition. No, that's not strictly accurate."

He stared at the slowly turning deckhead fan for inspiration and then continued.

"It is possible that our potential opposition has identified itself." He looked around the puzzled faces before continuing.

"It seems that there was another unfortunate terrorist incident in the Haitian capital of Port Au Prince this morning. A bomb exploded in the central bus station killing nineteen people and injuring thirty four more.

Their President has already broadcast a statement to the effect that the perpetrators and anyone connected with them will be punished. More unfortunately, he seems hell bent on blaming our new home for supplying the finance for the terrorists.

A note was delivered by the Haitian Ambassador demanding the cessation of support for the terrorists and reparations for the families of those killed. Needless to say, Andrew McTeal's government had nothing to do with it and of course have denied any involvement and have repudiated any such suggestion. Any comments?"

Andy Evans shifted uncomfortably before speaking.

"Boss, supposing they are the ones that are looking for a punch up. That puts Mrs 'K' and two of my boys in a nasty situation if the shit hits the fan."

Jake nodded.

"I know Andy, I'm going to talk to my wife tonight, she's in a meeting in the capital all day apparently according to Winston. I've asked for the nearest company Gulfstream to file a flight plan for tomorrow. I want them out soonest but that is just a sensible precaution not an indication of how seriously I view the threat."

He looked around the table.

"Everybody. We don't know what's going down out here or if there is anything going down at all. Whatever it is, I don't want us caught with our trousers down if something happens, so let's just be extra vigilant in everything we're doing. OK?"

Ian Halshaw spoke up.

"Boss, what about the families coming in tomorrow?"

The concern was evident in his voice, Jake remembered that Ian's wife Liz was on tomorrows' flight along with their daughter, Julia. Liz was going to be the practice nurse in their own medical centre and was apparently bubbling with the possibilities.

"Yes I've been thinking about that Ian. I cannot of course guarantee everyone's safety against every eventuality. I was originally going to take them all across on *Bismarck* but decided it wasn't perhaps the best idea to put our nearest and dearest on the only warship this country has."

He paused to let that sink in.

"I will be happy for individuals to determine the risk themselves and if they feel it appropriate, to turn their family members around and send them back either home after a night's rest, or perhaps to the US if they feel uncomfortable bringing them here."

Jake looked around the table to assess the mood, he was particularly interested in Kipper's response as the only representative of the 'lower deck'.

"I think we should meet the flight coming in tomorrow, get everyone a good meal and a bit of a rest then each make that determination. I've talked to Reiner and he's happy that those with incoming relatives will be allowed liberty."

Kipper was nodding and not looking too concerned so Jake presumed he hadn't any objections so far.

"In addition I will make available the very latest intelligence and even speculation so that people can make this choice based on all we have. What does everyone think?"

Ian looked sheepishly relieved while nodding his assent and there was a general murmur of agreement.

"Right that's settled then. We will sail for the island sometime after midnight tomorrow with the Minister and staff on board but the families which wish to continue will fly tomorrow afternoon and should all be still in bed by the time we get there in the early hours."

As everyone filed out, Jake took Andy Evans aside.

"Andy, how soon before we have the land based Giraffe AMB radar operational there, and how soon before we have our defensive systems on line?"

Andy looked at Jake for a moment.

"You really think something's going down boss?"

"Dammit Andy I don't know but I don't want us to get caught out. My personal radar screen has contacts all over it! Maybe someone out there is working to a timetable; we just have to go as fast as we can without panicking. Now, when will we be ready on the island?"

Andy took out a voluminous notebook and consulted it.

"According to the last report from the Saab technicians dated two days ago, they should have the radar up and running in four days and the defensive systems in a week."

"Jesus that's cutting it a bit fine if the man from Washington is on target with his estimates. I wish we could have another talk with him, I feel like a blind man with a five hundred piece puzzle made out of the smoothest material devised."

*

"But I'm telling you Sophie it all points to Haiti."

Jake listened again.

"Seriously darling, I'm very pleased that the talks are going well and that Francesca's hubby is a good bloke BUT you yourself said he wasn't in Farache's inner circle; he won't necessarily have a clue what they're cooking up, if they're cooking anything up at all. Now, the flight should be coming in tomorrow I'll get timings to Winston and Tetsunari, you can always go back if nothing happens, just claim a family crisis."

Andy could sense Jake's exasperation. He'd been trying for fifteen minutes now to persuade Sophie to leave Haiti. She was adamant that there was nothing unusual happening there and that she was as safe as houses, especially being the guest of a government minister.

Jake finished listening again.

"Look. Just please take it on trust from me darling, at the moment it's not just my considered opinion but Andrew's too, and I know how much you respect his opinion. Sophie we're not scaremongering, something is going down and if we are correct, you're going to end up on the wrong side of the wire."

Andy thanked the Lord again for not giving him a wife and children. They invariably cluttered your mind so that any decision making was more emotional than logical. He knew too that rational thought went out of the window when 'family' were threatened in anyway.

He sensed that Jake was winning his battle to convince Sophie. That was another problem with family, you couldn't just order them to do something you had to persuade and cajole.

"Right then, thank God. Look I'll get someone to tell Winston when the flight plan is in and they'll make all the arrangements from then on OK? Right I'm off then, put Winston on will you, Andy wants a word with him. Love you. See you tomorrow sometime, bye darling." Andy was embarrassed to see the relief on Jake's face as he stood up from the communications console and handed Andy the headset.

Still, he was relieved himself. It would be nice from a security point of view to have all of the König's where he and his men could keep an eye on them. He waited until Jake had gone before speaking to Winston.

"Now listen Winston, you and Tettas make sure that Mrs 'K' is on that flight tomorrow, it's just possible that you could be wandering around in enemy territory if you stay there, got me? Fine now you have the standard kit with you yes? Right, OK. You know the routine, keep your eyes moving and no one, no one, is a friend got it? Right. Full alert status until I tell you different, one of you no more than a room away."

He listened to Winston's reply.

"Fine. I'll see you both tomorrow sometime, just hop a charter out to the island."

He paused, his operatives were the nearest thing he had to family.

"Listen, be careful you black bastard, just you and your Jappo mate get here in one piece with the cargo, bye."

He sat back in the swivel chair and glanced around the OPs room thinking any PC Luvvies would be foaming at the mouth after that little chat. Of course Winston and Tetsunari wouldn't though. He saw that it was 'scouse' Smith as the duty radio/OPs man.

"Scouse. Scouse." He kicked the edge of scouse's chair and the Liverpudlian looked up from his displays.

"Yeah Andy, what can I do you for?" He asked taking one of his ear buds away temporarily.

"Just make sure tonight that anything about the Gulfstream comes to me first whatever the time, and if anything comes from George Town let me know. I won't wake the boss unless it's urgent. OK?"

"Rog Andy. What's happening mate? Is someone really looking for a 'bundle' with us?"

Andy noted the slight pitch of excitement in Scouse's voice. Never been near an angry bullet or he wouldn't be so bloody keen, he thought but didn't say.

"Not really scouse, just the usual panic over nothing I expect." He got up and left.

Wednesday 23rd May 2018

George Town, Grand Cayman

The next morning Reiner declared a Sunday routine, most of the crew that were not on duty later, went ashore for a last look around before they sailed for Little Cayman.

They all knew that there wasn't much on sparsely populated Little Cayman to entertain them, apart from a couple of bars at the other end of the island so they were making the most of it. Of course 'nothing to do' apart from the incredible diving and snorkelling but guys like a variety of relaxation options.

The best that the single men could hope for would be a night out across on Cayman Brac every week or so. Little more than four miles east of their island, its population was around two thousand and it had a number of bars and restaurants they could visit. A regular tender would be organised anyway for fresh foods etcetera and would ferry them there and back.

The day passed quietly for the most part, the aircraft bearing the thirty or so family members arrived and partners exchanged whoops and hugs as parent and children were reunited and after lunch at the Lobster Pot on the sea front they all went back to *Bismarck* and the serious conversations began in the wardroom for the parents while the children were kept occupied by a guided tour of the ship and or refreshments in the Senior Rates mess.

Jake and Reiner started off by stressing the confidential nature of the information and asked if it could be kept within this room until it was proven either way. Andy Evans gave a brief on security on the island and then it was discussion and decision time. Jake couldn't work out whether he was pleased that everyone decided to continue or whether he would have preferred it if everyone had decided not to go on.

Either way, everyone was waved away on the two charter flights which would take them out to Little Cayman and to a new life. Half an hour later they had landed and were on their way towards the new complex.

All the apartments were furnished but clothes and other possessions would be arriving in another weeks' time on one of Jake's regular mixed cargo carriers which would just be able to fit through the harbour mouth and turn within.

On *Bismarck* last minute stores were brought on board and finally at eight in the evening, just in time for dinner, Minister Roche appeared on the jetty with his three plain clothes MPP bodyguards.

Most of the sailors would remember that balmy evening simply because it was so peaceful and the clear skies littered with stars. The muted sounds of entertainment floated down the shore to the ship from the nearby bars and the lights along Seven Mile Beach seemed to twinkle extra brightly, or so they would remember.

Bismarck sailed at three minutes past one on the morning of the 24th of May, the eighty mile journey would take them about six hours at most bumbling along at 14kts or so and they would arrive in time for a break-fast reunion with their families, that was the plan anyway.

02.30 May 24th 2018

Snowden Pond, Maryland, US

At 02.30 Vernon Weathers mobile phone by the side of his bed started to chirrup with a particular tone. The persistent low toned 'chirrup, chirrup' was finally acknowledged by his brain after the third repeat. He rolled over grabbed the phone, cradled it by his ear, and spoke softly trying not to wake his wife.

"Weathers?" He whispered.

"Duty Officer Fort Meade Sir, sorry to bother you."

"Yeah what is it?"

"Your night orders Sir. There's a SatEval that needs your attention Sir, it's marked 'Immediate. Eyes only' no electronic forwarding, Sir."

"Send a car, I'll be waiting."

"On its way Sir."

Vern tiptoed out of the bedroom carrying a shirt, slacks and shoes with socks tucked in them. He dressed quickly and made himself an instant coffee to kick start his brain, all the time pushing thoughts of the SatEval out of his mind -it did no damn good to brood about something you hadn't even seen yet.

He checked his watch, he was only ten miles or so away from the complex and at this time of night the Baltimore Washington Parkway wouldn't be its usual parking lot.

Half an hour later he was viewing not only the evaluation but blown up copies of the relevant satellite shots. A stream of questions poured through his mind as he noted the projected courses appended to the photos.

He needed to get in touch with Nate and Miles that was for sure. It appeared that the three 'wandering' Haitian ships and Mr König's 'Pocket Battleship' were going to meet in about two hours' time and neither side were aware of it, yet!

It was like being God. He could see what was going to happen and he could change it -if he felt the need to do so. Right now he could pick up the phone and speak to two people in different countries and he could stop what was bound to happen. Or would it happen anyway with both sides forewarned?

The phone on his desk rang loud and stridently, shaking him from his reverie.

"Weathers."

It was Miles Carlson answering his bleeper.

"Vern, what the fuck you dragging me out of bed at this time of night for?"

Weathers didn't bother with small talk.

"The three 'wandering minstrels' are heading towards the 'little bears' right now; they changed course sometime in the last hour."

Miles Carlson tried to shake his brain into action finally remembering their pre-arranged simple codes.

The 'wandering minstrels' were the three Haitian ships and the 'little bears' were the two smaller Cayman islands. So what else was there that had prodded Vern into ringing?

"Ok Vern I've got that on board. What else?"

Vern was mildly surprised that Miles had grasped that there was more to come but after all these years he shouldn't have been. Miles had been a damned good field spook so old habits like being instantly awake, died hard.

"The 'magical mystery machine' is on a course to intercept and will arrive at the Little Bears just after the 'minstrels', in about four hours' time."

He waited for the expletives and wasn't disappointed.

Miles' mind raced to cope, König's mini battleship was the mystery machine!

"Jesus fucking wept. Could either of them know about the other, you know, somehow they got word?"

"I don't think so Miles, but like you I hate coincidences. He continued. "I've woken up one of our on-loan Pentagon naval boys and he's on his way in to try and predict a result for us."

He drew a deep breath.

"What I want to know is do we do anything? It seems to me that there have been an awful lot of coincidences around here lately. You know, like this morning's superbly timed terror attack in Haiti that coincides with a small strike force being in position to retaliate."

He paused expecting Miles to jump in but he didn't, so Vern continued.

"It's starting to stink even more of a setup."

"Hell Vern, that was a long speech for this time in the morning. But heck, I know what you mean. I'm even more certain now that Farache has got his eyes on the Caymans. The gang of three are going to need to meet again soon aren't we?"

"So it seems. The big problem is this. If we tip off the 'mystery machine' and it intercepts the 'minstrels' before they arrive and do whatever they're going to do, *he's* got no proof that anything was going to happen anyway and unless they fire on him, he can't really start anything. Which means the next time Farache orders a strike, if he has, maybe the 'mystery machine' won't be nearby. Shit that twists my brain at this time of the morning."

He paused to conclude.

"Well, I couldn't locate Nate so there's only us two to decide. If we don't do anything, then maybe more people are going to die in the long run. In the short term the simple fact is that we have no proof of intention. So I think we're just going to have to wait and see again, do you agree?"

Vern paused to let Miles digest his conclusions. It was a lot easier when you'd been up and tossing a problem around for a while.

"I hate it, but doing nothing seems the only thing to do. I guess I'm rooting for the 'mystery machine' let's hope it's a 'mean machine'. OK, I concur Vern."

"I guess there's nothing more for now Miles, is there?"

"Nope. I'll see you tomorrow, err, later today, Vern."

05:50 Thursday 24th May 2018

North of Little Cayman, Haitian missile destroyer
Dessalines -Ex-Chinese Sovremenny

Commander Emile Aristole gave the order to turn to port reversing their course whilst bringing his ship broadside to face the first target.   He had decided to start with the new installations on Little Cayman whatever they were -the intelligence brief hadn't been very specific- and then carry on eastwards to Cayman Brac.   On arrival a few minutes later, he would work slowly down from the northern tip and along the west coast.

The additional fear it caused to the islanders on Cayman Brac, wondering what was happening on their near neighbour, then the dawning realisation that the same fate awaited them, would be worth the few minutes extra that it would take.   After all, the purpose of the mission was to strike fear in to the hearts of the new enemy.

Now time to get down to some serious target practice.   He smiled at the thought, glancing around quickly to make sure that his Ukrainian adviser wasn't watching.   Dammit why does he always make me feel like a naughty school boy?

Aristole was young for his command, only twenty seven, but the suddenly expanding Haitian navy had been desperate for commanding officers for its new fleet.

He and several other Lieutenants had been immediately promoted to Commander and sent away to the Ukraine and China on courses appropriate to budding commanding officers, that had been eighteen months ago.

He had subsequently been given command of this old ex-Russian, ex-Chinese Sovremenny class destroyer and at first had been disappointed.   This ship was not as new as some of the others in the fleet and would probably have gone for scrap before long, a 'rust bucket' he'd heard someone call it, but actually after a good refit and some fresh paint it had been transformed.

The surprising pleasure of being in command had doubled and trebled when Admiral Ramade himself had come aboard and then explained the *Dessalines* role in the upcoming operations. The honour of striking the first blow of the campaign had been given him along with command of the assaulting ships.

Life was good and could only get better; he felt a surge of pure joy at the additional honour of having the President's only nephew as a very junior watchkeeper. It all added up potentially to a glowing future.

He cast a furtive glance towards the other two ships of his small fleet, a pair of modern *Houjian* class missile corvettes.

At first he'd wanted one of those sleek powerful looking ships, a friend of his had one, but then he'd gone off the idea. Although they were newer and had slightly more modern weapons, the *Houjian* class corvettes were still only escorts to the major units like his missile destroyer.

The voice of his gunnery officer intruded into his reverie. "Permission to open fire Sir?"

Damn, he must keep his mind on what was happening. "Yes, yes of course. You have your orders, now get on with it."

He couldn't resist putting the barb on the end, this was real power. He turned to look out over the bow as the twin 130mm guns crashed out their opening shots. The war had started.

At the other side of the of the bridge, Captain 2nd class Gorshky, late of the Ukrainian navy and even later of the Soviet navy, watched without much apparent interest but inside he was seething.

His dark hair and pale Slavic looks contrasted completely with the Haitians around him. Trained 'monkeys' was how he thought of them -not too well trained at that.

What the hell was he doing here anyway? These idiots were about to start a war by committing an atrocity against a lot of innocent civilians. He didn't believe for a minute the story that had been given the crew; it sounded very much as if the Haitian propaganda machine had been trained by those arse bandits in Moscow, so very convincing.

Ha! He picked up his glasses and scanned the intended target just in time to see the first two shells impact a hundred or so yards beyond the dockside buildings they were intended to hit. 'Bud' ya proklyatyy!' -*I'll be damned*.

They couldn't even hit a stationary target at a range of two miles. He finely focussed the glasses on the impact point, it looked like some kind of apartment block -what was left of it. Flames were licking up from inside the building as the second pair of 60lb high explosive shells ripped into what looked like a refuelling pipeline down on the dockside.

The filthy billowing smoke obscured the target of the next shells until a waft of breeze parted the curtain of oily smoke long enough to see that they'd hit some kind of office building. He could clearly see a couple of bodies lying in the open, unmoving and other people were now making an appearance, short darting dashes between cover.

Something clicked in his mind as he watched them, he'd seen people move like that before, a trained movement like soldiers, he thought.

He considered telling that pompous 'prick' Aristole about it, then decided not to bother. It wasn't his business and he wouldn't do anything to help that incompetent shit anyway.

He scanned again and noted that a fine house was now on fire and the apartment blocks had been hit again, accidental or deliberate he didn't know. He could see women and possibly children running from them. He'd had enough.

"Captain Aristole, how long are we going to be shooting at targets that can't shoot back?" He knew the question was provocative and didn't care.

Aristole controlled himself with a great effort and deliberately waited a moment before answering the Ukrainian buffoon.

"If you wish to return to your quarters whilst we give our answer to terrorist aggression, please do so, and keep your opinions to yourself."

Gorshky left the bridge rapidly, fuming to himself. It was either that or throw that jumped up little turd over the side. The little sod wouldn't even be given command of a berthing buoy back home.

He made it back to his cabin without killing anyone and threw himself on his bunk. The useless bastards thought that putting gold rings on your arm made you an Officer, gave you experience and the ability to command.

Fortunately for them, they were unlikely to encounter anything more dangerous than a harbour wall; just as well, he decided and contemplated the last six months of his contract.

He and the other eight advisers would then be able to return home and be damned to these ignorant baboons.

"Ublyudok!" –bastards- he shouted and turned on his side.

Despite the regular thump of the guns Gorshky fell asleep thinking about his return to Ukraine and the wife and two boys he'd left behind.

05:55 Thursday 24th May 2018

Bismarck 16 miles SSW of Little Cayman,
80 miles WNW of Grand Cayman

Bren tossed and turned in his sleep. The girl kept speaking to him. Every time she spoke he turned to look at her and couldn't quite see her face. It was frustrating. He tried to walk around her to look and still couldn't see her face. He thought it might be Lorraine playing games and then someone set a radio alarm going in his ear, louder than usual and it wouldn't stop.....

The persistent high toned *Beep, Beep, Beep*, pause, *Beep, Beep, Beep* of the Tannoy tore him from his dream catapulting his brain into a maelstrom of confusion.

The beeping was the Morse for '**S**' and meant just one thing to sailors on a warship 'ACTION STATIONS, Surface Warfare'.

More unreal than the dream, he watched almost detachedly as his body responded to the commands of that 'trained' part of his mind.

One hand reached for his trousers and the other reached for the waist belt containing his anti-flash gloves and hood, life jacket and immersion suit. Yesterday's number 8 shirt thrown over the top, socks in his pockets and steaming boots on without being laced up.

He was almost dressed before he was awake enough to realise that the Tannoy was now telling him what was happening. By the time Brendan left his cabin, less than a minute after the alarms had sounded, his adrenalin vs. blood ratio, was about one to one.

Even as he ran through the passages to his action station, the other, normal, part of his brain was trying to remember the words that had spilled from the Tannoy.

Something about the new base, the islands, under attack shit! Lorraine was there now.

The bridge was all noise, movement and apparent confusion as men, wrenched from sleep, mingled with those who had been on watch when the alarm sounded.

The raised dais around Reiner's chair ensured that the tide of bodies washed around and not over him. He sat, still as death, the eye of the storm, occasionally speaking into his boom mike. He checked the clock as the final reports came in, not bad, five minutes from a cold start to closed up at action stations all guns loaded and all systems in the green.

He felt the ship surge and lift under him as the gas turbines wound her up to full speed. The tide of movement slackened, all that was audible now were the muted commands spoken into boom mikes. A tense silence enveloped the whole ship.

Reiner looked around to see a worried looking Jake come and stand next to him.

Jake found the professional Naval officer in him was busy calculating variables, making estimates and 'guesstimates' and taking the decisions, whilst the husband and father was torn in two different ways.

His wife was in Haiti and his children were at the house on Little Cayman. He would bet his last fiver that the source of this attack was Haiti. Instinct, no shred of proof. Which meant that his wife would now be in real danger.

He tore all thoughts of his family ruthlessly out of his mind and pushed them away until later, he just couldn't afford them now. He was the overall Boss here.

Down in the OPs room information was being processed and collated; a situation map had been projected, as yet with few details, onto the 3D holo display. All of the passive systems were fully operational but none of the active systems, and Simon didn't like what they were telling him.

He'd been Officer of the Watch when the thunder had begun almost as soon as the sun had peeked over the horizon to his right -the east. The two events were so close together that it was seemed as if one had caused the other.

He'd been scanning ahead ever since, towards the still dark part of the horizon west of north, using the low light sensors.

Then had come the brief radio message from the base at Little Cayman.

Static then "....*under attack from sea, two poss three ships shelling. Apartments hit...Command centre hit...boss's house hit...*'then nothing.

That was when he'd reached over and punched the action stations alarm.

Minister Sandiford Roche arrived on the bridge at the first convenient time, almost as if he'd waited in the wings during a play. He immediately walked over to Jake and Reiner, leaving his minders by the doorway.

"What has happened Commodore, Captain?"

Jake noticed the switch from 'Mr' to 'Commodore'. Without a word he handed Roche the printout of the radio message.

"Quiet everyone." Said Reiner in a loud voice just shy of shouting. "Switch that damn air conditioning off, open the bridge wing doors." Reiner cocked his head to one side.

Puzzled, Roche did the same. There was silence for a few seconds before the jarring rumble of thunder came to them. Thunder not far away. It started with a discernible 'Craaack!' before tailing off to a rumble.

In the distance Little Cayman was visible as a dark low hump on the Northern horizon, from its North Eastern tip rose a tornado shaped plume of smoke.

Further to the right and half lit by the rising sun, it was just possible to make out Cayman Brac. Roche looked up from his scrutiny of the brief radio message.

"What are your intentions Commodore?"

Jake couldn't detect any inflection in the Minister's words, but it didn't matter, his course of action was clear to him.

"I intend to locate the attacking vessels and 'prevent' them from causing any more damage to your islands and my people. Do you have any problem with that at all Minister?"

He hadn't meant it to sound like a challenge but that's how it came out. He supposed that it was due to his long held belief that politicians couldn't act, they could only prevaricate and this wasn't a time for waiting around.

Roche simply smiled weakly but there was no humour.

"But of course I concur Commodore; will it be possible to communicate with the Prime Minister?"

"I'm sorry, that won't be possible until action is joined, you see it would be possible to detect the transmission and we don't want to give the, bast.. err, enemy any warning of our approach."

He'd nearly said 'bastards'. The emotion crept in unwanted, unneeded, unbidden and most definitely un-useful.

"Grand Cayman will be aware now because of the base's transmission; I expect they're just trying to whistle up somebody senior enough to enquire what we're up to."

Roche cocked his head to one side in that curiously boyish manner of his, processing, always processing.

"I see. Will it be possible to watch the battle from here?"

"I'm sorry Minister but you'll have to go ashore if we can fix that."

"Sir there's a motor cruiser directly ahead, range four miles."

Buller's shout, louder than usual, provided a way for Jake to mask his surprise at the request and to marshal his arguments for dropping off the Minister.

This cruiser may be the way out of a potentially awkward bind; he just didn't want to spare the time required to drop the Minister in a boat near Little Cayman, but he didn't want him on board in the forthcoming battle.

The unsuspecting motor cruiser could be, no, would be, commandeered to take Roche to the base, yes, a good idea. Minimum of delay before we get up to those bastards shelling my children.... he thrust the painful surge of rage away and explained his idea to the Minister.

"Now it will be a couple of minutes before we come up to the boat so I'm shifting to the OPS room and I want a council of war down there in sixty seconds. Get everybody gathered Captain."

He turned to the Minister. "Your people can get your stuff together Sir, perhaps you'd like to listen in on the planning up until we come up to the boat?"

A moment later the OPs room began filling with the ship's officers ready for an 'O' group or orders group. Jake didn't hang around.

"OK, Simon what have your magic machines picked up?" He said referring to Simon's array of passive sensors.

"Right, we have two possibly three contacts on ESM, the bearings are between 025 and 030 which, since they're not in sight, puts them on the other side of Cayman Brac from us. Strength of transmissions suggests that they are between one and three miles offshore.

Transmissions which have been identified, are a mixture of Russian and Chinese origin, 'Square Tie', 'Rice Lamp', 'Palm Frond' nav radar, 'Top Plate' air and surface search, 'Band Stand' FCS and 'Kite screech' gun FCS."

Simon proceeded to list the NATO code classifications for the various radar emissions which told them what systems were up and running.

"Basically, the only ships in this area, which we know of, which use these systems belong to Haiti and my best guess is two of the Houjian missile corvettes and a Sovremenny class destroyer."

Reiner stared at the holo display for another ten seconds before speaking.

"Drone control." Click then connection.

"How long before we could get useful data from a recon drone over there." He used a touch pen to designate the area north of Cayman Brac and the screen in Chief Kempfe's drone control centre showed a blue dot with an expanding circle around it.

"Wait one." Answered Kempfe as he calculated the time to prep and launch, then gain a useful altitude, then move just a couple of more miles for basic coverage growing to good coverage as it closed.

"Basic coverage in not less than fifteen minutes Captain. Good coverage not less than twenty."

Reiner debated. It was no good lamenting that they had deliberately curved to the east during the night in order to come up to the islands from almost due south; but on the upside they could now use Cayman Brac to shield their approach from whoever the attackers were, right until the last minute.

"Launch with full recon package as soon as you can and bring the sensors up when you have the altitude to help."

It would either help or it wouldn't, decided Reiner. No point in arming it either, nothing they could launch would do much damage and would certainly get the enemy using their optical scanners to find the launch platform.

Jake looked around the assembled faces, 'grim faces' was the cliché that sprang to mind.

"My initial proposal is to veer slightly further to our starboard, still heading north before we turn to port at the last second, just short of West End point."

He indicated the approach route on the holo display.

"I want to mask our approach for as long as possible and gain maximum advantage from a surprise attack. Any other ideas strategy wise anyone."

Jake was using the central holo display to point out the various points of approach, the 3-D projection made it so much easier to grasp the scales and in this case terrain effects.

The islands of Cayman Brac and Little Cayman were displayed along with *Bismarck's* current position and three yellow symbols indicating the suspected positions of the enemy ships. There was no directional line showing from the base of any of the vessels since their course was as yet unknown.

A number of suggestions were put forward along with a restatement of the various problems. From the slight change of the bearings it appeared that the enemy ships were slowly cruising in a westerly direction, probably south west, parallel to Cayman Brac. They had apparently ceased their attack on Little Cayman and now were shelling Cayman Brac.

Were it not for the fact that these ships were hitting shore targets and therefore probably killing people, the best tactical approach would be to come at them from around the top of Cayman Brac, putting *Bismarck* behind the enemy on a darker

234

sea. The down side of that was the extra time that it would take to get into position, forty four minutes as opposed to twenty four minutes the short way.

The short way was also the most dangerous, steering for the gap between the two islands, using Cayman Brac to shield them for as long as possible, would mean that they would suddenly appear in front of the opposition and couldn't be missed.

Jake however, resented even the slight curve to the starboard because it meant a few more seconds before they could engage. But it was better than playing safe and taking forty plus minutes.

He nodded to Reiner. Are you in agreement with that Captain?"

"I concur Commodore, though no doubt you have already dismissed an engagement from the northern end as well?."

"Indeed Captain. The time factor." He need say no more. He also changed his mind about something else and turned to Sandiford Roche.

"Do you really want to witness this action Minister? You will be in real danger especially if you go up on the bridge with me?"

He had only that second decided to be on the bridge for the action, he really didn't want to crowd Reiner and Simon, they knew what they were doing, anyway he'd hear the OPs room audio on the bridge so he could in theory intercede if he felt it warranted.

Roche looked at him carefully for a second as if trying to divine his seriousness.

"You will not be in here Commodore?"

"No Minister, I am the Strategic Commander, Captain Krull and Lt Cdr McClelland are the Tactical Commanders. The strategy has been approved, only if it changes for some reason will I need to be consulted again. I'd be in the way here; besides I have the utmost confidence in the abilities of this ship's company and its systems."

"In that case I accept Commodore. What now?"

"Well we need to kit you and your men out in appropriate clothing." He looked over at Kipper.

"Anything to fit these gents in the slops?" He said referring to the spare clothing store. "Ovies, anti-flash hoods and gloves Kipper?"

"Aye sir, no problem." He gestured to the minister.

"If you'll come this way sir and bring your two minders, we'll get you sorted."

Roche looked a little uncomfortable, as if he'd painted himself into a corner. He smiled grimly to himself as he left the OPs room following Kipper down the ship's 'Burma Way', its widest corridor running fore and aft.

"Is that wise Sir, going up to the bridge with the Minister?" Asked Reiner as the door closed. He was in his formal mode with a quizzical eyebrow raised.

Jake smiled back.

"Probably not old friend; but if we sink Reiner, you'll get wet before me."

With that he left the OPs room for the bridge, leaving behind a grinning OPs room gang preparing for a fight in which they were outnumbered three to one and up against modern missiles as well as guns. He had a last thought as he went up the steps to the bridge and spoke into his mike.

"Kipper." Click

"Kipper, hoist battle ensigns if you please."

"Aye, aye Sir." Responded a surprised Kipper Herring.

A couple of moments later a twenty foot by ten foot Caymans ensign unfurled and whipped out from either side below the Foremast crosstree. Properly dressed now, thought Kipper looking up as the ensign rippled in the strong winds.

06.10 Thursday 24th May 2018

'Blue Parrot' Inn, West End Point, Cayman Brac

Captain Jason Sims USN(rtd), hauled his considerable bulk up through the narrow trapdoor that led onto the roof of the Blue Parrot which was just a few feet higher than the palms nearby.

Huffing and puffing with exertion, the silver haired navy pensioner hauled the owner, Mike Farrow, through the same small gap after him. The third and younger man, Tim Martin, climbed through what he thought was a generously proportioned trapdoor and slammed it shut behind him.

All three ducked involuntarily as another brace of loud explosions pierced the early morning quiet. Jason Sims planted his bulk in one of the rattan chairs and hoisted the large naval binoculars to his eyes.

The roof of the single storey building provided a much better view than the rocky foreshore.

"Jesus, shit! That bastard is just calmly working his way down here. Wait a sec, one of the corvettes is getting in on it now."

The sharper crack of a 76mm gun could be clearly heard now.

"I wonder what the fuck is going on?"

Mike Farrow plumped himself into the chair next to Sims.

"Give us a shufty 'J'?" Sims handed the glasses to Farrow and continued to gaze around.

"Who do you think's pissed off with us 'J'?"

Farrow was trying to focus the glasses on the nearest warship, now only a couple of miles away.

Sims, staring hard across the four and a half mile gap to Little Cayman and the smoke rising from it, spoke through the side of his mouth.

"Hell I don't know. I've been out of the Goddamn Navy for ten years now. How the hell should I know who's flying which chickenshit flag nowadays."

He grunted as his eyes scanned towards the south, the position of the Blue Parrot right at the southern tip of the island gave them an uninterrupted three hundred degree viewing arc.

"All I know is that it isn't 'Old Glory' flying on them or the 'Hammer and Sickle', which is shit strange 'cos at least one of them is Rooshian built."

Tim Martin stooped down beside Mike Farrow.

"Can I have a look please Mr Farrow?"

"Sure Tim, see if you can make out the flag on one of them, tell us what it looks like?"

He winced as more explosions rippled over by the light on Deadman's point and the dish aerials, just inland, disappeared in boiling smoke and flames.

Sims continued his horizon search, now looking south.

"I guess we won't be making any long distance calls for a while." His eyes scanned left and right as he moved through the compass points and locked on a distant speck.

"Now who the hell. Gimme the glasses quick."

Sims leaned over and grabbed the glasses taking Tim Martin with him as the latter failed to unhook the strap from around his neck in time.

Sims yanked a bit harder, his eyes still locked to the south; finally he turned round to the struggling Martin.

"Now stop messin' around boy and gimme those goddamn glasses."

"What is it 'J'? What have you seen?" Chipped in Farrow as he turned his gaze in the same direction. Sims was quiet for a few seconds as he fine-tuned the focus.

"Mike, did they just take the Union Jack off the Caymans flag after independence? Or did they do something else to it?"

Farrow looking puzzled was squinting in the same direction as Sims, he could make out something just a little left of due south but his eyesight wasn't getting any better as he grew older.

"The flag is just blue with one large and two smaller green palms in the top left corner, nothing else. Now what can you see for Christ's sake?"

Sims paused for another few seconds before speaking.

"It's the cavalry boys, hot damn! It's the cavalry!"

What the fuck are you talking about 'J' for Christ's sake? We don't have a Navy."

Sims turned to them both and smiled.

"You do now. That boy steaming hard up here is flying your flag guys and I don't expect he's comin' to ask nicely what those bozo's are doing shooting up the islands."

Farrow snatched the glasses back as Sims stood up to look around. His mind wound back to long forgotten lessons in tactics and strategy. He swept his eyes all the way around from north coast to south coast, a deep frown crossing his features. His mind made up he turned to the others.

"Mike, Tim, we gotta get in touch with our guys. They're comin' in blind, don't ask how I know it's too complicated, but we gotta tell 'em where those bastards are."

He paced the roof peering one way then the other.

"Hey have either of you got a radio... nah forget it, we wouldn't have time to find the right frequencies and the emergency channel is out 'cos the bad guys would hear too. Sheeit."

Deep in thought he walked quickly to the stone parapet that surrounded Mike's rooftop haven, and looked down at the tables, chairs and parasols out at the front of the inn. Damn! He needed some way to get in touch, he slammed his fist down onto the stone in frustration and started to turn away, then he saw just what he needed.

"Mike, quick, go down and crank your generator and gimme some power to your spotlights."

He turned away from a confused Mike Farrow and rapped out an order for Tim.

"Tim, I want you to stand here and point when I shout. I want you to point at the big ship first then at each of the little ones. You got that?"

"Yeah, sure 'J', I point right?" Said an equally puzzled Tim Martin.

Sims scrambled his bulky frame down through the trapdoor into the gloomy interior, more explosions sent tremors through the floor and lent urgency to his stride as he moved quickly through the deserted bar.

Outside he chugged over to the nearest lamp on the south side, this one would usually illuminate the palms on that side of the inn. A quick check revealed the power switches on the back of the powerful spotlight.

Sitting down next to it on a big border stone he heard the generator cough into life and the hum of power through the lamp. He concentrated hard remembering the old way, then began to send his message to the ship now barely four miles away.

*

Four and a half miles away at East point on Little Cayman, the crackle of burning buildings competed with the muted cries of the wounded. It had been nearly fifteen minutes now since the first shots had been fired at them.

Down at the dockside, Jan Helders a big blond Dutchman, one of Andy Evans' security team, knelt down on the stone jetty next to his friend Piet Pibis. Pibis was dying and Jan knew it, but there was nothing he could do.

Piet's guts were hanging out, Jan had tried in vain to put them back in but there wasn't enough left to put them in. He talked quietly to his friend cradling his head, he didn't know what he was saying he just knew that he didn't want Piet to go alone and in silence.

He looked around at the devastation caused by the brief but brutal bombardment, the heat from the burning fuel pipes forty yards away was getting too intense now. He could feel the sweat evaporating from his face as soon as it formed.

Jan looked down at Piet and stopped mumbling. He was dead. He slowly stood up and turned inland, the Command Centre was a shambles. He looked further inland towards the burning apartment blocks, no point in staying down here now he thought, the comms are wrecked.

He could hear distant raised voices, above the roar and crackle of the burning fuel. Taking one last look at his friend he began to run up the shallow incline towards the residential apartments, God knows what I'll find, he thought as he ran.

*

Liz Halshaw RGN was doing her best to staunch the flow of blood from the child's neck but it was damn difficult when one of your own arms was broken. She looked over at Trudi Krull and thanked the Lord that Trudi had arrived with the others yesterday. Liz was perfectly confident of her own abilities, she'd been an emergency room clinical manager for the last eight years, but it was really useful having somebody else around who was medically trained.

The apartment building nearest the harbour had taken a couple of hits along with the communal lounge area, the two storey linked buildings were only of standard construction and it showed. She didn't suppose the designers had really given much thought to making them shellproof, unsurprisingly. Unfortunately though four, of the new families had just moved in, all of them technicians for the harbour systems.

Liz was busy doing the triage and stopping bleeding while Trudi with two hands was doing the doctoring. Liz's casualty experience meant that she was good at most trauma stuff and experienced at deciding who needed treating next, as well as getting people organised.

Trudi was an ENT consultant and therefore hadn't practised general medicine for a long time let alone basic casualty work.

So it was handy for her to have Liz feed her the patients in the best order for treatment.

Nearly done now, only the one that Liz's holding, she thought to herself as she finished packing the large hole in young James König's thigh, he'd been caught by a flying fragment as he and his sister had run for cover after the bombardment had started. Jake was going to be really angry she thought abstractedly, it could affect James' ambition to be a navy pilot. She knew she was trying to do anything but think about the four dead lying over the other side of the road.

The smoke from the burning complex was thinning, everybody had been got out now and the living casualties were sitting or lying by the side of the new road.

She looked up as she heard running feet, she didn't know who the newcomer was but Liz obviously did.

"Jan thank God. Where's Piet? We need you both up here. We need to get everyone down to the medical block, we haven't got everything we need here."

"Piet's dead." He mumbled as he came to a shuddering halt.

She looked closer at him.

"Oh Christ not you as well?" She said, as she took in the open gash on his forehead along with the torn and dusty clothing.

"Come over here let's put something on that before you leak to death." Muttered Liz, as she got him to open a field dressing which she then applied.

"Hold that hard against your head. Were you knocked out? Have you any nausea, is your vision OK?"

She could see he was really distressed but had to get through to him.

"Get someone to tie these ends. Look Jan I'm sorry about Piet but we need your help here, now. Is there anyone else down at the dock who can help?"

Jan slowly shook his head.

"All dead." He said simply.

He looked around noting the three radar technicians and Ian Hubbard of his own security team. They were all busily helping to comfort the wounded who were mainly children.

"I don't think there's anyone else." He turned to Trudi.

"*Bismarck* will be here soon Mrs Krull; I managed to get through on the radio before we were hit. Your husband will send help soon."

Trudi perked up at that until the next thought jumped into her mind.

"Oh, oh no! What about whoever attacked us, I can still hear gunfire. There'll be a battle won't there? Damn them all! More useless deaths!"

"Calm down Trudi. My husband's on that ship as well, they'll get here as soon as they can. It's no good worrying about something we can't affect. If there's a battle, then *Bismarck* will win and then it will come here."

She looked across at the sheet covered corpses on the other side of the roadway, eyes lingering on the last little bundle in the line. Her daughter Julia, a whole seven years old.

She turned her dirty face and singed eyebrows to Trudi. Features contorted in pain, her composure cracking, she hissed.

"I personally hope they kill the whole fucking lot of them, whoever they are. The bastards"

She bent her head down, hiding her sobs of grief as she checked the bleeding and unconscious child.

Oh hell! Muttered Trudi following her gaze to the little bundles, suddenly realising Liz's loss.

06.17 Thursday 24th May 2018

Bismarck 2.3 Miles South of Cayman Brac

Reiner was now in the OPs room at his command console studying the display in front of him. He spoke into the mike.

"Guns." He heard the click of connection.

"Jules, how long to lock and fire once we pass around the headland and the radar comes on?"

Up in the MGCC, Julius Kopf was preparing himself for his first proper battle. To say he was nervous would be rather an understatement but he was determined to do it right.

"Less than a second for the TV and laser rangefinders Sir, they'll hand over to the radar for the second and subsequent shots. It depends on how quickly we locate them all."

"Thanks. Are you all set?" He added.

"Yes Sir, we're ready." Julius relaxed a little, yes of course he and Carl were ready, they'd done nothing but practice for months, what was he nervous about? Could it be to do with the fact that these targets could shoot back?

Reiner himself wasn't as calm as his outward appearance would suggest. Nagging doubts assailed him from all points of the compass. Was he right to ignore the longer approach? Should he have argued for that despite knowing how desperate Jake was to get to their island base, hell, not just Jake he corrected himself.

How would the ship perform? He had no doubts about the crew, but high-tech equipment was prone to catastrophic high-tech failure just when you needed it most.

Jake's words on the day of the mock missile attack came back to him with a sickening thud.

'...There is truly only one circumstance in which a fighting man can be judged and that, as you know, is in action.' He wasn't tested that day, Simon had done nearly everything. Was he afraid?

Every battle was different, but he'd never fought a real one, very few of them had. His mind roved searching for reference points. There hadn't been a major ship to ship confrontation since the Second World War. This would be the first. There were no precedents for modern surface warfare! Can I do it?

A voice, full of barely suppressed tension, reached into his self-doubt.

"Visual signal Sir, bearing 355!" Shouted Buller.

On the bridge Jake quickly turned his viewer to the bearing. Buller started reading what was clearly Morse code and Jake started writing on a pad in front of him as he spelled it out. The signal read.

A, A, A.
ENEMY IN SIGHT. 1DDG. 2FFG.UNKNOWN.
DDG.BEARING 330. RANGE 8500.
FFG.BEARING 335. RANGE 15000.
FFG.BEARING 345. RANGE 12000.
GOOD LUCK.

"Take a hand lamp onto the bridge wing and acknowledge, please Stroder."

Stroder nodded and disappeared. Jake re-read the message into his headset for Simon and Reiner's benefit down in the OPs room.

"I wonder who the hell that is? He added to no one in particular. "Clearly done our job before. No matter. Let's see what we're up against."

Jake wandered over to where Roche was standing.

"There is a retired US navy officer who lives not far from the point Commodore. It may be him." Roche commented.

Jake considered the response, impressed that the Minister knew the name of a particular resident on the island, and shrugged.

"I'm grateful. It gives our Gunnery Officer a half second head start. Now anyway where was I..."

He shuffled through the pages on his data pad until he found the appropriate section.

"Ah, there it is. Haiti. Two destroyers, ex-Chinese Sovremenny class and five Chinese Luda D class. Luda Ds are about the same size as us but the Sovremenny is 7900 tons loaded, twice our size." He added as an aside, "more like a cruiser."

"Both have got two twin 130mm guns. Eight SSN-22 'Sunburn' missiles on the Sov, I wonder which variant?" He mused. "And six or eight C802s on the Ludas. Still at this range it won't matter a great deal, we'll only get one guess. Forty eight SAN-12 Grizzly missiles on the Sovremenny." He smiled at Roche's alarmed look.

"Don't worry about those SAN-12s, they're anti-aircraft missiles." He finished.

"Now the corvettes. Six *Houjian* class, 520 tons, 30kts, four 37m cannon, four C802 SSM, again I wonder what variant because they have different seeker heads."

Jake frowned as he glanced over the details, checked his watch and walked to the command chair where he pressed a button. With a servo motor whine the armoured blast covers rose up behind and in front of the thick Perspex bridge windows.

"Replacement Perspex costs a fortune." Jake added flippantly bringing a smile to Buller and Stroder.

Roche's eyebrows joined each other at the top of his head as projected images blinked into life and it was as if they were really looking straight through the real windows.

07.19, time for a pep talk Jake decided.

"Shipwide." Click then connection.

"Do you hear there. This is the Commodore speaking. Sitrep. In about two minutes time we will be engaging three vessels. We don't know yet who they belong to but presume they are Haitian."

He paused a second.

"That's not too important at the moment though since they are shelling the islands. As soon as they have been dealt with, we will land parties to assist the civil population on Cayman Brac and then make our way to Little Cayman just as fast as possible. Those with wives and partners on Little Cayman will not be included in the landing parties for Cayman Brac."

That'll bring a few sighs of relief he thought. How could you look after other people when just a few miles away your own family needed you? He continued.

"Sadly, this is not one of my more elaborate exercises, I'm afraid. Just remember, these people have fired upon defenceless civilians some of whom are our loved ones. Let's deal with these...whoever they are, and get to where our help is really needed. I won't wish you good luck, because you won't need it. That is all."

Jake checked his watch again and looked through the viewer in front of him 0720.

"Buller, we'll go as close as we dare to the headland, I make that 150m and as we pass it we'll turn ten degrees to port. Got that?"

"Aye Sir. With respect that's awfully close Sir."

"I have the utmost confidence in your ability Buller. That should put us broadside to them and give us a good course to steer for open sea."

"When the action starts, try to remember to steer a few degrees port and starboard."

Jake mused as he looked through the viewer at the rapidly approaching headland, was it Jacky Fisher who had said it? 'Hit first, hit hard and keep on hitting'. Well whoever said it, they were right. We've just got to make sure that we hit first.

Reiner spoke to Julius again.

"As soon as you are able to get a lock don't wait for permission, open fire and keep firing until I tell you. I realise that it'll be a ripple broadside but that should be a psychological factor in our favour, it'll be one long roll of flaming thunder to them."

"Aye Sir." Acknowledged Kopf, then realised he hadn't been going to ask permission.

*

Down in HQ1, the damage control centre, Lt Ian Halshaw tried to keep his mind on the screens in front of him each showing different electrical systems, but thoughts of his wife Liz and their daughter Julia kept on intruding. It was like a tug of war inside his brain, one half saying they would be OK, the other half telling him all was not OK.

He pushed the 'enter' key on his keyboard as the computer asked if he wanted to run a system check on the 76mm secondary guns. Yes, check it, he thought. How the hell do I know if they'll be used?

Another light went on as the four main gun turrets were powered up and began to train towards the expected bearing of the enemy as Jake's Broadcast began.

I agree Jake, thought Ian after it had finished, let's go and shoot these buggers then I can go and check that my wife and daughter are alright.

Ken Herring sitting next to him, watched the emotional play and was thankful he'd no one on Little Cayman. Of all things, this new paradise was supposed to be safe.

*

In the Wardroom the doctor, Surgeon Lt Lawrence Cribb was busy setting out his operating and triage areas. This was where any casualties would be brought after first aid treatment in situ and the Senior Rates mess was where those who'd been treated would be sent.

Granny Smith was helping him along with Louis Fovargue one of the two French chefs and no stranger to blood and guts. Medical work at sea was an ad hoc trade-off between location and practicality. There was no way there could be enough space in the sickbay itself if the ship started taking damage and suffering casualties, hence the Wardroom had as usual been co-opted.

All the men had received good basic first aid training. The likes of Granny, his sidekick the Spanish Steward Jorge Vivarre, the other chef Mark Braime, no relation to the Engineroom Chief, and Louis, had received advanced training as well as some after care techniques from both Lawrence and Bren the medical senior.

Lawrence looked around, satisfied he had done what could be done to create a logical flow system. Now it was just the waiting. Feeling a little like a spare part he moved to the bar area and switched on the screen. Using the remote he flicked through the available external views until it showed the hump of an Island which appeared to be dead ahead.

Granny was watching him and saw the alarm that lit his face.

"Don't you worry Doc, they'll turn before they hits it. You see."

Granny went back to fussing over the Balmoral chair covers, he was every bit as concerned about properly covering all the wardroom furniture and dismantling the great table which was stowed below, he didn't want sweaty sailors bleeding all over this nice stuff.

*

Jason Sims noted the brief acknowledgement then clicked off the power switch to the spotlight. He stood up with a groan and massaged some life back into his oversized buttocks. A voice floated down from the roof of the Blue Parrot.

"Did I do alright 'J'? Did they answer?"

Sims began making his way toward the front entrance.

"Sure Tim you did fine and yeah, they got the message. Do me a favour, wait by the hatch will ya, I'm comin' back up."

Back on the roof he whipped the glasses from around Mike's neck and levelled them first at the unsuspecting enemy and then at the ship he dubbed 'Retribution' as it swiftly closed with the island.

Boy was that ship moving, he thought, as he noted the great white moustache at the bow. It was less than a mile away now and he guessed that she would turn slightly at the last minute in order to avoid the headland and to line up for her intended victims.

He didn't know why he was so sure of the result but he couldn't see it any other way. There was something menacing and implacable about that shape racing towards battle.

He put down the glasses, he didn't need them really now and without taking his eyes from the approaching Bismarck, he spoke to the other two.

"In just a couple of minutes guys, the shit is going to hit the fan, and if my guess is right, most of it will be going thataway."

He said, pointing towards the unsuspecting Haitian ships.

"...and we are going to get a grandstand view.

Shit it's like watching a goddamn film."

He checked his watch, it was 06:20

*

Lt Julius Kopf wiped the sweat away from his forehead for the sixth time in as many minutes, then immediately pressed his face back into the gunnery viewer.

The cross hairs for the laser range finder were laid over the headland less than 500 yards away. In less than a minute or so they would centre over an enemy ship. His guts had little fluttering spasms running through them, he could feel the raw adrenalin pumping into his bloodstream.

Steady, steady. Standby!

The mental refrain repeated endlessly.

He kept his eyes pressed into the viewer, his right index finger sweated over the 'lock' button which would lock the computer onto its first target. His left hand gripped the joystick control, that index finger hovered near the flip up cap that would allow him to shoot.

He spoke quietly to his partner sitting in the chair at his side.

"Not long now Carl, everything set?"

Steady, steady. Standby!

"Yes sir. All set. You take out the big bastard I'll sort out the little ones."

Steady. Standby, standby!

More sweat trickled down his face but he no longer noticed it, his body tensed like an athlete on the starting blocks. *Bismarck* started its ten degree turn to port, some one hundred and fifty yards short of the headland which immediately started changing shape. Not long now, seconds only!

Standby! Standby!

There were no human sounds on *Bismarck* at that moment as everyone held their breath.

Standby! Standby!

The words screamed in Kopf's brain, his eyes searching beyond the receding headland as the sea behind it moved into view with increasing speed. *Bismarck* steadied on her new course and slowed slightly.

Standby! Standby!

He'd said it out loud he knew, but he didn't care.

There it was, the bastard.

Right index finger. Lase.
Thumb on lock button! Engage.
Cross hairs flash red!
Locked.
Range data transferred to the guns.   Answering ping in his headset –guns aligned.
Left index finger flip the safety up.
Squeeze trigger!
SHOOT!!!
The time was 06:23.

*

Sims too sweated in anticipation. 'Retribution' seemed to swerve, the stern actually drifting round as it changed course slightly and visibly slowed.

He gasped as the full profile of the ship became visible for the first time. They all watched the four main gun turrets glide swiftly on to the new target bearing and he imagined he could hear the servo motors whining as the turrets turned.

The eight long slim barrels rose slightly as if sniffing for the enemy.

Now he knew this one would be the winner. It wasn't only to do with the number of guns pointing at the bad guys, he reasoned, this ship resonated menace.

"Jesus fucking H Christ."

He gasped out as the full extent of what was about to happen hit him. He turned quickly to look at the Haitian ships still steaming unconcernedly along the coast. His head snapped back instinctively to face Bismarck as it started to clear the headland and then all hell broke loose.

Angry flames and belching grey smoke erupted from the foremost guns followed by successive, percussive claps of thunder as one by one guns fired along its side just as soon as they had a target.

It rapidly became one long roll of roaring sound, gouting flame and smoke as the automatic guns reloaded and fired again and again and again, each time adjusting slightly as the now active radar fed back minute changes in their relative positions.

Sims turned to observe the fall of shot and noticed his two companions lying on the roof with hands over their ears. Grinning at the sight he whipped his eyes up just in time to see the first shells strike. Hot shit!

*

Jan Helders on Little Cayman looked up quickly as the sound of rolling thunder hit the island. Unlike thunder it didn't stop though. He smiled grimly, the repayment had started.

Then he got back to work. Why was it, he wondered sadly, that the dead are so much heavier than the living?

06.23 Thursday May 24th 2018

North West of Cayman Brac. Haitian missile destroyer
'*Dessalines*' ex-Chinese *Sovremenny*

Commander Emile Aristole turned at the shouted warning. His brain yelled that his eyes were lying. It could not be. Then he knew with a sickening certainty that it was so. He knew at the last that he'd screwed up.

The ship that had a second ago suddenly materialised to their front, completely disappeared behind gouting flame and banks of black and grey smoke. Voices came to him distantly. He watched in morbid fascination as his forward turret began to turn away from the shore and towards the intruder.

There followed a blinding flash, momentary pain and then nothing. *Bismarck's* first shells had arrived on the bridge of the *Dessalines*.

Down in his cabin, well aft and one deck below the main deck, Captain Second Class Gorshky was picked up and then thrown onto the deck, or so it seemed to him. His nose sprang a leak. He was trying to lever himself off the floor as the second salvo of shells ripped into his ship, throwing him back against the side of his bunk and clouting his head.

Cursing loudly and fluently, he managed to get himself upright and to the cabin door. He'd just got the door open and had lurched into the passageway when a titanic explosion lifted the ship and him with it, bodily upwards and then he was once again thrown down with a bone jarring crash.

He thought he might have broken an ankle this time because the pain that shot through him when he tried to place weight on it to stand again, was off the scale. That was the death blow, he knew it instinctively.

Picking himself up for a third time and cursing even more fluently, shuffling and hopping he made his way forward through the thickening smoke towards the single flight of stairs that led to the upperdeck door. Using railing and one foot he got to the top of the stairs, unclipped the door and pushed. It moved about three inches.

A wave of panic briefly swept over him as visions of being trapped in a sinking ship leapt into his mind. He viciously suppressed them.

The smoke was thicker and the deck had taken on an ominous forward tilt, explosions still racked the stricken ship. The scream of incoming rounds was almost continuous.

The professional part of his mind noted that the sounds were consistent with 130mm artillery, just like theirs. Marshalling his muscular frame along with his most descriptive curses he launched his shoulder at the offending door.

It burst open as the blocking object gave way and he fell through onto the canted main deck, and into the remains of one of the crewmen whose head had been wedged under the doorsill.

He vomited explosively, partly from disgust and partly as a result of the smoke he'd inhaled and lastly from the dagger of pain stabbing through his right ankle. Looking around the upperdeck, which was now about twenty degrees down towards the bow, he saw it was a shambles.

There were flames, thick smoke and roasting bodies everywhere he looked. It seemed that many of the crew had come up to watch the fun as their ship shelled defenceless targets, and had now paid the price for that curiosity.

Rounds started cooking off somewhere close by and above. Must be one of the AK630's, an unbidden thought rose to tell him, as he then hopped and skipped further aft to avoid the potential mayhem of random 30mm heavy shells.

Stepping to the rail he could see several life rafts in the sea nearby, he made his decision, standing on his good leg he vaulted the railing into the warm Caribbean Sea without a backward glance.

*

Even within *Bismarck's* armoured bridge and OPs room, the sound of all the main batteries firing simultaneously was stunningly loud.

Jake had flinched when turrets Anton and Bruno commenced firing, followed swiftly by the starboard secondary armament, and lastly Caesar and Dora, back aft, as the ship cleared the headland completely.

His eyes strained to see the fall of shot as he waited the eight seconds or so before the first shells landed, the noise was continuous as the guns maintained a high rate of fire.

A stunning thought struck him. By the time the first shells arrived, there would be no less than thirty six others on their way to the target. Thirty six! And that was without counting the secondary shells! Modern guns, he thought, are grossly underrated.

The first four shells arrived. Jake observed a sudden blossom of crimson flame as at least two struck the enemy destroyer's bridge, another landed close alongside giving a leaping column of white that rose nearly as high as the Sovremenny's funnel.

The fourth must have missed the bridge by a whisker and exploded somewhere aft, Jake couldn't tell where since the destroyer was almost end on to them and going so slow that it made a perfect target.

Four more shells, another four and a further four arrived in a monotonous, deadly, slamming succession. Separating out individual salvos was now simply impossible. Smoke and explosions blossomed all over the doomed destroyer as a mixture of semi armour piercing and high explosive rounds fell on it in a veritable deluge. Still, even under that rain of fire the forward turret opened up on *Bismarck* and the vessel began to swing to starboard, evidently trying to get its after turret into action.

Sandiford Roche very nearly wet himself as the first guns opened fire. Even though he knew it was about to happen it still took him by surprise; he was slightly mollified when he noted Jake flinch a little too.

Jake watched through a viewer and tried to remain clinically detached from the carnage he had unleashed. After watching the first dozen or so strikes with only one miss, he knew it was simply a matter of time. He heard and felt a crash somewhere aft and knew that the enemy was striking back.

Reiner too watched the carnage. He wondered whether the enemy would be able to get their anti-ship missiles into action before they were destroyed.

The *Sovremenny* continued its slow turn and as it did the missile tubes alongside the bridge structure became vulnerable to direct shell strikes and sure enough a brace impacted on the port side missile housing. The resultant explosions visibly shook the ship and debris could be seen raining around the slow moving vessel. The next pair did it though. He thought they landed near the base of the *Sovremenny's* forward gun turret. A short pause followed and then a scorching bright flash chased by a thunderous detonation, ripped through the crippled ship.

The *Sovremenny* came to a halt as abruptly as if it had run into a harbour wall. A magazine explosion, Jake presumed. There was a collective gasp from those glued to viewers. Glimpses through the thick smoke and secondary explosions showed, that the enemy ship appeared to have lost its bow almost as far back as the bridge, it was already much lower in the water and clearly in danger of sinking. Men could be seen jumping from her into the water.

Reiner in OPs gave the order to switch fire from the destroyer but could only watch helplessly as shells already in flight, kept landing on the stricken and defeated ship. Shuddering he reduced the magnification on his viewer, trying to blot out the sight of shells bursting amongst those trying to launch boats and rafts. The momentary jubilation of the victory was quickly replaced by pity for fellow seamen in distress.

Up in the MGCC Carl Dettweiler lined up his viewer on the two corvettes, blotting out the explosions on the destroyer in the foreground and the jubilant sound of his boss's voice as the hits rolled in.

Now that the radar was up the process for shooting had changed, all he had to do now was to select the target priority from the list offered by the digitized radar picture, either touching them or clicking the mouse over them had the same result.

Going old fashioned he used the mouse and clicked once over the nearest corvette then once over the farthest, that was it, he'd made his selection.

The computer would now assign more weapons to the first target than the second and keep on shooting both main and secondary armament until told otherwise. He noted, all high explosive fusing had been selected by the system as the corvettes were not in any way armoured. It 'knew' what the targets were and it would select the appropriate munition settings for them.

This was all time saving stuff he mused, especially if you were in a multiple target environment, where it was nice to know that you were firing the appropriate fused shell at the right target. The corvettes were harder targets to hit for two reasons. They had started to speed up and turn away for one and they were much smaller for two.

He watched with interest as the computer quickly adjusted to the first target's changing course and speed, shells were dropping all around and on it now as it tried in vain to escape.

Switching the viewer to the third target, he noted that it was firing back even as it tried to steer the best course for escape.

He could sympathise with the enemy Captain's problem, the missiles pointed forward and he could not turn and tackle *Bismarck* and still run away. His little 37mm guns wouldn't do more than fetch the RAD paint off. The poor man was in a bind, fight or run. Having seen his larger consort destroyed within a blink of the eye and noting the shells already landing around his sister corvette, he would only have seconds to decide.

Carl dragged his gaze back to the first corvette and immediately ordered the computer to cease firing at it. The once sleek and graceful ship was stopped in the water, on fire and clearly sinking, he could see men jumping overboard as it listed further and further to starboard.

He closed his eyes quickly as a searing flash filled the viewer, when he opened them again there was nothing but smoke and raining debris where the corvette had been. Their missiles must have cooked off he decided.

Scratch one, he said to himself as he switched his mind and guns to the remaining enemy. He could see the last corvette had a big bow wave now and was headed away from them, but almost immediately it veered to port and began a turn that would allow its missile batteries to bear on *Bismarck*.

Shit! Thought Carl as it managed to get far enough round for its portside pair of missiles to launch.

The whole vessel briefly disappeared behind a screen of flames and billowing smoke as first one then another C802 missile leapt from their canisters toward *Bismarck*.

Instantly the Sea Giraffe, radar now rotating at once per second, picked up the missiles and activated the two AK630M2 Gatling batteries on *Bismarck*'s starboard side.

Carl noted with relief that it overrode his ammunition and target commands to the secondary armament, switching them to attack the incoming missiles.

The two starboard 76mm guns fired the ready loaded HE shells and reloaded with the new 'shotgun' ammunition for the next rounds. The radar and computers knew that the first two HE shells hadn't much chance of a hit but they provided ballistic information all the same. It was certainly faster to fire them and reload than have the rounds removed and then new ones loaded.

Down in the OPs room Simon McClelland activated his ECM suite and began trying to jam any radar emissions from the incoming missiles. He didn't think they'd be using TV guidance with the corvette jerking around like a hooked fish. Now having completed its turn it was trying for an escape around the north end of Cayman Brac, all the while being chased by *Bismarck's* main battery shells.

He realised that the corvette hadn't fired its second pair of missiles and wondered if they had been damaged by a hit since it was now trailing smoke and on fire. He fired chaff patterns to the stern and starboard quarter trying to spoof the missiles into thinking *Bismarck* was at least two and a half times as long as it was and hoping they'd aim for centre mass on their radar or infra-red picture. He'd used a modified chaff rocket which had an added flare package to lure any infra-red seekers.

Almost everyone had forgotten about the drone but all the while its sensors had been adding to the image in the central fire control system and updating the holo image continuously. This provided even more information to the battle management system on drift, speed and altitude of the missiles as the TV cameras sent their images directly to the ship's fire control system which converted them to useable data.

With the chaff clouds billowing and flares dropping through them, *Bismarck* veered a little to port to add even more to its radar length.

The AK630M2's now added their sheet ripping cacophony of 4000 rounds per minute from each barrel to that of the main batteries which were still shooting at the corvette, albeit at a slower rate now. In addition the two starboard 76mm twin turrets were chugging out rounds at the phenomenal rate of 260 rounds per minute each. The action would not of course last a minute.

Reiner irreverently wondered how much money was being spat out of various barrels per second. There was nothing he could do now but let the ship defend itself. He had brought up the ammunition status on to his main screen and noted the frightening rate at which the green lines were sliding down the bar towards empty on the 76mm and the AK630's. He made a note to practice the reload systems more often –if they got out of this.

*

Jason Sims had never seen the like. The nearest he'd come to it was as an Ensign on the USS *Berkely* when it escorted the heavy cruiser USS *Newport News* a traditional built heavy cruiser, on one of its fire missions off Vietnam in 72'. But even that paled into insignificance with what he was witnessing now.

"Hot damn will you look at that you two."

Without taking his eyes from the scene in front of him he nudged Mike Farrow with his foot.

Get up Mikey, you ain't ever going to see anything like this again pal, come on you're quite safe unless a stray round lands here and lying down won't help if it does."

Mike Farrow stood up slowly. The noise was incredible and seemed to be getting even louder. The ship that was on 'their' side was heading away and almost invisible behind a bank of smoke or what looked like smoke to his untrained eye.

Over to his right there was what was left of the big ship that had been shelling them earlier. It was now clearly sinking and its stern was up out of the water. Further right he could see remnants of smoke drifting away and just disappearing around the cliffs north of Spot Bay seemed to be one of the smaller ships trailing smoke.

Sims picked up the narrative for Farrow.

"Any second now we're going to see how good our good guys are, that last damned corvette fired a pair of anti-ship missiles at our guy and he's firing like hell to hit them. See those puffs of smoke in the air there, they must be some kind of flack shell and that ripping sound is some sort of Gatling point defence gun. Shit this is intense."

Farrow flinched as a bright yellow flash blossomed in the sky about half a mile from the ship and then almost immediately another further out. Then the noise ceased, almost as if someone had flicked a switch. The smoke drifted away and the ship which had come to their rescue turned in a graceful arc back towards Cayman Brac.

Sims lowered the glasses a final time, gone was the whooping cowboy of minutes ago and in his place was someone reflecting on the power of modern guns and the savagery of conflict.

"Seems like they got the missiles. Hot damn they're good! Only one got away."

The surviving corvette had just disappeared around the northern headland and silence reigned once again. He looked across to the friendly ship and noted that she was slowing and turning towards the sinking destroyer. He looked at his watch.

Jesus H Christ! Three and a half minutes was all it had taken, two sunk or sinking and one damaged and running. He suddenly felt his age and looked at his two colleagues one still lying on the roof.

"You can get up now Tim, it's all over."

Tim got up and brushed the dust from his shirt and trousers.

"What do you mean it's all over? They just got started!"

"Take a look for yourself Tim, it's finished. We won, the bad guys are either dead or running."

Or drowning, he added to himself.

*

Jake noted that the last remaining corvette had now decided to 'run' having done its duty. So be it.

He didn't blame them one bit. The survivor would be allowed to escape. Her crew would take the horror stories with them, back to their cronies. Let them sweat at the thought of taking us on, he thought, as Reiner ordered a cease fire. He had more pressing matters to attend to.

Reiner ordered the drone north to make sure the last uninvited guest didn't sneak back for another pop at them then spoke into his mike.

"Shipwide." Followed by a click.

"Do you hear there, this is the Captain. Secure from Action Stations. The immediate threat has been dealt with, the enemy has been either sunk or has retreated out of range.   All departments report any damage. We will now commence the search for survivors. Standby all boat crews and security staff. Well done everyone."

08.25 Thursday 24th May 2018

Bismarck off Cayman Brac

So far it had taken the better part of an hour for the majority of survivors to be picked up from both locations, by which time Jake had worked through his fingernails and had started on the skin at the sides.

All any of them wanted was wanted was to turn around and head for the base. But they couldn't. The Law of the sea? Whatever. They just couldn't leave men in the water struggling for their lives.

Jake had no viable excuses to quit the area, the radar was on air search/sea search mode and no way was the escaped corvette going to be coming any time soon. Of course there could be other ships nearby but he didn't think that was the case and anyway the drone would give plenty of warning of anything else approaching. The drone Chief had it up at 5000 feet now so the visible horizon was about a hundred miles.

Five minutes later, having conferred with Reiner, he decided to leave two of the ship's RIBs in charge of what was left of the rescue. The two boats would be sufficient, there weren't many bobbing heads remaining now. At last they'd be able to get across to the base and find out what had happened. It was worrying that there was still no radio contact.

Roche had gone ashore in the first boat with his minders to organise the locals. It might also benefit the Minister to see the results of the ultimate expression of government policy.

The preliminary casualty list was staggering, out of the four hundred and twenty five crew of the two sunken vessels, only eighty five had been picked up and he knew they wouldn't add many to that now. He turned away and walked back into the bridge.

Reiner gave the orders and seconds later came the rising whine of the gas turbines and *Bismarck* slowly turned away from the flotsam that was once a destroyer and pointed her sharp bows towards Little Cayman. As soon as they cleared the debris field, the turbines were let loose again and they hurtled towards Little Cayman.

A few minutes hard running later, but three lifetimes for those waiting for news, they were edging through the mouth of the new harbour. Men lined the upperdeck rails all of them impatient to get ashore.

The first to go though would be the Chief Petty Officer Medic Bren, with his first aid and rescue party, made up mainly of the chefs, stewards and stores people, all dual trained in first aid with a sprinkling of engineers for the light rescue stuff.

Brendan was standing in the ship's waist, tense and fidgeting waiting for the go, as he and the others surveyed the debris and destruction ashore. He tried not to think about what might have happened to Lorraine, kept pushing it aside each time it slid into his mind; he had to concentrate on what he was doing.

Lawrence Cribb, the doctor, was staying below with the wounded from the two ships they'd sunk, and that fact had been the cause of a brief row with Jake only minutes before, he'd wanted the doctor to go ashore.

The exchange had taken place in a wardroom packed with casualties, the moans and cries of the wounded a background to the crisp orders Cribb was giving to the team of three helping him on the emergency operating table set up by the bar.

Jake had blundered in through the packed bodies all being monitored by the wary eyes of one of Andy's security team, who was casually cradling his stubby machine pistol as he watched the proceedings. He had come down himself because Reiner had just filled him in on the organisation for the first landing parties. When Reiner had detailed the make-up of the emergency first aid party Jake had stopped him cold.

"Reverse that." He'd said. "I want the doctor to go, Bren can stay here."

Reiner had turned away and used his mike to change the orders. But had come back just a moment later shaking his head, having talked briefly to the doctor, and relayed Cribb's' message 'that he was needed where he was and that the first aid parties were perfectly OK as they were.' and he is 'up to his elbows in someone else's guts' at the moment.

Jake had then blown a fuse, post action stress or whatever, he not in the mood to be told what to do by one of his own officers and set off for the wardroom. On arrival he noted the intravenous tubes sticking out of arms, the splints and fresh bandages, some of which already had a darker red stain, and the strong smell of fuel oil as he approached the emergency operating area.

Red splashes made a colourful line down the bulkhead behind the table itself. Some of his anger began to evaporate as he noted a new jet of bright red blood shoot up into the air and the doctor's quick but calm 'clamp that will you Granny, I've got a thumb on it'. Jake slowed as he approached the half screened table, the peculiar ferrous smell of blood pervaded the air, you could taste it in your mouth.

He looked around the screen. Lawrence Cribb had both hands deep inside a wide open abdominal cavity, the patient was a big black man and by the looks of him, he'd been hit in a couple of other places as well, since Jake could see shell dressings on both feet.

Jake heard a metallic click and the doctor stood up quickly and dropped a 'marble' sized lump of metal from his forceps into a kidney dish on the trolley next to him. Cribb spoke to one of his assistants.

"Just pack that so that all his 'bits' stay where they are and then put a light 'steri-pad' over it. We'll let a proper surgeon sew him up later."

He ripped his surgical gloves off and put on another pair quickly wiped his brow with a bar cloth.

"I'll pick the next one and you get him ready." He looked over the table and noticed Jake for the first time. "Hello boss. Come to watch me earn my exorbitant pay cheque?"

"No doctor. I've come to ask you why you refused an order to go ashore with the first aid party, actually."

Lawrence noted the cold clipped tones.

"Oh." He said and reached for another mask.

"Simple logic really boss." He waved his arms at all of the wounded.

"There are any number of these men who will die without surgical attention -soon. They've only had basic first aid."

Jake glared at him and snapped.

"The people ashore doctor, may not even have had that yet!"

Lawrence summoned up his arguments and carried on as if the interruption hadn't occurred.

"Brendan is an expert in casualty assessment and recovery, that's what he was trained for and what he practiced in action, in the Navy."

"He can do it better than me. He knows light rescue as well as battlefield trauma care, I wouldn't do it as quickly or as well as him." He took a deep breath and looked around. I'm the best at the next stage and that's primary care -making sure they survive the next hour -that's why it's better to send Bren."

He looked into Jake's unflinching gaze and started to get angry.

"For Christ's sake boss he's into all this combat casualty recovery and light rescue stuff, it's his bread and butter -I'd just be in the bloody way. Believe me, if it's possible to keep someone alive until they get to a medical unit, then Bren is the guy who'll do it. I'd want him to come hunting for me if I was injured and that's about the best reference I can give anyone."

Jake immediately relaxed.

"That's all I wanted to hear doctor. They are our families out there after all.`

"That is precisely why I am here and Bren is going, I'd never forgive myself if I cocked up out there."

Jake just stared intently at Lawrence for a moment.

"Fine, if you need any more hands down here, give Reiner a buzz. I'd better get back to the bridge."

Roberts looked over at Granny. He knew Jake's mood better than most on board, being his steward while he was on board. Granny just shrugged and continued to pack the abdomen.

"You done right Doc. You need to show that you believe in what you done. But," he added with a grin. "You need to 'ave a bag packed if you're wrong though."

He chuckled at his own wit. Cribb shook his head puzzled, and went to look for his next casualty.

A major concern at the moment was that a fair proportion of the casualties would be HIV positive, simply because they came from Haiti.

Up on the bridge Jake and Reiner were scanning the area as *Bismarck* tied up and the first aid team and light rescue party went dashing along the harbour wall. It was a pity that they couldn't moor up to the inner wall, but the fuel fire made it dangerous, it was too close to where the stern would be.

Jake looked down as the Chief Engineer and his party moved off at a trot towards the fuel fire, Scotnikov would get that under control and then decide whether it was safe to move the ship to the inner berth.

Using binoculars rather than the ship's viewers his gaze travelled up the gentle slope a little, to where the smoke rose from behind the trees fronting the accommodation areas. Guilt surged up inside as he realised for the first time that people known to him had been injured or killed because of his orders.

He was dreading the first reports from the shore parties; it was obvious that the accommodation area had been hit as well as the temporary communication centre on the jetty.

How many casualties? Who was fatherless, motherless, husbandless or parentless because of him? Feeling sick he turned away, looking out to sea, only to be confronted by a canvas draped hump at the end of the left arm of the harbour wall. As he glared at it, his anger and frustration rose like a tide and threated to swamp his mind completely.

It was just a canvas covered hump, but it mocked his efforts and became the focal point for his anger. Underneath the canvas on its dais was a 'Dardo' system, a radar controlled, remotely operated twin 40mm cannon. Or, he corrected, it would be remotely operated when installation was complete. On the other arm of the harbour wall sat another canvas covered hump, a 76mm remotely operated gun, again, or would be. So too would the radar on Weary Hill and the other defence systems. Shit! Shit! Shit! 'It's just not fair,' he almost said to himself but caught it just in time. Self-pity is as much use as tits on a bumble bee, he recalled one of his instructors telling him decades ago.

Cold logic took over. We just weren't ready, so stop wallowing in self-pity, it said, buck up and get organised. Let's just be ready next time if there is one, eh? He looked over at Reiner and saw his own frustration mirrored there.

"Reiner, I'll make it my number one priority to get all our defence systems in working order, all this high-tech stuff lying around like so much junk, it's embarrassing. I'm sure your imagination has come up with a few 'what ifs' too."

Reiner could hear the barely controlled anger in Jake's voice and shared it wholeheartedly, the only time a target was ever likely to come into view of their new super anti-aircraft anti-surface systems, the bloody thing wasn't ready!

No, he corrected himself, perhaps not the only time. He had the distinct feeling that this was only the start. Something was nagging him about today's date.

Static crackled in both their ears -the start of a report from ashore no doubt- it sent a chill right through him.

Selfishly he thought, please God let them be safe, and then felt ashamed, his son and daughter were but two of those he was responsible for. He forced himself to listen as the first reports came in.

*

Bren and his team left the remains of the temporary Comcen on the jetty and huffed their way up the incline toward the apartments. They huffed because, even though it was only just eight in the morning, it was hot and they were carrying a lot of gear. They all wore denim overalls, a webbing belt with hand axe and torch, plus hard hats of the industrial kind.

He had decided to add Petty Officer Rautsch and another stoker to the party, since they might have to shift rubble. The

263

two engineers carried a heavy 5 foot 'crow bar' each along with a 'block and tackle', aluminium 'shear legs' and ropes.

Bren's five man first aid team each carried a satchel of large shell dressings, airways, triangular bandages and a pair of industrial grade scissors. In addition to that, Bren shared the weight of a 30kg emergency case with one of the others and all of the rest carried a back pack with extras in them, like cervical collars, intravenous fluids twinned with their giving sets and cannula, plasti -splints etc. All in all, it was a lot of weight to hump about.

He stopped at the crossroads part way up the hill and decided to radio in partly because he was 'knackered' and partly to let the two man security team scout ahead.

He hadn't wanted the MP5 toting posers with him but Andy Evans had insisted -'we don't know for sure that they didn't put anyone ashore OK?'

Bren had been even more pissed off that Andy wouldn't allow his 'wonder boys' to carry some of the kit -'they need to be able to react instantly and I don't want them weighed down with anything they don't need OK?' He heard the words echo in his mind.

Well so far all they'd needed was five body bags, which he had forgotten to bring anyway, for the poor buggers in the temporary Comcen. He took a deep breath and began his report.

"Bravo Kilo this is Foxtrot Alpha, over." Chance for another big breath whilst the reply came back.

"Foxtrot Alpha. Report." Bren recognised the Captain's voice.

"Bravo Kilo there are five 'KIA's', repeat FIVER KIA's on the jetty by the Comcen." Another deep breath. He thought he'd better mention them since he didn't think they'd be visible from the ship, given the debris and smoke.

"No sign of anyone else down there. We've moved toward the accommodation and are waiting for security clearance to proceed, over."

"Roger Foxtrot Alpha. Keep us advised, Bravo Kilo out."

One of the security guys was trotting back towards them now, slinging his MP5 over a shoulder.

"What's the gen?" Bren asked as the man trotted up to him. Bastard, he thought, the bugger's not even sweating despite the heat and the 'cammo'd' body armour he's wearing. Seeing all that flashy lightweight armour and fancy gear hanging off them made him feel like he was in a Star Wars movie rather than on a Caribbean island.

"It's all clear 'Doc'. Don't seem to be anybody about. We're going to check out the boss's shack and the other flats before moving up the hill." He pointed to the right arm of the crossroads.

Bren consulted his map and traced a finger along the route that the security men proposed to take. He looked up and around to check his bearings and thought how ironic it was that *Bismarck's* crewmen had to use maps to get around their new home, none having seen it before.

He let the security team disappear then moved out himself. "OK guys. Let's get down to the roadway opposite the entrance to the first block. We'll leave the extra kit there and get searching. I'll stay central and wait for a call from you guys. Right?"

The seven men nodded and began to jog towards the apartment buildings.

*

Several miles away to the East, the Number 1 RIB nudged in to the concrete jetty at West End. This was the nearest landing point to the 18-bed Faith Hospital along the road at Stake Bay, Cayman Brac's only hospital. *Bismarck's* other rigid inflatable boat was about a hundred yards behind. All told they'd picked up another twenty one survivors from the corvette.

The crews scanned the foreshore as they tied up. Smoke was still rising from several fires nearby and a sizeable crowd had gathered on the seafront road to watch their arrival.

Roche was waiting impatiently for the boat to come alongside, he was desperate to get ashore and speak to Andrew McTeal. He stepped ashore as soon as the boat had touched and accompanied by one of his guards, made straight for the single policeman in view. The man saluted smartly, having immediately recognised his boss and the gun toting MPP guard.

He studiously ignored the wet, blood stained clothes the minister was wearing and stepping forward asking how he could be of service. Roche simply told him to keep the people back and to organise transport to take the casualties to the hospital.

That organised, he pulled out his mobile phone and speed dialled Andrew McTeal whilst passing through the crowd. Roche could feel the undercurrent of anger and tension, the mood was potentially ugly, his guard sensed it too and began to take more notice of the gathered crowd. Having cleared the press of people they moved to a clear spot on the foreshore. The crowd were advancing down the jetty now and Roche told his minder to warn the others that trouble was brewing and to make sure that the Haitian survivors were not molested by the crowd.

Despite the early morning horror of his baptism into the realities of warfare, his political mind was still working. He had recognised the importance of retaining the international moral high ground and a massacre of survivors on the beach would not do their case any good.

Down at the jetty, big Trev Kent and three of his mates, all with their overalls turned down to the waist, sweated as they moved the wounded over to the jetty. All of *Bismarck's* crew were first aid trained to some extent, a fact of which Jake was proud, so even without *Bismarck's* doctor and medic the wounded had been well attended.

Trev was so busy making sure that their unfortunate erstwhile enemies were comfortable, that he didn't notice the approaching angry crowd. The first he knew that something was wrong was when a piece of coral the size of a hen's egg, probably meant for one of the casualties, tore a bloody furrow in his shoulder.

He gave a howl of pain and looked up to see the three remaining MPP guards backing down the jetty towards him. As he watched, a guard briefly went down to one knee as something hit him in the face. The mob grew noisier as they sensed their advantage and pressed on towards the Haitian survivors now only ten yards away. Trev tapped Dave Page's shoulder and whistled to George Gulobovich, the nearest of *Bismarck's* crewmen.

The three men moved quickly to support the beleaguered MPP's. All of the landing party were armed with holstered Browning automatics, in case any of the survivors had ideas.

But, thought George Gulobovich, they wouldn't be of much use here since you could hardly start shooting up the very people you had just put your life on the line to protect. With a quick look at his two colleagues George decided that he was probably the most diplomatic of the three and smiling, stepped forward to talk to the crowd.

He passed between the surprised MPP guards and stood in front of the surging crowd with his arms held high above his head in a peaceful manner and shouted "Wait!" George, a Ukrainian that everyone said was a nice guy, had always believed that people were basically good, despite coming from a place with a turbulent history.

That was why it was such a surprise to him when the black man in front of him, jerked his right arm forward and made his 'gutting knife' do its job.

George sank slowly to his knees, wearing a look of pained disbelief, hands clutching at his lacerated stomach. The front of the mob ceased moving and all eyes were on George as he looked at the bright red blood and faeces spurting out from between his fingers and managed one whispered word as he looked at the man holding the knife.

"Why?"

Then his eyes glazed and he crumpled to the wooden planks, with a final gush from his severed mesenteric and renal arteries.

Silence reigned as even those at the back of the mob realised that something had happened and they all strained to hear what was said. Trev drew his Browning, parted the three MPP guards with one hand and looked down at his friend of four months, there was a frightening calm about him as he reached down to George's neck and checked for a carotid pulse.

Standing up slowly he looked directly at the culprit as a surge of happy but disjointed memories passed through his mind. George had had a calming influence on Trev which was good because fighting had always prevented Trev from advancing very far in his service career.

Excellent seaman he might be, but he had a short fuse. Commodore König had got him this job and George had promised to help him keep it, for Captain Krull had been reluctant to employ him.

Now George was dead.

The man with the knife stood still and watched the strange play of emotions cross the big blond man's face. He knew he was watching a human roulette wheel of temperaments and that wherever it stopped, he would face the consequences.

A tremor of cold dread squeezed his guts as he watched the emotional wheel slow and stop. The look in those cold blue eyes told him that his knife wasn't going to be much use to him. He blurted his excuse to the stranger.

"They killed my wife man, those bastards."

Trev's left hand snaked out and closed over the wrist of the hand holding the knife, he held the Browning high and fired three rounds quickly into the sky.

"Get the fuck back you ungrateful bastards or I swear the next bullet and all those after will be in your direction you dumbshits."

The crowd backed away as sense returned.

"You," He spat at the murderer, "are lucky they don't have a death penalty here or I'd fucking volunteer to carry it out."

The man quailed and tried to take his hand back still holding the knife but Trev just brought the Browning round and pistol whipped him.

"No you fucking don't, that's evidence you bastard, that will get you 25 years or more if I can swing it. George was a good man you bastard." He looked into the frightened eyes. "He was a very good man and you didn't know him, you didn't even let him speak. I think you're a waste of fucking oxygen."

Nobody moved. Nobody spoke. All eyes that could see, were locked on either Trev's face or the frightened eyes of the culprit

"George was always the one who tried to stop arguments you know, he never started them. He kept me out of trouble a number of times. You just killed a very kind and generous man you fuckwit."

He turned to the policeman.

"Officer arrest him please before I waste a bullet on him."

With that he twisted the guy's arm and spun him round.

"Got a bag for the knife, I wouldn't want to spoil the evidence."

Now he needed to get on the radio and tell *Bismarck* they had another casualty. Fuck what a waste, he sighed to himself as he holstered the Browning and turned back to help.

*

Two minutes after their arrival at the apartment blocks, Bren knew that there wasn't much point in looking further.

The debris on the roadway indicated that someone had been here before them -with medical gear. He blew two blasts on his whistle to recall the team, and turned to look for the security bods; now why hadn't they spotted the empty shell dressing packets, and blood stains.

He consulted his map, time to report in again and then move down to the community centre, with or without the sodding security boys.

"Bravo Kilo, this is Foxtrot Alpha."

"Foxtrot Alpha go ahead, over." Came Scouse Smith's not so dulcet tones. Bren's eyes continued to scan the area as he made his report.

"Bravo Kilo the first apartment area is empty. There is evidence that casualties have been treated here though, so we are now proceeding to the community centre and medical block, over."

"Roger that, Foxtrot Alpha. Will relay your message to the bossman, Bravo Kilo out."

Bren clipped the radio back onto his belt and began picking up his kit. The Captain's wife was a doctor wasn't she? I wonder if she's been busy, he thought as he gathered the gear together.

As Bren gathered his team to move on he glanced back to see Jake, Reiner and a disgruntled Andy Evans appearing from the direction of the ship. So they joined together for the final approach to the community and medical centres.

A tense, hushed expectancy fell over the group as they jog trotted the 200 odd yards further up and around Weary Hill. The collective wisdom had it that the survivors of the attack just had to be around the corner.

Nobody except Andy Evans noticed the excellent landscaping job that had been done, the tall native trees and flowering bushes had only been there for a month or so, and Andy only looked at the trees and bushes out of a professional interest in case they were a hiding place.

The near rhythmic drumming of their boots was the only sound, it echoed back from a forest that was unnaturally quiet as they went through, almost at a run now.

Suddenly a voice shouted *'Bismarck*' and everyone hit the deck, a second later a figure appeared from the undergrowth fifty yards up the side of the road.

"It's me, Jan Helders." Shouted the figure, carefully placing a gun on the tarmac surface. Andy walked forward slowly eyes scanning right and left, there wasn't much light with the trees overhanging like they did and he wanted to be sure there was nobody holding a gun at Helders' back.

Finally he lowered his MP5.

"Shit Jan, you scared us half to death, I nearly coughed in me rompers. What's the score?"

"All secure. They're just around the corner." Replied Helders not wishing to give out any more information.

Everyone started off again at a gallop now that they knew there were no 'hostiles' about. Lungs straining they pelted the last fifty yards and into the clearing fronting the community centre and skidded to a halt. They were greeted by a spontaneous whoop of relief and delight from the survivors sitting on the community centre patio.

Jake ran to his son and daughter. James was sitting with a heavily bandaged leg resting on another chair with Helen sitting next to him. She rushed into his arms sobbing and Jake pressed his son's shoulder with his free hand, the lump in his throat making it impossible to speak.

Bren spotted Lorraine and with a surge of relief ran to her where she sat clearly comforting someone but stopped short as he realised she was in 'counselling mode', their eyes locked and she gave a tiny nod to indicate she was OK. Reassured he re-joined Reiner as he headed towards the medical centre.

Reiner couldn't see Trudi anywhere on the patio area so hurried on towards the medical centre. He and Bren piled through the entrance to be greeted by a waiting room occupied by half a dozen adults and children bearing various bloody dressings tightly pressed against wounds. Without a word they both carried on to what was labelled 'Treatment Room' and there they found Trudi and a one armed Liz patching up another casualty. Trudi finished tying a sling and gave the child's mother some paracetamol and advice about keeping the wound clean, then she looked around. Seeing Reiner she rushed into her husband's arms. He held her tightly, ashamed at his relief for her not being on the casualty list.

Bren immediately took charge of Liz, carefully examining the broken arm, the injury made, she told him, by falling masonry. He broke open a packet containing a triangular bandage and carefully lifted Liz's arm putting the bandage underneath before tying it around her neck finally allowing the arm to rest inside the sling. Then came the crunch as Trudi led her husband by the hand to a double door leading to another treatment room. Without a word she opened it and stood aside. The four looked down on the line of body bags, the last clearly with only a small occupant.

Liz spoke in a quiet voice that chilled both men to their hearts.

"That's my baby in the last one, the other three are the wives of the harbour technicians. They were killed by the pool."

08.30 Thursday 24th May 2018

Prime Minister's Study, George Town, Grand Cayman

Andrew McTeal held the receiver in his hand for a few seconds before putting it back onto the cradle. The world slowed down and almost ceased to exist as his mind raced through the import of Roche's information.

The call had lasted five minutes or more during which McTeal had just grunted, yes and no a few times. All the while his mind crackled sequentially with anger, indignation and sadness at the information that Sandiford Roche was passing him.

He just had sufficient wit at the end of the call to tell Roche to wait locally for a helicopter which he would send, and to get as much information from the able bodied survivors as possible.

The Grandfather clock in the anteroom outside his study chimed the three quarter, it had just struck the half hour when McTeal had replaced the receiver, and still he sat frozen at the desk, his features empty of expression as his mind raced along unfamiliar pathways. Pathways that led to war, death and mutilation no matter which one he followed. The biggest problem, he realised, was response time.

He had no doubt that the UN and certain 'friendly' countries would eventually give aid to his islands, possibly even military aid from Britain who would be affronted if its newest former dependency was swallowed up, but people would die because these governments would waffle and prevaricate, much preferring to wait and see.

He only had to think of Ruanda or the Yugoslavian problems to be reminded of how slow and ineffectual international response could be. Even when faced with hard evidence of multi-sided atrocities, the world sat back and allowed the slaughter to continue.

The scenario repeated itself in North Africa and the Middle East although his deep suspicion remained regarding the origins of the so called 'Arab Spring' revolutions. It had seemed obvious to everyone that the warring factions would prevaricate at the conference table and 'carry on regardless' on the battlefield as witness Ukraine and Syria now in their '*n'th* year of trouble.

He rubbed his eyes and sat back remembering the discussions in this very room back in 2015. Response time was the key. It was invariably much slower in a democracy simply because consensus and factional support was most often required, so Haiti could and would react quicker than *his* potential allies.

At the moment, he mentally reviewed, it was obvious that the vague warning of the American agent had been a reference to Haiti. It was equally obvious that Jonathan König, bless him and his ship had, as it were, inadvertently 'trashed' the leading pawns in Farache's bloody game of international chess.

What he had to do now was to formulate a response - international presswise- to Haiti's aggression, because he had no doubt at all that Farache would somehow try to turn this reversal to his advantage on the international stage.

He buzzed his secretary and ordered a full cabinet meeting for 11am, in about two hours, also asking that the Duty Communications Officer report to him immediately.

He must speak securely to Downing Street and see what the British would do, also he needed to summon Commodore König and invoke the agreement that they'd made. It hardly seemed necessary, almost insulting, considering Jake had already been in action, but he wanted no misunderstandings, friendships couldn't be weighed against a nation's needs.

God that sounds pompous, he thought, I'll have to play it carefully with Jake if I'm not to give offence.

He needed the military potential of Jake's vessel for the simple reason that at present, it was all that stood between Haiti and an immediate, almost unopposed, invasion of his islands. How long Jake could stand in the way, he just didn't know. That ship of his, and its people would just have to buy them as much time as was possible.

McTeal put his head in his hands, what price freedom now, he thought sadly as his broken dreams, littered with the dead of two years independence, paraded their way through his mind. It had all seemed so uncomplicated and painless when they set the Caymans on the road to independence.

Now he was about to commit one of his oldest friends and other brave men in a desperate gambit which could only lead Jake, his crew and his ship, into a nightmare of death and destruction. He put a mental clamp on his negative thoughts and activated that acute QC's brain, which had seen to it that he rarely lost a court case, and concentrated on what his enemy's strategy might be.

09.25 Thursday 24th May 2018

NSA HQ, Fort Meade Maryland, US

Vernon Weathers yawned again, reached for his eighth coffee and continued to study the 07.40 satellite photo.

Fucking incredible, he thought as he checked the verbal evaluation next to it. He never ceased to be amazed by the clarity of photographs taken from eighty or so miles up in space.

Well the Pentagon's Navy man was going to be pleased with himself, he got most of it right he just hadn't predicted that one of the Haitian ships would survive.

He chuckled to himself as he remembered the bleary eyed Navy Commander's early morning reading of the summary of *Bismarck's* construction and armaments. He'd looked up and asked if it was some kind of exercise or test or something. But then he'd got to work and intrigued, had asked to wait around to see what would actually happen.

Vern's eyes skipped across to the larger scale photos of the rest of the Caribbean which showed the remainder -and largest portion- of the Haitian task force heading on a mean westerly course. Well one thing was for sure, there'd be no more speculation about who was going to be invaded, and that meant that they'd have to try again to convince the state department that Farache had his eye on the Caymans

The other thing that had become obvious was that Miles would definitely have to go over to the Caymans soonest and put them properly in the picture. He chuckled again at the thought of what that bastard Farache had been served up for breakfast.

10.00 Thursday 24th May 2018

Residence of Louis D'Orville, Haitian Minister of Agriculture and Natural Resources

Louis D'Orville had never seen the President so agitated before. When he and his colleagues had been dragged from their beds, at a quarter after eight that morning, to this emergency cabinet meeting, he had been fearful of another ministerial reshuffle or perhaps yet more atrocities committed by this government against its own people.

The truth as told was far worse than the speculation, although how much was truth was difficult to assess. Not being in the inner circle meant that he had not been privy to the planned attack on the lesser Cayman Islands. The fact that the raiding ships had been intercepted by some kind of mercenary warship which had sunk two of them and driven off the third, suggested to him that someone had slipped up on the intelligence side of things.

The 'General' had ranted on for fifteen minutes about the revenge he would take if his only nephew, on board one of the lost ships, was not a survivor.

Louis had then spared a thought for that 'someone' in the intelligence services, the scapegoat, who would probably be screaming for mercy at this moment. Farache would never have allowed his precious nephew to be anywhere near a real battle since he fancied him as a replacement one day.

All through the session the General had swung from anger to pleasant anticipation as he'd outlined how this setback could now become part of the international excuse for the invasion of the islands.

Louis had gladly sat at the periphery of the meeting, not saying a word. Glad, that was, until the end of the meeting when Farache's last diatribe was subsiding.

Just when Louis thought it had petered out, Farache looked up and, apparently staring straight at Louis, carried on.

"Our man in George Town has supplied the name of the person who is responsible for this setback. The owner of this 'mercenary' vessel is called Jonathan Henry König."

Louis had felt the blood drain from his face and his heart do a double beat. In that terrible moment he foresaw his own execution. Nobody would believe that it was a mere coincidence that put König's wife under his own roof; they would see only a conspiracy.

He wondered briefly whether it was possible to get away with it, after all, she would be flying out -he checked his watch- in the next few minutes or so.

Perhaps he could play dumb? It shouldn't be too difficult since he hadn't known anything of her husband's intentions and he was sure she hadn't either, else why come to the one place that would put her in danger?

No, it had to be an obscene coincidence. But even so, he was now guilty of treason by not revealing her presence to the man across the table from him, the Interior Minister, who would have her flight cancelled if Louis opened his mouth now.

Instead, Louis just got up and smiled to everyone as he left, unaware of the Interior minister's cold eyes following him out. All the way home he pondered the morning's revelations and most especially that there was someone in the Cayman government passing information, incredible.

At least that was how he interpreted the significance of 'Our man in George Town'. Thank God that Sophie would be on her way now, he hated to think of the problems it would have caused if she hadn't left when she had.

I might just survive, the way things are, he mused. I might.

As the Ministerial car turned into his drive he glanced back down the road towards the capital and all his problems. He noticed a jeep and an army truck back along the road in the distance and vaguely wondered where they were heading. His front door was opened by the butler Albert. Stepping into the large hall he noticed hand luggage on the floor in one corner, Sophie's stuff? He thought, puzzled.

Time slowed as his mind raced away, making connections. Francesca appeared and seemed to be walking across a hall covered with treacle. She was saying something and looking really angry, he thought, as his ears picked up the sound of a heavy truck noisily changing down through the gears.

Connections!

Sophie was standing in the doorway to the drawing room. Why hasn't she left? She should have been away at least an hour or so ago. More noisy gear changing.

Connections!

The maniacal scream of a big engine in low gear, Francesca's voice louder now and more insistent "...flight cancelled and they were so rude to me..."

Connections!

Spinning towards the door, briefcase noisily hitting the tiles. Time galloping now.

Realisation rushing at him as he looked out toward the driveway and saw soldiers leaping from the back of the still moving truck, blue uniforms, red piped trousers, sheathed machetes.

Ton Ton Macoutes!

The old cold fear, an involuntary shudder of the bowels. No not the Macoutes, not any more.

Worse. Interior Ministry police. He watched paralysed as the man people called the 'Mad Major'-but never to his face-stepped down from his jeep.

Time returned to normal speed.

Not so his heartbeat.

Polite knocking at the door but no boots kicking it in. A shameful relief flooding him. So they'd just come for Sophie had they, his political instinct informed him. He opened the door.

"Yes Major, what can I do for the Interior Ministry Police?"

It was impossible to read Mercier's expression behind those mirrored glasses.

"I think you know Minister."

A smile spread slowly across Mercier's ebony features.

"But to avoid embarrassment. Sir, I believe you have one, Mrs JH König as your house guest. I respectfully request you to hand her over into my custody whilst certain irregularities are investigated. She will be held at the local police station but will not be allowed visitors at present. Secondly, her bodyguards or servants. We wish also to keep them in protective custody until this is resolved. Where are they?"

"No!" A shout brimming with pain and horror was torn from Francesca as she launched herself across the entrance hall to her husband's side.

Sophie stood immobile unable to understand the rapid fire French, but she knew this was serious trouble simply from the look of fear on Louis's face.

Out of the corner of her eye she watched the door to the servants' quarters close slowly as Winston moved back out of sight. I don't blame him, her reason said. Liar! Selfishness shouted, of course you do! Huh! Said reason, surrounded by soldiers he just wouldn't have a chance of saving me. But dammit that's what he's paid for! Selfishness screamed back, knowing she was being unfair.

"Is there a problem?" She asked with a confidence she didn't feel.

Louis looked at her and felt a painful lump rise in his throat, such a lovely woman and I have to hand her over to this pig, he thought, as he turned to face Mercier again.   Anger rose to replace the fear, he was still a Minister after all.

"The Lady's assistants are out Major."

He didn't know then why he lied and waited for Mercier to defy him or argue or anything. But the man didn't. Louis knew Mercier had got what he'd really come for and his anger rose to a dangerous pitch as he leaned towards him.

"Don't for one minute think that you are beyond the laws of this country or beyond a man's retribution. Remember, this Lady is the wife of one of the world's richest men and is also my wife's dearest friend. Have a care Mercier!"

He hissed the words, and saw spittle decorate Mercier's mirrored glasses. Without even waiting for an answer Louis turned to face Sophie. Taking her to one side away from Mercier he spoke quietly and calmly to her.

"I am most eternally sorry my dear but this policeman has an order to detain you at the local police station I, err…."

He faltered.   How to tell someone that they may be subjected to torture and degradation?

"Please be warned, these vile ministry police think they are a law unto themselves. I will do what I can to have you released but prepare yourself for an ordeal!"

He knew it sounded pompous but he couldn't think of any other way of saying it.

Francesca could stay quiet no longer.

"Louis, you can't let them take her."

He recognized the immense effort she was making to control herself and loved her more for it.

"We have no choice at present my love."

He was frantically trying to gauge his own position.

"I will try to ascertain the problem when I speak to my good friend the Interior Minister."

He said, louder and more for Mercier's benefit than for Francesca or Sophie. In fact the Interior Minister was a cold fish but he hoped Mercier wouldn't know whether they were friends or not.

As Sophie walked towards the man with the mirrored glasses, a chill crept down her spine.   She instinctively recognised a man who enjoyed his work, especially if it involved inflicting pain or humiliation.

He took her by the upper arm and led her out to the jeep. Oh God! What now, she thought recalling how frightened Louis had looked at first.

Francesca let out a sob and ran to the window at the side of the closed door. Another great sob of despair and anguish escaped her lips as she saw the salacious, knowing looks that Sophie received from the guards as she entered the jeep and they drove off.

The door to the servants' quarters burst open and out tumbled an angry Tetsunari and a worried Winston.

All at once the hall was filled with voices each demanding to be heard. Something snapped inside Louis. Something that had been stretched and stretched over the years.

"Silence!" He shouted. "Silence! This instant. How can a man think with all this noise? Everyone come into the drawing room, we must calm down and think this through." He led them into the drawing room and seated himself without waiting for the others.

"Precipitous action will not help Sophie's cause in the slightest."

Francesca had allowed him to lead her by the arm. She had never seen this side of Louis before, he suddenly seemed harder in some way, less pliant than usual.

Tetsunari and Winston both nodded acquiescence to Louis's request but carried on their own 'sotto voce' debate as they followed the Minister and his wife into the drawing room.

"...no way Tettas. That's a load of bollocks. If I'd have let you go out there, Mrs 'K' would still be a prisoner, you'd be dead or a prisoner and I would be short of fifty percent of my prisoner recovery unit!"

Winston was starting to get tired of Tetsunari's fanatical Samurai bullshit. But his anger was real and Winston had rarely seen him angry.

Louis interrupted his thoughts.

"Winston, Tetsunari please be seated, I have some information to impart which will allow you to see why I could not object too strongly to them taking Sophie."

He got up and walked over to the French windows staring out over the terrace. It wasn't a dramatic pause it was just that imparting this information would make him a traitor for the second time that day, so he composed himself first before turning to speak.

"This morning at approximately 07:30, near the islands of Cayman Brac and Little Cayman, a naval battle took place between a Haitian force and a ship owned by Mrs König's husband."

He noted the sudden interest and a certain guile in Winston's eyes, the Japanese's face betrayed nothing.

"I see you are aware of this ship Winston?"

Winston thought quickly.

"Aware of it, yeah. But of its movements and specifics, no."

"Well no matter. It was an ill-conceived plan anyway but the point is this. That ship of his inflicted a stunning defeat on the Haitian force, sinking two of the three ships."

He paused to let that little nugget sink in.

"One of the sunken ships had General Farache's nephew, Francois, on board. This information came out during the meeting I was summoned to early this morning. I had hoped that Sophie would have been on her way by the time I returned but obviously not."

He paused for a second time to let everyone absorb the information, Francesca had paled at the mention of Farache's nephew and he hoped that she was beginning to understand his own delicate position.

He continued.

"The fact that this information was imparted at the meeting and that Sophie's flight was cancelled before the meeting seem to indicate to me that the Interior Ministry have been keeping a close eye on her visit and were quick to link the two events. If I had objected strongly or refused to allow the police to take her, I suspect there would have been a warrant for my arrest too in the Major's pocket."

He noted something he didn't like in Winston's expression and his anger surfaced briefly.

"Winston you may think what you like, but I am of little use to Sophie if I am myself in prison, I can only help from the outside."

He saw the barb go home but Winston said nothing.

"I still suspect that my arrest is not far down the road. Now I want to know what you gentlemen plan to do about getting Sophie out, I suspect that she is in great danger from that animal Mercier but she may be reasonably safe until this evening."

Winston's mind went into overdrive, this is fucking nutty, he thought, here I am talking to a Minister of this fucking country about breaking into a police station and helping a prisoner of his fucking government to escape! He turned to look at Tetsunari and receiving a nod, spoke to Louis.

"Sir we must communicate with Mr König as soon as possible but I suspect he will only be able to help with extracting us from your country once we have rescued Mrs 'K'."

Winston paused a second before pressing his luck.

"That being the case, could you give us any information about this police station? Also, do you have maps of your country at all?"

Winston and Tetsunari left the Minister rummaging in his bureau and headed for their room and the satellite phone which they only turned on at pre-arranged times because really, it was a bitch with only 30 or so hours standby time, so it was best off unless they needed it.

"We have failed her Rinston."

Winston nearly laughed but thought the better of it, Tetsunari always had problems with his w's when he was excited even though he had conquered the 'L' problem.

"Re should have gone around the back and surprised them. Surprise 'rud' be enough against these primitive people."

Tetsunari felt dirty. He felt ashamed of himself and Winston. The first time that they had really had any problem to deal with they had failed and were still alive to feel the shame. All they'd had to do in the past had been to discourage amorous advances or give a purse snatcher corrective therapy.

Winston didn't know for sure that Tetsunari was wrong, his instincts were excellent. However, Tetsunari had not seen their opposition or their positions and that's what counted.

His retreat had been the instinctive withdrawal of a trained soldier facing overwhelming odds in a bad position, not the fleeing of a coward. He had to get Tettas out of his 'I'm dishonoured' mode and back to thinking again.

At least they knew where Mrs 'K' was being held. However, the really bad news was that he'd recognised the 'bad ass' from the airport and that could only be trouble, it also meant that they would have to be quick getting her out. He mentally vowed to pull that fucker apart if he did anything to Sophie. Winston meant it in the most literal sense.

Jake's cabin, *Bismarck* in Harbour, Little Cayman

Jake had just finalised the discussions regarding funeral details when the door opened and Andy Evans walked in. The aftermath of action was something that he'd dealt with before, but never had it affected him as personally as it had this time. They'd lost nine people killed and eleven injured ashore. *Bismarck* had received just one hit and that had exploded on impact, unable to penetrate the toughened Titanium skin.

The ship had only one grieving father, Ian Halshaw, who with his wife Liz was trying to come to terms with their loss. But the rest of them had the loss of George Gulobovich to come to terms with, he'd been immensely popular. Then there was the horror of the technicians who survived when their wives did not. Most of all, the burden rested on Jake's shoulders for all of their losses, and he could feel that weight like a physical presence.

Thank God for social workers, he thought. Got to be the shittiest job in the world at times like this. Although the ship didn't carry such a person they fortunately they had one ashore in the shape of Brendan Crellin's wife, Lorraine. It was a job he knew he couldn't do, it involved too much listening for a start, and he marvelled at the ability of such people to soak up the misery of others without being overcome themselves.

I empathise I don't sympathise', had been Lorraine's response when he'd quizzed her in Bermuda. He felt bad about leaving such a job to someone else but shamefully recognised his own relief and her ability.

He returned to the present noticing Andy. Now what the hell's the matter with him? He looks like he's just been told not to play with guns any more. Jake held up a hand to interrupt Reiner's dissertation upon the arrangements for refuelling and looked directly at Andy Evans.

"Reiner hang on a sec please. Andy, what's the matter?"

Evans looked to be in shock, the big ex-Marine was plainly out of his depth and simply handed a message form to Jake. Reiner watched Jake's expression and felt a sudden chill of dread, the play of emotions across his boss's face were frightening to behold. He reached forward, took the message from Jake's unresisting grasp and read it.

Oh Sheisse! The message simply stated that Winston had contacted them and that Sophie had been taken into the custody of the Interior Ministry Police. He would stay near the receiver until Jake called back.

Jake's mind was a blur of thoughts and he knew it was useless to try and stop them so he let the surge pass and waited for coherence in his mind.

Andy watched Jake's face and particularly his eyes, he waited for what seemed like ages before Jake seemed ready to speak. As he opened his mouth, the telephone on his desk trilled and Reiner reached over to take the call. Without a word Reiner passed the receiver to Jake and turned to look at Andy Evans' troubled features.

Jake listened for a minute without interruption.

"Yes. Yes Andrew, I'll be there. Oh, is your pilot is aware of the Heli-pad behind our community centre? Fine. I'll see you some time after eleven then. Yes it was a bad business, we lost ten adults and one child. Thanks I'll pass that on to the men. No, I've no idea about the casualties on Brac? Really? Oh hell! Bye Andrew."

Everyone waited expectantly for Jake to give details of the island's casualties, all had shamelessly tuned in to the one half of the conversation they could hear.

"In case you hadn't guessed, that was Andrew McTeal. Reiner please pass his gratitude on to the ships' company. He just said, without us turning up unexpected, there'd have been lots more casualties. As it was they've had thirty dead and seventeen injured."

He made a conscious effort to return to the present problems.

"Right Andy. I want you to get some heads together and come up with a way of getting Sophie out. I don't care how much it costs or even what method you select."

The room cooled to about minus 140 degrees with Jake's last words.

"But it must succeed."

He paused a second.

"I'd find it difficult to justify keeping anyone in my organisation who tries to get her back and fails. I think that's clear."

Andy nodded and made to leave. Jake added a slightly warmer note as Andy was exiting.

"Tell Winston and Tettas that I know *they* would have prevented it if they could."

They watched a hard faced Andy Evans leave Jake's stateroom. Jake knew that the man would go himself if necessary, he also knew that it was best not to get in the way of the planners, knowing that emotion would prejudice his input to any plans. The experts in the world of infiltration and extraction/rescue did their job without the encumbrance of emotion and that gave them an edge. He turned back to face Kipper and Reiner.

"We've some signals to send gentlemen, we don't know what's coming down the pipe yet but I want *Bismarck's* ammunition replenished ASAP. Anything else at the moment? Kipper, any problems with the boys below?"

He asked with a deliberate lightness he didn't feel.

"No Sir. But I'd just as soon get rid of our prisoners and patients then get to clearing up. Things might get a little tense if we keep 'em on board much longer."

He shifted in his seat before continuing and Jake knew there was something else.

"By the way boss, Trev Kent had his chest prodded about the Geneva Convention by one of their officers. Right stroppy bugger he was too, by all accounts."

Kipper stopped speaking and looked across at one of the mock brass scuttles on the bulkhead.

"Well I'm waiting Kipper." Jake had recognised one of his coxswain's 'excuses before the revelation'.

"Well Sir he'd just come back from escorting Lt and Mrs Halshaw Sir, and 'o course he'd just lost his real best 'oppo' George Gulobovich and got a bit worked up -I had a big lump in me throat too Sir- just seeing them like that, she was such a cute little kid an'..."

Uncharacteristically Jake lost his temper. Normally he would be happy to wait for Kipper to get to the point but at present he felt time slipping helplessly through his fingers, like a handful of sand.

"Kipper! For fuck's sake get on with it."

Herring sat up stiffly in his chair.

"Well Sir, begging the Commodore's pardon, before the sentry could intervene, Kent had belted this bloke a good 'un across the chops and walked off Sir. The officer has made a formal complaint Sir seems he can pull some strings back home Sir. Says he's the Presidents nephew or something."

You could have heard a cockroach wiping it's feelers at that moment, or so Kipper would tell his messmates later. Jake looked like he'd just been slapped and Reiner looked like he'd been propositioned by the vicar's daughter.

Kipper stared at them a little apprehensively, thinking only of 'looking out for one of his lads'. Not aware of the card he'd just placed in Jake's hitherto weak hand, he deduced that Kent was 'for it'.

"I gave him a bollocking Sir, a right good 'un too, he's a good lad Sir, I'd have probably done the same meself."

He trailed off as he realised that neither Jake nor Reiner were listening. Recognising his escape cue he stood up to leave.

"Right Sir I'll be off then, there's plenty to see to."
He closed the door quietly.

Jake's mind slowed down to sub warp speed and he spoke into his mike "Zero, zero." Click.

"Andy Talbot." Came the answer from the security room.

"This is the Commodore. Talbot I want the Haitian officer who was assaulted, separated from the rest. Put him in a cabin and he is not to be left alone for a second, is that clear? Oh, and have the doctor check him over please."

Reiner felt his spirits lift as he saw Jake smile for the first time that day. It wasn't a nice smile though, it was the smile of a victim suddenly scenting revenge. Still it's an improvement, he thought, as an identical smile crept onto his own countenance.

11.15. Thursday 24th May 2018

Prime Minister's Office, George Town, Grand Cayman

"Do sit down Mr Carlson, what did you say your position is within the Central Intelligence Agency?"

"I didn't say, Sir. But after today I expect it will be picking gum off the floors at Langley -if I'm lucky. Or maybe our incumbent 'administrator' will have them throw me in prison."

McTeal noted the disparaging reference to one of the current President's off the cuff remarks about 'the new job' and Carlson's assessment of his own future. He determined that if this man had now brought the information that he desired, then he would do all in his power to see him commended and not chastised.

"So, your visit to us is totally unofficial? Why then have you put your career at risk Mr Carlson?"

McTeal was genuinely curious.

"Ah, that's a long story Mr Prime Minister but it basically boils down to the 'good guys and the bad guys'." He proceeded to relate the information that had been dug up over the last two years by him and his co-agency colleagues.

By the end of Carlson's narrative McTeal was both relieved and dismayed. Relieved because he now knew the roots of the problem, and dismayed at what his people now faced. He continued to study the satellite photographs that Carlson had brought with him.

Carlson sat back and sipped his Earl Grey, the ninth or the tenth so far today, while he reflected ruefully that not only was his career in the shitter but prison was not out of the question now too. The director would be real pleased that he'd gone alone and not involved him, but he could expect no help from that quarter, the man was a career bureaucrat.

He smiled to himself, at the very least they're going to be mighty pissed off that he authorised himself a company jet in order to get here. Well at least that guaranteed that there'd be no more pretence, because before long somebody was bound to ask why the ADDI was going to Grand Cayman, since that was who he'd booked it out to.

He sighed and wondered whether the British would manage to do anything in time, their Prime Minister was every bit as useless as his own President. At least, he thought, if the Brits do come up with something it would let poor König off the hook, they surely wouldn't expect him to go up against the whole Haitian invasion fleet on his own.

Still, Carlson reflected, he did make short work of that destroyer and corvette this morning. I'd really like to meet him, he mused. McTeal broke into his thoughts.

"I would like to thank you and your colleagues Mr Carlson for having the courage of your convictions and since your involvement cannot for long remain a secret, would you object to my using you and your information to promote assistance from the British?"

"Well as I said Sir, it doesn't really matter now. I'm in it for better or for worse. Sure you can quote me."

"Again, the heartfelt thanks of my people are yours. Would you be available for the cabinet which meets shortly?"

"Sure thing Sir, providing you can keep topping this up." He held up his already empty tea cup. The early morning flight and a late night beforehand meant that he was staying awake on the caffeine only now. He spent the next fifteen minutes or so in the cabinet anteroom which fortunately had a bathroom, waiting for the summons, but before it came another man joined him in the room.

*

Jake nodded to the various assistants and secretaries that lined the way to the cabinet anteroom. If asked, some would have said that he looked saddened and others that he looked pre-occupied and angry. All would have been correct, for these emotions flitted like shadows across Jake's face as they followed in the wake of his thoughts.

The somewhat bumpy flight from the base on Little Cayman to the heli-pad at the rear of Government House on Grand Cayman, a distance of some eightyish miles, had been one of introspection.

He'd declined the crewman's offer of a headset and had sat in noisy isolation at the rear of the AW101 Merlin helicopter. His two security escorts, a patched up Jan Helders and a taciturn Yorkshireman ex-SAS called Peter Crutchley however, were plugged in to the command circuit and had discussed threat levels and such with the Government House security team.

The AW101, very fast, by helicopter standards at nearly 200mph, had skimmed low over the shimmering Caribbean the crew ever alert to the possibility of an encounter with unfriendly ships.

Jake was unaware and uncaring of these concerns and arrangements, his mind was still replaying his two recent emotionally charged encounters firstly, with Ian Halshaw and his wife Liz and secondly with his wounded son James.

Ian and Liz were sitting, quietly and introspectively, drinking tea in the doctor's office just along from the ward where the surviving injured lay in the base medical centre. Trudi was doing her rounds at the time. Jake had decided to look in on his son before continuing on to the heli-pad at the rear, he was surprised to find Liz and Ian in Trudi's office.

He felt a rush of guilt for not having spoken to them sooner and then he was angry with himself for feeling guilty at all. But deep down he knew that he'd avoided the contact because he felt responsible for putting them there on the Island, a place where it was supposed to be safe.

Jake felt clumsy, then even angrier with himself that he should feel so with his own son laying a few yards away nursing a serious leg wound. What words can you use in such a situation? What could anyone say that would make their grief easier to bear? How are you? *Stupid*. What about 'I'm so sorry'? *Utterly inadequate.* Or 'I know how you must feel'. That was probably the worst because, how could he?

Just meaningless platitudes. In the end he said the only really meaningful thing he could think of.

"She was a lovely little girl, I *know* she was liked very much. I will miss her and so will James and Helen."

The grateful look from Liz was reward enough, but the lump that rose in his throat, when Ian stood with tears in his eyes and embraced him, was more than he could bear. With glistening eyes and mumbling something about James he left them guiltily, to their grief. He was more relieved than he dared admit that they did not appear to hold him to blame.

James had been quite active despite the encumbrance of the heavy bandaging on his left leg, and consequently already bored. Full of beans and chat, notwithstanding the terrifying suddenness of the attack and his injury, his unquenchable vitality had restored some of Jake's good heart. He left promising to return as soon as he could, his uninjured daughter trying to behave like a nurse, was fussily tucking a reluctant patient in.

*

Carlson instantly guessed the identity of the man who entered the anteroom. His dossier said medium height, about 5'10". Average build, about 180 pounds. Dark salt and pepper hair with grey temples and no face hair, yep that's him. However, he confessed to himself, the smart white naval tropical uniform with the single broad gold band below a gold circle on the shoulder boards, was a bit more of a giveaway.

He was surprised there were no medal ribbons. He knew for sure the white blue and green of the South Atlantic Medal should be there, it being the 1982 Falklands War British campaign ribbon. Jake could wear it with the bronze oak leaf superimposed, the mentioned in despatches clasp.

Nice to meet you Mr Jonathan Henry König, he thought, as his practised eyes took in every nuance of the man's body language, or should I say Commodore König, owner and master of the Merchant Protector *Bismarck,* dollar billionaire to boot.

He shrewdly gauged Jake's mood as being a little unstable at present. Carlson waited until the man had set his cap down and poured himself a coffee from the silver coffee service, he then stood to introduce himself.

"Hi, Miles Carlson. You must be Jonathan König, pleased to make your acquaintance at last. You're quite a celebrity at various US agencies."

Then he wished he hadn't said a word, the neutral expression on the man's face was exchanged for one of pain and then anger as he made the connections.

"Ah so you're the super spy that gives out tidbits of information." Then the anger spilled out.

"Too fucking little, too vague and too fucking late mate." A finger was wagged at him and the expression on the man's face was of barely restrained fury.

"Because of your little games, around four hundred and sixty people are dead or injured and my wife is a hostage of a foreign power. Pardon me if I don't clasp your hand as a good old buddy should do."

The last was said in such a scathingly sarcastic manner that despite himself Carlson felt his own anger rise.

"Listen pal, you got the information you got because that was all we could release at the time. We didn't have to give any out. And you can't blame me if your wife chose the world's worst place to go and start do-gooding, at the world's worst time."

He thought for a second that he'd gone too far, König had all but leapt off the seat but curiosity was overcoming the man's anger, time to calm down myself he thought.

"Listen, we weren't certain that Haiti was going to come this way, hell until this morning we were just going on guesswork. Oh by the way König, just for your information, my visit here isn't sanctioned."

Jake looked puzzled.

"I'm so far out on a limb that I can't see the goddamn tree trunk. When I get back I'll be lucky to stay out of Leavenworth, so don't give me any hard shit stories."

Now he had his attention.

"I'll have a wife, three kids a mortgage and no goddamn income. Besides you don't want to worry about me Mister, I reckon your friends next door are lining you up for the nautical equivalent of the Custer's last stand!"

"What the hell are you saying? Are you telling me there's more to this? You don't seriously think that Haiti is going to carry on with whatever crazy scheme they've had cooking, now that the cat's out of the bag, do you?"

Carlson was truly contrite for a moment, they obviously hadn't mentioned the Haitian task force when König had been summoned. Oh shit! In for a penny as the Brits say.

"Mr König I suggest we start again, we are after all on the same side of the line?"

He waited for Jake to nod his agreement before continuing and then proceeded to lay it out for him as he had done for the Prime Minister.

Jake didn't interrupt once but did come out with a couple of astute questions which, again, made Carlson upwardly revise his opinion of this unusual man.

"So in a nut shell, it is drugs again isn't it?"

Jake ruminated for a moment, his pathological hatred of anything to do with 'drugs' was well known but the reason why was a little more obscure. He spared a thought for his pretty sister in law, a younger version of his wife, gang raped and dead because of cocaine. Then he turned his gaze back to Carlson. But before Carlson could continue, the Cabinet Secretary opened the ornate double doors and led them into the cabinet room where Carlson had another bombshell to drop.

Andrew McTeal asked them to be seated and then asked Miles Carlson to introduce himself and give his brief. Carlson looked absently around the table, his eyes briefly locking with Sandiford Roche almost opposite him.

"Good day gentlemen thank you for allowing me to address you in this time of crisis. Err, before I get to the situation regarding Haitian intents I have one other matter of business that I'm sure you'll agree is of considerable importance."

Jake was sitting and listening intently, he sensed something unusual in the big CIA man's words and demeanour.

Carlson was playing to the gallery now and dramatically produced a pale green folder with an embossed DEA logo on the front. He held it in front of himself for a few seconds and then gently skipped it across to Sandiford Roche who simply stopped it and turned it correct way up, unopened.

"That gentlemen, is a little present from my colleagues at the DEA. At the request of Mr Roche there, we did a little investigating for him into the activities and accounts of various people and surprise, surprise you have a traitor in your midst."

Jake could see that he was plainly enjoying this charade but was obviously annoying the other cabinet members, particularly Erskine Buerke, he noted with great interest and not a little pleasure. Carlson continued placidly on.

"Would the traitor please stand up?"

He glanced up and down the table but got no response other than furious glares and indignant mutterings. His eyes moved to Erskine Buerke and locked in place, the lightness of his tone was betrayed by the steel in his posture.

"Come now Mr Buerke, don't be shy, please stand up and take your place in the rogues gallery."

Uproar! It took some minutes before the Prime Minister, obviously in the know thought Jake, could re-establish order. The only person apart from Jake and Carlson who hadn't joined in the furore was an evilly smiling Sandiford Roche. Not very surprisingly the meeting closed shortly afterwards with the arrest of Foreign Minister Erskine Buerke.

Roche, Jake found out later, had carefully pieced together Buerke's web of treachery starting with the laundering of drug money years before and culminating in his assistance to the Haitians. Having 'turned' one of Buerke's confederates, Roche had then asked the DEA to assist in tracking down the ill-gotten gains the foreign Minister had accrued.

After the meeting McTeal, Jake and Carlson along with Roche retired to the PM's private office. Jake finally got to look at the satellite photos.

McTeal misinterpreted the look of dejection on Jake's face.

"I'm so sorry Jake but your ship is the only thing that stands between us and them."

He said, indicating the Haitian task force in the photos.

"No Andrew, it's not that so much, although I could have done without it, but I haven't had a chance to tell you yet, Sophie's been taken."

McTeal sat down with a thud as Jake continued.

"I was hoping to use *Bismarck* in some capacity in her rescue and recovery. But obviously I can't go trotting off to Haiti with that lot on the way here and there might not be an afterwards anyway. That's what I mean."

He too sat down heavily and a gloom descended over the office, none wishing to verbalise the horror of being a prisoner without rights in Haiti. Jake struggled vainly to get a grip on the situation.

"Surely they won't still come on after this morning? I mean it's out in the open now.`

He addressed his remarks to no one in particular but it was McTeal who answered him.

"It appears that we've just given them further justification.`

He handed Jake a copy of a press release issued by Reuters central office at eight forty, local, that morning.

"The Haitian Defence Ministry have just announced that in a savage and unprovoked attack early this morning, off the lesser Cayman Islands, the Haitian destroyer 'Dessalines' and a corvette the 'Cap Haitien' were sunk by a mercenary vessel in the employ of the Cayman government. Incidentally this is the same vessel which foiled an attempt to blow up a cruiseliner in the Mediterranean earlier in the year.

The spokesman went on to point out that the Haitian ships were about to land a severely injured crewman at the local hospital when without warning they were attacked. Loss of life is said to be severe and the Haitian government will be taking the matter up with the UN Security Council later today.

This attack comes in the wake of some serious verbal battling between the two nations and calls for retaliation are already loud in the Haitian capital of Port au Prince.

Counter accusations by the Caymans that the Haitian ships were shelling shore installations when attacked, have been greeted with scorn and disgust by the Haitian defence ministry which claims that any civilian casualties would have been caused by the guns of the Cayman ship overshooting their targets. Reuters."

Jake was flabbergasted, such an incredible distortion of the truth could not possibly be believed, surely? They'd made him and his men out to be murderers. McTeal and Carlson looked on in sympathy as Jake set down the wholly fictitious report.

"Bastards. They didn't waste any time did they?"

Was all he could manage by way of comment. It was Roche who gently explained.

"Mr König, truth or fiction, right or wrong, they matter little on the international stage. The Haitians made the first statement, and it's plausible too, so the onus is on us to discredit them, which will not take too long I feel. Unfortunately the man who should be leading the counter attack is indisposed."

His oblique reference to Erskine Buerke raised no smiles.

With a great effort Jake began to concentrate on his most immediate problem, the approaching task force.

"It's obvious gentlemen, that despite the capabilities of my vessel, I could not stand alone against this force, not toe-to-toe anyway, so we'll be looking at deception to even the odds. I should get back to the ship and give it some thought. Their average speed of advance is only eight and a half knots so we have at least forty eight hours to prepare a reception I think."

He studied the photo's for some seconds.

"Mr Carlson, are we able to get any more of these? And would you by any chance have a Pentagon appraisal of this task force?"

Carlson smiled.

"I can't believe you're even considering it König. It's suicide man. But anyway, it just so happens that I did in fact bring such an appraisal."

He passed it to Jake for study.

"As for the satellite updates, they depend on Mr McTeal really."

McTeal raised his eyebrows.

"How so Mr Carlson?"

"Well Sir it's like this. I have no doubt that you've been in touch with the British?"

McTeal nodded.

"Well I think that you should get in touch directly with the President Sir. Just explain that you rang to give your personal thanks for the assistance of the CIA in bringing this grave situation to your attention and particular thanks to the CIA for providing the incontrovertible evidence of Haitian aggression."

Roche smiled at the man's duplicity.

"You see you'll put the President on the spot, this morning's battle won't be news but the fact that the CIA supplied any information will be news. Finally, you rang to seek the President's personal assurance, that whilst you realise that you can expect no overt military assistance, you would deem it vital for the satellite information to keep flowing and expect Great Britain would too."

He finished with a mock bow. McTeal and Roche locked eyes for a second before McTeal asked the question that Jake had wanted to.

"But Mr Carlson, why do you think the President will agree?"

Carlson began to list the points on his fingers.

"One, the President will be madder than hell that the White House didn't know that you'd received intelligence. Two, they'll be grateful that you've let them off the hook militarily it would be too late by the time they decided to help anyway. And three, there is an implicit threat in the fact that you've already received information from us. i.e. It could really be very embarrassing if it got out that you'd been cut off in your hour of need so to speak. And finally, I expect that the British will give you some assistance and they're going to want the 'sat' info anyway."

Roche nodded silently in appreciation of Miles Carlson's manipulative skills.

"Mmm, but why do you think Britain will help us Mr Carlson?"

"Well politically I'm not sure, but I dropped a big hint to a very senior military man some time ago and I expect he's got a contingency plan already made up and ready to go."

He smiled winningly.

"It's very likely built into their deployment plans for a 'Red Flag' exercise we've coincidentally got coming up in the States soon. That's a test of our air defence systems by the way, we get friendly forces to come and attack us."

He collected the photos and put them in a folder with the appraisals.

"I managed to get a friend in the Pentagon to request the Brit's to take part in the one coming up. Because of that, the British military will be able to say that they have units in position to intervene immediately. That obviously shoots down the first stalling ploy the British Prime Minister will have."

McTeal stood up and smiling hugely shook Carlson's hand once more.

"I thank you again Mr Carlson for your covert assistance and marvel at your devious mind. If we should fail in our endeavours it will not be through lack of effort by our friends."

No, Jake thought ruefully, it will be because the *Bismarck* will be sitting on the sea bottom full of fools who've followed me to their deaths.

The conversation curled around him but did not include him. I have a reality problem here, he thought to himself, the problem is that none of this seems real. How the hell has it happened? Do I have any choices left? Or are they already made for me? I'll surely wake up in bed soon, drenched in sweat, remembering every detail of this nightmare. I must do, surely? It felt rather like he was being pushed slowly towards a cliff edge by some irresistible force. How could his dream of being a Merchant Protector, a deterrent to pirates have led to this?

M40 Motorway, Oxfordshire England

The black Jaguar staff car cruised through the thickening afternoon traffic towards Northwood and the headquarters 'bunker' of Britain's Defence Chiefs.   Its main passenger, Air Chief Marshal Sir Andrew Kirby-Moore, currently CDS or Chief of the Joint Service Defence Staff sat next to his driver instead of in the back.   Moore suddenly stiffened and leaned forward to turn up a breaking news alert on the radio.

After listening for a minute or so he sat back in the plush leather seat and contemplated his options.   His aide, Squadron Leader Jeff Bakewell sat in the back of the car, knew something was up but not what.   He decided to sit back and wait until the 'old man' wanted him in on it.

CDS wasn't terribly surprised that he'd first heard the news about the Caymans from the radio rather than from his staff or the Foreign Office.   He supposed they'd get around to passing along something eventually but Britain had really very little 'presence' left in the Caribbean nowadays so real-time information about the area very often came from third party sources, mostly the media.

He turned to Bakewell with his hand out.

"Sat-phone please Jeff."

Bakewell took out the Iridium sat-phone from the secure briefcase next to him, switched it on and made sure there was a good charge on the battery before passing it and the antenna jack plug to his boss.

Moore began dialling then stopped and sat back again deep in thought.   Obviously Miles Carlson's prediction earlier in the month had turned into grim reality, and by what he'd been able to piece together from that warning, as much by what was not said as what was, the Americans were not going to lift a military finger to help the Caymans.

Carlson had finally suggested that the RAF might look favourably on any request to participate in an upcoming 'Red Flag' exercise basing the deployed units in Belize.

The CDS had smiled at that point recognising the political advantages of denying preparedness later and also the common sense of using the exercise to get the units into theatre.   It was also a good way of testing his staff's ability to put together an OP-plan in short order rather than the six months or so warning they usually got.   If anyone said anything the answer was that rapid deployment units, by definition, deployed rapidly and were not always the ear marked units.

So he'd ordered an operational deployment plan prepared along his own lines of thought, which of course had nothing to do with attacking land based targets in the USA.

He chuckled quietly to himself remembering the astonished expression of the Vice Admiral in planning, to whom he'd passed his requirements not three weeks ago, the man must have thought I was losing it, he thought. You could see the question on his face, 'why the hell do you need Ghurkhas for a 'Red Flag' exercise?'

Still, it was time now to get the ball rolling, better to start the preparations and save time later. He picked up the phone and dialled again speaking briefly.

"CDS. Have exercise 'Crossover' activated immediately. Have Air Command commence now with the logistics, but tell them to put the aircraft on to 12 hours' notice and have an emergency briefing set up for the Joint Chiefs when I get there in about thirty five minutes."

He looked across at the driver and got the nod on the timescale.

"And err, one last thing, delete exercise and insert 'Operation'. Classified Top Secret. Fine. Thank you."

He unplugged the phone from the external jack and handed it back to Bakewell.

Squadron Leader Bakewell, an ex-Tornado pilot, was still waiting to be put in the picture, but from what CDS had just said and the connection to the news report, he guessed that some of his erstwhile colleagues could be going into action fairly soon. He suppressed a twinge of envy as the car sped towards Northwood, but he had a different job now.

End

Part two, *Retribution*, the dramatic concluding part of the *Bismarck* Folly is also available on Amazon Kindle and in paperback. An Omnibus edition will be out soon in both paperback and Kindle.

If you enjoyed this book, please take a moment to review it on the Amazon site, many thanks.

Printed in Poland
by Amazon Fulfillment
Poland Sp. z o.o., Wrocław